Landscapes

Joss Kingsnorth

First published in 1996
by HEADLINE BOOK PUBLISHING

First published in paperback in 1997
by HEADLINE BOOK PUBLISHING

A HEADLINE REVIEW paperback

10 9 8 7 6 5 4 3 2 1

ISBN 0 7472 5468 0

Printed and bound in Great Britain by
Cox & Wyman Ltd, Reading, Berks

HEADLINE BOOK PUBLISHING
A division of Hodder Headline PLC
338 Euston Road
London NW1 3BH

Landscapes

PROLOGUE

The old man sat on the centre bench of the gallery, balancing the bones of his almost transparent hands on top of his ebony cane, his eyes fixed on the object that meant more to him than anything in the world. It was his treasure, his fixed star, mercifully still surviving unchanged in a changing world; it was a lodestone, a shrine preserved from month to month as if for him alone.

The painting was large, very nearly the dimensions of Grant's *Bathers*, so that its subject, a single nude figure, was almost life-size. The label on the wall beside it gave the title as *Emily Asleep*, painted by A. J. Monk in 1932 and acquired by the Tate in 1960. The canvas dominated the room, drawing the eye inexorably even if one didn't normally care for the work of A. J. Monk, which the old man did not. There was nothing revolutionary about the painting, Monk was no innovator, but what he had in abundance was audacity, a careless, confident brio, an insolent disregard for public taste or moral judgements.

The woman in the painting was posed in such a way as to have caused a furore even in an age that considered itself sophisticated and immune to shocks. She lay with eyes drooped in what appeared to be post-coital languor, with the swathe of yellow earth, ochre and terre-verte that stood for hair, tossed over the face. The same colours appeared again in the pubic hair that framed the pudenda; these had been rapidly brushed in against the shadow of the thigh, while in the background a faint suggestion of an oriental rug reflected dashes of Indian red and cobalt on the lusciously painted flesh. A hollow filled with violet and viridian seemed to have been burned, by the heat and weight of the body, into the crumpled sheet on which the figure lay. It was a painting that owed much to French Impressionism yet with a flavour of its time. It was

1

easy to imagine one could hear the distant echo of a trumpet, the wail of a saxophone and the panic notes of a flute. And it was quite apparent that A. J. Monk had been in a fine state of artistic and sexual arousal when he had attacked the canvas with loaded brush. Never before or since had Monk managed to pull it off as he had in this, his very best painting.

But when Aiden Chase gazed on the sleeping Emily it was not for once as a connoisseur of fine art; for on one day a month his eyes were not those of a highly regarded art expert and dilettante, but of a lover. What he was seeing was Emily herself. In an elevated moment of insight Monk had caught the essence of the woman as Chase remembered her. That way of curling her fingers into her palm, of tilting her head and tossing her short unruly hair impatiently across the pillow.

Chase's worst nightmare was that the painting should disappear, be damaged by some feminist zealot, be relegated or stolen. (It being stolen had preyed on his mind ever since his home had been burgled and two important paintings taken from his collection.) This was the chief reason why he was now glad that he did not, after all, own the painting of Emily. It had become apparent that he would not be able to give it the protection it deserved without turning his home into a fortress. He might not possess it but at least it was now available to him, when for years it had eluded him in private collections. Nor was it French. In spite of his contempt for British art in general, the painting that Chase valued above all other was the work of a man who, though his origins were somewhat mixed, had been placed firmly in the company of English painters of the early twentieth century.

As Chase contemplated the familiar image, he was, as usual, seized by a tumult of paradoxical emotions that made him tremble, caused his pulse to flutter and his eyes to sting in pain. How he loathed Monk! Yet how dependent he was on the man's vision of the woman he himself had worshipped, loved and finally lost. His thoughts, as he sat alone on the bench, were bitter and vindictive.

At last, exhausted by his emotions, he heaved himself to his feet and made his way, of necessity slowly, through the rest of the Tate's galleries of British art. The nineteenth century, sweet sentiment as was fitting in this shrine of the Sugar King. On to the twentieth century, to the Bloomsbury crowd, the vorticists painting up a blizzard of angles; then the one-offs, the eccentrics like Stanley Spencer. But Chase was blind to them; today he noticed them even less than usual, as he dwelled on love and loss.

He had been reared on a diet of classicism in his early career and had later been seduced by the delectable goodies emanating from Paris. Finally he had been completely won over to Post-Impressionism and to Matisse, Picasso and Braque. His renowned collection of modern work amply reflected his interest.

There was a moment, in the press of tourists, students and even occasional art lovers, when his frail but upright figure wavered. He was saved by the arrival of his chauffeur, who took his arm and shepherded him through the revolving doors to the Daimler, waiting on a dim and rain-drenched Millbank.

Inside the vehicle, with a rug tucked round his bony knees, Chase's thoughts remained with the painting while his fingers fumbled in a silver pillbox. Shakily he placed a small tablet under his tongue. Every time he came he felt more upset, not less.

All at once a whole lifetime of detestation and jealousy crystallized into a single second.

'Damn the man to hell,' he muttered with tears in his eyes.

At that moment, a hundred miles away in Dorset, A. J. Monk whispered hoarsely, 'Bugger it, Queenie, I'm going!' and, obliging his distant enemy at last, he died.

CHAPTER ONE

The day they buried Jacko was fine but still the wind had a keen edge to it. Emily's decision to attend the funeral had been made on the spur of the moment, belatedly in fact, so that when she turned up at the church the service had already begun. (A church service for Jacko, she thought, when he had been a life-long atheist. Ha!) Irritated by this inconsistency, she slipped almost unnoticed into one of the pews at the back.

It had not dawned on her that Francis would be present at the last rites of a man he had spent a lifetime detesting, until she found herself standing next to him. He thrust his Order of Service sheet under her nose. She pushed it away.

'What are you doing here?' she hissed. 'I thought you thoroughly disapproved of Jacko and all his works.'

'So I did and do,' he whispered hoarsely. 'But now that the fellow's dead—'

It hardly needed explanation. Her brother had always been voyeuristically fascinated by each scrap of gossip and every titillating scandal that had marked out Jacko's career, seizing on one deliquency after another as if to heap fuel on the fires of his disapproval. There was a chance that even in death Jacko might yet provide Francis with a juicy morsel or two.

To Emily's surprise, the church was full, yet among the ranks of backs there was not one which Emily recognized, and, she thought, even had she done so there was not one that it would not have been an embarrassment to meet.

Bugger! she cursed inwardly. Turning up like this had been a mistake after all.

'For a thousand years in thy sight are but as yesterday: seeing that is past as a watch in the night.'

She glared at the great sheaves of arum lilies that stood about the barrel-vaulted church as if in mourning for a Pre-Raphaelite heroine instead of a rascally old reprobate. It was too much.

'I have to get out,' she said to Francis through gritted teeth.

'You've only just come,' he objected.

Her leaving so soon after she had arrived, and followed closely by Francis, caused a little local stir in the pews. Outside, Emily sat on the flat top of a handy tombstone and removed the man's old trilby hat she'd been wearing, laying it tenderly on her lap. Francis watched critically while she struggled with a few flying wisps of pearl-white hair, most of which was screwed up into an untidy topknot. She appeared to be wearing a horse blanket, cut and stitched at the neck with purple wool. He wondered if the old girl was going senile.

Emily sighed. 'That's better.'

'What's the matter with you? Are you ill?' For a moment, until he saw that she looked as indestructible as ever, Francis's heart gave a little leap of terror. 'Don't tell me you were overcome with grief because I shan't believe you,' he added, relief sharpening his tongue.

'Nothing of the kind,' she snapped. 'It was the enclosed space. And all those people.'

'Kind? Not like you to be kind.'

'I said, "Nothing of the kind," ' she repeated loudly. 'All that mumbo jumbo. Of course, you know he was an atheist?'

'Atheist you say?' Francis dived into his pocket and produced a large white handkerchief. 'What else could the man have been? I ask you?' He removed his gold-rimmed bifocals and dabbed at his pale and rheumy eyes. 'It's been a good few years since you saw Jacko,' he said. A look of sly satisfaction settled in the vertical creases of his slightly vulpine features.

'Years and years. They stick like bloody leeches, sucking away one's lifeblood.'

'Salt. That's what you need,' Francis said vaguely.

'Salt? What the hell are you on about now? Salt is very bad for you, if you must know; furs up the arteries.'

'What? What are you talking about?'

'Age, Francis. Age.'

'You've lost me. I thought we were talking about leeches. Leeches like Jacko, for instance.'

'Forget it,' Emily said irritably. Was the old chap going senile? She squinted up at him, at his stork-like legs trousered today in dark grey suiting, his elegant hands speckled brown as a kittiwake's egg as he fumbled again for his handkerchief, catching a stupendous sneeze. Recovering, he smoothed the thinning rusty strands above his ears and nodded towards the church porch from which a low drone emanated.

'It is sown in corruption; it is raised in incorruption: It is sown in dishonour; it is raised in glory:'

'Astonishing,' Francis said. 'All those people turning up like that. You wouldn't think that anyone who'd known him in his heyday would still be alive, would you?'

'I'm alive. You're alive . . . just.'

'Bitchy as ever then?'

She said, 'A. J. Monk was a name once, even though he has since been relegated to the down escalator. Who knows, he might yet be collected for his quaint period charm, if nothing else.'

'Charm, did you say? Jacko had about as much charm as a charging rhinocerous.'

'He had his moments. In any case, I was speaking of his work.' She glanced at her brother sharply. 'Are you sure you don't need a hearing aid?'

Francis bridled. 'What makes you say that?'

Emily shrugged. Slightly puzzled, she had noticed that a small crowd of people, women mostly, had assembled just beyond the lych-gate that led from the churchyard.

'What do you think *they* want?' she said, before turning back to Francis. 'You seem to forget,' she went on, 'that there are a hell of a lot of collectors still around who bought his work. You don't suppose they're going to sit on their hands and watch their investment depreciate indefinitely, do you? Two of his *Acrobats* sold for quite a respectable sum at Sotheby's last month, did you see

7

that? His earlier stuff, needless to say.'

'In that case, now's the time to flog anything of his you've hung on to. God knows, you need the money.'

'What makes you think I still have any of the old scoundrel's work?'

Francis buried his nose in his handkerchief once again. His comment came out muffled. 'I suppose you sold off what you had years ago. Oh, well!'

The crowd round the church gate had bunched together and were staring stonily in the direction of Emily and Francis. From the church there came the sound of a young female voice accompanied by a recorder and what might have been a lute.

'Don't tell me all the whole congregation are coming to Burr Ash for the wake?' Francis said.

'Wake! People don't have wakes these days, do they?' She glanced at her brother. 'Coming? You said "coming"? You're not going on to Burr Ash yourself, surely?'

'I thought I might. Do I take it then, that you are not?'

'Has old age addled your brains? Of course I'm not. I have a taxi picking me up as soon as this is over.' She looked towards the church, an edifice of knapped flint with bands of limestone, inside which the tremulous song was just ending. 'I just thought I'd see the old ruffian off. I might have been the first idiot to marry the man, but we all know who will be Queen of the Night at this final performance.'

'Queen of the Night?'

'I was speaking of *her*. Queenie.'

'I should have thought you'd have buried the hatchet after all this time. At least you should have been grateful that she took the bounder off your hands.'

'Is that how you see it?'

'God Almighty, Em! It's all ancient history now and I'm damned if I remember what was supposed to have happened anyway.' He lowered his scrawny bottom cautiously on to the grave slab next to his sister. Above their heads, newly arrived house martins wheeled and whistled. The crowd round the gate were murmuring amongst themselves and fidgeting with what looked like broom handles.

'You can please yourself,' Francis said, 'but I certainly intend

8

going on to Burr Ash. I was looking forward to something to sustain me for the journey back, if you must know. You've probably no idea what it costs to get even a halfway decent meal out these days.'

'Good old Francis! You never change. A hundred miles for a free nosh. Don't tell me the grub at that crammer of yours is even worse than I remember?'

'That was all of thirty years ago. It was probably the last time you went anywhere at all outside Devon.' He cocked an ear, straining to hear what was going on inside the church. 'And I wish you wouldn't keep referring to Rudyards as a crammer. In any case, that reminds me, you never answered my letter.'

Emily raised her voice. 'Francis, there was nothing to answer. For the last time I do not want to live in London!'

'You would be near me. I could keep an eye on you. It's merely stubborn self-indulgence to keep on living in the back of beyond as you do.'

'It's a bloody poor lookout if one can't be self-indulgent, as you call it, when one has reached our age.'

Francis's brow creased, anxiety and irritation both evident in his expression. He nodded in the direction of the church. 'Now Jacko was self-indulgent from the day he was born. You were supposed to be intelligent. It's always been a wonder to me that you didn't see it; in fact it absolutely beats me why so-called bright women get themselves lumbered with the likes of egotistical beasts like A. J. Monk. I just don't get it. Never did!'

'Even so-called bright women didn't have much choice in those days, as you are well aware. All men were more or less egotistical. Still are, for all I know,' Emily said imperturbably. 'In any case, even if I hadn't misguidedly fallen for him, I think I can be excused for imagining that I had hitched my wagon to a star. I was extremely young, don't forget, and probably thought the lustre of a famous husband would rub off on me a little. In my innocence I could have thought I might make a modest name for myself under his wing.' She gave a hoarse chuckle.

'You made a name for yourself all right!' Francis seized on her last words as he lunged for his handkerchief again and mopped his eyes. 'Yes, I think it can be said that you made a name for yourself!

Thanks to that disgusting painting.' He blew his nose. 'Damn this pollen!'

'All right. I wouldn't have chosen that particular road to fame. But there was nothing disgusting about the painting, unless you consider human flesh innately disgusting, which I rather suspect. You're very like Muriel was in some ways, you know. Damn it! That painting was the best thing Jacko ever did. The Tate were lucky to swipe it from under Aiden's nose like that.'

'What's this? Praise for Jacko! And there was I assuming you loathed the man.' Francis stowed his handkerchief back in his pocket. 'You can keep your countryside,' he said irritably. 'All it's ever done for me is to bring on my hay fever.'

'Are you sure you want to go on to Burr Ash? It will be far worse there. Besides, you don't suppose the Queen of the Night will recognize you after all this time, do you, let alone put out the welcome mat?'

There were signs from inside the church that the service was coming to an end.

'What about the will?' Francis said, getting to his feet. 'Jacko's will?'

'What's that to do with me?'

'There are the children. *His* children when all's said and done.'

'You don't imagine that there's any of his own money left, for goodness' sake?'

'And Burr Ash?'

'Queenie's now, presumably. After all, she lives there. She was pretty fly with money. Jacko never had a bean.'

'I don't understand you,' Francis reiterated peevishly. 'You're taking it very calmly.'

'Stop fussing. It's been over forty years since I had anything to do with Jacko. I wish I hadn't come at all. I think I'll go and see if my taxi's turned up.'

But before she could act on her intentions there was a stir inside the church, and the doors were opened and hooked back to allow for the passage of the shining oak coffin and its solemn pallbearers. Simultaneously, the small posse at the gate unfurled a number of banners lettered blackly with feminist slogans: 'PORN AS ART IS STILL PORN' and 'PATRIARCHY BREEDS PORN – GOOD RIDDANCE PORN PATRIACH.'

Emily nudged Francis. 'What do the banners say? I haven't got my specs with me. What do they say?'

Francis demurred until she poked him more vigorously in the ribs whereupon, whispering, he delivered a summary of their message.

Emily chuckled. 'So that's their game.'

'Disgraceful!' Francis spluttered. 'But serve the old bugger right.'

Oblivious of the minor demonstration came the great painter's family, walking behind the coffin to a grave that had been reserved long before.

Most noticeable among them was the slight figure of the widow veiled in a mantilla of heavy lace, supported on one side by a young man with pale spiky hair and metal-rimmed spectacles and on the other by a man of middle age who, in contrast to the following relatives, looked the embodiment of conventionality. The woman on his arm, the widow, was dressed in an expensive shade of deep purple and, under the veiling, was as pale as an image in wax. Her ink-black hair was drawn severely back into a huge knot at the nape of her neck; because of her apparent age, the effect of this was startling.

'There she is,' Emily said in a stage whisper. 'The Queen of the Night herself. I like the veil, marvellous touch of theatre, that; and with such *very* black hair ... very Spanish. Just like Goya's mistress, that Duchess person.'

'For Christ's sake, Em!' Francis hissed. 'Pipe down, can't you? You're a spiteful old woman.' He stared openly and admiringly at the bereaved woman's trim figure; even now it remained apparent that it was the figure of an ex-dancer.

'She looks just the same,' Francis said in an awed whisper. 'Just like the paintings of her.'

'I expect she's had herself embalmed,' Emily confided into her brother's good ear. 'And so clever of her to keep her hair black. No problem about being recognized.'

'At least she hasn't let herself go!' Francis gave Emily a look that was supposed to be meaningful.

As she followed her dead husband's coffin along the flagged path of the churchyard, there was an immobility and impassiveness about the woman Emily called Queenie that was powerfully

11

reminiscent of the portraits of her that the painter had rattled off in his later period, now pronounced his decline. To everyone except Emily she was known as Regine Monk. Although she passed quite close to where they were standing, she gave no sign of having recognized either Emily or Francis; neither did she acknowledge or even appear to notice that some of the women at the gate were shouting an occasional uncomplimentary valediction to her husband's memory.

Peering, Emily scrutinized the feminist demo carefully, half expecting to see that her granddaughter was part of it. Relieved that, as far as she could make out, there was no one she knew among them, she was then able to let her attention stray to the widow's supporters.

'What a handsome young man,' she said. 'Pity about the hair. Is he related, d'you suppose? I don't remember a grandson that age.'

Francis shushed her angrily, remembering too late Emily's aptitude for embarrassing him, for now the rest of the family were filing past.

First came a dark woman with a swarthy complexion, possibly in her forties, followed by another middle-aged woman who looked like a poorly contrived replica of Regine. Then a tall, stooped man, two pre-adolescent girls and a sulky, heavy-lidded boy of about thirteen. Of all of them he looked most like Regine, with the same features and slight, graceful figure. Except for the stocky man who walked beside the widow, the boy was the only member of the family who was conventionally dressed, being in the uniform of a local private school. The rest all had an odd whimsical appearance: dipping skirts in black or brown, heads of long braided hair, much-worn corduroy, fringing and idiosyncratic footwear all added up to an impression of slightly dated eccentricity. Like Regine, none of them gave either Emily or Francis a second glance.

However, when he saw Emily, Aiden Chase, who had been following close behind, stopped dead in his tracks, visibly shaken. *He* had recognized Emily at once. But then so a lover should, even when the affair was as dead and done for as the remains they were here to inter.

* * *

12

It took Aiden several seconds to recover from the shock. He had never expected to see Emily here, or ever again. He wasn't sure why he was here himself unless it was for the satisfaction of seeing Jacko put into the ground.

'Emily!' he said at last, leaning forward to kiss her. He caught at her hands and the sudden exertion caused him to stagger ever so slightly. His lips were thin as paper on her cheek. 'Enchanting as ever,' he said, with an attempt at gallantry to hide his dismay.

'I don't know about that but at least my eyesight's up to scratch,' she said, which was, in fact, a lie. With difficulty she focused on the old man masquerading as the handsome Aiden Chase she remembered.

'As is my own,' he said severely.

Impelled by the forward motion of the mourners, they made their way to the newly dug grave at the far corner of the churchyard. With them went a young man not yet introduced, who walked by Aiden's side and who helped him over the rough grass. Now here, Emily thought, was someone who resembled the Aiden of the old days; in fact the likeness was quite startling and confusing, reeling back the years to her time at the Slade. In spite of the fact that the young pretender's hair was worn longish and tied back in a pigtail, it was of an identical colour, like fine amontillado. Good bones too. Only his complexion was different: it suggested an outdoor life rather than one spent in galleries and auction rooms.

Standing with Francis at the very back of the small crowd round the grave, Emily was surprised at how completely detached she felt as she heard the last rites said over the man who had once been her husband and her lover.

'. . . to take unto himself the soul of our dear brother here departed, we therefore commit his body to the ground; earth to earth, ashes to ashes, dust to dust;'

The solid wall of backs parted momentarily and she found herself looking straight into the eyes of Regine Monk. At this distance the heavy veil was less effective and Emily peered at the woman, searching for signs that the pure venom of her thoughts had been

13

rightly understood. She was disappointed; there was no answering flash of hostility, nor any indication that she'd even been recognized. The woman's tragic mask was not disturbed by so much as a tremor. She looked straight through Emily as if she didn't exist.

It was all over and there was a stir among the mourners. A stir too amongst the feminist protesters. One had climbed on to the church wall in order that her banner should be more visible. 'BOW OUT' and 'BUG OFF, MONK', it read. A man from the funeral directors went across to remonstrate with her, sotto voce, and she seemed to agree to descend and join her companions. However, he appeared unable to persuade the women to move any further away.

Several black saloons with tinted windows waited. As Regine's young, blond acolyte handed her into the first of these, the widow stumbled slightly as if blinded by grief.

'That's a good touch,' Emily murmured half to herself. Francis hadn't quite caught the remark but stepped aside to dissociate himself from what he guessed was his sister's malice. Aiden and his young companion approached with another man whose face was vaguely familiar to Emily.

'Emily, allow me to introduce my son,' Aiden said, without actually mentioning the name of the young man with the pigtail. For a moment she had the impression that he might even have forgotten it. Son! More of an age to be a grandson surely. But then, when Aiden had eventually married he had been well into middle age.

Emily inspected Chase the younger. Same intelligent eyes, but not, she thought, an aesthete. More powerfully built and lacking Aiden's fastidious hauteur.

'I'm Gideon,' the young man said, compensating for his father's omission.

'Your father and I are old friends,' Emily said. 'Did he tell you?'

Aiden cut in abruptly. 'And Francis. It *is* Francis, isn't it?'

They shook hands. Francis approved of Chase. He thought Emily had been mad to throw him over.

'And you remember Mr Davidson, of course?' Aiden said, turning to his second companion.

'Bruno! Thought the face was familiar,' Emily said. The hair she remembered as black was now a silvery white, but the dark eyes were as watchful and warm as ever. 'Still in Cork Street?'

Bruno retained Emily's hand. 'I'm afraid Lombards and I parted company,' he said. 'I'm on my own again.'

'Goodness. I thought you *were* Lombards.' Bruno had started his highly successful art gallery in the fifties and had at one time handled Jacko's work.

The dealer searched for a reminder of the Emily of the portraits, for the halo of wild wheaten hair, the handsome, paintable planes of her cheeks and the dark, cornflower-blue eyes. Something remained, though the hair was now white and the extraordinary eyes were rimed with age; there was also something else, something more elusive that interested him more than her physical beauty had once done.

'I suppose you'll be considering a retrospective for Monk now?' Aiden said to Bruno.

'That will be up to Regine.'

'He'll make money for you again one of these days,' Emily said slyly.

'I wouldn't be too sure of that,' Bruno said. He looked at Emily thoughtfully. 'I could have handled yours, you know. If you had produced any more like those two canvases you did in Provence. You know, I still have them.'

'Couldn't sell 'em, I suppose.'

'Wouldn't. Wouldn't sell them. They are where they've always been – on my wall at home.'

'Early stuff. Youthful enthusiasm,' Emily scoffed.

Bruno frowned. 'I never knew why you gave up.' A lie. He did.

'Well, now.' Aiden was impatient, seeing the mourners dispersing and the black cars disappearing down the narrow road that led away from the church, through the village and out into the Dorset countryside. He vouchsafed a passing glance of distaste in the direction of the demonstrators – feminist activities made him anxious – then studiously pretended that they did not exist. Turning back to Emily he said, 'Well, now. Since you are not, after all, totally entrenched in the country, Emily, what about coming up to town or to Riversfoot? Francis too.' His invitation was simply a gesture. He knew Emily would never accept it. But he was afraid Francis might.

Emily was trying to remember what had become of Aiden's wife. She couldn't even recall her name, only that she had been much younger; which would account for Gideon's extreme youth. Suddenly she recollected that the woman had died.

'No thank you, Aiden. I never stay away from home these days.'

'And the children?' Aiden said, absent-mindedly looking round as if he expected to see five-year-olds romping among the tombstones.

'Three thousand miles is a long way to come for the funeral of someone you hardly remember!'

'Ah, yes. The boys went to Canada, didn't they? And the girl?' He never could remember their names.

'Fern is still teaching, as far as I know, poor soul.'

Aiden thought it better to close the subject of Emily's children. He had never been very interested in them anyway. He was relieved when Bruno Davidson and Francis began to make arrangements to share a taxi to Burr Ash. He himself would get Gideon to drive him back directly to Riversfoot. He'd had quite enough for one day.

Emily noticed Gideon glancing surreptitiously at his watch, impatient no doubt, with the desultory maunderings of the elderly. She couldn't cope with meeting Aiden like this. It was unreal. So much could have been said but the thought of raking over the dead embers of old loves, old quarrels and customs long past was too frightful to think about. And much too exhausting. There remained nothing but the intervening years of silence.

Aiden kissed her once more before he left. She, Bruno and Francis watched Gideon lead his father slowly back to where their car waited.

The women at the gate were lowering their banners and chatting among themselves, satisfied that they had made their point. A minor victory in the general scheme of things. Davidson nodded towards them and chuckled. 'Never expected that!' he said. 'Though I can't say I'm surprised.'

'Disgraceful,' Francis repeated. 'This is a funeral, after all!'

'I think it's most conscientious of them to bother with an old boy like Jacko,' Emily said. She nodded towards a young man just departing. 'Press,' she said. 'I wonder if he'll mention it.'

'Bit of a waste of the women's time if he doesn't,' Francis commented with some satisfaction.

'I sometimes wonder about you,' Emily snapped. 'Here's my taxi. I'm off. You two toddle along to your wake. I just hope that the Queen of the Night doesn't chuck you out on your ear when she finally decides that she knows who you are, Francis.' She kissed Bruno on the cheek. 'Good to see you again, Bruno,' she said gruffly.

'Wonderful to see you, Em,' he said. 'For goodness' sake, look me up when you come up to town, won't you?'

'She never will,' Francis said irritably, sneezing. He opened the door of Emily's taxi.

Emily reached up and put a hand, tanned as dark as a tree root, to her brother's flushed face. 'Look after yourself, Francis. It's high time you retired, you know. You're getting past it. Time to take things easy.'

The two men stared after Emily's departing car. Francis cogitated about his sister's bewildering switches from truculence to sudden and unexpected flashes of affection and perspicacity. Though they rarely met, he drew constant comfort from the knowledge that in his darkest moments there was always Emily, a stalwart older sister and ultimately a stout ally against a hostile world. Tough, but not tough like their older sister, Muriel, had been – dead now these twenty years – whose strength of character had been stained by bigotry and intolerance. Emily had no petty prejudices, would ask no questions, her courage would be enough for both of them.

His thoughts were interrupted by Bruno.

'Our taxi,' he said. 'Let's get this over with.'

CHAPTER TWO

Holly Wyatt prised open the catch of the kitchen window with a rusty knife she had found in the garden. It was ridiculously easy. Except for those painted into immobility, the catches of most of the windows were either loose or missing. The sash of this one shot up with a rather unnerving crash, but fastidiously setting aside some pots of geraniums from behind the sink, she pulled herself over the sill with no trouble at all. Then she hauled a large multi-coloured patchwork bag in after her.

The owner of Sandplace did not appear to be much concerned about the possibility of intruders, perhaps with good cause. It could hardly be called a desirable residence. Its name, scarcely legible on the rickety gate, was appropriate since it was practically on the beach; and in spite of forget-me-not-blue shiplap panelling, new windows and some decorative bargeboards, there was no disguising the fact that it had once been a railway carriage belonging to the GWR. Deprived of its wheels but propped three feet up on brick piers, it had dreamed away nearly a hundred years, going nowhere. It was surrounded by a roughly fenced patch of sandy grass interwoven with sea holly, creeping mallow and horned poppy. Parked beside Sandplace and inclining tiredly towards it was an ancient, tarpaulin-covered cabin cruiser that had obviously not cruised anywhere for some time. Less than twenty yards from both, the sea broke briskly on to the deserted shore, leaving a tideline litter of plastic bottles, ends of orange nylon rope and seaweed; further along some turnstones rummaged in a patch of pebbles.

The salty aroma of seaweed followed Holly into the long, narrow interior. The space where passengers had once sat had been opened out and repartitioned to form several small rooms. The kitchen where Holly now stood had once, a long time ago, been painted blue-green. The fading evening light and the dim presence of the leaning cabin cruiser combined to drown the room in shadow, giving it an underwater appearance. Holly would hardly have been surprised to see little golden fish swimming between the bunches of mint, fennel and samphire that dangled from the ceiling. Pegged on a string across one corner of the room was a jersey with an unravelling sleeve, a faded much-worn swimsuit and a beautiful pair of lavender-coloured silk knickers with pale grey lace trimming; the only clues to the personality of the occupant.

Holly passed through what had once been the corridor into one of the two bedrooms. The walls here were tomato red, which had paled near the windows to rose and darkened in the corners to oxblood. Just below the ceiling was a hand-painted frieze, a repeating pattern of shells and gulls in flight. The only other decorative touches were a patchwork bedcover, some rag rugs and a painting of a red nude standing against a ground of green and gentian blue. Holly scarcely gave them a glance but dumped her variegated holdall on the bed, taking from it a plastic bag containing a wholemeal loaf, an apple, a tin of soup and some cheese. The cheese was of the mousetrap variety but it would have to do; she was very slightly skint, student grants being what they were.

Back in the kitchen with her groceries, she found an electric kettle which she filled at the sink and switched on; the only food on the premises as far as she could see (not counting the half-empty bottle of Teachers), was a stack of packets of Darjeeling and a cupboard full of tins, mostly baked beans, tuna and Ambrosia creamed rice. A glance into the minuscule bathroom was enough to put her off risking the antiquated water heater so she used some of the boiled water to wash the grime of the journey from her face and hands. She had come a long way, now she was tired and hungry.

Starving, in fact. It seemed ages since she'd had a decent meal. She searched for a tin opener and a saucepan, and put the soup to heat on an electric stove similar to ones usually seen in pictures depicting life in the 1950s. While she waited, she laid a perfunctory place at the table and sawed off large chunks of bread and cheese which she ate standing up.

Through the open window came the rhythmic silky rustle of waves breaking on the beach and the subdued squawks and pattering feet of gulls as they settled to roost on the roof. There was a faint reek of seaweed and something else that might have been drains. Holly turned on a light that hung low over the table, drowning it in a glowing yellow pool and leaving the corners of the room in darkness. Now and again she stopped chewing and listened for sounds that might herald the arrival of the rightful owner of Sandplace.

Swearing to herself that she would ban absolutely all thoughts of the looming finals for at least twenty-four hours was proving more difficult in the execution than in the resolve. Four years of more or less continual conflict with those who had the power seriously to affect her future had not made her sanguine about her degree results, since Holly and the North Withering College of Art and Technology had fallen out almost from day one. She had begun the course in a glow of enthusiasm, equipped with some very creditable A levels, hoping to add to her skills and to learn at the feet of practising artist-craftsmen. She had been bitterly disappointed. At first, being unsure of herself, she had bowed to what appeared to be the requirements of the course but later as her intransigent nature reasserted itself and her confidence in her own work grew, she began to question those requirements and, as a result, found herself up against a stone wall of disapproval and even ridicule. Eventually, later than most, she had learned to keep her own counsel, pay lip service to the prevailing ethos and quietly go her own way. Her marks suffered but by that time she felt that she knew where she was going. She *had* to follow that route, no matter what. Of the few who had, like her, struggled to work in their own way, most eventually gave in to the lure of the high marks that resulted from conforming.

'But where's your rationale, Holly?' her chief opponent was fond of saying. 'Where's your rationale?' So she had sat down and written a screed which had kept him off her back for some time. In the meanwhile and strictly on the quiet because such subversion, had it become known, would have heaped more coals of fire on her head, she took independent action. Having long since despaired of finding help at the college, she had spent every evening she could

21

spare and a great many weekends at the side of a master carver called Stan, who had nothing whatever to do with the North Withering College of Art and Technology. In fact, he specialized in ecclesiastical restoration but what he didn't know about wood and carving, and the use and care of tools wasn't worth knowing. Her tutors, the ones she despised as lovers of 'rationales', of 'concepts' and of tongue-in-cheek parodies, would have had a fit. They thought craftsmanship was both elitist and reactionary.

Now, at Sandplace, she managed with an effort to put the course, the college and everything to do with it, to the back of her mind – but thoughts of home were not so easy to dispel right at this moment; or to be more specific, thoughts of her mother.

She poured the heated soup into a bowl and sat down to eat it with more chunks sawn from the loaf.

She had noticed before anyone that something was amiss with her mother. Even her mother denied the problem until she had been forced to face it: that is, when the school where she taught English had suggested she sought treatment. Taking for ever to accomplish certain everyday actions and being late for everything wasn't at all like her mother, since she took pride in being super-efficient and always punctual, almost obsessively so. Which was the root of the problem. The moment Holly had first realized that something was terribly wrong had been quite a shock. She'd found her mother standing motionless by the front door of the small basement flat they shared in Bath, seeming to be speaking to herself under her breath.

'Mum? Are you all right?'

No answer.

'Mum?'

Her mother stopped murmuring, coming abruptly out of a daze. 'Yes, darling?'

'I asked you if you were all right?'

'Of course,' rather shirtily. 'It was the post. I was waiting for the post.'

It happened several times – not only before work but on other occasions. Holly would catch her mother staring at the floorboards or with her attention glued to a single page of a book for a quarter of an hour at a time. Ultimately the school where her mother worked must have noticed how long it took her to see a class into a room or out of it, or to get books marked or reports written; the head had strongly suggested a trip to the doctor.

After that there had been appointments with the community nurse attached to their GP's practice, appointments with a clinical psychologist and a long period when her mother appeared to make no improvement at all. In fact, for a time she got worse. Holly began to be terribly afraid that her mother was going mad.

Celia, the psychologist, speaking to Holly alone, had allayed her fears.

'We all have rituals, Holly. But in some of us and at some times, the rituals run out of control.'

'Rituals? What rituals?'

'With some people it's washing or checking to see if the door's locked. With your mother, it's counting. She has to count to a certain number at certain times. If she doesn't she becomes unbearably anxious. The ritual becomes a compulsion.'

'But Mum hasn't been particularly anxious lately. The divorce was years ago. She has a good job now.'

'You don't need me to tell you that teaching can be very stressful. But we can't be a hundred per cent certain that the condition is caused by stress. Sometimes it runs in families. Your mother says that she was brought up by an aunt who could have been afflicted the same way.'

'Afflicted! My mum's aunt was a control freak. And a bigot, by the sound of it. Though I never met her.'

'Just the right sort of temperament as it happens,' Celia smiled. She was a very reassuring kind of person. Holly liked her.

'Mum isn't like that.'

'But she herself agrees that she's a perfectionist.'

'Yes, she is. Or was.' It had sometimes made life difficult because Holly was only a perfectionist herself when it came to her work.

Celia said that it would be very beneficial if Holly could help Fern, her mother, stick to the routine that had been devised for her. It was a process of desensitization that was supposed to wean the sufferer off entrenched rituals. Holly had agreed. It meant being encouraging and patient, and checking, without appearing judgemental, the diary her mother was supposed to keep. It meant making a huge effort at home on top of keeping her head about the coming finals. Sometimes her supportive role, even with Celia cheering her on, became an onerous burden and she needed desperately to go somewhere on her own and quietly – or noisily – freak out.

Which was why she was here. She had borrowed her mother's Metro and taken herself off to Devon. She needed space and she needed the sea.

Holly wiped the bowl with the last chunk of bread and ate it hungrily. Then she sank her teeth into the apple, propped her feet up on a chair and began to relax for the first time for weeks.

The series of thumps in the darkness outside the railway carriage cabin came as a surprise. There was the sound of someone fumbling with the lock and then the door was flung open with a resounding crash.

'I warn you!' Emily's voice rang out commandingly. 'I'm a dab hand with this boat hook!' She stood framed in the doorway like an avenging angel.

'Well done!' Holly said with her mouth full. 'I'm impressed. Never mind a citizen's arrest. If I'd been a burglar I would have had a cardiac arrest by this time.'

Emily stared at Holly. 'How did *you* get in?'

'I was spoiled for choice, but through the window as it happens.' She pointed with her half-eaten apple.

Emily tossed her hat on to the dresser and sat down heavily on one of the cane chairs. Holly went over and gave her grandmother a peck on the cheek, the only intimacy she had so far risked. 'Hallo, darling Em.'

Emily sighed. 'I'm like a dead dog.'

'Would you like a cup of tea?'

'No thank you. I need whisky.'

'Whisky isn't good for you.'

'Nothing's good for me at my age. There's no cure for anno Domini.'

Holly reached over and took a bottle and one glass from the dresser. She poured a small tawny pool into the bottom of the glass and handed it to Emily. Emily looked critically at the amount before putting the glass to her lips.

'You went to the funeral, I suppose?' Holly said.

Emily nodded and laid her head on the back of the chair.

'Poor Em. Was it awful?'

'Funerals *are* awful. I don't usually go to them. Why can't they just turn us into something useful, like bone meal, or chuck us in the sea and forget about all this palaver?'

Holly grinned. 'I'll see what I can do when the time comes. Why didn't you ring? I could have come with you.'

'There was a moment when I rather feared you might have.' Emily drained her glass.

'What do you mean?'

'There was a feminist demo at the church gate. "Good riddance to an old chauvinist," that type of thing.' She chuckled. 'I felt sure you would have agreed with their sentiments.'

'I don't know why you went at all!' Holly blurted out hotly. She didn't trouble to point out that only a small minority of women in her year bothered about feminist demos, let alone about a painter who was as prehistoric as A. J. Monk. As the course progressed most students had shed their defiance along with their dreadlocks, their coloured hair and their ragged jeans. Holly thought it was rather sad.

'I hate what that shambolic old—' she had been going to say 'git' but changed her mind out of deference to her grandmother – 'what that shambolic old fraud did to you. I'd die of shame if my friends knew I was related to him. I'm sorry, Em, but it's true.'

'Your friends are art students. Terrible snobs in their way, art students. But once, you know, he was *somebody*. In those days even the ordinary chap in the street had heard of A. J. Monk.'

'Did you meet anyone you knew at the funeral?' Holly got up and went to over the stove. 'Would you like some soup? There's some left.'

'No, thank you. I've gone past eating. My brother was there, Francis. And Aiden Chase of whom you will not have heard.'

'He's an art collector and historian.'

Emily turned her head to look at her granddaughter. 'Yes!' Surprise. 'Then there was the Queen of the Night herself, naturally.'

Holly sat down again and cut herself more slices of bread and cheese. 'Why do you call her that?'

'You'd understand if you saw her. And her name is Queenie, after all.'

'I thought it was Regine?'

'A little free translation. Dancers liked something foreign-sounding in those days. Her real name was Queenie Tapp. Her father had a pie shop in Hackney.'

'I thought she *was* foreign.' Holly took a bite out of her makeshift cheese sandwich. 'I saw her on the box in that programme about English painters. She had a French accent.'

'So she has. But she's as English as I am and more so than you.' Emily referred to the fact that A. J. Monk, Holly's grandfather, was part Argentinian. Emily put her empty glass on the table.

'Yes,' she went on with a certain amount of ill-concealed glee, 'Regine was her idea but it was Jacko who turned Tapp into Fawcette – as a joke at first. Later she claimed it was her real name.'

Emily ran her gnarled, tree-root hand through milk-coloured hair. The difference between their tones reminded Holly of a photographic negative. On the middle finger of her left hand Emily wore an enormous gold ring, a single garnet surrounded by a swirling art nouveau mount. The last time Holly had come to see her grandmother she had asked if Jacko had given it to her. Emily had answered sourly, 'You're not seriously suggesting I'd still be wearing the old ruffian's ring, I hope?' Holly had supposed not.

'Well, I feel better now,' Emily said. 'I hope you've found enough to eat. If I'd known you were coming I'd have got something in.'

'It was a spur-of-the-moment decision.'

'Oh yes?' Emily glanced sharply at Holly. She still found Holly's physical likeness to Jacko disconcerting. Like his, her skin was deep olive and, like his, her hair sprang from her head in tight spirals. But Jacko's eyes had been a curious shade of amber whereas Holly's were nearly black. But she had his strong, stocky build.

At first Emily had resented the girl's intrusion. By mutual consent, ever since it had become apparent that being separated while Fern, Holly's mother, was still a child had created an unbridgeable gulf between them, Fern and Emily had given each other a wide berth. Getting rid of Holly, since the girl had taken it into her head to seek out her grandmother, had been easier said than done. From resenting her occasional visits Emily had moved on to merely tolerating them; finally she had begun to look forward to them.

'I'll make some tea,' Holly said, getting up. 'Would you like some now?'

'It'll keep me awake, but, yes, perhaps I will.'

Later, when the tea cups were on the table, Holly asked if the feminists' demo had upset the mourners.

'I don't think the Queen of the Night even noticed them,' Emily said. She added sugar to her tea straight from the packet. 'I must say they were very discreet. Does that disappoint you?'

Holly grinned. 'Was there anyone at the funeral from your Slade days?'

'Only Aiden. My greatest friend used to be a girl called Pan. Talented, she was. But she got married and went to Kenya and I never heard from her again. Then there was Tom Wylde; he became an engineer and a Sunday painter, I believe. Otherwise, the only person at the funeral I knew was Bruno Davidson who owns a gallery in London. He told me he still has some of the work I did in Provence. Can you beat that? Stuff from the 1930s presumably, done while Jacko still permitted me to paint.'

'Like the one in the spare room?'

'Bloody execrable colour, Jacko called it. Like a mandrill's backside.'

'But the colour in that red nude is fantastic!'

'It isn't bad. I do know that now, as it happens.'

'You *were* joking just now when you said about Jacko permitting you to paint?'

'You modern girls wouldn't understand. Let's just say that it was like water wearing away a stone. I might try to explain some day. I'm too tired tonight.'

Holly picked up the tea cups and took them over to the sink. 'Does this gallery-owner chap keep in touch then?'

'Bruno? Not lately. He wrote once, rambling on about an exhibition to include my stuff with the work of Winifred Nicholson, Vanessa Bell et al. You've heard of them, I suppose?'

'Yes.'

'So they do teach you something at that art school of yours. I thought it was all do-as-you-please these days.'

Holly said grimly, 'Do as you please? You must be joking!' She turned on the tap. 'So what did you say?'

'He seemed to think I might still be painting.' Emily rose from her chair with a sigh and picked up a drying-up cloth. 'There's talk about a retrospective for Jacko, of course.'

'What a waste of time,' Holly said dismissively.

'The Queen of the Night will see to it, you may be sure of that.'

'Why were women so shitty to each other in those days?'

'Aren't they still?'

'No, I don't think so. Not in my experience anyhow.'

'That's because of the feminist movement. Solidarity amongst the troops and so forth.'

They finished the washing-up in companionable silence. Outside the fall and drag of the surf was louder; the wind had got up and the tarpaulin cover of the cabin cruiser slapped monotonously against the hull.

'Who does that boat belong to?' Holly asked.

'I can't remember. Nobody ever comes near it. Been there years.' Another silence, then: 'How's your mother?' Emily asked.

'She's – not too well.'

'What's wrong?'

'She's had a sort of breakdown.'

'Where is she? Is she in hospital?'

'No. She's at home. But she's having therapy. One of her friends on the staff's looking in this weekend. But she wasn't well enough to come to the funeral.'

'There was no reason why she should have come to the funeral. She didn't owe Jacko anything. She hardly knew him. Poor Fern. Is there anything to be done?'

'Not really. Every so often I have to have a session with the therapist too. I hate it. Though the therapist is very nice.'

'I should think you did hate it!' Emily hung up the drying-up cloth. Holly emptied the water from the sink. 'I'm afraid Fern had a rotten childhood; as a mother I was a complete wash-out. Your head-shrinker will have a field day.'

'She knows it wasn't your fault,' Holly said sharply. 'Mum told her about you having to go to the sanatorium, and Aunt Muriel and everything.'

'Ha! All the same, the mother is always to blame in these cases. Anyone will tell you that. Don't you know your Freud?'

'I don't think Celia's a Freudian,' Holly said, drying her hands. 'Anyway, what about fathers?' Holly's father had walked out soon after she'd been born, when Fern had been in her mid-thirties. Holly had the impression that Fern preferred to face the difficulties of single-parenthood rather than those of marriage. Her father, who had since married again and now lived in retirement near Chepstow, had been even older than her mother when Holly had arrived on the scene.

'Bed,' Emily said. 'You're tired, I suppose? How did you get here anyway?'

'Mum lent me the car.'

'Good. Better than hitching. It was all right in my day but now they've let out all the maniacs, it isn't safe.'

Holly giggled.

They went to their beds. Emily made no grandmotherly fuss as to whether Holly had made up the spare bed or needed sheets or anything, which suited Holly very well. At Sandplace it was quite all right simply to toss off one's outer layers and doss down under the threadbare eiderdown, or in Holly's case, in her sleeping bag. She was asleep almost at once.

But it wasn't only the tea that kept Emily awake. She lay listening to the familiar sough and hiss of the sea and the slapping of the canvas cover (she would have to fix some extra ties).

Going to the funeral had been a mistake. It had given a prod to sleeping dogs who should have been allowed to lie. Now they were up and prowling about ill-humouredly, looking for someone to bite.

Holly's face, glowing like amber (how those Argentinian genes persisted!) swam across the ceiling, dissolved and reformed imperceptibly into Jacko's. In the twenties and thirties, Jacko could afford to be oblivious of such racial slurs that came his way. It meant nothing to him that the mean-minded and the envious called him 'that bumptious dago'. He had already created his own legend and his star was in the ascendant. He was an *enfant terrible*,

29

the wild man whose reputed genius excused even his most out-rageous exploits.

He had been ten years older than Emily. She had been younger than Holly was now when she had first heard his name.

With her share of the money left to Muriel, Francis and herself by their parents, who had been carried off by an epidemic of viral encephalitis within days of each other, she had elected to enter herself for the Slade. Muriel had taken her role as elder sister *in loco parentis* all too seriously and had fought bitterly to prevent Emily from entering what she called 'that den of iniquity'. But Emily had won and was soon besotted by the myths of the Slade's golden age, echoing with names like John, Orpen, Spencer, Gertler and a strange, gifted woman called Carrington. Later, during a brief visit to Paris, she had discovered Matisse, and having a glimpse of his vibrating primaries had found that the shining auras of her predecessors had begun to fade somewhat; a bright new rainbow had exploded in her head. If the results of this had puzzled her tutor, Wilson Steer, he gave no hint of it; indeed after sitting behind her dozing for some time, all he would usually say was 'muddle along then, muddle along.' On the occasions when he took her brush and worked on her painting himself, she learned more than in a hundred lectures. Even Muriel could not have faulted this rcumspect student existence. Until Emily met Jacko.

Jacko had radiated dynamic energy such as she'd never experienced before. She hadn't stood a chance, for goodness' sake! That he should even notice a green young student like herself would have been enough, but it went much further than that.

They met for the first time at a studio party in Fitzroy Street to which Pan, Emily's friend and a fellow student, had managed to wangle an invitation. The atmosphere was made up of all the elements they both found most exciting: a blend of London fog, cigarette smoke, the smell of turpentine and paint, the blazing fire, the canvases stacked round the walls, the half-light, the noise. And here they were! Two eighteen-year-old nobodies. And here was the obligatory cast of outrageous characters, just as they'd hoped, all vying for attention, including the young painter, sulking ostentatiously on the sofa, whose attitude shrieked, 'Look at me!' But Jacko Monk had no need to employ such tactics, he had just to be his brash and provocative self. They had heard that he was sensational to look at and they were not disappointed; his Argentinian mother had bequeathed him her extraordinary colouring, his aristocratic profile he had from his English father; his audacious amber stare was all his own. Even the bold Emily Troy trembled a little under it.

He completely ignored Pan. But his first words to Emily were absolutely typical.

'You know, I suppose, that you have the best arse in the room. A woman's most important attributes are a seductive neck and a good backside. Clever girl to have both!'

She thanked him drily for his approval with a pretence at sophistication, but underneath she was alight with apprehension and excitement.

'We must arrange for you to pose for me,' he said, oblivious not only of the roar of the party around them but also of a young woman with orange hair and a tortoiseshell cigarette holder, who was doing her best to wrap herself round him.

'Bugger off, Bunny!' he said, good-humouredly. 'Can't you see I have serious business here?'

The woman made her lips into a strawberry-sized pout and drifted off into the crowd.

'I would never have thought you were short of models,' Emily said.

'I'm never short of women who'd murder to pose for me, best beloved,' he said, grinning, but with the air of one reiterating a boring fact. 'What I am short of is models who look like you.'

Emily had a sudden urge to see his self-satisfaction dented a little. 'What do you pay?' she asked.

He gave one of his yells of laughter. 'Pay! My God, woman, are you demanding filthy lucre as well as a place in history?'

Women turned to look enviously at Emily. They recognized, if Emily did not, that she was to be the next of Jacko Monk's willing victims. Pan gave her up for lost and began an unsatisfactory conversation with the effete young painter on the sofa.

And how astonishing it had seemed to Emily to be taken up by the great man. Later still she came to know that she had no choice in the matter. She was profoundly in love with him; and she loved him to the detriment of her work and of her former closeness to her circle of friends.

It didn't take Jacko long to overcome her modesty and persuade her to pose nude, for she had already decided that prudishness was old-fashioned, something she associated with Muriel and her boring husband, Cedric.

'It's blasphemy to cover that dazzling body with these wretched rags!' Jacko dismissed the latest clinging skirts and her rainbow scarves with a wave of his hand. 'For Christ's sake get rid of them.'

Then later: 'You know, best beloved, that nothing must come between a painter and his muse? Not even your precious maidenhead. You do realize that, don't you? A painter has to know his subject absolutely, and that means in the biblical sense too. Even with that ghastly bourgeois upbringing I dare say you've just about heard of the concept of the new woman?'

She hadn't seriously questioned his argument. In any case, her circle of friends considered that they were not only casting off the shadow of a terrible war but also the last trappings of Victorian morality. There was not one of them who didn't pay lip service to the blessings of the new sexual freedoms, though Emily was convinced that in fact they were all as virginal as she was herself. Even Aiden Chase or, when she came to think about it, particularly Aiden Chase was, she believed, sexually innocent in spite of the fact that he was looked up to as the epitome of sophistication among the students; for Chase usually had the last word when it came to matters of taste and style. His paintings may have been academic and uninspired but he was the only one of Emily's circle whose background was thoroughly civilized and cultured. He was also the only one whose parents were rich. But Chase had looked upon Emily's attachment to Jacko Monk with public disapproval and private anguish; only she hadn't know about the anguish until much later.

When the nude portrait was exhibited it became the subject of notoriety for a few giddy weeks, bringing Emily furious letters from both Muriel and Francis, both of them berating her for bringing the name of Troy into disrepute; but by that time she and Jacko were married, leaving the London art world wondering if there were any ways left for Jacko Monk to astonish it.

* * *

Emily stirred restlessly, listening to the sound of Holly's regular breathing on the other side of the partition. It was all too apparent that Holly felt more at home at Sandplace than she did at the flat in Bath. Emily hadn't had the heart to tell her granddaughter that the days of the old railway carriage, along with all the other shacks, chalets and makeshift dwellings round about, were numbered.

CHAPTER THREE

The airy depths of the vast studio dwarfed the figures of the two people inside it. One was a young man who, with an air of deference, set down a tray on which were arranged a tiny bottle, a glass of mineral water and a bowl heaped with crushed ice and covered with a folded white cloth. Regine herself sat immobile in a high-backed chair, her face in shadow.

The young man measured out two drops of liquid from the bottle to the glass which he held to Regine's lips.

'Rescue Remedy, Maman dear.'

She remained motionless but took several sips before pushing it away. The young man took up the freezing cloth and pressed it gently to her forehead. She gave a delicate shudder and seemed to relax.

'Good boy. Good boy.' Her voice was barely above a whisper.

He put his mouth to her ear. 'Is that better, Maman?'

'*Beaucoup mieux*, Zak.'

Lowered blinds had plunged the studio into perpetual twilight since the day Jacko died. He had fought death to the bitter end, amazing the doctors by his capacity to survive to over ninety with a liver a mess from his days of heavy drinking, his heart clogged with fatty tissue and his bloodstream poisoned by his early and nonchalant disregard for the properties of flake white.

'It's been a strain, poor darling,' Zak said.

From the folds of the shawls that lay on her lap Regine raised a narrow hand the colour of candle wax, and touched his blond head.

'Did you make that telephone call?' she asked.

'Of course. And Mr Davidson suggested Thursday, if you think you'll be up to it.' He returned the cloth to the bowl and pressed it into the melting ice.

'I shall have to be, *tout de même,*' she said. 'I owe it to darling Jacko.'

'It could wait.'

'No. These things take enough time as it is.'

'Just as you say. You know best. As long as you feel strong enough.'

'For Jacko's sake,' she reminded him quietly.

'You drive yourself too much. You're a saint.'

She flinched as he once more applied the cloth to her temples. 'You spoke to Davidson about the early paintings?' she went on. 'We must have more of his early work. It's of the utmost importance. I myself much prefer his later oeuvre but the collectors all seem to think more highly of his youthful, more exuberant canvases. I find some of them just a little slapdash.' It was the nearest she would come to criticizing her late husband.

'He says he'll try to track down more of the early work.' Zak thought it might be tactless to mention the Tate painting, knowing she still clung to the belief that the most important canvases were the ones in which she herself figured. He lifted the cloth and straightened up. Then it could have been seen that beneath his David Hockney haircut his face had almost the same pallor as his employer's, except that his skin was firm and taut over his cheekbones. There was about his well-shaped head and hollowed temples a look almost of vulnerability; though he had removed his trendy spectacles, the narrowness of his eyes made it impossible to make out their colour, only that they were needle-sharp. He wore a fashionably baggy shirt of coarse linen and slate-coloured chinos.

'*She* must have some,' Regine said doggedly, almost to herself. 'I'm convinced of it.'

'His first wife, you mean. Yes, Maman, I'm sure she has,' Zak agreed. Though he was no relation whatever he had slipped easily into using the same diminutive as the rest of the family.

'As you know, Zak, there is a problem about the early paintings. So many are missing. He used to give them away, you see, in payment for paints and food, poor dear.'

And the rest, Zak just stopped himself from saying: booze, women and wild living generally.

'Have you put the appointment with Mr Davidson in the diary?'

'Yes, Maman. He's coming to Dorchester by train. I've arranged to meet him in the car.'

'Good boy,' she repeated. 'How did I manage without you?'

'Brilliantly, I'm sure,' he said. He fetched a large black diary from the desk in the corner of the room and flipping over the pages, showed her an entry. She nodded.

Inside the cavernous studio the isolation from the outside world was almost total; all that could be heard was the faintest twittering of sparrows high up in the eaves, and more faintly still, the complaint of collared doves and the drone of a tractor working in some distant field in the Dorset countryside. The former barn had once had two storeys but, soon after she'd come to live here, Regine had had a floor removed and windows let in along the north slope of the roof. The unplastered walls had been whitewashed and on them hung the canvases that represented every phase of the artist's career. Tier upon tier in the dim, greenish light, they reached almost to the apex where the walls met the exposed rafters of the roof.

The idealized gypsy had stood in her idealized landscape for fifty years or so, hand on hip with pitcher or amphora resting with improbable ease on one shoulder; labour made safe and romantic, for no trace of effort clouded the almond eyes or disarranged the cerulean dress and cinnamon-coloured shawl. An acrobat in pink tights wheeled against a ground of umber sawdust and women, clothed and nude, sat at tables, slept, bathed and combed their hair as if they had nothing else in the world to do. And everywhere there were portraits, the likenesses of long-forgotten sitters. The sustained gaze of a battery of eyes still looked out from another age; gypsies and circus people as well as many of the painter's own children and grandchildren. The battalions of portraits that had been commissioned by the famous, infamous and the *nouveau riche* were distributed throughout the country in stately homes, clubs and boardrooms, for to have been painted by A. J. Monk had once been the supreme endorsement of success.

Below them Regine and Zak, the living, looked insignificant in comparison, almost crushed by the weight of imagery. The collection composed all the paintings in the artist's possession at the time of his death and, as in the last twenty years he had sold very little, yet more canvases had been stacked round the walls as if in expectation of being discovered by posterity.

On a dais stood an oversized armchair, the twin of the one in which Regine was sitting, heaped with colourful drapes and shawls. Over the back was thrown an old, paint-stained corduroy jacket, unworn for the last six months of the artist's life, and beside the chair a battered straw hat was tilted at a rakish angle on top of an immense easel. Next to it stood a kitchen table that Jacko had used as a palette; it was thick with craggy lumps of scarlet, umber, viridian and cobalt, now all collecting a powdery layer of dust. Batteries of brushes of all sizes were clustered in earthenware crocks. Illuminated dimly from the obscured windows in the roof, the whole took on the aspect of a *mise-en-scène* for a period play, or even a shrine to the dead artist which, in fact, it was already in the process of becoming. Zak had seen to it that the studio had all been copiously recorded in stills and on film; just as the painter's life was already being painstakingly chronicled, filed and documented, as well as ruthlessly edited, by his adoring widow, with the help of the young man by her side and an Apple Mac which stood incongruously on the desk beside the very latest type of printer.

Regine stood up, steadying herself on the arm of her chair, allowing the dusky shawls to fall at her feet, revealing her unexpectedly crow-black hair and her blackberry-coloured dress whose straight folds suggested a figure on a Gothic cathedral, except that they finished abruptly to show off her remarkably elegant ankles. Against the front of her dress rested a heavy onyx and silver necklace from which depended a long silk tassle. In the space between the darkness of her hair and the dress, her face hung like a pale moon. In the aqueous light of the studio it could almost have been the face of some drowned woman. Her skin had curiously few lines, being as insubstantial as tissue paper pressed on to a mould. Not even the ghost of an emotion appeared to have disturbed its surface since the time of Jacko's youthful portraits of her fifty years before.

Zak leaped to assist her as she made her way to the door. She laid a hand on his arm.

'*Écoute*, Zak dear. Be so kind as to tell the others that I'm going to my room and don't want to be disturbed for an hour. Then Auriel could bring me some tea if she would be so kind.' Regine never wore a watch or had a clock of any kind about her; she relied entirely on the family's timekeeping and Zak's handsome, but unfortunately fake, Rolex.

'Of course, Maman.' Zak saw her out. He would be only too delighted to convey the message, thus emphasizing his dominant position in the household. He was well aware that, although they were all eaten up with jealousy, they would say nothing. In Regine's eyes he had become an honorary and favourite son.

Left to himself he would put in an hour or two categorizing the painter's canvases. Zak's initial role as disciple, admirer and general skivvy to Jacko had been steadily upgraded since he had arrived. Responding to an advertisement in 'Painting Now', he had immediately recognized that the job at Burr Ash, albeit low paid, would suit him admirably. He had seen to it that Regine now regarded him as indispensable. It had been he who had enthusiastically supported Regine's tentative proposal for Jacko's biography, something she could not have contemplated alone. Not bad, when at the beginning all he had in fact required was a sufficiently sequestered spot in which to disappear for the time being. He reckoned he now more than earned his keep.

Minutes passed before he became conscious of and then irritated by, a noise above his head. A sparrow had found its way into the studio and was making panic-stricken attempts to extricate itself. Zak made an impatient gesture. This was always happening; they had hired a local builder to find out where the birds were getting in but his repairs had obviously been completely inadequate. The sparrow fell to the floor, momentarily dazed and exhausted, its wings outspread. Zak seized the opportunity and scooped it up. He opened a side door that led into the garden and hurled the creature into the air. It landed, still dazed, in a patch of emerging arum lilies, before flying off into one of the surrounding beech trees. Bloody birds, he should have broken its neck while he had the chance. But he disliked violence; it wasn't his scene.

He paused for a moment, looking resentfully at the thrusting green of the arums and thinking how much he disliked the compulsive fecundity of nature. He found it obscene and somehow threatening. The hot-house arums in the church yesterday had made him feel almost physically sick with their sinister waxiness.

He shrugged and relocked the door, remembering the funeral. It amused him to reflect on the fact that there had been a certain person present at it who, in another context, might have recognized him. Here at Burr Ash and in his present incarnation he felt safe in the knowledge that this was highly unlikely, though he had to admit that the possibility of discovery had given him just the slightest pleasurable buzz.

His work finished for the moment, Zak sauntered across the cobbled yard. Given that he wasn't one for the countryside, in fact normally he detested it, he could have chosen a worse place than Burr Ash to retreat to.

It was situated in one of Dorset's lush valleys, surrounded by small, humpy hills, their sides clothed in the varied greens of fields and woodland, the lanes winding tortuously from one village to another. Looking at it as a dispassionate outsider, Zak guessed that a place so remote and so untouched would, sooner or later, be bound to attract the attention of despoilers, in the form of road builders or the designers of some leisure park or other. The thought did not disturb him a great deal. As far as he was concerned, as long as it served his present purpose, he was satisfied.

He approached the main house, unconscious of the fact that he was watched, or if conscious of it, indifferent.

From his bedroom window, Fergus stood behind the curtain, his almond-shaped eyes narrowed, his thirteen-year-old brain busy with a variety of possible ways to engineer Zak's downfall.

CHAPTER FOUR

The trio were playing a selection of classical music, there was a murmur of conversation and a subdued tinkle of cutlery as the young waiters whipped off covers and relaid tables.

The Pump Room was soothing, if expensive – not one of Fern's regular haunts, but Holly had insisted she came here with Audrey. Holly insisting! Somehow or other, in the last few weeks their roles seemed to have become reversed. Or had the reversal taken place much earlier? Fern wasn't sure now; in fact she wasn't sure of anything. She hesitated before helping herself to a scone, fighting an intense inner battle. To smother her impulse she grabbed the scone somewhat inelegantly and blundered into speech.

'I haven't been here for ages. We should do this more often.'

'Yes, we should,' Audrey said. Sensible, matter-of-fact Audrey. 'Yet when it comes to it, I always seem to be too busy at weekends. Only come when I have visitors, as a rule.'

'I know what you mean. When one does the rounds – Pump Room, Roman Baths, the Abbey and so on.' She began to butter her scone with thoughtful deliberation.

'You're better, aren't you?' Audrey said, appraising Fern with her slightly protuberant eyes. 'Not quite so sallow and a bit less lethargic.'

Audrey meant well but she could have put her comment more kindly, Fern thought. Audrey had no idea about the nature of Fern's problem; just that it was some kind of 'breakdown'.

Telling even Celia about the counting had covered her in agonizing shame. When at last it had all come out, Celia had received the confession in a completely straightforward manner as if Fern had simply said, 'I brush my teeth every morning', or 'I usually drive to work'. It was almost anticlimatic. Her therapist asked only how often the counting occurred, for how long, and were there any special situations that triggered it. And she wanted to know if certain numbers were significant, as if she'd come across such oddity every day of the week. Perhaps she did. All she said was that she'd had other clients with similar problems. That was the part Fern found almost impossible to take in. Other people, it appeared, could be as peculiar as she was!

After that it was easier. She could explain how it all started with an apparently harmless habit of counting floorboards and fence posts. Then it became essential to her to count her classes into the room and to count them out afterwards; then having to do it all over again from the beginning if the least thing distracted her, which with a flock of thirteen-year-olds giggling at her eccentricity it almost always did. Twenty-seven had been the number of her tutor group and that number had steadily become an obsession. She found herself counting to twenty-seven on all kinds of occasions: before opening a door, or a book, before putting her key in the lock of the car, before turning on the cooker. Twenty-seven became a talisman against some unimaginable disaster. Other people might cross their fingers or touch wood but she knew they didn't take it seriously; part of her too knew that her actions were totally without reason but that made no difference. The anxiety she felt if she stopped was too awful to make stopping worthwhile.

When Celia had asked her what she thought might happen if she failed to carry out her ritualistic counting, it was impossible to answer. All the same, she felt she was getting better. She'd made a real effort and still the sky had not fallen. There were two more successes to write in her diary tonight. Holly would be proud of her.

Still no one but Celia and Holly knew about her miserable secret. It would have been easier to admit to a dependency on drugs or booze; at least people presumably obtained some initial pleasure out of those. Her compulsions brought her no pleasure whatsoever. Only shame.

She had attended one or two group sessions and discovered that others had terrible secret obsessions that seemed as strange to her as hers did to them. There was a girl with hands raw from washing; a woman her own age with a compulsion to check doors, windows, taps and plugs; a young man plagued by involuntary twitches. Fern was thankful that at least her body hadn't let her down; she should have felt compassion but she had to admit to herself that her first reaction had been guilty relief that she wasn't as bad as some of the others.

'I was thinking of booking up for this painting holiday in Umbria this summer,' Audrey was saying. 'I suppose you wouldn't be interested? Might be something different.' Audrey taught maths. 'How about joining me? I thought of asking Pat but I was forgetting she has the family.'

Oh Audrey! Blunt as usual.

Fern prevaricated. 'I'm not sure how well I'll be in the summer. I wouldn't like to let you down.' Besides, she could not explain to Audrey that painting had always been a no-no. Not that she didn't have some talent. When she was a child at school the art teacher had constantly praised and encouraged her but she had always resisted; somehow or other she equated following it up as being an attempt to compete with her father, setting herself up in competition, which was unthinkable. Her father was a genius, a real painter, his work as far above her puny efforts as the sun above her head.

Audrey was impatient with her excuses. 'Goodness, Fern! Surely you'll be all right by then? These things settle down in no time these days, what with the modern drugs and what-have-you. You'll be back in the fray by next term, you'll see.'

Fern studied Audrey's good-natured face, high-coloured from her love of tramping round the countryside at weekends. She wore her mousy hair sensibly short, and a speckled grey Marks and Spencer jersey over a silk shirt, with a string of carnelian beads. Her expensive quilted anorak in shades of grey and tan lay over the back of her chair. Fern was tiredly aware that her own appearance left something to be desired; a black polo-neck that had seen better days and a long grey skirt together with her old tweed jacket looked distinctly shabby in her present surroundings. And she couldn't be bothered with jewellery nor with having her frizzy salt-and-pepper mane tamed. Next stop, bag lady, she thought despairingly. Audrey was probably ashamed to be seen with her. Nothing in Audrey's experience would help her to understand.

There would be absolutely no point in trying to explain about her compulsions. She would simply say, 'It's just a matter of pulling yourself together and getting out more.'

Audrey put the full amount of the bill on the table. 'Look, this one's on me. You stay put, my dear. I'm afraid I have to dash, I want to catch the post office before it closes and I haven't even begun the letters yet. Don't forget about coffee at my place next Thursday.' She humped on her jacket. 'And think about that painting course. It should be fun.'

'Yes, of course I will. And thanks for the coffee.'

'I'm sure Holly would think the holiday's a good idea.'

'Yes, she would.'

Audrey left, leaving a faint suggestion of Tweed in the air. She was of the type of unmarried career teacher that Fern admired. She wore good clothes, took her holidays abroad, often with some cultural interest attached, had her own house and arranged her life as she pleased.

Fern ordered another cappuccino and sat over it for a further quarter of an hour.

The trouble as she saw it was that she, Fern, had always tried too hard to please other people. First, her wonderful, awe-inspiring father, then her stern, unforgiving aunt. It had never been so necessary to please Emily since for years she had taken her mother's approval for granted; until that is, Emily had disappeared from her life altogether. Fern could remember all too clearly the last terrible days at Burr Ash that led up to her mother's departure. They were the culmination and realization of the sense of dread that had haunted her childish dreams for months; after that everything began to change and go wrong.

Just before, she had begun to notice that the great bearded presence of her father was missing more frequently, for which it was hard to know if she was thankful or desolated. When he was in a good mood the days were golden and the fun continuous. There were the unexpected bonuses of being allowed to stay up late, to mingle with the exciting strangers he brought home, of being made a fuss of; there were the spontaneous decisions to take a picnic on the river or to charge round the countryside in some newly acquired, high-powered but ultimately short-lived motor car. With petrol rationed, she had no idea how he managed this but, since it was her all-powerful father, she never questioned it. These were the high spots. But there was the reverse of the coin; times when Jacko came back to Burr Ash to nurse one of his black depressions. Then she and the twins learned to make themselves scarce. At best he would ignore them, at worst he would snarl like an animal and for behaviour that had previously delighted or amused him they would as likely as not be sent to their rooms without supper. If their mother objected, which she invariably did, the ensuing row would be harder to bear than if they'd simply crept away hungry to bed.

Fern had since realized that it was her mother's failing health that had prevented her from challenging Jacko more often, until, that is, that shocking weekend.

It was a strange time anyway, with the war in Europe nearing its end. The privations of rationing and making do had taken their toll. Fern and the twins had been recovering from whooping cough. It was evening and they were already in bed, but voices from the kitchen heralded the arrival from London of her father and some of his friends and she had crept to a point halfway down the stairs, clutching her little tortoiseshell cat to her thin body, hoping perhaps that Jacko would be in an expansive mood for a change, that he would sweep her into his arms and press her against his great barrel-like chest. The twins remained asleep; they were two years younger and lay snuggled down together like two baby birds in a nest. She hesitated. She could hear Jacko's voice, louder even than usual – he always insisted the children called him Jacko – just as they knew their mother simply as Em. Fern stayed where she was. The sounds from downstairs had taken on a sinister and disturbing tone: Em's laugh, mocking and unnatural, not like a real laugh at all, thumps and crashes, the rasp of tearing cloth. And then her father's laugh, which was suddenly more frightening than his snarls.

They were shouting at each other. The visitors seemed to have fallen silent.

'Can a cunt think?' she heard her father roar.

'Better than a effing prick!' Her mother's shriek was almost unrecognizable in its rage.

They were bad words her parents were using, she knew that. She had heard them used before, but casually, not in uncontrollable anger; words used by demented strangers. The sequence of the rest was confused in her memory. She listened in horror to Em's scream; there were sounds of a struggle, the grunting of men in conflict and then the sudden harsh bellow of Jacko's laughter that sounded to Fern more like a howl of rage.

'Sweet Jesus preserve me from a jealous woman!' her father yelled.

In her dark refuge on the stairs Fern froze with fear. She thought her mother dead since no one came to comfort her, put her back to bed and soothe her to sleep. The only sound was the murmur of strangers in the kitchen. An hour later, Fern caught up the cat, who lay asleep beside her, and crept miserably back to bed. She lay awake in the dark, feeling as if the end of the world had come.

It wasn't quite the end of the world but it was the end of the life Fern had known. Em hadn't died but she now spent hours either lying on the sofa in a feverish sweat or locked in the bathroom coughing almost as much as Fern and the twins had at the height of their illness. Being too young even to have heard of tuberculosis, she supposed at the time that her mother had caught whooping cough too. She wasn't to know that the fixed light that was Emily was about to be extinguished for ever, at least as far as she and the twins were concerned, and that her energy and gaiety were about to be replaced by the severe regimen of an unknown aunt's household; that the sweet, wild countryside round Burr Ash was to be exchanged for the dingy streets of post-war London. Jacko, established at Burr Ash with a new woman, never knew Fern's pain when her beloved father refused to come anywhere near Aunt Muriel's dour establishment.

Aunt Muriel had died twenty years ago of cancer of the spine and Cedric had followed soon after by choking on a fishbone, a bizarre and haphazard end for a man of his conventional respectability. The twins, Piers and Perry, were by that time already in Canada, sufficient unto themselves as ever, running their own business designing house interiors for upmarket clients. Fern rarely heard from them and their Christmas cards were as impersonal as publicity hand-outs. They had neither of them married; she supposed they might have been gay but thought it was more likely that they were completely asexual.

Perhaps she too should not have married. She had never had much success with men. There had been no difficulty in attracting them initially, since they assumed that her olive skin and dark hair denoted a passionate Latin temperament, but they soon discovered that her hidden fires, if she had them, were hidden too keep to be worth bothering with. They said she was cold and inhibited, though that was not how she felt inside. Jonah was the only man who had seriously attempted to penetrate the barriers she was scarcely aware she had erected. Both teachers, they met on a walking tour of the Pyrenees and had married a few weeks later.

'Let's face it, we could both be said to have reached the age of discretion,' Jonah said, for by that time he was forty-three and Fern was in her thirties. She had come late to everything, not having taken a degree until she was twenty-five. When she had first left school Aunt Muriel had insisted she took a secretarial course and it was only a chance meeting with her old English teacher that had encouraged her to think again and study for a qualification.

'We both want the same thing,' Jonah went on. 'A home, companionship and moral support in this vale of tears!' He said it smiling. His expressive dark eyes moved her. He held her gently. He was a gentle man.

'I'm not exactly a sexy dolly bird!' she said drily, warning him, for it was the age of the mini-skirted, wide-eyed vamp; the child-woman.

'God preserve me from sexy dolly birds,' he'd said, and she'd been comforted. If she'd realized it at the time, his pose of carefree bachelor was beginning to wear a bit thin among his friends, becoming a joke rather than an occasion for envy. Some suspected him of being a closet gay. Fern herself was weary of her single state and tormented by loneliness. 'At least we like doing the same things,' she'd said. 'We shan't quarrel about what to do in the holidays.'

'I don't think either of us is the quarrelling type,' he responded fondly.

They found they had the same taste in most things: in music, books and food. Their 'sensible' marriage, though sudden, promised to turn out to be more successful than those of their more impulsive friends, many of which were stagnating or breaking up.

One of the things they imagined they agreed on was their decision not to have children. It was true that she had once longed for a child but she put such feelings behind her as soon as Jonah made it perfectly clear that he wasn't at all keen on the idea. All the same, Fern did not take contraception all that seriously and was secretly delighted when she conceived. It was like being given a marvellous and unlooked-for gift. It was almost impossible to conceal her joy. But Jonah was furious; when he had said he didn't want children, he had meant it.

She remembered how he had looked up from his A level marking, incredulous and hostile.

'But you're on the sodding pill, for God's sake!'

She had turned away, her face flaming. 'Nothing's one-hundred per cent, Jo. Accidents happen.' But she suspected that he guessed the truth about this 'accident'.

'The doctor will say you can't go through with it, not at your age.'

'He says there's no reason why not.'

She did go through with it, against Jonah's stubborn opposition, keeping her morning sickness and her tiredness to herself and promising to go back to work as soon as the baby arrived. It should not impinge on Jonah's life at all.

He had never forgiven her for the deception he insisted she'd played on him. 'It's sod's law,' he'd said bitterly. 'Out of all the women I could have picked I chose one who was both frigid *and* broody.'

'That's not true!' she cried. 'How dare you say that!'

Later, when their tempers cooled, they had both apologized in a civilized manner. All the same, Jonah had no intention of sharing his comfortable environment with an inconvenient and noisy intruder and a few months later he went back to his soothing, bachelor existence, to his sixth form maths set and his walking holidays. Later, much later, he had married a nursing sister who was past child-bearing age and in any case had had a hysterectomy at a fairly early stage of her career.

Being a single parent was more difficult than Fern could ever have imagined but there had been a kind of tranquil contentment at being alone with her easy-going and sturdy daughter. When Holly had reached the age of fifteen and shown such an aptitude for art, Fern was both proud and fearful. She had never dared compete with her famous father, whom she had not seen for very many years, but it seemed that Holly had no compunction about it at all. She discovered to her amazement that Holly's life was not one that would be circumscribed by fear, as hers was . . .

The Pump Room trio finished their selection of popular classics to polite applause. Fern left her table and settled the bill. Now she had to think of some way to fill the day that would keep her occupied mentally and physically. She decided to go round the Roman Baths, feeling like a tourist and wondering how Holly was getting on with Emily. She herself would never have had the inclination or the courage to get in touch with Em after all these years, but she would never have dissuaded Holly.

Some years before, Holly had contacted her father; she had written to him suggesting she visited him in Chepstow, just for one day, but his response had been so delayed and unenthusiastic that, in the end, she had never gone. The message had come over loud and clear that he had still not forgiven Fern for Holly's existence.

But Holly was not a quitter. She simply transferred her attentions to her other mislaid relative. When, eighteen months before, Holly had tracked down Francis and extracted her grandmother's address from him, Fern had been extremely worried. The last thing she'd wanted was for Holly to suffer another rejection. But her fears were unfounded and Holly was regularly at Emily's, though Fern could never imagine herself visiting her mother. Not after all this time.

CHAPTER FIVE

'Your coffee, Mr Troy.' Mrs Bessemer dumped the cup down on his desk. Some of the coffee spilled into the saucer but she affected not to notice.

'Thank you so much,' Francis said. 'How kind.'

Mrs Bessemer departed without a word and Francis sat down at his great carved desk. It had been chosen, like all the furnishings of his study, to convey the impression of solid reliability and scholarship rather than elegance; a makeweight against a fear that parents might consider him deficient in these qualities.

From inside his tweed jacket he took the leather case that held his bifocals. These he rested on his long nose, which was still red from his recent attack of hay fever, and adjusted them behind his ears. He had felt under the weather for a few days but nevertheless he was glad that he had taken the trouble to go to Jacko's funeral. It might well turn out to be worth the discomfort. Meeting Bruno Davidson again had been a stroke of luck which he fully intended to follow up, now that he had got over the novel concept of Jacko as fund-raiser. If Davidson was right in saying that Jacko's daubs could be about to fetch high prices, it didn't matter to him in the slightest that it was because of their period appeal or the changing tastes of the art-buying public rather than because of their intrinsic aesthetic value. All he cared about was the exciting possibility that they might be exchanged for hard cash.

Some of the governors and even a few parents were beginning to cut up rough about the postponement of the start of the proposed new science labs and he would very soon have to do something about it. Lately there had been one or two excessively uncomfortable interviews in which enquiries as to the fate of certain substantial gifts and legacies, earmarked for the Laboratory Fund, had been couched in rather unpleasant terms. Just in time it looked as if his erstwhile brother-in-law's doodles might help him out in a quite unexpected manner. Davidson would surely know where to place them without Francis's own name being brought into it; presumably Davidson had customers who went in for that sort of thing. In a way he would be sorry to let them go, but he had to admit that they didn't do as much for him recently as when he had first stolen them from Jacko's studio. That was years ago, of course. Fortunately no one had missed them at the time (Jacko was notoriously careless) nor would have associated their disappearance with one of his rare visits to Burr Ash. That was when Jacko and Em were still together.

From the metallic bundle that weighed down the pocket of his venerable tweed jacket, Francis selected a key that unlocked the bottom drawer of his desk. From it he extracted some flat objects wrapped in a Marks and Spencer bag. Carefully, as if newly aware of their possible market value, he slid out two framed engravings and laid them side by side on the desk top. He studied them intently, commercial considerations in mind.

The first one was entitled *Embrace*, which was a relatively mild term for what was going on inside the sober gilt frame. A woman had apparently been leaped upon by an assailant, for the impact had knocked her half off what was presumably a bed. Her head was tipped back and her mouth was wide open as if in a cry of ecstasy or terror. Her assailant, who looked remarkably like Jacko himself, had laid a great paw-like hand on her chest as he kneeled between her chunky thighs and flying feet. Bracketed by the two struggling figures, like a third party about to intervene, a huge phallus rose up from a nest of scratchy black lines that extended to surround the dark gaping space between the woman's flailing legs. The style was lyrical, the detail explicit and the general effect exuberantly bawdy.

The second engraving, *Lovers in a Provençal Landscape*, was in much the same vein, except here the drama was being played out in a setting of fields and rocks with cypress trees standing symbolically erect.

Francis sighed. There was no doubt about it, as stimulants the engravings had lost their old appeal, but as investments they were just beginning to acquire it.

He became lost in a cash-induced trance. How much would his pictures bring him? Hundreds? Thousands? Indeed, was it possible that they would realize enough to resolve his financial embarrassment entirely?

There was a sharp rap on the door which sent Francis's gaunt frame into overdrive as he fumbled to stuff the engravings back in the bag, meanwhile managing to knock over his half-drunk cup of congealing coffee. He succeeded just as Mrs Bessemer, carrying an empty tray and grubby J Cloth, stumped into the room in her usual cracked and stained tennis shoes.

'All right if I take your dirty cup now?' A rhetorical question as always. 'Tch, tch! You should've drunk it while it was hot.' He longed to say that it had never been hot in the first place but he would not have dared.

She advanced with the J Cloth. 'Never mind, let's mop it up.'

She dabbed at the desk and the papers on it while Francis held the Marks and Spencer bag aloft almost as if he feared she were about to wrest it from him.

'You men!' she scolded matily, for she was suddenly in a rare good mood. 'Messrs by name and messers by nature! Did you hear that? Messrs by name—'

'Yes. Ha, ha,' Francis nodded, frantically praying that she would make herself scarce before he struck her across her fat, red face.

Taking her time, she picked up a pile of school prospectuses and flicked coffee from their corners. 'There,' she said, 'you can hardly see the stain. You'll be able to use them after all.'

'Thank you, Mrs Eh—' Francis said. 'Thank you. That will be all. As you say, one can hardly see the stain.'

Mrs Bessemer swept the cup and saucer on to her tray and Francis tentatively returned the plastic bag and its precious contents to the top of the desk. Mrs Bessemer fixed her eyes upon it.

'Would you like another cup?' she asked, the obliging mood continuing. 'I can soon boil one up.'

'I'm sorry?'

Mrs Bessemer repeated her question laboriously and loudly.

Francis suppressed a shudder. 'No thank you, Mrs Eh – that was delicious.'

'If you're sure?'

'Absolutely.' Francis struggled with his uncharacteristically violent urges.

Mrs Bessemer closed the door behind her, absent-mindedly she gave the handle a little polish with the J Cloth, coating it with a layer of cold coffee. Her mouth was twisted in a knowing smile. She didn't know what he wanted with those dirty pictures, a man in his position. Pornographic, that's what they were! He should've married long ago. Better to marry than to burn, like St Paul said. And what would the parents and governors think if they knew the Headmaster's grubby secret? What if, indeed!

During the first week of her employment Mrs Bessemer had discovered that access could be gained to any of the desk drawers that her employer chose to keep locked by the simple expedient of removing the drawer above; a problem that could be solved by a half-witted six-year-old. (A half-witted six-year-old was her favourite character.) It was pathetic how stupid these so-called brainy folk were in practical matters. Like children themselves really. Yes, finding those pictures had been a nasty shock and had upset her for almost half an hour, after which she had been forced to have another look at them to make sure she had seen aright the first time.

Francis sneezed explosively. He removed his spectacles and mopped his eyes and nose. Blast the woman! Now his hay fever had come back, just when he thought he was getting the better of it. Mrs Bessemer had been very far from what he had looked for in a housekeeper. He had visualized a refined, ladylike creature. Genteel. Yes, that was the word, genteel. An old-fashioned quality, but then he supposed that in many ways he was old-fashioned himself. He would have liked someone who would have added status to his establishment, but after interviewing half a dozen candidates he had come to the conclusion that the money he was offering would not buy such a paragon. All he could afford was Mrs Bessemer.

He leaned back in his swivel chair, seduced by the vision of his stolen engravings solving the problem not only of the new science labs but his domestic help as well. He shut his eyes and dreamed of money, for cash had long since taken the place of sex in his fantasies. A vintage Lagonda, a holiday in Amalfi (was it still as he imagined or a high-rise hell?). Or perhaps a pent-house flat overlooking Hyde Park and clothes from Savile Row. Plus an obliging housekeeper to cook and clean and answer the telephone. He dreamed of being able to retire. He had been advised to sell the school but he doubted if anyone would buy it as a going concern; and in any case he would first have to sort out the little matter of the Laboratory Fund. He had also been advised to hand over the Headship to a younger man but the financial difficulties made this an impossibility. And, at the back of his mind, there was another consideration. As Headmaster and owner of Rudyards he had a certain status, he was somebody, he counted. As a retired schoolmaster on a tiny pension he would be a nobody and he would be alone.

Like Emily. Except that Emily evidently didn't mind being alone and appeared to fill the days somehow in that seaside bungalow of hers, a place that he could never have brought himself to visit even if she had invited him, which she never had; the very thought of a retirement bungalow filled him with horror and he couldn't understand how his unconventional sister had ever come to settle in one.

Yesterday, to his astonishment, he'd had a telephone call from none other than Aiden Chase, enquiring as to his sister's present whereabouts. He had been highly intrigued and had wasted no time in giving him Emily's address. If the rich collector took it into his head to play the philanthropist towards his old flame there was no knowing what it could lead to. He would give it a week and call back; it was a connection worth following up. He sighed, coming down to earth. It was too much to hope; knowing Emily, she would tell the old codger to buzz off. Yes, it was all very well for her, being alone.

For him the school in Muswell Hill was both business and hobby. It had taken the place of everything normal people took for granted, such as wife, home and family. Not least it enabled him to live in the sort of grandeur that he could never otherwise have afforded. This great house with its ancient (Victorian, in fact) panelling, massive carved oak staircase and rooms on a palatial scale, satisfied a very special need in him, notwithstanding that the place was as cold as the tomb in winter.

The words cold, winter and tomb chilled his mind and reverberated through his body in an involuntary shiver. He sensed that the shadow which had stalked him throughout life was closer these days. If he could only have persuaded Em to come to live with him it would have been some comfort; Emily's presence would have kept the darkest shadow at bay, it would never have survived the burning ferocity of her personality.

He got up and paced to the window; he looked out on the drive which was overhung by a magnificent copper beech, its already unfolding leaves a vivid coral. The beech tree had become the hallmark of the school, featured on the front of the prospectus and fostering the impression that Rudyards had existed from time immemorial. In a few days from now the drive would be full of the bobbing heads of the boys, back for the summer term, some of them the sons of men who themselves were old boys of the school. So terms and time rolled on.

Francis shivered again and, in an almost panic-stricken burst of activity, he went back to the desk and riffled through his address book until he found Davidson's telephone number. As he punched out the digits he suddenly thought about the strange telephone call he'd had some months ago from a girl called Holly who had turned out to be Fern's child, and who had asked for Emily's address. Emily had written to tell him soon after that she had been down to see her. To his amazement it seemed that Emily had not given the young woman her marching orders, which was what he would have expected. In fact it now appeared that the mislaid granddaughter was a rather frequent visitor.

CHAPTER SIX

Holly sat huddled, her arms round her knees, watching the figure at the edge of the sea. Like a cormorant with wings outstretched it stood, until the wings dropped to the sand in a heap of purple towelling and the illusion was snuffed out. Emily stepped into the water and dipped under the little waves; she swam a stately breaststroke to what was evidently a preordained distance before turning and swimming back, her chin level with the water.

The sea was the colour of lead except where olive and sepia glimmered briefly as the small waves turned smoothly over and disintegrated in a soft hiss of creamy foam. Beyond them Emily's purple towelling turban ploughed on undisturbed. The sky was pearly grey, a thick mist obliterated the horizon and in fact everything else more than fifty yards away. They could have been on a desert island.

A whisper of breeze blew in from the sea and Holly, fully clothed, shivered. The sand felt harsh and gritty on the verandah under her boots. Verandah was probably too grandiose a name for the structure in which she sat. It had been stuck jauntily on to the end of the GWR carriage and was just about big enough to accommodate a couple of deck chairs; from it one could descend to the beach by means of a few wooden steps. Holly sat with her feet on the topmost one.

Like all the makeshift shanties around about, Sandplace had been embellished over the years with its share of gables, carved bargeboards and shaped windows (Gothic arches seemed to be the favoured style – some even had stained glass) as well as many coats of bright-hued paint. But salt air and bombardment by sand had given the original colours the appearance of an ancient fresco. On the timbers of the verandah where she sat, Holly could detect evidence of dark green, chrome yellow and white as well as the present incarnation of forget-me-not blue. It seemed, Holly thought, that the owners of the shanties used them to realize fantasies they would never have dared carry through on a regular house. In fact the whole small settlement reminded her of a random collection of cut-price *cottages-ornés*, all hedged about with their rudimentary gardens and tamarisk bushes. She knew that Emily lived in Sandplace all the time but she had never figured out how many other shanties were occupied year round. But she loved it here, even in winter when the old railway carriage vibrated in the wind and salt spray abraded its windows. It was her ambition to live in a place like this, it had just the right sort of atmosphere. I could work here, she thought.

Emily emerged from the water, retrieved her towel and rubbed her arms vigorously as she came up the beach.

'Do you do that every day?' Holly flinched as icy drops pattered down on her and scattered dark circles on the wooden floor.

'Every day,' Emily said. 'Pretty well.' She towelled her legs.

'I don't know how you stand it. That water would stop a polar bear in its tracks. I know, I tested it. Aren't you afraid you'll have a coronary or something?'

'Why should I be afraid of that?'

There didn't seem to be an answer to that. Holly squinted up at her grandmother. She looked indestructible, like a piece of knotty driftwood. Her navy swimsuit sagged slightly in places and Holly noticed a neat darn. Except for some rounding out of the spine between her shoulders and a broadening of the haunches, Emily could have been twenty years younger.

'I saw Jacko's painting of you in the Tate,' Holly volunteered.

'You did, did you?' Emily pulled off her turban and patted the nape of her neck. Her topknot unfurled itself and her hair collapsed on to her shoulders. It was still thick and Holly found its milky whiteness disturbing as she remembered the rich colour of it in the painting. Now it looked more like the winter pelt of some arctic animal. 'So. What did you think of it?' Emily said.

'I suppose it's good of its kind,' Holly admitted grudgingly. 'Just as long as you can take the idea of woman as a sex object, which I can't personally.'

Emily chuckled. 'So the women you carve are different, are they?'

'Naturally. They're not representational in any case. More allusive.'

'Illusive?'

'Allusive.'

'Ah. Then you think the Tate painting is pornographic?' With an end of the towel in each hand Emily energetically dried her back.

'Don't you?'

Emily shrugged. 'You may be right. All the same, that and a couple of the ones from the South of France era were just about the best he did. We were staying in a little place called Vaux. All we did was paint, swim, drink and make love. He called me his Muse – they said things like that in those days – just a high-falutin name for something much more down to earth, you know. I didn't care. He could have called me any bloody thing he liked; I was an idiot girl, witless with happiness. I thought I had everything. And so I did for a time: days on the beach, the little tan-coloured house with its blue shutters, the whole place reeling with the scent of mimosa, sea like jade—'

'I see,' Holly said with studied irony. 'So when did it change?'

There was no answer. Emily had gone inside. Holly followed, leaning against the door of Emily's room where her grandmother had stripped off her wet swimsuit and was rummaging through some clothes that were draped over the back of a chair. She stood naked in the middle of the room without any attempt at concealment, as oblivious as ever over the conventions of physical modesty while yet as emotionally inaccessible as the limpets that clung to the rocks further up the beach. Holly considered herself fortunate not to have been slung out already, so she framed her next question casually as she bent to pick up Emily's discarded swimsuit.

'Obviously things *did* change?'

Emily's sparse pubic hair and leathery shanks disappeared into an expensive pair of violet-coloured silk knickers; she reached for the matching bra as if she hadn't heard the question.

'When Jacko's jealousy got the better of him,' she said at last.

'You had another fella?'

'Are you being deliberately obtuse?' Emily was offended. 'I told you! I was in love with Jacko.' She pulled a cotton tee shirt over her head. It had a patch on it of a different colour. Holly grinned. Emily cared nothing for outward show but her underclothes were immaculate.

'I still don't understand.'

'Think, girl!' Emily completed her attire with a pair of men's trousers and a multi-coloured jersey that had been knitted in one piece on huge needles. 'I was a painter too, remember. And good. I won prizes at the Slade. At first both Jacko and I used to paint; I painted the landscape and Jacko painted me.' A low, mirthless chuckle. 'Two incompatible activities you might say.'

'Tough,' Holly commented drily.

'When one is scarcely out of art college and confronted with a talent as established as Jacko's the outcome wasn't in doubt.'

'Why not?'

'Stupid girl! In any case it was all pretty subtle at first. Subtle for Jacko, that is. Remarks about my painting like the reference to the mandrill's backside.' Emily tugged a comb through her tangled hair. 'Jacko had rather traditional views about colour—'

'Like what?'

'That it was icing on the cake, not the main ingredient or intrinsic to the work.'

'Bit out of date even then, wasn't it?'

'I was young. I rebelled but I believed him ultimately because I trusted his judgement. Besides, I was still in love with him.'

'You mean you still had the hots for him?'

'Blast you, girl! No! I was in love. It wasn't only sex.'

'Right. If you say so.' Holly straightened up. 'Want some tea? I'll put the kettle on.'

As they drank their tea Holly tried more questions but Emily wasn't to be drawn further. Holly realized she'd have to be less outspoken if she wanted to get anything more out of her grandmother.

Even before they left Vaux it had become clear to Emily that her knack of handling colour, her growing self-assurance as a painter, her unorthodoxy and above all her refusal to rework her style into a pale reflection of her husband's was becoming a thorn in Jacko's side. No matter how much he belittled her developing talent she knew that he was already beginning to see her work as part of the future, just as his was even now of the past.

But he was still at the height of his powers, and with a vision excited by Emily's potent physical beauty, he was in no mood to have it denied him while she trotted off into the countryside with her easel and paints. She realized that he regarded her insistence on pursuing her own agenda as trivial and perverse; but it was equally apparent that, at first anyway, a confrontation over it would have seemed too much like jealousy, and jealousy between such unequal contenders was surely out of the question. Instead he hit on another issue altogether. He decided that he objected to Celestine's cooking. Celestine came up from the village every day to clean and cook them a meal in the evening.

It was a languid late afternoon: the sea like polished lapis, the heat stifling, the air full of the rasp of cicadas.

'Her cooking tastes all right to me,' Emily had replied to his grumbles.

'What the hell do you know about cooking? You were brought up on English stodge. And it's not you she's trying to poison.'

'Poison! Don't be ridiculous.'

Jacko's tawny complexion became brick-coloured.

'Don't patronize me!' he roared. 'I tell you every time I eat that woman's food I get a pain in the belly.'

'You'd get a much worse one if I cooked for you. Besides you've never mentioned this before, and it doesn't seem to have affected your appetite.'

'I've only just tumbled to it.'

'Well, *I've* never noticed anything.'

'Christ! Can't you understand, woman? It's *me* she's got it in for.' He stabbed his stomach with a paint-stained finger. 'She's a bloody witch!'

Emily laughed at the idea of the good-natured Celestine casting spells. It was her full-blown gutsy chuckle in which Jacko normally took such delight against which he now reacted with sudden violence.

He seized the earthenware pitcher in which they cooled their

61

wine and hurled it at her. It grazed her arm and smashed on the paving of the terrace. The wine was like blood as it ran down the front of Emily's white dress and over her sandalled feet.

'Bitch!' Jacko yelled as he flung out of the house.

She stared after him in shock. He had never before acted like this towards her, though naturally she had heard stories of the fights he'd been in. Stories that in the retelling had always amused her. But what had *she* done to provoke such an outburst? It was unreasonable and extreme. Was she in some way to blame? For hours she agonized over this disastrous flaw in their Provençal idyll before she satisfied herself that Jacko's outburst was due entirely to the heightened susceptibilities of genius. Allowances would have to be made.

He came back at last, flushed and boozy, the incident apparently quite forgotten. He had four brand-new friends in tow: a White Russian painter, an American writer and his wife, and a French sea captain.

In the end Emily had to learn to cook. Jacko insulted Celestine and she left; undomesticated Emily had pleaded with her but she had refused utterly to return, even to clean. Emily did the cleaning and on the occasions when they stayed at home in the evenings, produced a succession of rather peculiar meals. Strangely, Jacko didn't seem to mind. She had the obscure feeling that her efforts somehow made up for some unnamed failure of which, as a wife, she had been guilty. And she didn't comprehend until later that while she was spending hours posing for him, stretching his canvases and then cooking his meals, she could not be fostering her own talent. She thought that, in any case, there was plenty of time. Besides, Jacko had never been more exuberantly good-tempered; he was exhilarated by the knowledge that he had never painted better and with an almost Romany superstition that the muse might suddenly desert him, would brook no interruption.

Were things so different now that it would be impossible to make Holly understand? The two women drifted back to the room that had a view over the verandah, the beach and the sea as far as the now visible indigo line of the horizon. Emily's towel and swim-suit were hung outside to slap themselves dry in a sharp spring breeze which was already dispersing the fog.

Holly chafed her arms. 'I'm cold,' she said. 'Could we have a fire?'

'You should have come swimming.'

'Stupid of me. I didn't think to bring a swimsuit. And it's April already!'

Emily showed a gleam of strong teeth and went over to rake life into a wood-burning stove that sat like a little black god on an improvised hearth. She gathered an armful of driftwood and crammed it into the open door. 'How long are you staying?' she asked, busy with matches.

'The weekend. I've brought some sketchbooks. I thought I might have a go at rocks and waves. I have an idea – it might take a couple of days. Would you mind?'

'Not at all. You're still persisting with antediluvian concepts like drawing, then?'

Holly's mouth had a stubborn set. 'You bet.'

'How's it going?'

'OK as far as I'm concerned but as I told you, they still don't like my stuff. They're still saying I should get rid of the craft element. You talked about art students being snobs and I know where they get it from. But it's not the sort of snobbery you were talking about. They think that the work of the artisan, the craftsman, has by definition to be inferior to the intellectual process.'

'In the case of art, how do you separate the two?'

'You'd understand if you saw the end product. Anyway, I have serious doubts about my degree marks.'

'All they indicate is how good you are at passing examinations.'

'Unfortunately how you pass exams has a bearing on one's future.' Holly gazed into the stove where the driftwood had caught and was blazing brightly. She grinned suddenly. 'In a lecture the other day one of the tutors announced that painting was dead. Then he marched out of the room. That's the kind of thing that happens.'

Emily shrugged. 'That old chestnut! D'you know, I remember an almost identical occurrence. That was fifty years ago, of course. *Plus ça change—*'

One of the reasons Holly liked coming to Sandplace was because she could talk to her grandmother about the course. Not something she could discuss at length with Fern. Fern became far too anxious about Holly's conflicts at college and would plead with her not to make waves. Somehow Emily's comments always seem to put things in perspective.

'When does Fern expect you back?' Emily asked.

Holly thought guiltily of her mother. 'I'll wander up to the phone box later and ring her; see how she's getting on. I might be able to stay the extra day if she's OK.'

'You're a kind girl to think of your mother but you're an artist too. You must live your own life. Do you believe your mother would expect you to dance attendance if you were a son?'

'She doesn't expect it of me. I want to do it, otherwise she might never get better.'

Emily watched the blue flames hovering about the burning logs. Sometimes they looked as if they burned quite independently. 'I expect Fern thinks I let her down. Well, I did.'

'She doesn't blame you. She told me.'

Emily grunted. 'That's very civilized of her. It remains that I allowed myself to be put away at a very critical time in the children's lives.'

'Come on! You couldn't help having TB. I expect it was that shitty, damp farmhouse.'

'Who knows if we can help our illnesses. But two years is a long time out of an adult's life, let alone a child's. Longer still if you count the convalescence. Besides, Burr Ash might have been damp but it was extraordinarily beautiful. Tucked into the Dorset countryside, it was a dream come true at first. There was a stream overhung with willow and hazel, apple trees in the paddock that in spring looked as if they were covered in pink snow, a walled garden, swallows nesting in the eaves. Yes, I suppose that in the beginning I did deceive myself that Jacko could settle down to a rural existence.'

There was a long silence. Holly poked at the burning logs.

'When I came out of the sanatorium,' Emily said, almost to herself, 'I found that life had moved on. The children had settled down with Muriel, happily she said. I was told not to upset them, or even worse, infect them with my disease. She treated me like a leper.'

'Mum says that Muriel had religious mania and was frightfully strict.'

'I suppose I thought the children were better off with an overdose of sermons than homeless and fatherless.'

'But even Jacko wouldn't have kicked you out of Burr Ash, would he? You could have lived there.'

'Yes. As you say, I could have lived there. It's just possible, I suppose, that Jacko might have tolerated my presence. If I didn't mind living with the Queen of the Night in a sort of *ménage à trois*.'

'Oh, I get it,' Holly said. She glanced at Emily, who had closed her eyes. Holly understood that the conversation was over. There was no sound in the white panelled room except the crackle of the logs and the snap of Emily's swimming things on the line outside. It was indescribably peaceful.

CHAPTER SEVEN

'Here is the traffic news. A tanker has overturned on the M5 and drivers are warned of a four-mile tailback on the westbound carriageway just north of the Wellington turn-off. On the M25—'

Gideon Chase stopped listening as he crept past the tanker where it lay on its side like a huge upturned beetle. Firecrews were hosing a tide of milk off the motorway, a police squad car was parked, blue light flashing. Gideon emerged at last from the tedious enfilade and put his foot down.

The delay had not improved his usually equable temper; he hadn't wanted to come on this errand in the first place but his father had insisted. Insisted in the gentle but relentless manner Gideon knew only too well. He had been on a job in Somerset when his mobile phone had bleeped and his father's quavering voice had come over the line. It had taken a moment to drag his concentration away from the difficulty of attempting to explain to his clients the problems of landscaping a garden in which so many mistakes had been made; for starters, a water-logged lawn, too many trees planted too close together and in the wrong place, and a whole border of calcifuges slowly giving up the ghost in entirely the wrong soil. He had been in the process of warning the bemused couple that a certain amount of violent activity was going to be necessary before their dream garden could actually take shape.

'I want you to do something for me, Gideon,' Aiden had said.

'If I can,' Gideon knew he sounded less than enthusiastic. He glanced at his clients, who were pacing the awful crazy-paved patio (*that* would have to go), looking thoughtful.

'I expect you remember meeting Emily Troy – she was once Emily Monk?'

'Remind me?'

'At the funeral, Gideon,' impatiently.

'Ah, yes. I'm with you.'

There was a pained silence, then Aiden spoke again. 'I want you to go to see her. I don't mind telling you that I was a little concerned by her appearance that day. She has always been somewhat eccentric but it seemed to me that she might be in need, financially that it.'

'She did look a bit wacky,' Gideon said.

'I wasn't asking for your opinion, I just asked if you remembered her,' Aiden said severely.

'Sorry. What d'you want me to do? Where does she live?'

'She lives in Devon, a mere stone's-throw from you.' Gideon lived in Dorset. 'I should like you to pay her a visit and report back to me. I have managed to extract her address from her brother who appears to be of the opinion that she's perfectly all right. But one is naturally a bit worried. I would go myself but as you know, these days my health isn't really up to the inordinate amount of travel involved.'

Aiden, reading his wobbly handwriting with some difficulty, gave the address to Gideon. Gideon read it back.

'That's right,' Aiden said. 'It's a bungalow, I believe. Probably on one of these seaside retirement developments. I believe they call them estates.' His appalled tone made Gideon smile to himself. To his father an estate was somewhere like Riversfoot, which had been the country home of the Chase family for several generations.

'One would have supposed that Monk would have seen to it that she was well-provided for – she certainly once led me to believe that was the case – but now one begins to wonder.'

'So, as I understand it, you want me to suss out her situation and report back. Is that it?'

'I want you to notice if there are any signs of difficulty, yes,' Aiden said crisply.

'Apart from having to live in a bungalow on a retirement estate, you mean?' Gideon grinned to himself.

'Sarcasm doesn't suit you, dear boy. I'm sure you know what I mean. And Gideon, one other thing—'

'Yes?' warily.

'I would like you to try to persuade her to visit me in town or at

Riversfoot. For a protracted stay, d'you see? She might listen to you. Then once she was here one could, if necessary, sort something out.'

'Sounds like a tall order.'

'Please do as I ask for once, Gideon?'

For once! Gideon thought wryly. Oh well, perhaps he should humour the old chap.

At the other end of the phone Aiden was congratulating himself on his astuteness. His son had turned out to be quite presentable, apart from that regrettable pigtail, that is. Not unlike himself when young, which might affect Emily's judgement. After all, when he had been much the same age as Gideon was now, he had been of the opinion that Emily loved him, in fact he was sure of it. He couldn't believe, even now, that her feelings were the result of being on the rebound from Jacko Monk.

At the same moment Gideon, sliding back the aerial, was wondering what on earth his father was getting him into, his imagination galloping wildly ahead to cringe-making scenes with flaky old harridans. As he'd remarked, it was a tall order.

Released from the traffic hold-up he sped along the motorway on his errand of mercy, being passed by an articulated lorry doing at least eighty-five. He glanced at the earth-stained envelope on which he had written the address. East Ashpool was not a part of the world he knew very well, and according to his father the Saltings was a mile or two further on, near the coast; he ought to have allowed himself more time to find the place, but time was a commodity always in short supply. In spite of the recession, he had never been busier. Fortunately for him gardens were something people were still prepared to spend money on.

His father had been deeply shocked at his son's choice of profession and had for a time prevailed upon him to study architecture instead. Gideon had completed a year of the course before rebelling. Even now Aiden wasn't absolutely sure what a landscape designer did, it was so far removed from the rarified world with which he himself was familiar. And though Gideon had been brought up in what amounted to a museum, he realized that he was just as far removed from the ambience of paintings, sculptures and *objets d'art* amongst which his father felt most at home.

69

The only aspect of Gideon's former home that had ever interested him was the garden; and although by the time he was twelve he knew the difference between a Samuel Palmer and a Kandinsky, what really inspired him were the achievements of Capability Brown and Gertrude Jekyll. At the time his elderly father was as remote a figure as the artists themselves. Once he had come across Gideon wandering in the sculpture-lined corridor near the library and had asked him who he was and what he was doing there.

'I'm Gideon', the puzzled ten-year-old had replied.

'Gideon?' His father had stared at him, mystified. 'I have a son called Gideon.'

'That's me. *I'm* Gideon.'

Chase had examined his offspring in embarrassed silence before turning on his heel and walking off with his strange bouncing gait and ramrod back.

Gideon had hopped it to the library to immerse himself in a cache of gardening books he'd recently discovered there. At least his father left him in peace to follow his own preoccupations. Some of the chaps at school had tyrannical parents who pestered them unmercifully, even to the extent that they were actually glad to get back after the holidays. As for his mother, he'd hardly known her. After she died he had been raised by various nannies and housekeepers who had all tried their best to make up for his loss; in fact they'd been pretty decent in their way.

Since he had grown up and had managed to remain roughly the same height and size between sightings, he had tended to be recognized by his father more frequently and for some years now they had been on quite amicable terms. This was in spite of, or perhaps because of the fact that while Aiden remained firmly in Buckinghamshire at Riversfoot, or in London, Gideon had established his landscape design and consultancy firm in the West Country.

Aiden was renowned for never going anywhere except to his club, the soberer type of eating establishment or to one of the great auction houses, so although Gideon had been startled by his father's decision to attend the funeral of the painter A. J. Monk, he had been sufficiently intrigued to offer to drive him there. He already knew that there was some obscure connection that had something to do with his old man's periodic visits to the Tate where, Gideon had been told, he sat for hours at a time in front of one painting; a painting, moreover, that wasn't the type of thing his father went in for at all as a rule. The explanation had dawned on him when he had seen the effect that Monk's former wife had on the old man. He hadn't seen his father so animated since the time he'd come across a genuine Picasso aquatint mixed up in some worthless book plates.

Gideon had been aware that there was a curious unexplained period of his father's life just after the war, and some time before his mother had come upon the scene, about which Aiden was more that usually reticent – which meant very reticent indeed. For some reason Gideon connected it with the visits to the Tate. When he had discovered which painting his father went to see he had been surprised and then lost interest, until he heard about the funeral. The nude of the painting whose title he had forgotten, had certainly not been the dark, rather sinister-looking female Gideon had seen following the coffin. He had recognized her immediately from a BBC programme he once saw by accident when he had switched on for the cricket score. It was almost impossible to tell, but it looked as if the flamboyant nude of the painting was the same woman that he was on his way to see now.

CHAPTER EIGHT

Holly washed up. Emily dried and restored the heterogeneous collection of crockery to their places on the shelves.

'You'll be drawing again this afternoon?' Emily asked.

'I thought so. But I could go to the shops first if we need anything.'

'Just bread, and I shall go into Ashpool myself on my bicycle.'

Holly wasn't keen on the idea of Emily cycling but it was more than her life was worth to comment on it. Noticing small hesitations in Emily's movements and an increasing maladroitness when she picked things up had once prompted Holly to suggest her grandmother invest in some stronger glasses; she had been well and truly slapped down for her impertinence. All the same, she hoped that Emily would be unlikely to come to much harm on the road to East Ashpool since she knew it like the back of her hand.

There was a small store at the Saltings but it was open only in the summer. Holly resigned herself to another dose of Emily's cache of tinned tuna. Not that she minded – she wasn't fussy. Busy with the greyish-looking washing-up mop, she stared out of the window. It would be a good day for working, mild and sunny, not too windy. 'Did you come straight here after you left the sanatorium?' she asked, glancing at Emily.

'Straight here? Good heavens, no.' Emily gave her usual hoarse chuckle. 'First I was spirited away by a knight in shining armour who shut me up in his castle along with all his other pretty things.'

Holly grinned. If Emily wasn't in the mood to be drawn it was going to be no good probing. 'You don't mean Aiden Chase, by any chance, do you? Did he shut you up?'

'This is the twentieth century, Holly. People don't do things like that.'

'But you never saw Jacko again after you left Burr Ash?'

Emily adjusted some wisps of hair that were still wet from her morning swim. The garnet ring gleamed on her finger. Could it be Aiden's ring? Holly wondered, since it was not Jacko's apparently.

'Yes. Once or twice.'

'I should've been glad to see the back of him. I can't stand guys like that.'

'So you've already made abundantly clear.'

Holly opened the door of the kitchen and emptied the washing-up water into an old plastic dustbin which acted as a reserve for watering Emily's geraniums. She looked around the rust-streaked bows of the cabin cruiser to the small shed on the far side of the garden. 'Who does that belong to?' she asked.

'Who does what belong to?'

'The shed.'

'It belongs to me, of course,' Emily said, rather coldly.

Holly glanced at her. 'I only asked,' she said, offended.

Emily relented. 'None of it's going to be here for much longer anyway,' she said.

'What d'you mean?'

'The Saltings is to go. We're all to be booted out, evicted, given the push. They want to knock the lot down.'

Holly's black brows drew together in disbelief. 'You're joking!'

'I wish I were.'

'I don't believe it. The Saltings are practically listed buildings. It's special. Besides, they can't. You own Sandplace, no one can make you sell if you don't want to.'

'I thought you were supposed to be bright. These days anything is possible. Even things we thought sancrosanct are up for grabs.'

Holly remained where she was, still holding the washing-up bowl. She felt as if someone had punched her in the stomach. 'Who wants to knock it down?'

'A so-called developer. A consortium is offering the owners good prices for the freehold and as most of them are old and poor, they're tempted, naturally.'

'But what would a developer want with a grungy piece of land like this. I mean I like it, but it's not what these goons usually go for.'

'They want to build an hotel and a what-d'you-call-it, place where you keep boats?'

'A marina,' Holly said numbly. 'But you can fight it, can't you?'

'They have the council on their side. And the council think it will bring more money into the area. You can't blame them, councils are up against it. Besides, some of the counsellors think this place is an eyesore anyway.'

'An eyesore!' Holly gazed out of the door. 'They're out of their trees!' She turned back to Emily who was putting on her outdoor things. 'Can't you mount a campaign? Get a petition up or something?'

'Too late. There were so few of us and most of us are old fossils.'

Holly shook her head. 'But where will you go? What will you do?'

'We've been offered alternative accommodation.'

'No prizes for guessing what that would be like,' Holly said, furious and disgusted, and aghast at the idea of Emily being homeless. Sharing Fern's small flat would surely be out of the question; she could not even imagine it. Neither could she imagine Em living with her brother in Muswell Hill; London would drive her mad. And as for 'sheltered housing', that was totally unthinkable. Not for Emily.

'If only you'd told me before,' she grumbled.

'And what d'you think you could have done?' Emily wound a scarf round her trilby and tied it under her chin. 'Living eighty-odd miles away, taking your degree and looking after your mother is enough of a burden as it is. *That's* why I didn't tell you about this before.'

Feeling that the day was already spoiled, Holly watched Emily wobble along the sandy pot-holed tarmac that passed for a road and went back inside to gather up her sketching materials. She was touched that Emily, looking to spare her anxiety, hadn't told her about the proposed marina. But why the sod did life have to be one long battle against apparently deliberately placed obstacles? she thought resentfully.

Emily followed the track between the ramshackle dwellings of her neighbours, waving to old Mr Watts as she pedalled along; he was, as usual, out walking his gingerish mongrel. Mr Watts raised his stick in gloomy salute. Watts was one of the originals who'd arrived at the Saltings about the same time she had.

Her moves from one place to another had never been accomplished smoothly, with due consideration and forethought. Impulse and romantic notions of a rural idyll were what had beckoned her and Jacko to Dorset in the thirties, though a moment's reflection would have reminded her that Jacko was an essentially urban creature. The idyll had ended in an electrical storm of rage, desire, jealousy and pain which had thundered with such destructive power that the repercussions still echoed down the years.

Often alone at Burr Ash, she had fought a long campaign against his particular kind of horse-trading but he had defeated her in the end. The outbreak of war had changed their lives in all sorts of ways. Jacko was too old and too unfit to be called up but he made the war an excuse for spending more time in London. Air raids had kept her and the children in the country. The final skirmish had taken place one weekend when the war was drawing to a close. Jacko had returned to Burr Ash after being away for several weeks. With him he brought a crowd of friends. Among the friends was a dancer called Regine, the ex-wife of the scoundrel Inky Petheridge who was later to become a solid establishment figure of apparently blameless respectability. Regine had also just parted company with the Ballet Rambert; she was younger than Emily, a gorgeous creature of gazelle-like grace. She materialized in the Burr Ash kitchen from behind Jacko's increasing girth, an exotically fragrant wraith, quiet and submissive to his bluff affection. Jacko himself was in an exuberant mood.

'Come here, mole-face,' he commanded Regine. 'Meet Em. Em will look after you.' He caught Regine by the shoulders and shoved her forward. To Emily he said, 'She damaged her ankle dancing in a bloody canteen, would you believe? She needs a rest but she might like to give you a hand with the young sprouts if she feels up to it.'

Emily glowered, feeling as if sparks were shooting out of her eyes. Jacko's jocularity was all the harder to take because he had left Burr Ash all those weeks previously in the foulest of foul humours, the blackest of black moods. Since then all three children had contracted whooping cough and they were only now getting over it. Because it was becoming increasingly difficult to get Jacko to take an interest in the upkeep of the house it was gradually falling into a state of disrepair. Naturally he blamed the war and the difficulty of obtaining materials and labour. The drains overflowed, the ceiling of the twins' bedroom collapsed after heavy rain, fortunately without hurting anyone, and one night she had come downstairs to find a rat on the kitchen table. Usually she could cope but now she herself felt ill. By the time Jacko arrived with his entourage, she was volatile with fatigue and anxiety.

She directed a savage gaze towards the proposed helper. 'Oh, you've brought her here for me!' she cried. 'To help, and all this way! Mind you, a nurse might have been better, but there you are, beggars can't be choosers, can they? A dancer will be perfectly splendid and looking after the children will be a lovely rest for her – perhaps she can help them with their *pliés*!'

It seemed to her that Regine was scouring every part of her with those heavy-lidded eyes and her half-smile, that she had not missed Emily's unkempt hair, the faded skirt and the old jersey that had shrunk in the wash. In fact that she was noting all the ratlike processes that had gnawed away at both Emily's looks and her self-respect.

'I'd love to help with the children, Mrs Monk,' the dancer said softly. She spoke with an accent that Emily could not quite place. 'Perhaps I could read to them.'

'The children can read for themselves,' Emily said shortly, 'but how are you at clearing up sick?'

'Stop that!' Jacko roared. 'I've brought Regine a bloody long way to meet you. The least you can do is to be civil. She's an artist, not a damned skivvy!'

Jacko's friends – an alcoholic poet, a lugubrious sculptor, now in the army, and a transvestite gallery owner were all that Emily could remember afterwards – watched with voyeuristic interest as one of the scenes for which Jacko was famous, unfolded before their eyes.

'Then what d'you think I am?' Emily cried. She lunged forward towards one of Jacko's bags that he had dumped on the kitchen table. She flung up the lid and pulled out the dirty shirts and smocks he had brought home for washing. The bread knife seemed to leap to her hand and she began ripping long gashes in them while the others stared at her with ghoulish attention. Regine's eyes were huge with enquiry and, it seemed to Emily, suppressed excitement.

'A skivvy,' Emily screamed, slashing at the fabric, ripping wildly when it resisted. 'A bloody skivvy – that's me. Not an artist. Absolutely *not* an artist!'

Jacko stepped forward, dextrously grabbing the knife as it plunged into one of his shirts. He appeared quite unperturbed.

'That's enough!' he bellowed, as to an unruly child. He turned to the others with a loud laugh. 'You know she's putting on this performance in your honour. I hope you're appreciating it. She can't get it into her bloody noddle that nobody's stopping her from painting.' He put the knife back on to the kitchen table but out of Emily's reach while he restrained her with a huge hand. 'I tell her that if she wants to go on hurling colour around like a demented infant that's up to her.'

The others laughed or made noises of commiseration according to their temperaments. Jacko made a sweeping gesture. 'The truth is,' he informed the world at large, 'that women haven't it in them to be painters. For Christ's sake let's face it – it isn't in their natures to be generators of art. Interpreters if you like, like mole-face here, but originators—' He blew a tremendous reverberating raspberry and the others laughed obediently. Regine merely smiled. She gave the appearance of hanging on Jacko's every word.

'A woman is a womb.' Jacko was on his favourite topic. 'Isn't that bloody well enough? What more do they want? Can a cunt think?'

For Emily a veil of unreality came down over the scene. She began to yell at him.

'Better than an effing prick!' she screamed. 'Tell me – whatsyourname – Regine, don't you think he should be satisfied with being the biggest lecher in the Western world? I think so. You see, he's so damned proud of it. Has he ever told you he's had half the women in London? No? So why should he want to paint too, especially now he's wasted his substance on riotous living and his stuff's not selling any more.' Emily lowered her voice now she knew she had everyone's attention. 'In fact, to tell you the truth, the rumour's going round that he's burned out, that all he's good for is sentimentalizing the mugs of rich scrap metal dealers from Birmingham—'

Jacko, who had listened to the first part of her diatribe with mocking good humour, reacted to the damning conclusion with ungovernable rage, extreme even for him. He snatched up the knife that he had only recently laid down and hurled himself at Emily. The knife grazed her shoulder and she screamed. Fortunately the sculptor's voyeuristic amusement had not blinded him to the hazards of the situation and he was able to grab Jacko round the waist with arms thickened by the wielding of a stonemason's mallet; somehow the others managed to wrest the knife from Jacko's grip, at which he suddenly relaxed and began to roar with laughter, a sound hardly less terrifying than his roars of rage.

'The sleep of reason,' he bellowed, 'brings forth monsters! Old Goya was right. That's what you get from tangling with a woman! Because we all know what that was about, don't we? Sweet Jesus preserve me from a jealous woman.'

Emily scooped up one of Jacko's ripped shirts and pressed it to her shoulder to staunch the blood which had begun to stream from a surface wound. The wound itself was, anyhow, not important; what was causing her to shake and catch her breath was the look of murderous hatred in Jacko's eyes when she told the terrible truth about his work. A truth she had long known but would never have voiced except under provocation. As one of the others stepped forward to help her patch up the damage she was thanking God for their presence for there was no saying how things might have turned out if she and Jacko had been alone. For the first time she was afraid.

In spite of his laughter Jacko never forgave her for putting into words the knowledge that haunted him day and night; neither could she forgive him this final betrayal. It was the end. Jacko went back to London the next day, taking Regine and his other friends with him. As far as he was concerned, Burr Ash was not functioning for him as it had once done, when Emily had presided over this, the fecund incubator for his imagination, when it had been the sponge that absorbed and soothed his dark depressions, enabling him to emerge stronger than ever. Not least it had been the place where he could recover physically from the excesses of his London life.

After that weekend everything changed; it was as if sorcery was at work, whipping up the children's peevish convalescence, causing the rain to cascade through bedroom ceilings and Emily's usually robust health finally to fail her. No matter that peace was at last coming to a Europe ravaged by war, the end of hostilities saw Emily's children packed off to Muriel's and Emily herself incarcerated in a sanatorium.

The love between Emily and Jacko, even before that last explosion, was being stealthily bled to death by a thousand barbs and scratches. The rough exchange of insults that had once been playful, inspired by mutual passion and leading only to their enjoyment of each other's bodies, had turned into purposeful wounding. A common urge to create had turned into conflict and conflict into a rage for self-salvation. Jacko needed her to diminish so that he could grow, but it was not in her nature to be self-effacing, at least not for long. She had made a sacrifice for the greater glory of Jacko but had finally discovered that he was unable to live up to her expectations, or indeed his own.

It was the end of the marriage and the start of Regine's stratagems to tighten the net that would eventually ensnare the bull. She knew nothing about painting but she was absolutely convinced that if she stopped Jacko drinking and put him to work, he would at last emerge a great man and a great artist.

Now Emily was thoughtful as she left the last of the Saltings shacks behind her. It was time for another move, another stage of her long life. But where and what next?

Holly picked up a thick wax crayon and rubbed an area of extra dark into the monochrome wash. The denseness of each rock form plunged into its own land-locked pool and was festooned above by crunchy black weed that underneath the waterline became a slippery, secretive forest. The rocks themselves, which were blotched, pitted and encrusted with a myriad colours and life forms, gave the impression that they were sentinels or watchers on the beach, standing singly or in sombre groups. The quality of light in this place was quite exceptional, enhancing not only colour but tone, deepening darks and bouncing brightness from one object to another. Ideas came and went, were pondered, tried out or rejected. Often, what appeared to work perfectly as a sketch would not survive the transformation into three dimensions, and the results of weeks of effort had to be discarded. She could never understand why her work was dismissed by several of the tutors as 'navel-gazing'. It seemed to her that she was forever reaching out to something beyond the self and they, on the contrary, were content to gaze into the intellectual navel that existed in their own heads.

'As if they'd be likely to discover anything worthwhile in such an unlikely environment,' she'd complained to Emily.

'You follow your own path, my girl,' Emily advised robustly. 'And don't let them put you off for a moment. They'll be back numbers by the time you really get going.'

That was what was so bracing about coming to see her grandmother.

The wind was getting up again and was snatching at the corners of Holly's paper. She narrowed her eyes critically, surveying the dark area, then began to pick out minute highlights with the point of a blade. She leaned back and the image of the rock on the page immediately reminded her of Emily standing on the beach, her towel draped round her gaunt shape like a tatty cloak. She pondered on the human brain's capacity to anthropomorphize; primitive people saw gods in their own image in trees and stones and what was more, thousands of years of civilization hadn't diminished the tendency. She looked towards the clouds now massing on the horizon in creamy and mussel-coloured heaps and at once saw the form of a sleeping giant. A giant who stirred and eyed the distant land.

The drawing wasn't coming out as she hoped. There was a restlessness at the back of her mind that was preventing her from concentrating. It felt like guilt; as if she should be somewhere else instead of here. It had been too soon to leave her mother after all; taking the extra day had been a mistake. Left alone for more than twenty-four hours her mother could regress and all the work they'd already done would be wasted.

* * *

Gideon's dusty-blue Volvo bounced down the lane that had once been properly surfaced but was now full of pot-holes and blown sand. On each side, hedges of sea buckthorn, escallonia and tarmarisk were punctuated by the occasional stunted pine, and behind them he had glimpses of a motley collection of cabins and wooden bungalows dumped down in apparently random fashion. All of them looked too small for anyone of normal size to inhabit. A few were freshly painted in bright colours and sported hanging baskets of spring flowers but there were some that had evidently been abandoned to the processes of decay, their windows boarded up and their shingled sides deep in dusty weeds. He passed a copse of windswept pine, poplar and sycamore. Beneath the trees was a huddle of dinghies and small boats, their masts pointing skywards at crazy angles. He stopped the car and got out, stretching his limbs. A breeze monotonously rattled the rigging in the boatyard and gulls screeched overhead. There seemed to be no one about from whom to ask directions so he had no idea where to start looking for the place whose name was scribbled on his piece of paper.

To start with the Saltings wasn't at all what he had expected from his father's description. In fact he was fast coming to the conclusion that his father had got it wrong. He began to walk. As he approached the last few cabins before arriving at the beach, he paused for a moment to appraise the sight of a large tarpaulin-clad cabin cruiser leaning precariously against the side of a blue-painted shanty that could once have been a railway carriage. He peered at the name on the gate which had been rendered almost illegible by time and weather and had just discovered that he had inadvertently arrived at his destination when a young woman came round the side of the eccentric dwelling from the direction of the beach. She was scruffily dressed in a long dark-coloured coat with bulging pockets, old jeans and a red cotton shirt, and was holding a large plastic-covered board. She had the dark skin and hair of a gypsy and was staring at him suspiciously.

'Are you looking for something in particular?' she challenged him.

'Someone, in fact.'

The hostile scrutiny continued. His traditional country wear of

Barbour vest and green cords that were perfectly acceptable at Wisley and Chelsea were evidently cause for alarm in the circles in which she moved.

'Who d'you want?'

He was becoming impatient. He was tired, fed up and hadn't wanted to come to this godforsaken hole anyway. 'I'm looking for Miss Emily Troy, as a matter of fact. Who are you?'

'Never mind. What d'you want with her? You're not from the council, are you? Or,' fiercely, 'from the consortium?'

Gideon sighed. The girl was a basket case. If his father's old friend (old flame?) was being subjected to harassment from would-be squatters or New Age travellers he had clearly arrived not a moment too soon.

'Is Miss Troy in?' putting on his most official manner and his most cut-glass accent. 'I've come a long way to see her.'

'Who wants to know?'

'I do.' Gideon opened the gate and strode purposefully to the steps where the young woman was standing. 'And my name's Chase. Gideon Chase.'

There was an immediate and noticeable change of attitude. He saw dawning comprehension. Comprehension and curiosity.

'Are you related to Aiden Chase?' she asked.

'Look, are you Miss Troy's housekeeper or something?' He banged on the door. It had a knocker in the shape of a bearded head. Neptune, presumably.

'No, I'm not her housekeeper. And it's no good doing that, she's not in.'

'Who *are* you?' he asked.

'I'm her granddaughter.'

His hand dropped away from the knocker. 'I see.' He inspected her more carefully. 'And do you live here too?'

The girl shook her head. She seemed suddenly to make up her mind about something. She turned round and unlocked the door. 'Would you like a cup of tea?'

'How I feel at the moment, I'd kill for one.'

'I don't think that will be necessary.'

They went inside and while he took in his surroundings in a bemused manner, she filled the kettle at the sink.

'By the way, my name's Holly Wyatt.' She switched the kettle on.

'How d'you do?' Formally, Gideon offered his hand. She took it and gave a small explosive laugh.

'My grandmother lives alone,' she explained. 'I come down to see her sometimes. You *are* Aiden Chase's son, aren't you?'

'Yes. How d'you know about me?'

'You were at the funeral.'

'Yes.' Gideon sat down on the safest-looking of the basket chairs. 'Tell me, what was all that about a consortium?'

Holly, leaning against the sink, pursed her lips. 'They're a pack of bloody rip-off merchants who are trying to get rid of the Saltings so that they can build some shitty marina for millionaire yachtsmen. They're turfing out all the residents, who are all old so it's assumed it'll be a walkover. I could spit nails.'

The kettle boiled and Holy put a teabag in each of the two mugs she had arranged on the draining board. 'Milk? Sugar?'

'Just milk, thanks.' He reached out for the mug she offered. She hooked another chair over to the table with her foot and sat down.

'I suppose they've tried all the usual oppositions to planning permission?' he said.

'Ages ago. It's all a foregone conclusion now.'

'What will Miss Troy do?'

'Search me.' Frowning, Holly encircled her mug with her hands. 'Anyway, what brought *you* down here?'

'Providence, by the sound of it. Or more prosaically, my father. He met Miss Troy at the funeral, as you know, and has been fretting about her ever since. He seems to think she's in need of care and protection.'

'Bit late for that, isn't it?'

'I'm not sure what you mean by that. He only found out where she was living by giving her brother the third degree. You would have thought that the brother would have cared that she was living in a dump like this, wouldn't you?'

'What d'you mean, dump?' Holly was offended. 'I love it. So does she.'

'Well, anyway, it seems that my father and your grandmother were chums from way back. They went to the Slade together, I believe.'

'Yes, she's told me that much.' Holly grinned. 'I get the impression they were lovers at one time.'

'Lovers?' Gideon looked doubtful. 'Oh no. I don't think so. He wasn't one for having a bit on the side.'

'I mean *before* he married but after she left Jacko. But I'm only guessing.'

'I see what you mean. He married late, the old man. My mother was much younger.'

'She died, didn't she?'

'When I was little. She had a pulmonary embolism after a minor op.' Gideon drank some of his tea. 'You seem to know more about my family than I do about yours. Trappist monks are loquacious compared to my father. He never tells me anything.'

'All I know is what my mother has told me and what I can pump out of Em.'

Gideon said, 'Did you ever meet Jacko?'

'No, thank God!'

He raised his eyebrows. 'I've seen pictures of the famous A. J. Monk. You've been told, I expect, how much like the old guy you look?' he said slyly. 'When he was young, of course.'

'Shut up! He was appalling! Besides, I haven't got a beard.'

He looked at her flushed face with renewed interest. 'You really meant that, didn't you? I don't mean about the beard.'

'Listen, if you know anything *at all* about recent art history, you must have grasped the fact that the man was a simply God-awful old poseur.'

'But I don't know anything about recent art history,' Gideon explained patiently. 'Or any art history for that matter.'

She gave him an incredulous look, which was not necessarily disapproving, more as if she'd just come across a member of a rare and exotic tribe.

'I'm a landscape design consultant,' he said in an effort to throw light on his unorthodoxy. 'I expect you'd call me a landscape gardener.'

'Are you *really*? You mean that Aiden Chase has a son who's a gardener? A landscape design consultant.' She savoured the words. 'Mm, I like it. I think that's neat.'

'Thank you.' He grinned. 'You appear to feel strongly about a grandfather you never met. Was he that bad? Surely it's all water under the bridge now?'

'You're talking about water as if it were innocuous, neutral stuff, not something that has knocked down the houses and drowned all the inhabitants.'

'I'm not sure I'm with you. Wasn't Monk supposed to be a great painter?'

'I expect he thought he was. I expect he thought that excused everything. I've made it my business to find out as much as I could because my mother thought he was seriously hot shit,' Holly said. 'She worshipped him in spite of the fact that he dumped her, along with Emily, in favour of his other female. It wasn't until I started to read art history myself that I found out the truth. If he was mentioned at all it was as a second-rate dauber with occasional flashes of brilliance, that's all. So it was all for nothing.'

As she spoke Holly heard sounds that heralded Emily's return. She got up to open the door.

'Gideon's here,' she called.

Emily remembered him from the funeral. 'Ah, Gideon,' she said, appearing in the doorway, laden with plastic bags, 'have you come to smite the Midianites?'

'I don't suppose Midianites give you much trouble in these parts, do they?'

'You'd be surprised,' Emily said darkly.

Gideon held out his hand politely. 'Nice to meet you again, Miss Troy.'

'What's all this about Midianites?' Holly said, puzzled.

'Take no notice of her,' Emily said to Gideon. 'She's terribly ignorant.'

'Pardon me for existing,' Holly said, putting the kettle on again to make tea for her grandmother. 'I only went to a comprehensive and I didn't do RE anyway.'

Emily sat down and accepted a mug of tea. She scrutinized Gideon narrowly, forcing her troublesome eyesight into action. Now she had got over the shock of his likeness to Aiden it was easier to see him as a person in his own right. There was the pigtail, of course, and his expression was open where Aiden's was suspicious and guarded; even the way he sat, with his legs sprawled across the floor, was in contrast to his father's habitual rigidity of posture. She speculated on the implications of the sudden appearance of Chase the Younger. He had not come here for the good of his health or of his own volition, of that she was convinced. He expected something of her, or rather his father expected something of her. Damn! She had known it was a mistake going to that dratted funeral.

They took their mugs of tea into the room that overlooked the beach. Holly lounged on the windowseat. Gideon looked round him at the boarded walls, painted a dusty white, and at the basic blue-painted furniture. The place wasn't too bad inside, in fact the setup as a whole was beginning to grow on him.

'Not quite what you're used to, eh?' Emily said.

'Not quite. My cottage is usually a bit of a mess, I'm afraid. More like a workshop. I never seem to find time to tidy up.'

His answer hadn't been what Emily expected. 'So you don't live at Riversfoot?' she said.

'Good heavens, no,' Gideon laughed. 'My work is in this part of the world these days. My cousin, Will, spends more time there than I do. He's an art historian and a member of a rather special branch of the Metropolitan Police.'

Emily let that pass without comment. 'So you work?'

'It seemed a waste not to put my training to use,' Gideon said, straightfaced.

Holly frowned, suspecting him of making fun of her grand-mother.

'Are you a collector too?' Emily asked.

Holly butted in impatiently, 'No. He's a garden design consultant.'

'A what?'

'I'm a landscape gardener.'

'I don't suppose your father approved of that?'

'He's come to terms with it now, fortunately.'

Emily laid her empty mug on the floor beside her. 'Well, I'm afraid you're wasting your time here. As you see, there's not a lot of scope for gardening round these parts.'

'As a matter of fact I didn't come here to offer my professional services,' Gideon said. Gingerly he stretched out his legs which were beginning to feel cramped in the small space. 'I've come with an invitation. My father would very much like you to stay at Riversfoot. He apologizes for not coming himself but his health isn't too good these days.' He stopped. Perhaps he shouldn't have given the impression that the old man was past it.

'He always lived too well, that was his trouble,' Emily said. 'He never gave life a chance to put a bit of ginger into him. No wonder he's cracking up.'

Gideon changed tactics. 'I think you could be right. I think you should tell him this yourself. I'm sure he would listen to you.'

Emily glanced at Gideon, summing him up. She was coming to the conclusion that for all his outdoor looks and his landscape gardening, this young man was no fool. He was clever, like Aiden.

'You can't teach an old dog new tricks and your father is a very old dog. He was set in his ways by the time he was twenty – a creature of habit. Do you take after him?'

'I've no idea.' Gideon was thinking that, all the same, his father was still capable of springing some surprises. Like the possibility that he and this woman had been lovers, for instance. 'But what I believe is that now that most of my father's old cronies are dead, he gets a bit lonely. I was hoping that you might take pity on him and come to Riversfoot. If train travel is a bore, I'm quite sure he'd be delighted to send a car.'

'He still likes to play the emperor, then?' Emily laughed.

Gideon grinned and waited. Holly hummed a tune and examined her stubby fingernails.

'Well,' Emily said at last. 'Will you thank your father for me, but tell him that I rarely go anywhere these days? Like him I've become boringly set in my ways. I confess that, in my dotage, I've become attached to my routine. Besides, I think that it would be most unwise to leave this place unattended just at present. By the time I came back it could very well be just part of a landfill site.'

Gideon glanced at Holly and back again. 'You mean—' he began.

Emily nodded. 'The Midianites,' she said. 'I shouldn't put it past them to knock this place down while my back was turned; sort of accidentally on purpose.'

Gideon's first thought was that with Sandplace razed to the ground his father's purpose might yet be served but it would hardly do for Miss Troy to be forced to stay at Riversfoot because she had no alternative accommodation. He seemed to have run out of options and turned to Holly as his last hope. She had stripped off her disreputable old coat and was sitting with her arms round her knees. She had rolled up the sleeves of her geranium-coloured shirt and was studying the worn toe of one of her boots. A momentary shaft of sunlight suddenly illuminated her, casting a warm reflected glow from her shirt on to the underside of her chin. A small pulse beat in the soft hollow of her neck and it seemed touchingly at odds with the image she otherwise presented. This vision so absorbed Gideon that when he became aware of two sets of eyes fixed intently on him, waiting for him to speak, he said the first thing that came into his head.

'Did you say you were an art student, Holly?'

'No, I don't think I did.'

'But you are?'

Holly chuckled. 'Yes. I sculpt.'

'Stone? Wood? Metal?'

'Wood, when I can get it. Good seasoned stuff's hard to come by. And expensive, naturally.'

'I might be able to help you there,' he said. 'I sometimes have to fell timber.'

Her eyes lit up. 'That would be great!' Then she slumped. 'But it'd be too late for my degree show. That's next term. Afterwards perhaps—' But by that time they would have lost touch, she thought. He would forget or be too busy, anyway.

'I'd like to see some of your work,' he said. 'Clients often ask me if I could suggest a sculptural alternative to fauns and goddesses.'

'Why don't you show him photographs of your work?' Emily suggested, relieved that the earlier topic of conversation had been abandoned.

'You wouldn't like them,' Holly assured him. 'They're not meant as decorations, you know.'

She sounded almost offended by the offer, Gideon thought. 'Why don't you try me? I'm not just an ignorant compost-basher, whatever you think.'

'He wasn't brought up at Riversfoot for nothing,' Emily interjected. 'Something is bound to have rubbed off.'

'Thank you, Miss Troy,' Gideon said smiling. Knowing now for sure that he wanted very much to know Holly better he felt himself ready to applaud and recommend any type of work she cared to show him, even if it turned out to be a string of pink plastic sausages tied up with yellow ribbon.

'Why don't you stay to supper?' Emily said to Gideon, suddenly expansive.

Holly stared at her grandmother. This was a most un-Emily-like gesture. Besides, she'd be bound to offer him tinned tuna and creamed rice; as far as she knew they were the only things in the cupboard.

'I've just been down to the village,' Emily said, 'and bought some fresh bread. And there are plenty of tins. What about it?'

'Thank you,' Gideon said. 'That sounds great. I should be delighted.'

Holly felt put out. It had taken her ages to break down Em's reserve and here was this stranger, walking in and twisting her round his little finger in no time at all. It was probably because while she, Holly, resembled the despised Jacko, Gideon looked like lover-boy Aiden. Abruptly she left the windowseat.

'In that case I'd better think of something else to do with tuna,' she said briskly. 'We shall have to eat early because I have to get back to Bath tonight.'

'I thought you were staying an extra day?' Emily said, raising her voice because Holly was already in the kitchen.

'I've changed my mind. I think I should get back to my mother,' Holly called.

'Her mother?' Gideon's question hung in the air.

Emily shook her head, frowning. Suddenly, like a light going on in her brain, she saw how her prolonged solitary existence had cut her off from human concerns and human emotion. Holly was anxious about someone other than herself, was putting herself out for her mother. Emily had been slow to accept her granddaughter but increasingly she missed her when she went home. Now it was her absences that were painful, like when sensation returns to a numb tooth.

Fern had filled her day as she had promised herself, ticking off her achievements in her notebook. The Pump Room, the Roman Baths, the Abbey. Even as she was congratulating herself she realized that she had been standing in the tiny hall of the flat counting to twenty-seven before she took off her coat, then again before she put her hand on the handle of the living-room door. To be made anxious by the everyday act of entering a room was clearly ridiculous. Did she think the gods would strike her down if she failed to carry out the ritual?

Filled with a sense of failure that immediately cancelled out the successes of the rest of the day she went into the kitchen. She wanted a cup of tea and forced herself to go through the process of filling the kettle and switching it on without counting; it cost her a renewed attack of nerves as bad as any she'd had at the beginning of the treatment. Dry mouth, sweating palms, and not just butterflies in the stomach but a painful turbulence, and a feeling of tightness round her head. Celia said this might happen, not to worry, that she was unlikely actually to faint, which was what she feared. But Celia wasn't here. Neither was Holly. If she collapsed nobody would find her until tomorrow when Holly was due home.

According to Celia, some very famous people had suffered with this disorder. Dr Johnson, for instance, and Howard Hughes. As if that were any comfort! On the other hand, neither of them had known about modern treatments which Celia had assured her had a high rate of success. It was just a matter of confronting one's fears. If doing it was as easy as saying it, I would have had the courage to accomplish it by myself, Fern thought. For she wasn't a coward. No one who has successfully brought up a child on their own could be called a coward, could they? She was used to handling problems on her own, to not asking for help. What made the group sessions particularly difficult was that most of the others were so much younger, adolescents, some of them. She remembered that last time a young lad of sixteen with a washing ritual had singled her out to confide in during the coffee break. Perhaps he saw her as some kind of mother figure; it had given her a small warm glow somewhere deep inside, making up in part for what she saw as her loss of esteem in Holly's eyes.

She sat on the sofa drinking her tea. The television, which she had deliberately left on while she was out, was now devoting itself to football. There were things to be done, a meal to be cooked, the gas fire to be turned on, ironing to be finished. But to do any of them without her rituals would mean at least three separate battles against her fear. She remained where she was until the light faded from the room, which it did early in the basement flat. Perhaps tomorrow she would have more courage. Courage. It seemed to be a constituent that had been left out of her make-up from birth. Somehow she had muddled through using instead other, more boring, characteristics like stoicism and tenacity.

CHAPTER NINE

Regine never entered a room unnoticed, unless it particularly suited her purpose. It had something to do with the hypnotic power of her extreme consciousness of self. So when she appeared at the kitchen door Auriel put down her sewing and Arlette paused with floury hands round a ball of dough – Burr Ash made its own bread, no matter what. Questioning lines creased Arlette's broad forehead and her flushed cheeks grew even pinker. Only the cats, stationed round the room in a variety of poses, scarcely bothered to give the mistress of the house a second glance.

Regine shook her head slowly and Arlette's hands moved in the dough.

'Auriel, a chair!' she said sharply to her sister.

With nervous, jerky movements Auriel hastened to clear the piled-up curtain she had been mending from the armchair next to the Aga. Regine sat down. She rested a cool hand on Auriel's arm by way of thanks before adopting an attitude of repose, hands folded on her lap. Auriel bundled the ancient fabric into a basket on the dresser.

'A drink, Maman?' Auriel asked. Regine had always insisted on the French form of endearment.

Regine shook her head. Arlette glanced at her mother anxiously before she returned to thumping the dough. She knew her mother was here with a purpose but would divulge it in her own good time.

Although they were very close to each other in age, there was at present little resemblance between Regine's daughters. This had not always been the case. A faded photograph on the dresser, taken when they were children, showed them sitting astride a fallen tree with their younger sister, Aimée, who had died of meningitis at the age of six, and their older brother, Alain. All four had bushy dark hair cropped off at the ears in a vaguely medieval fashion and wore loose smocks tied round the waist with a cord. All had inherited their parents' dark colouring. Jacko, whose full name was Aurelius John Monk, had taken it into his head that all his offspring should have first names beginning with A, like himself; a fancy that Emily had resisted but which Regine was only too happy to indulge.

Over the years, Arlette's body had thickened, her skin had become swarthy, rather than smooth and exotically tinted, and her abundant black hair which she wore in a plait round her head, had coarsened and was threaded with grey. There was a suggestion of a moustache on her top lip, and years of unremitting housework had turned her speckled arms into those of a weightlifter.

Everything about her sister, Auriel, had on the other hand, diminished. Originally so like Regine, she had become attenuated and lacklustre. Her hair was dust-coloured and her once-fine eyes had sunk into brown hollows. The movements that had at one time been graceful like her mother's were restless and gauche; in short there remained nothing to be seen of the beautiful child who appeared in so many of Jacko's paintings.

Auriel bent over her mother solicitously. 'Are you sure you wouldn't like some lemon tea?' she coaxed.

There was no answer and Auriel bit her lip. She had been fussing again, something that Maman hated. One was expected to know precisely what she needed without having to ask. Her mother had prided herself that she was able to sense and supply Jacko's least request almost before he knew it himself.

Except booze, of course, Auriel thought with a guilty ripple of spite. When it came to alcohol Maman had been marvellously adept at outwitting her father in ways that were far too subtle for him to fathom. Auriel had never got the hang of this much-vaunted perspicacity herself even though it had been drummed into her from an early age that it was one of the essential ingredients of being female. Passivity, intuition, maternal nurturing and the instinctive wisdom of the female were all qualities expected of Jacko's women. To men, and in particular to himself, he ascribed intellect, potency and the responsibility of initiating action. Of course, he believed in the nobility of physical toil just as he spoke about such concepts as motherhood, home and the mysterious earth-rhythms of the seasons. He would sometimes throw himself into bouts of violent but short-lived activity round the farm such as chopping wood, hacking down hedges or lighting tremendous bonfires. However, boredom usually set in after a few hours of this and he would return thankfully to his painting. To him, man was the originator and the terminator; women presided over continuity, routine and the pulse of life. There were no exceptions to this rule. It was, he said, a matter of gender. Auriel, having separated from her husband after a short-lived marriage and, what was worse, never having had children, felt herself a failure twice over.

Glancing at her mother from time to time, Arlette divided the dough and plumped it into the waiting row of tins. With the deftness of long habit she transferred them to the side of the Aga to prove. The Aga, which was already thirty years old, was one of the few concessions to modernity at Burr Ash; otherwise little in the room had altered for fifty years or so. There was very little plastic, no polyester, no convenience foods and no washing machine. There was no television in the house and the only radio the family possessed was a battered old portable in Jacko's bedroom. It was believed that Zak had one too but as he kept his room locked no one knew for sure, except Fergus, and he kept his knowledge to himself. There were, however two telephones, one in the kitchen and one in the studio. Otherwise little of the outside world permeated the massive limestone walls.

When the children burst into the kitchen from their trek to fetch logs from the Burr Ash woods, they brought with them at least a flavour of the twentieth century. But their boisterous mood changed as soon as they caught sight of their grandmother. Two almost identical long-haired girls of about ten and twelve immediately stopped chattering and went to sit on the floor by Regine's feet. One of them fingered the tassle at the end of Regine's long necklace, the other caught up her favourite cat and stroked it, murmuring endearments. The boy Fergus skulked on the periphery of the room, his back against the wall. When Regine's gaze, sweeping past the girls, searched him out, his heavy lids dropped and he bent to fondle one of the cats behind the ears. The animal sensed his tension and took a swipe at him with unsheathed claws; Fergus withdrew his hand smartly and saw triumph flicker on his grandmother's face.

He was very afraid of her yet he took an almost masochistic pleasure in the fact that everything he did attracted her anger and contempt. He was small for thirteen, with a long head and olive skin as smooth as a baby's, but his eyes had a look of oriental watchfulness that made his kinship with Regine unmistakable. His rebellion was costing him dear but he was convinced that anything was better than becoming like his father, Donald. Donald's one act of rebellion had been to insist on naming his son after his own father, after which he seemed to succumb to his powerlessness. Fergus observed his father now as he loped into the room with his shoulders bent, though not necessarily by the load of logs he carried.

Even though he drove daily to his bookshop in Dorchester Donald had, by marrying Arlette, made himself part of the Burr Ash setup and was therefore expected to put its priorities before his own; the bookshop had never been taken seriously at home and now Donald hardly took it seriously himself. He envied his brother-in-law, Alain, intensely for getting away from Burr Ash as soon as he was of age, but his own inertia was such that he had never, or at least not for long, contemplated the idea of following his example.

He dumped his load in the corner of the kitchen and brushed bits of moss and bark from his sleeves. Alain, who had been relieved to relinquish his burden outside in the yard, sat down heavily at the table and took out his pipe.

' "Ash logs smooth and grey—" ' he quoted with an attempt at bluff good humour, ' "burn them green or old—" '

One of the girls, Adina, the eldest, chimed in triumphantly, ' "Buy up all that come your way, they're worth their weight in gold." '

'Though we can't promise they're all ash, some of them may be beech,' Alain said, packing tobacco into the bowl of his pipe. The activity enabled him to observe his mother without appearing to do so, for it was as well, where Regine was concerned, to ascertain which way the wind was blowing, as it were. He had long ago discovered that the best way of dealing with the problem of a powerful father and an implacable mother was not to deal with it at all. By putting up a show of acquiescence and filial dutifulness he had somehow survived childhood and adolescence on a time-serving basis, after which, having said nothing of his ambitions, he had left home for good to become a structural engineer.

His wife, Margaret, had refused to come to Jacko's funeral. Her first visit to Burr Ash soon after the wedding had been her last. Unprepared for the way her new father-in-law expressed himself and for his opinions about women, and intimidated by Regine's arctic appraisal, she had returned to their home in Winchester resolved never to accompany her husband there ever again. She considered everyone at Burr Ash to be quite mad.

Alain had agreed to stay on for a few days to 'comfort poor Maman in her bereavement,' as he put it, as if the event had not affected him too, which in truth, it had not. Actually, he had done very little except comment on the weather, smoke his pipe and get in everyone's way. In any case, Zak had seen to all the funeral arrangements. All that remained was a visit to the solicitor that afternoon, about which he was gloomily resigned. His mother had always controlled the purse strings so there would be no useful little legacy that would help, for instance, with the building of an extension he'd planned at the back of the Winchester house to accommodate his model railway; the inconvenience of using the loft had always rankled, but Margaret insisted that holidays in Tuscany and the children's education came before the gratification of personal whims. She had never understood that the model railway was not just a hobby.

However, the condition of the family finances could have been worse. If his father had had access to the money there would not only be nothing left but he and Margaret could quite easily have been saddled with looking after Regine for at least part of the year. The prospect of his mother and his wife sharing a house was absolutely unimaginable.

'When had you planned to return to Winchester, Alain?' Regine asked him.

Alain puffed complacently at his pipe. He was a larger, plainer version of his father but even if he had grown a beard and attired himself in smock and ancient corduroys, nobody would ever have taken him for an artist.

'I'll toddle on as soon as we've seen Mayfield, Maman,' he said, 'if that suits.'

'As you please,' Regine said tautly.

Cold bitch, Alain thought. She would much rather I'd have snuffed it than Jacko. All that's ever mattered to her is Aurelius J. Monk as Artist and herself as Muse. The great collection of unsold works by his father, which of course were all hers now, were as nothing to the edifice she herself had created.

'I don't suppose Mayfield will have anything new to report,' he said aloud. 'It's just a formality. Hardly worth staying for really.'

'Nevertheless,' Regine said crisply, 'I would appreciate it if you did. One continues to hope for these little acts of thoughtfulness, although consideration for others was never your forte, was it, Alain?'

Arlette, busy washing her floury hands at the sink, gave her brother a reproachful look. How could he be so unfeeling to poor, brave Maman! Anyone could see how she was suffering beneath that quiet composure.

Fergus intercepted his mother's glance and hesitated. He had been about to steal away to see what Zak was up to, but sensing hostility that was not for once directed at himself, he stayed on, hoping for developments. He was not disappointed.

'Let me come with you to Mr Mayfield's, Maman,' Auriel said gushingly, a remark she immediately regretted.

'What an angel you are, Auriel. Unselfish as ever! But as Alain knows,' Regine's glance swept across Donald to Alain, 'Jacko believed, rightly I think, that the ultimate responsibility for the legal side should lie in the hands of the men.'

Fergus sniggered and Regine immediately transferred her attention from Auriel and Alain to her grandson, gesturing for him to come and stand beside her.

'Has something amused you, Fergus?' she asked, as he reluctantly approached. 'And at such a time?'

'No, Grandmère.'

'So why do you laugh? Only idiots laugh at nothing.'

Fergus went dark red and was furious to feel the sting of tears.

He shook his head, not trusting his voice.

'Do you think we find it easy to afford your school fees, Fergus?' Regine went on relentlessly. 'I would not like to think that we were spending all this money in an attempt to educate a simpleton.' This was Regine's trump card, for she knew that the threat of sending Fergus to the local comprehensive was enough to bring him into line. It had always been the custom of the family to refer to state education as beyond the pale. 'My advice to you, Fergus, is to try to emulate your sisters. Their application to their music was so beautifully demonstrated a day or two ago when they performed in the church, don't you agree?'

The younger of the two girls, Andra, modestly pressed her face against her cat's warm tabby flanks as her grandmother laid a hand on her shoulder.

'*Charmante, ma petite,*' Regine said. 'Jacko so adored his girls.'

Satisfied with her victory Regine waved Fergus away. He went to sit near the door. He felt the heat leaving his cheeks at last while at the same time noticing that his aunt, Auriel, had an uncharacteristically high colour in hers. Probably jealousy because she had no girls for Jacko to adore; no kids at all, in fact. And her old man had left her, anyway, Fergus thought. Having failed to entice her away from Burr Ash, he'd stuck it for eighteen months and then bunked off.

Fergus studied his father, who had propped his loosely jointed frame against the wall next to the Aga as if he were perfectly at ease. Fergus knew different. His dad had knuckled under. It seemed to him that Donald hardly counted as a man at all in Grandmère's eyes. Certainly he himself did not – he was considered far too young – but when he was older he fully intended to show them all what power really meant. He had learned a lot from Jacko but even more from Regine. When he was grown up he would sell Burr Ash and all his grandfather's naff paintings and put Grandmère in a Home. He would buy a labour-saving bungalow for his mother, Arlette, but the others would have to fend for themselves which would do them good. He would live in London and be something in the city; he would make masses of money so that he could buy all the videos and video games he wanted, and an Alfa Romeo and a yacht.

'So it will be just you, me and Donald this afternoon?' Alain asked pointedly, looking across at his mother.

'I've asked Zak to accompany us since I entrust so much of the business side to him,' Regine said, meeting Alain's gaze.

Alain sucked at his pipe, which had gone out. 'He's hardly family though, is he?' he said mildly.

'I don't know what I should have done without Zak in these past weeks. Of course Zak's coming!'

'I think you are being most unwise.'

The effect of this remark was highly gratifying to Fergus. His grandmother stiffened in her chair like a lurcher scenting a rabbit.

'Unwise? Am I to understand that you think there's something not quite *comme il faut* about that?'

Alain's jaw set stubbornly. 'Please, Maman. I was just wondering if you thought it was a good idea to allow him such a free hand with the running of the place. I mean, just how much does he know about your affairs, our affairs?'

'Alain?' Arlette cried warningly.

Regine said, 'I take very great exception to what you are inferring, Alain. All I can say in reply is that it's been a blessing that I have someone who is not only not afraid to take on responsibility but who does it with such efficiency and with so little regard for his own convenience.' The air round her seemed to crackle with the icy particles of her anger.

'All I meant, Maman,' Alain said immediately conciliatory, 'was that I don't know why you need him; you yourself are better at business than anyone I ever met.'

'So you think I could have done it all? Nurse darling Jacko *and* run the house? I see.'

'No, of course not, Maman. But I should have thought that with Arlette and Auriel—'

'*You* were the one I should have been able to turn to!' Regine said. 'But no. You chose to run away from your responsibilities a long time ago. Now, all of a sudden, you question the arrangements I have been forced to make here.'

She'll say she's a poor weak woman next, Fergus thought, hugging the scene to him to ponder in a quiet moment. He noticed that his uncle had gone brick-coloured and was fussing with his pipe, clearly wishing he hadn't started the argument in the first place.

'I'll make some coffee,' Arlette said, thumping the huge kettle on to the Aga hotplate. 'I think we could all do with some.'

Regine said, standing up, 'I'll have mine in my room, if you don't mind, Arlette, *chérie*. I'm rather tired.'

When she'd left the kitchen there was a charged silence during which several pairs of eyes converged on Alain reproachfully.

'Well, don't you think I'm right about this Zak person?' he blustered. 'When it comes right down to it, what do we know about him, after all? He just appeared out of the blue in answer to that advert, saying he was an admirer of Father's – which is a bit suspicious in itself.'

'Alain, how could you?' Auriel cried. 'If you knew how that sounds!'

Alain succeeded in getting his pipe going again. 'I am quite aware of how that sounds,' he said. 'It's just that Father's work is not fashionable these days, not with youngsters like Zak.'

'Where is Zak, anyway?' Donald remarked.

'I'll go and see,' Fergus said, slipping out of the room.

'Yes, Mrs Monk. The results came back from the lab earlier today.' Dr Evan Griffith observed his patient with compassion though she gave no indication of inviting it. She sat very straight in her chair, her face as pale as a bowl of cream, a smile barely creasing the corners of her mouth.

Dr Griffith cleared his throat. 'I'm afraid it's not good news, Mrs Monk.'

She nodded as if she'd known all along. One never knew how people would react. Sometimes the old took it harder than the young, the will to live not necessarily diminished by age. Regine Monk had never been easy to deal with – and Monk himself had been impossible, but for different reasons. As far as Regine Monk was concerned, nothing a doctor could do was good enough for the great man (one was never allowed to forget that A. J. was Somebody), but of her own health she was stubbornly negligent except in so far as it affected her capacity to care for her husband. The doctor had frequently admonished her for overdoing it and this last business was a case in point. If she had come earlier something might have been done. But she'd come too late, much too late. The blunt truth now was that there was nothing that could save her.

She was sitting quietly, waiting for him to continue.

'The tissue samples we took were positive, I'm afraid,' he said. 'And the scan rather confirmed what we feared.'

'Is there any treatment?'

He tried to be encouraging. 'Oh, certainly there's treatment. I have to warn you that it would not be particularly pleasant but I will gladly arrange for you to see the consultant at the hospital.'

Regine stopped him with a gesture. 'Dr Griffith,' she said sternly, 'I want you to be perfectly honest with me. What is the prognosis? It really is essential that I know.'

The doctor glanced away from the level stare. 'It's not good. It's true that treatment might slightly prolong your life but I'm afraid that things have gone too far. You see, in the end—' He lifted both hands to express his feelings of helplessness. 'I'm terribly sorry.'

'I see.' The only indication she gave of inner disturbance was the gentle rocking of one elegant foot in its amethyst stocking and youthful black pump. Today she looked very much the *soignée* French lady, not an old woman confronting her end.

'All the same, I would like you to see Mr Dent again.' He began to scribble busily, glad of a chance to avoid her penetrating eyes.

'No!' Regine stood up. 'Absolutely not. I don't want treatment and I don't want hospital. That is my last word. Besides, I have a great deal to do; I shan't be able to spare the time. Neither do I want the family told. I imagine I haven't got very long?'

'It's very difficult to say, Mrs Monk, but it is quite far advanced. I would think six months, perhaps more—'

'Thank you for being honest, Dr Griffith,' she said matter-of-factly. 'I appreciate it. I need to know because there are arrangements to be made, as I expect you realize.'

'Of course.' The doctor got up from his chair and held out his hand. 'Please don't hesitate to come to see me about anything at all. There's no need to suffer unnecessarily these days.'

He watched her leave with a mixture of relief and regret. One had to hand it to the old girl, she was as hard on herself as she was on other people. She was a tyrant in her own home and he had never liked her, but he admired her for taking it on the chin like that. He suspected that she had not been altogether surprised by what he had to tell her; she had lived so exclusively for her husband that she might even be glad that she was to follow him so soon.

Zak was waiting in the car outside. 'Everything OK?' he asked.

'Just anno Domini. There's nothing to be done about that,' she replied lightly.

In the car on the way home, Regine discussed the A. J. Monk retrospective with Zak as if everything was as usual.

'As you know, Zak, his later period is very well represented at Burr Ash. What we need are examples of his earlier work.'

Zak nodded as he steered the old Rover through the country lanes. There was an encouraging scent of spring blowing in at the window at his side; the one on the passenger side was tightly closed. At least this was better than the gloom and mud of winter.

'Perhaps this guy Davidson will be able to tell us more about that when he comes this afternoon,' he said. He shot her a keen glance. Regine spoke as if all Jacko's work were of equal consequence but she must surely know that only his early stuff was going to be of any interest to the punters.

'I shall have to rely on your energy, Zak dear. So much has disappeared. Jacko was generous to a fault. I think I told you he gave countless paintings away.'

Zak nodded again, but he smiled, running a hand through his short strawlike thatch. He knew for a fact that in the days before Regine had taken over control of his finances, Jacko's generosity had been mostly inspired by the demands of importunate creditors, who frequently had to settle for one of his canvases or nothing at all.

'Sometimes he made a note in his diary,' Regine went on, 'but more often not. Davidson will be able to recommend a course of action, I'm sure. He might approach Chase because Chase is so very knowledgeable. For some unknown reason the man was antagonistic towards poor Jacko but I don't suppose he'll be averse to a chance to display his scholarship.'

'Why did he dislike Jacko?' Zak asked. He glanced at his fake but otherwise reliable Rolex and slowed down. There was plenty of time. Besides, he took a professional interest in Aiden Chase.

Regine was in an uncharacteristically forthcoming mood. 'I'm afraid it was jealousy. He was and probably still is a pathologically jealous man. It's said that he wanted to be a painter himself, in fact he trained at the Slade, I believe, but all he ever produced were a few rather dull canvases after the style of Cézanne. But amateurish, you know.'

'But he came to Jacko's funeral?'

'Yes. That was odd,' Regine said, snipping off the words.

They cruised along between the renascent trees and hedges.

'There was only ever one man for you, wasn't there, Maman?' Zak said softly.

'One man,' she said reverently. 'From the moment we met.'

'Where was that?'

'It was at a house party. One of the very few at that time. The war put a stop to that sort of thing. It had indirectly put a stop to my career as a dancer too.'

'Why was that?'

'We had to dance in all kinds of places for CEMA. That was the Council for the Encouragement of Music and the Arts, you know. Factories, canteens, that sort of thing. It was horrible. I never remember being so cold and uncomfortable in my life. I tripped on some unsafe steps and sprained my ankle very badly. It was while I was still hobbling about that I met my first husband, Inky Petheridge. I'm afraid it was all a great mistake. The marriage only lasted a few months. I was only just getting over it when I went to the party and met Jacko.' She didn't mention that, although her ankle had healed, she had retained for the moment her dramatic and sympathy-attracting limp.

She smiled. 'But never mind, Jacko could always be relied on to be the life and soul of the party, war or no war. Of course he was rather too old to be called up. Do you know what his first words to me were?'

Zak glanced at her, smiling encouragingly.

'He said I had a beautiful behind! A beautiful behind and a beautiful neck. Although he didn't use quite those words, as I expect you've guessed, knowing Jacko. He was always very down-to-earth, it was what made him such a colourful character and what drew people to him. They always got the truth from Jacko.' She gave the faintest sigh. 'But in spite of his apparent *joie de vivre* Jacko was actually deeply unhappy when we first met.'

'Yes?'

'He was weighed down with family responsibilities. Absolutely weighed down. It was all a terrible mess. He had a wife who had let herself go and did nothing but pester him with trivial domestic worries. You see, she had turned out to have the *âme de boue* in spite of having been trained in the arts. You would have thought that a woman with her background would have known instinctively what the needs of genius were, wouldn't you? But no! Her problem was that, *au fond*, she was completely selfish. No use to Jacko whatsoever. He was just beginning to discover this when we met. I think he knew at once how I could help him. And I did.'

'You did indeed, Maman.'

'And we knew immediately that we were destined for each other.'

'And the other women,' Zak said carefully, 'the ones who came later? They didn't count at all, did they?'

Regine made an impatient and very French gesture of dismissal. 'Poor man. They literally threw themselves at him all the time. You wouldn't believe it. He'd hardly have been a man if he hadn't taken what was offered, would he? And Jacko was very much a man. But, as you rightly say, they didn't count, these other women. They came and they went. As for me, I saw it as my duty to run Burr Ash, to make sure he had a peaceful home. Very fortunately I had a little alimony.'

'I suppose the attentions of those other women were quite flattering to your good taste in a way,' Zak said with a sly smile.

'Put crudely, yes, I expect that's true.' She laid a hand briefly on Zak's arm as he changed gear. 'You're wise for your years, Zak dear.' She smiled a tiny, economical smile. 'I don't expect you remember Mona Leech?'

'No. Before my time, I expect.'

'Well, anyway. She was the last. That was three years ago.'

Zak shook his head in wonder and admiration. 'Three years! And still pulling the birds! Christ, but wasn't he the most amazing guy?'

105

'He was absolutely exceptional. He was a genius,' Regine said simply.

Zak smiled privately to himself. 'What happened to his first wife after that? You don't mind me mentioning her?'

'Not at all. It brings us on to the subject I wanted to discuss. Fortunately, she left Burr Ash of her own accord and went to live with Aiden Chase, having conveniently dumped her children on a relative. But Chase got tired of her and set her up in a certain amount of style somewhere in Devon, I believe. One thing that can be said of Chase is that he's a gentleman at least. A kept woman, I suppose you'd call her, unlike some of us who have to work so hard for what little we have. But there you are! I wouldn't exchange my life for any other!'

'I should think not.' They had arrived back at Burr Ash. Zak parked the Rover in the yard, the cobbles of which were threaded with bright green moss.

'Is she still alive, the first wife? You didn't mention her name.'

'Emily. Her name's Emily. And yes, I have reason to believe she is still alive.' Regine closed her eyes momentarily, remembering a stony, blue stare. 'And Zak, I want you to find her.'

Zak narrowed her eyes. 'Find her?'

'I don't want anyone else involved at this stage, not Davidson, not anyone. But I want you to find out where this woman is living and I want you to discover just how much of Jacko's early work she's hung on to. I estimate that she must have quite a collection.'

'Right. That doesn't sound like it would be a problem.'

'This is the point. I think it may. Chase will know her address but I don't want him warning her that she has something I want, or even worse, getting to her before I do. The chances are he may not know what she has. She was very secretive and extremely stubborn.'

'I see what you're on about. Never mind, leave it to me.'

'I can give you one possible lead. Emily had a brother. You might remember that extraordinary man who turned up here after the funeral.'

Zak brought his pale eyebrows together.

Regine smiled thinly. 'He ate an inordinate amount.'

'Ah, I'm with you. The codger with hay fever.'

'Francis Troy. He'll know where she is. All I can tell you is that he has a school somewhere in London called Rudyards. He was boasting about it.'

'That'll be a breeze then.'

'But I don't want him to know who it is asking for her address either. She simply must not get wind that we want the paintings. If she does, she'll do anything to deny us access to them, simply out of spite. I'm afraid she's like that.'

'And when I've sussed out where she is?' Zak lowered his voice. He had caught sight of Fergus, who was watching them from the corner of the yard. Zak would be glad when the school holidays were over, if just to be shot of Fergus's relentless snooping. The kid's curiosity was something he hadn't previously taken into account and it was turning out to be a bloody nuisance.

'I want you to pay her a visit and without mentioning my name, find out what we want to know. Once she's taken you into her confidence it shouldn't be too difficult. Not for you. After she lost Jacko I think she went slightly off her head, poor woman, so she can't be looking after Jacko's work properly. Besides, she's very old.' Again the faintest smile. 'Even older than I am. You would be doing posterity a favour if you could get them away from her as unobtrusively as possible. Offer her a good price, naturally. I just hope you're able to get some sense out of her.'

'Of course I could get them off her for nothing, if you like,' he said grinning.

Regine wagged her finger at him indulgently. 'Now, Zak, don't be naughty! I know you can charm the birds down from the trees but we mustn't take any risks when it comes to Jacko's exhibition, must we? Everything above board.'

'Just as you say, Maman,' Zak complied, though his entire life so far had been about taking risks. He had observed Arlette at the kitchen window apparently washing up and thought: Christ, but how this place reeks of jealousy!

With one eye to Arlette, he took his hand from the wheel and laid it briefly on Regine's shoulder. She felt the warm pressure and was comforted. Not for much longer would she know that reassuring male touch. Without it, there was no way she could have survived thus far, or would even have wanted to.

107

'I promise I'll be good,' Zak said. 'Leave it all to me. I expect the quack told you to take things more easily now, anyway.'

'Yes, he did as a matter of fact.' She glanced at him. Sometimes Zak was a little *too* intuitive.

'There you are, then. You never spared yourself, did you? I wish I could have done more.'

'You already do enough.' She looked at him steadily. 'Do you know what I wish?'

'Tell me, Maman.'

'I wish you were truly my son. In spite of having three children of my own, it seems to me that you are Jacko's true heir. There!'

After the reading of Jacko's will, which produced no surprises since he left everything to Regine, Alain had lost no time in pushing off back to Winchester.

Zak leaned across and kissed her cheek. 'That's the nicest thing anyone ever said to me,' he said. 'I'm truly touched because sometimes that's exactly how I feel myself.'

As he opened the door of the Rover Andra rushed out into the yard searching and calling for her cat. Arlette was still ostensibly washing up and Zak was more conscious than ever of the watching eyes. Sod the lot of them, he thought. In any case, his time here was almost up and he could hardly wait to get the hell out. Jacko's biography was nearly finished and besides, laying low had served its purpose. His instincts indicated to him that it was safe to move on to the next stage of the game.

CHAPTER TEN

Holly stuffed her few belongings into her bag. Gideon had left half an hour earlier, having apparently given up, at least for the time being on persuading Emily to shift from Sandplace and pay his father a visit. He had made a convincing pretence of enjoying his meal of tuna sandwiches followed by heated up creamed rice. Holly grimaced. She couldn't bear creamed rice; it reminded her of school dinners at the comprehensive she'd attended. Gideon had quite happily eaten her share.

'So Aiden Chase thinks I'm losing my marbles, does he?' Emily said as she watched Gideon drive away. 'Thinks I'll come running, does he? He always did like to control. I can't see any other reason for this fit of busybodying.'

'He must still fancy you. He saw you at the funeral and suddenly it all came back to him,' Holly said.

Emily looked fierce. 'It's all a joke to you, isn't it? Well, don't forget, young lady, you'll be old too one day!'

'I wasn't joking. Why shouldn't he still be in love with you?'

Emily maintained a hurt silence.

Holly stopped cramming things into her bag and looked at her grandmother curiously. 'Don't you care for him at all?'

'Yes, of course I do. What made you think I didn't?'

'Then why—'

'Haven't you been listening?'

'I reckon all these blokes showed you a hard time, eh? Can't say I blame you giving them the air but I don't see why you had to give up on everything else?' Holly hesitated, fiddling with the strap of her bag, knowing she'd gone too far.

Emily pounced. 'What do you mean by that remark? Niggle, niggle! You're like a bloody terrier. Who says I gave up?'

Holly reddened but set her lip defiantly. 'I mean, what have you got to show for the last forty years?' There. It was said. *Now* Emily would throw her out!

'You are an extremely rude girl and know nothing whatever about it!'

Emily sounded furiously angry but at least she didn't tell Holly to get lost and never darken her door again.

'I must blow,' Holly said stiffly. 'I have to see how Mum's managed today.'

'Go then,' Emily said.

At the door Holly leaned over and kissed Emily's unresponsive cheek. 'See you. Take care.'

'Take care? Well, really!'

Emily remained at the door while Holly made several attempts to start the Metro. When the engine was running at last Emily called out, 'I suppose you know you haven't seen the last of Chase? You better watch out. He probably has the same appetite for playing God as his father.'

Holly waved out of the window, relieved that her grandmother was at least speaking to her, she steered the car along the dark track where lights from the wooden shacks painted haphazard golden patches on the blown sand. Behind her the sea was a strip of pearly luminescence.

The last glimmer of the day. The previous two days had just been an interlude. Tomorrow she would return to all the same old problems: her mother's illness; a carving almost ruined by having to use a badly seasoned piece of wood; the pressure to complete all her work by the final assessment deadline and the probable outcome of that assessment. It was enough.

Emily went back inside the van and poured herself a stiff whisky. Then she went and sat on the verandah, now in darkness, watching the frosty gleam of the surf unfurl with a constant asthmatic hiss. Gulls pattered restlessly on the roof and the salty aromas of the shore filtered reassuringly through the whisky fumes.

She was sorry that she and Holly had fallen out but the girl would keep stirring up old embers, poking around in the past about things that didn't concern her. Perhaps a jolly good run-around with young Chase would put her off the scent. And be the most extraordinary irony into the bargain. She couldn't get over how like his father at the same age Gideon was, which had been a very long time ago.

Chase became the natural leader of the student group that stuck together because they were all bright, talented and thought themselves rebellious. Aiden Chase was also taller, better looking and more erudite than the other men in their circle, which somehow made up for the fact that he was a better theoretician than painter. He had been far more expensively educated than anyone else and Emily had the impression that his father, who was a dilettante collector as well as having interests in Far Eastern trade, had agreed to the Slade idea as a necessary letting-off of steam for his eldest son before the serious business of life began. School and background had already primed Aiden for his role in society, whereas Emily's precocious talent and irreverence had by that time put her at odds with her middle-class family. She had for all practical purposes already cut herself adrift.

While they were still students there had never been any question of romantic feelings between Aiden and Emily, or so she believed. The custom in the group of calling each other by nicknames and surnames was a kind of underlining of the platonic nature of their relationships, based on good-humoured rivalry and argumentative fellowship. It had come almost as a disappointment to Emily when, years later, Aiden himself had shattered this illusion. It was as if a god had descended from Mount Olympus to mingle with *hoi polloi*.

It had happened in the most unromantic place it was possible to imagine. Perhaps that had been part of the trouble. The visitors' room in the sanatorium, with its mourning garb of now defunct blackout material, its empty fireplace and reek of floor polish and disinfectant, was cold and unwelcoming. Outside the window the recovering patients could be seen half-heartedly digging the plots that had been cut out of the once-fine lawns in order to plant vegetables. Emily herself was recovering, no longer having to trail round carrying a sputum flask filled with disinfectant; she was allowed to walk in the grounds on the understanding that there was no sunbathing. Not much chance of sunbathing that day!

Emily sat down uneasily on the arm of an overstuffed but

decrepit chair. She was profoundly shaken by the sudden reappearance of the friend she had long since lost contact with; her marriage to Jacko had effectively broken all her old ties. But Aiden (and it took an effort to think of him by his first name) was no longer a student and she was on the point of being no longer a wife. Jacko had filed for divorce as soon as she entered the sanatorium; she hadn't seen him since. In fact Aiden was her first visitor for more than a year.

'Don't look so shocked, Emily,' Aiden said. 'Surely you knew how I felt about you? I just wish I'd been able to come sooner. As you see, my time hasn't been my own lately.' He was wearing army officer's uniform. 'Besides, I didn't know what had happened to you and Jacko.'

The room became intolerable suddenly. 'Let's go outside,' she said. They walked in the grounds at a distance from the gardening patients. Aiden discovered an old iron bench beside the smooth grey trunk of a beech and persuaded her to sit down. He remained standing, with one foot on the rails of the seat.

'You seemed surprised back there when I spoke about my feelings for you,' he said.

'Your feelings for me?' She pulled her old blue cardigan more tightly round her as if the spring day were bitterly cold and not merely mild and overcast. 'What do you mean?'

He was standing in front of her now, looking down at her intently, his hands folded behind his back. 'I worshipped you, Emily. Don't pretend you weren't aware of the fact?'

Coming from his lips the admission shocked her as if he had uttered some obscenity. In these surroundings the words seemed so incongruous as to be indecent.

'Of course I didn't know. How could I?' She looked helplessly at the institutionalized surroundings and was suddenly painfully conscious of her unkempt hair and ill-fitting dress. She felt humiliated. Why had he *really* come? Was it to see the proud young Emily Troy of former years chastened and laid low by her foolish blunder. She had married the wrong man and had paid the price. Now look at her!

'I never dreamed it would be necessary to tell you in so many words,' he went on. 'We were so close in those days. I thought you knew right from the very beginning.'

Emily shook her head dully. What did it matter now anyway?

'Muriel has taken the children,' was all she could think of to say.

'Oh, yes. The children,' he said without enthusiasm. 'You most certainly won't be well enough to have them back for some time yet, even if you get out of here tomorrow.'

She could hardly deny it. But it was impossible to convey to him that the worst, most painful part of her illness had been missing the children. He would never have understood the emotional and almost physical grief of the separation.

'You're wearing uniform,' she remarked as if she had just noticed.

'I'm in Army Intelligence. I'm hoping for demob soon but it doesn't seem imminent, I'm afraid.'

'You used to be a pacifist. You used to say you were.'

'This was a different kind of war.'

'Was it? Are there different kinds, then?'

'I think so.' He continued to stand with his hands behind his back as if he were waiting for something.

'You look very handsome,' she said. 'And I look — oh God!'

When she had been told she had a visitor she'd done her best. The nurse had helped her with her hair but there was nothing to be done about the frock. Once it had fitted. Now it hung like a sack.

Aiden sat down beside her, twitching his trousers at the knee fastidiously. He laid a hand on hers and stroked her fingers gently. 'You look even more beautiful than I remember,' he said.

She made a noise of disgust and disbelief.

'No. I mean it. Less robust but more refined.' He grasped the hand he'd been stroking. 'Look, my darling girl, when you leave here I want you to come back with me to Riversfoot.'

'With you? No, Aiden, that's ridiculous. I shall have too much to do. I'll have to go back to Burr Ash for a while but only until I manage to find work and a place for me and the children.'

Aiden looked at her pityingly. 'You wouldn't want to go back to Burr Ash, dear. Jacko's there with Regine.'

The silence stretched out. She hadn't known that. Very little news filtered through to her here. In her dutiful letter Muriel never mentioned Jacko's name.

'As I said,' she repeated at last, 'I have to find somewhere for me and the children.'

'Naturally, you will. But first you have to convalesce and give yourself time to look about. Things have changed a great deal in two years. The shortages are in some ways worse than during the war.'

'I know, I know. I do read the newspapers and listen to the wireless.'

'As a matter of fact, I'm stationed not far away from Riversfoot myself. I manage to get home quite frequently.'

'Am I to be a camp follower, then?' she said with an attempt at humour.

'Listen to me, Emily dear,' he said severely. 'As things are, this will present a perfect opportunity for you to get yourself absolutely well. You won't have to do a thing. My housekeeper and her husband are very efficient.'

'You managed to hang on to your staff despite the war, then?' she teased.

'They're quite old,' he replied starchily. He sensed her vacillation and his voice changed. He said softly, 'I'll be back frequently to see you. And listen, Emily darling! There will be absolutely no strings of any kind. Do you understand what I'm trying to say?'

She stared at her feet in their much-mended shoes, thinking. As if aware that he had made something of a blunder, coming out with his feelings when she had clearly not previously thought of him in the romantic sense, he was silent.

But her next comment was not what he expected and evidently tried his patience to the hilt. 'I'm sorry, Aiden, but I have to ask this. You've seen Jacko lately. How was he?'

Aiden coloured. 'He was obviously well. He's always well! I can't imagine how the bugger got exemption unless it was his age! I'm sorry about the bad language, I'm not given to it as a rule.'

'He's never been to visit me, did you know that? Well, he wouldn't. He always had a horror of illness. He thinks it's an aberration.'

Aiden's usually pale features became even darker with rage. He said harshly, 'Forget Jacko! He's behaved abominably!'

Emily gave him an angelic smile. 'Oh, I have forgotten him,

Chase, believe me. I just mentioned him, that's all.'

'And for God's sake call me Aiden. The old days are over now, Emily. We've all grown up. All except Jacko!'

'Muriel came to see me once or twice. She didn't bring the children, of course. She says they're settled now and she doesn't want them upset. Francis came once as well but he said it brought on his hay fever so he hasn't been back.'

'So much for your family, then.' Cautiously, Aiden placed his hand on her shoulder. 'That's agreed then? You're coming to Riversfoot to convalesce?'

It seemed she had no alternative. She finished up at Aiden's Buckinghamshire home almost by default. She had no money and there was nowhere else for her to go. Muriel had made it abundantly clear that a convalescing adult in the house for more than a few days was out of the question. Besides, there was no room; the house was already full. Moreover, Francis had no home of his own – he was a resident teacher at a boys' prep school in Hampstead; to his great relief his weak chest had kept him out of the services.

As far as Emily was concerned, Riversfoot was only ever meant to be a temporary solution to her problem but it didn't take her long to work out that this was not how Aiden saw it.

He was often at Riversfoot. Both his parents had died during the war – from distress, Emily was told, at seeing their home fall into disrepair and the fear that it might be commandeered and used as a billet or home for displaced persons, though it never actually was. Aiden's younger brother, Ruskin, turned up once, before disappearing again en route for Europe to track down stolen art treasures amongst Nazi loot. He was a more robust version of Aiden and in other circumstances Emily could have fancied him.

From her first-floor window she would watch Aiden arrive in a staff car, handsome in uniform with his sherry-coloured hair falling boyishly forward when he took off his cap. He would have already arranged with Mrs Hume, the housekeeper, to prepare a modest candlelit supper over which he would attempt to draw Emily into an exchange of ideas. She began to respond, intellectually at least, to feel like a person again, to come to life.

She compared these civilized meals with the ones she shared

with Jacko, which she would have cooked herself and to which he would turn up, more often than not, with an entourage of friends, acquaintances and hangers-on. While the wine flowed he would hold forth on any subject under the sun and relished brow-beating the opposition. He never thought women worth arguing with; their role as far as he was concerned was not to think or to have opinions. Emily slowly learned to keep hers to herself, in any case, the gradual onset of her illness meant that she was always tired. The old fire had died in her. Jacko and the illness had all but extinguished the bright, shining Emily of student days.

She began to get used to and even enjoy the ordered flow of life at Riversfoot. The talk, the quiet suppers, the country walks, Aiden's kindness, his patient wooing. She found out more about Aiden's attitude to sex. He seemed to regard what he called lovemaking, and what Jacko described as a good fuck, as a hurdle which had to be approached with caution and accomplished with due ritual and fastidiousness to avert the dreadful possibility of farce or indelicacy. Emily had been accustomed to Jacko's robust and bull-like virility about which the only cause for blushes would have been a temporary lack of performance. At first her response to Jacko had been in kind and for a time her body seemed to blossom, her passion to equal his. Eventually, under his domination and subjected to his unpredictable moods, the blossoming became a withering. She already knew that she had become just one woman among many, with the added humiliation that she was also a drudge, marooned in a decaying and ramshackle old farmhouse.

Aiden never expected her to lift a finger, let alone become a domestic drudge, but things were not going well in other directions. He had at last got round to visiting her bedroom, but only occasionally and he would never stay the entire night.

'Why are you leaving?' she asked him once, feeling his unspoken rejection.

'I'm only going back to my own room, darling.'

'Why do you always? Why don't you stay?'

'I'm sorry. I can't really.'

'Was it so awful for you?' she said, smiling. 'I can buzz off, you know. If there's someone else.'

He reacted almost angrily. 'Of course there isn't! It's always been you. Always. I adore you! Worship you, but when we make love I feel . . .'

'Feel what?'

But he never would tell her. She had to work it out for herself. The guilty manner in which he would leave her bed said it all. He evidently thought that impregnating the object of his adoration was a kind of defilement and that when the temptation to do so got the better of him he always regretted it. She even wondered if he regarded her as well as himself with equal disgust as soon as it was over. She thought that probably he did.

The revelation was a bombshell, though she realized how perfectly it fitted the personality she was only just beginning to understand and how little he had revealed of himself in the Slade days.

Sex between them practically ceased, even in the ritual-encumbered style he preferred. It seemed to Emily that he was relieved to have got it out of the way and could concentrate on grooming her for the role of mistress of Riversfoot. He had never suggested she brought the children to live there and Muriel was still adamant that to move them would be to disrupt their education and their emotional stability, so she left it for a few months longer, aware that Fern and the twins now regarded her as some sort of visiting aunt rather than a mother.

Her looks and her health were improving and both Aiden and the doctor suggested that it would be a good idea if she took up painting again.

Reluctantly at first, she made a few tentative attempts, fearing that something important had been lost for good. Then it was like an obsession returning, not at all the gentle hobby that Aiden had in mind but a serious rival to his own plans for her future. She painted furiously to escape the grief for her children whom, she was already beginning to realize, could also be lost to her for ever. Aiden was hurt by her preoccupation, complaining gently but firmly. She sensed that the walls were closing in again and that it was time to move on. Riversfoot had been merely an interlude. She had to get out, find a job, now that she was fit enough. Perhaps she could after all have the children back.

Early one morning, even before Mrs Hume was up and about, Emily packed a small suitcase with the meagre set of belongings she'd arrived with. She left behind the silk underwear and soft wool suits that Aiden had somehow managed to obtain in spite of clothes rationing, but at the last minute she slipped silently into the library and tucked a pair of Modigliani drawings in amongst her knickers and Kestos bras. Aiden could hardly grumble since he had boasted that he had purchased them cheaply from a man who had originally bought them for a mere two shillings at the Mansard Gallery in Heal's and who had failed to understand their potential value. Selling them to one of the less fastidious London dealers should raise enough boodle to see her through a few weeks while she looked for a job. With money in her pocket, though not as much as she'd hoped, she headed west, further west than Burr Ash, because in spite of everything she still felt that the West Country was home.

A flurry of rain and a stiffening of the breeze brought Emily back to the present. Hastily she swigged the dregs of her whisky and heaved the chair on which she'd been sitting back inside. It was all Holly's fault, this raking over old husks. Francis should never have told the girl her whereabouts in the first place.

CHAPTER ELEVEN

Francis took the cheque out of his wallet and laid it on the desk. His hands made the sound of dry leaves as he rubbed them together.

'Not bad,' he said to himself. 'At least not bad for a couple of salacious scribbles.' But all the same, he had to admit that it was not nearly as much as he had hoped for and not nearly enough to solve his financial problems.

He had taken the engravings in their Marks and Spencer bag on the tube to Whitechapel station and finally tracked Davidson down in his cramped office behind the gallery. The transaction had not been as embarrassing as Francis had anticipated. Davidson had examined them as dispassionately as if they'd depicted apples on a plate.

'Monk insisted on giving them to me,' Francis lied in a rush of explanation. 'Years ago. I must have done him some small favour or other, can't remember what. Lent him some money, I expect. His peculiar way of showing appreciation, I shouldn't wonder. Thought I'd fancy 'em. Funny chap. They're not quite the kind of thing one would want to hang on one's wall, ha, ha! So they've been in a drawer collecting dust ever since. Not my cup of tea, you understand.'

There was an uncomfortable pause while Davidson closely studied the engravings. Then he looked up. 'Well, they're Monks all right.'

'What?' Francis' bad conscience and his poor hearing caused him momentary confusion. 'No, no. Sorry old chap, but they're mine. Definitely mine.'

'I meant that they're genuine.'

'Of course they're genuine! You didn't think I'd done 'em, did you? Ha, ha!'

Davidson continued soberly, 'So. There's no doubt about their provenance. You were thinking of selling?'

'Didn't come all this way for nothing. They're no good to me. I just thought that they may have increased in value now that—' He cleared his throat.

'Quite. And what were you expecting to get for them?'

Francis stared at Davidson. Then he sneezed, reaching urgently in his pocket for his handkerchief. 'Look, old chap,' he said when he'd finished mopping up, 'I rather thought that was your department. That you'd make me an offer?'

Davidson tapped his teeth with a gold Parker. 'This isn't quite my field. I shall have to make a few enquiries and get back to you. I could sell them privately or put them with one of the auction houses, but I have to warn you that the latter process, though it might be more profitable for you, would take considerably longer. We should have to wait for a suitable slot for them.'

'What about this retrospective they were talking about at Burr Ash?'

'The works in the retrospective will not generally speaking be for sale.' Davidson's eyes showed a glimmering of humour. 'And this is not the type of thing Mrs Monk would be willing to put on display. She is hoping to enhance her late husband's reputation.'

'She'll have a job on her hands then. Womanizing old bounder.'

'I was talking about his reputation as a painter.'

'Shouldn't be any difference,' Francis grumbled.

'Ah, now that's what one might call a whole new can of worms,' Davidson said.

'What about Chase? D'you think he might be interested?' Francis suggested. 'I could go to see him myself.' He had suddenly remembered that Davidson would certainly ask a substantial commission; and in any case, he had been promising himself that he would contact Chase again, see if he had got in touch with Emily. He just hadn't got round to it.

Davidson shook his head. 'Not his terrain, I'm afraid. It's a limited market. But leave them with me, I'll see what I can do.'

Francis had left then. Davidson had shown him out through the attractively laid out and new-looking gallery.

'Had some trouble finding the place,' Francis said. 'You used to be in Cork Street, didn't you?'

'My business partner and I parted company. I decided to come back to somewhere near where I started.'

Francis seemed to remember that Emily had told him Davidson had been shipped over to England with other Jewish children just before the war.

Davidson offered to ring for a taxi but Francis declined. It would cost far too much. He returned to the school exhausted and dispirited but after a surprisingly short space of time Davidson had rung him to say that he had a potential buyer. The offer was not as much as he had hoped but, on Davidson's advice, he decided to accept it all the same. It was only the smallest drop in his particular financial ocean but it was better than a kick in the teeth; he just prayed that Providence would intervene again over the business of the Lab Fund.

There was a perfunctory knock on the door and Mrs Bessemer erupted into the room. Without preamble she launched into an apparently rehearsed speech about extra cash to cover overalls and bus fares, while she looked pointedly at the cheque Francis hadn't had the presence of mind to conceal.

'Not just now if you don't mind, Mrs eh – Bessemer. I have rather a headache.'

'I'm afraid I do mind, Mr Troy.' She pressed her overalled stomach against the desk while she craned her neck to read the figure on the cheque. Francis strategically shifted a paperweight replica in the shape of Shabti of the Psamtik inscribed with Chapter Six of the 'Book of the Dead', but he guessed that it was already too late.

'May I remind you of Luke, ten, seven,' she went on.

'Luke, ten, seven?' Francis queried. Oh, God! Not quotes from the scriptures again. He could actually feel a real headache starting.

'Now, Mr Troy, I thought you read the Bible every morning at assembly, even if at no other time!'

'That isn't to say that I actually know it verbatim, Mrs Bessemer,' he said testily. Assembly indeed! At Rudyards it was called Prayers.

' "The labourer is worthy of his hire," ' Mrs Bessemer quoted triumphantly, 'and that includes overalls and bus fares!'

'Indeed,' he said loftily. 'Then I'm afraid I must have read a different translation. I don't recall anything about overalls and bus fares. Now would you mind if we dealt with this next week? I'm very busy just now.'

'That's what you said last week, if you remember, Mr Troy.'

'Yes, yes. I really will see to it when I have a moment. Now would you mind bringing me my tea? I really have the most frightful head. I think I shall have to take some aspirin.' He turned his attention dismissively to the desk drawer from which he eventually produced a bottle of Boots paracetamol.

' "Charity suffereth long, and is kind," ' Mrs Bessemer announced threateningly, 'but if I don't get satisfaction quite soon, Mr Troy, I really shan't be able to see my way to remaining in this employment.'

'Come now, Mrs Eh – let's not be hasty,' he said soothingly, missing for the moment the implications of this remark. 'I really will give it some thought just as soon as I have time.'

'It's not thought I want. It's cash,' were her parting words.

After the door had slammed behind her Francis drooped. His head pounded. He gulped down two of the pills with the dregs of his morning coffee which Mrs Bessemer had deliberately forgotten to remove; there was no saying when or even if the tea would be forthcoming. Then he eased the cheque out from beneath Shabti of the Psamtik and fingered it absent-mindedly, his housekeeper's quotation buzzing in his head. Charity suffereth long indeed! And envieth not, thinketh no evil, beareth all things, begins at home. No, no. That last one was wrong. Blast the woman. She had upset him so much he wasn't thinking straight. He couldn't cope with her constant complaints at his age. He was getting old. He was afraid he *was* old. Emily was old too, older than he was, in fact. If charity did begin at home then perhaps the cheque, strictly speaking, belonged to her. She and Jacko had still been together when he had taken the wretched engravings. Conscience dictated that he send the money to Emily.

All at once he felt seven years old again, mortified and guilt-ridden over the time he had been discovered filching cake from another boy's tuck box. There had also been an undetected incident with a beautiful set of coloured pencils. He stared at his clenched hands on the desk. Surely there were more ugly brown patches on the backs of his knobbly knuckles than he remembered? And wasn't the tremor more pronounced then before? All inexorable signs of age. His time was nearly up. His heart began to flutter like a trapped moth and he imagined it struggling against overwhelming odds to keep his lifeblood flowing in its courses. He visualized it giving up, ceasing to beat, his life ending. Nobody would care if it did; some people might even be glad. Tears squeezed out of his eyes and ran into the back of his nose. He reached for his handkerchief yet again and for the next five minutes endeavoured to staunch the combined onslaught of sobs and sneezes. How had he come to this, that he had reached the end of his life without having acquired a single friend to mourn his demise? His existence was not even essential to Emily – she never came to see him anyway.

His melancholy train of thought was shattered by the whinny of the telephone at his elbow.

'Rudyards school. Headmaster speaking,' he said automatically, his handkerchief still pressed to his eyes.

'Would that be Mr Francis Troy?' A cultured male voice which he couldn't place.

'Yes, speaking.'

'I represent the Ventriss Tracing Agency. I wonder if it would be possible to speak to Miss Emily Troy.'

'No, I'm afraid it would not, and if you're selling double glazing or offering free holidays you're in the wrong box.'

A rich chuckle came down the line. 'No, I assure you it's nothing like that. The Ventriss Tracing Agency is a private firm employed by the National Savings Bonds and Stock office to trace holders of winning premium bond numbers. I expect you've seen the current publicity about unclaimed prizes on television?'

'I don't possess a television and I'm perfectly convinced that my sister never purchased any premium bonds.'

'You'd be surprised how many people have actually forgotten they ever bought any. I'm glad that I seem to have reached the right address at last. Your sister will be very pleased to know that she has won a considerable sum of money.'

'As it happens Miss Troy doesn't live here.'

'I'm sorry to hear that. Perhaps you could tell me how I can get in touch?'

'I'm afraid I couldn't possibly give her address to a perfect stranger.' He thought guiltily about giving Emily's address to Holly. He had asked very few questions of her. Not that she wasn't perfectly genuine.

'I hear what you're saying.' The man on the phone was sympathetic. 'Your caution is very commendable. Look, I'll tell you what I'll do. How would it be if I put something in the post which I think will prove to your satisfaction that it's all above board? Then you can get back to me. Our last address for her was in the West Country. Could you perhaps tell me if that is still the case?'

'Yes. As a matter of fact it is.'

'Good. You'll be hearing from us. Thank you very much for your help.'

Francis rang off. He continued to sit at his desk, frowning at the blotter. If the call was genuine and Emily had won 'a considerable sum of money' then he could change his mind about the possibility of sending her the money he'd got for the engravings; his conscience would be clear. The man sounded like one of the boys' parents, youngish, middle-class, well-spoken and polite. The sort of accent Francis was predisposed to trust.

His headache was worse and still the tea did not arrive; he went without, lacking the courage to go to the kitchen and face the gorgon a second time.

CHAPTER TWELVE

Gideon laid down his compasses and pushed his set square aside. He sat at his desk staring out of the cottage window, his attention straying yet again from the survey drawing he had been working on. But the sinking feeling he was experiencing had nothing whatever to do with either his drawing or with his attractively laid out garden, with its pergolas, seating areas and abundant planting now almost lost in the indigo shadows of late evening. He had, in fact, just made a momentous decision and all on the strength of a grumpy young woman in an old red shirt and big boots. His decision was that he would end his affair with Sarah Henderson.

In theory it shouldn't have been too difficult to extricate himself from a relationship that was already worrying him profoundly, but the two-year liaison was not of the run-of-the-mill variety. It had *ramifications*.

He had first met Sarah when he had surveyed her parents' garden in preparation for certain improvements Mr Henderson had in mind. Vanessa, Sarah's younger sister, was getting married and the reception was to be held there. No expense was to be spared.

At first he was completely bowled over by Sarah's looks, her vivacity and her enthusiasm. At twenty-six she was already well up the promotion ladder of the insurance firm for which she worked. He supposed she was what was known as a high-achiever. The whole family were high-achievers. His first impression of them was what he could only describe as their 'graciousness'. It had very soon given him the sensation of being part of it himself. It was all very pleasant, particularly when he and Sarah found themselves attracted to each other. Into the bargain the redesigning of the garden had been particularly gratifying because the Hendersons were perfectionists, something he could understand.

Sarah's parents, Elizabeth and Douglas, had a puzzling attitude to their daughters' sex lives which had been demonstrated by their preparations for Essa's wedding. They all knew perfectly well that she and Tony had been sleeping together for months but this was assiduously glossed over. The bride, whose lost virginity, according to Sarah, was already shrouded in the mists of time, was being directed towards the wedding night via all the tribal rites and taboos of the ritualized sacrifice of the maidenhead. The wedding dress, the bridesmaids, the presents, the vows were all nevertheless studied with a meticulous attention to custom. It seemed to Gideon more than just the wish to have a blockbusting rave-up.

Sarah was a very modern girl; she had her own car and her own flat, though she visited her parents frequently since they all got on so well. However, after what he now saw as a ridiculously long time, it began to dawn on Gideon that for a girl like Sarah to be career-oriented was simply not enough. It was only part of what was expected of her and what she expected for herself. He had come to the conclusion that the old-fashioned concept of being beaten to the altar by a younger sister was beginning to fester like a thorn in Sarah's flesh. Lately there had been oblique hints, not only from Sarah herself but, jokingly of course, from the family. He almost expected that any day now Mr Henderson would take him aside and ask him about his 'prospects'; not that he'd tried to conceal what they would doubtless see as the advantages of his birth nor had he exaggerated them. All the same, he had the uncanny sensation that he was caught up in a twentieth-century replay of a nineteenth-century novel. It was getting out of hand and it worried him. He wasn't against marriage; he found the idea of a wife, a home and children intensely appealing in spite of, or perhaps because of, the fact that he had so far very little experience of such things. But he liked to think he had some choice in the matter. He had begun to feel trapped, mostly because he knew that he no longer felt the same about Sarah.

He wanted to see Holly again. Not when he had news of a possible commission for her, but right now. Not that this was easy; he lived in Dorset and Holly in Bath. Besides, she had degree work to do and he had a particularly demanding work-load himself.

Spring was a busy time of year. And 'doing something about Sarah' would have to come first, wouldn't it?

His eye strayed to the phone and on an impulse he reached over and dialled the number Holly had given him.

'Yes?' a voice said abruptly, as if he'd interrupted an important conversation.

'It's Gideon.'

'Oh, Hallo.' She sounded marginally more friendly.

'I'm coming up to Bath tomorrow to look at a garden.' This was pure fabrication. 'Any chance you'd be free?'

'You must be joking?'

'All right. I'm busy too,' he said severely. 'But you eat lunch, don't you? We could go to a pub or something.'

'Well—'

'Just for an hour. Maybe I could see your work. You could bring your photographs?'

'I could,' doubtfully.

'That's settled then. I'll pick you up.'

'OK. Look, what about a picnic?'

'Sure. Anything you like.' He had rather visualized the corner of some nice cosy pub but guessed this was her way of dealing with the expense. He didn't like to point out that of course he'd pay.

Holly put the phone down and went back into the kitchen. Fern was standing like a statue in the middle of the floor, her hands hanging uselessly, her attention fixed on the pile of washing-up.

'Stop!' Holly cried, loudly and suddenly.

Her mother started, a look of terror flaring momentarily in her eyes, before she came out of her apparent trance.

'There's no need to shout,' Fern said, angrily pulling on a pair of rubber gloves. She ran hot water into a bowl.

'Celia said I had to,' Holly grumbled. 'And you did agree to it.' She picked up a drying-up cloth and began to dry the dishes as Fern fished them out of the suds.

'I know I did. It's just that it gives me a fright. And I sometimes think you enjoy it.'

'Enjoy it! You can't be serious.'

'All right. I'm sorry, darling. It's not easy for either of us and

127

you've been so good about everything.'

Feeling stricken, Holly put the plates away in the old Welsh dresser, bought when they'd first moved into the flat and Fern was feeling optimistic about the new home. She had sanded the wooden floors and strewn them with kelims, painted the walls white because, being a basement flat, it tended to be dark, and hung floor-length curtains of cheap hessian-like fabric she'd bought in the market.

But for nearly two years Fern had displayed very little enthusiasm for either her appearance or her surroundings. She came home from school exhausted, taking progressively longer to mark books and prepare lessons until she was sitting up into the small hours and waking in the morning unrestored.

'Who rung?' Fern said, emptying water from the bowl.

'Gideon. The guy I met at Emily's.'

'Oh dear. Poor Emily. What are we going to do about her being turned out like that?'

'There's nothing you can do. Stop worrying about it. If you like I'll go down next weekend and see if she's made any arrangements. She probably has but is keeping them to herself.' Holly wouldn't have been surprised. After all, neither Fern nor Emily had seen fit to communicate with each other for more years than Holly had been alive. It was the fact that she had found this faintly shocking that had driven her to seek out her grandmother in the first place – or at least partly. The cool brushoff from her father was another not insignificant incentive.

'I wish she'd go to stay with Mr Chase like Gideon suggested.'

'I don't know the old guy but somehow I can't imagine that working.' Holly stowed cutlery away in the dresser drawer. 'To be honest I don't think Gideon can either.'

'What did he want? Gideon?'

'He's coming to Bath tomorrow. He suggested lunch.'

'Will you go?'

'Yup. I said I would.'

'That will be nice.' It was the sort of comment that used to drive Holly wild when she was a teenager. Luckily she had grown up. All the same, Fern hoped it didn't sound too patronizing or too optimistic. She sometimes worried about Holly. Holly got on extremely well with the female students at the college but was invariably scathing about the men. She had only ever had two boyfriends, neither of whom lasted very long. Not that Fern had any doubts about Holly's heterosexual preferences, but good relationships with men did not appear to run in the family. Maybe Holly would be better off not attempting one in the first place.

'So how is your ma?' Gideon asked.

'Oh – you know,' Holly said uncommunicatively.

'No. I don't.'

Holly plucked a stalk of grass and put it between her sharp white teeth. She watched a distant stand of trees turn from pale jade to a dark inky green as a cloud passed over it. The shadow travelled on to engulf a hillside studded with sheep. In winter this was an inhospitable upland – the places round about had names like Cold Ashton and Freezing Hill – but on days like this it offered a secluded, pastoral setting for a picnic. It was unseasonably warm, the sky a pale azure turning to cobalt on the horizon. A plane droned across it, chalking a white line overhead. On the breeze came the faintest scent of primroses, cut grass and the farmy whiff of cow dung.

They had finished the picnic Holly had brought and were drinking from cans of lager supplied by Gideon.

'You said she had some kind of breakdown?' Gideon persisted.

'Teaching's hell. I'd never go in for it.'

'Is that what caused her problem?'

'Who knows? Probably. They've buggered teachers about with their endless curriculums. It must have been that or her weird upbringing. Or both.'

'She's not in hospital, then?'

'Look, butt out, will you? I don't want to talk about it.'

Gideon was lying back on the rug, watching her. She sat with her arms round her knees, the sleeves of her red shirt rolled up. Gideon wondered if it was the only one she possessed. The tawny skin on her forearms was taking on a soft warm glow in the sun but there was nothing fragile about Holly Wyatt. Compared to Sarah's pale, expressive and well-manicured hands, Holly's seemed to come from another species; brown, square and capable, with nails worn down to the fingertips. Perhaps it was too fanciful but he suddenly saw Sarah as a hothouse plant, an orchid perhaps, that had been carefully cultivated and protected from chill winds. Holly was more like a *Rosa rubiginosa* – sweetbrier – rugged and prickly.

'You say you've no intention of going into teaching when you're through finals,' Gideon said, heaving himself up on his elbow. 'So what will you do? An MA?'

'*If* I get through finals. An MA's out of the question but obviously I want to get on with my own work.'

'What about dosh?'

'I could get a part-time job,' she grinned. 'I might even go for an Arts Council Bursary or get an artist-in-residence posting on the strength of my degree stuff. If I'm lucky.'

'I'd like to see your work. Did you remember the photographs?'

To his surprise she blushed as she fished in her bag and handed him the folder. The photographs had mostly been taken outside in the grounds of the college. There were massive shapes hacked out of logs and even parts of whole trees. But there were also smaller, finely finished pieces that displayed the carver's developing skill. They all alluded to the human form, mostly female, or parts of it, but hugely modified by the material – tree-women.

Gideon looked through the folder attentively, without comment. Then, leaving the folder open, he sat back.

'Wow,' he said. 'Strong stuff.'

'What did you expect?' she said loftily.

'I think they're great. Absolutely great. I can just see them in an outdoor setting – like the ones in the Forest of Dean.'

'I got pretty frustrated by the wood I had to work with,' she said in a burst of confidence. 'None of it was properly seasoned. I expect they'll crack to hell in a few years.'

'Pity. Still, that might not be a complete disaster. But what you couldn't do with a nice bit of seasoned stuff, eh? Look, I'm sure I can lay my hands on some. Leave it to me. What d'you like to work on?'

'Anything decent. Lime, oak.'

He glanced at her as she kneeled beside him on the rug. There was a dash of pink from the sun across her tawny cheekbones; her dark eyes were intense, her jaw strong, her mouth full. He wondered what it would be like to kiss it. But not now. She'd probably stick one on him.

'I have to be going,' she said. 'I have some work to finish.' She stood up and began to gather up the remains of the picnic. 'How did this morning go? Are you going to take on this garden?'

'What?' For a moment he was confused. 'Oh, that. No.'

She giggled. 'It didn't exist, did it?'

He grinned. 'Party pooper!'

Back in the car, Gideon pulled out of the layby. He drove slowly, eking out the remaining time.

'So, you think your grandma and my old man had a wild affair?' he said.

'She clams up if I ask too many questions but I get the impression that they did. Not at the Slade but later, yes. She stayed with him – until she got itchy feet. But I don't think it was wild.'

'Knowing my old man I'm absolutely sure it wasn't. He's always got his kicks from Art.' Gideon chuckled. 'He was never so upset as when the Cézanne landscape and the Chagall went missing.'

'Missing?'

'Pinched, in spite of a so-called fail-safe alarm system. Never recovered.' Gideon negotiated traffic lights. 'Will, my cousin, has been trying to track them down ever since. So you see, in your grandma's case he probably fancied the painting above the real thing.'

'What d'you mean?'

'He goes to the Tate every few weeks to gaze at Monk's nude painting of her.'

'No shit?'

'No shit.'

'Poor old guy. That's really quite sad.'

'D'you think so? Yes, perhaps it is.'

Gideon drove home on a high, hardly conscious of the passing miles. As he soared up towards Shaftesbury, north Dorset spread out before him in a patchwork of every kind of green, punctuated with small, pale explosions of blossom. Hardy had called it 'the Valley of the Little Dairies'. In the distance Bulbarrow was a smudge of ultramarine.

He plunged down to the wooded Stour valley and on to Blandford. It dawned on him suddenly that he was not far away from an estate that boasted an impressive stand of managed woodland, and whose owners always kept back some of the best timber for long-term seasoning. Eighteen months ago he had landscaped the couple's garden; he reckoned it was time he checked up on its progress.

Impulsively, he called them on his car phone. Then he turned off and made the necessary three-mile detour. In the end, he not only inspected the satisfactorily maturing garden but was given some solid lumps of seasoned oak into the bargain. He also stayed to dinner. It was late when he set off for home. Almost immediately the car phone bleeped.

'Where the hell are you, Gideon?' Sarah's voice scorched down the line.

'Near Blandford. Why?'

'Because you are supposed to be here, that's why. At Tony and Essa's.'

Then he remembered. Vanessa and Tony had lately moved into a newly converted cottage. Tonight was their house-warming. 'Oh, Christ. Their party! Look I can be there in under an hour.'

'Don't bother,' Sarah said furiously. 'It'll be too late now. I've been trying to get you all evening. What was the point of me giving you that expensive electronic bloody organizer if you don't bloody well use it?'

CHAPTER THIRTEEN

Fergus was lurking. It was a favourite occupation and one that drove his sisters mad, though he had no interest in their paltry concerns. They were nothing. The only secrets worth knowing were the secrets of adults and to date he had unearthed quite a haul. He knew, for instance, that his father regularly met a rather plain woman who worked in the local library and that their meetings took place in pubs and teashops. As far as Fergus knew, that was all there was to it. It was pathetic and wimpish that his father could not even do *that* properly; no wonder his grandfather had despised him. Then there was Auriel, his aunt. He just happened to have stumbled on the fact that Auriel was a secret gin drinker and that she disposed of the empties in the dustbin carefully wrapped in newspaper. Though alcohol was not expressly forbidden at Burr Ash, except where his grandfather had been concerned, Grandmère nevertheless kept an eagle eye on any that entered the premises. Solitary drinking would most certainly have raised eyebrows.

But the prize was neither of these. The prize, if he could only pin him down, was Zak. Because if Fergus knew nothing else he knew that Zak had to be some sort of con artist, or a thief, or was into peddling drugs. Since he'd arrived Zak had made it his business to worm his way into Grandmère's affections and now she trusted him absolutely; Fergus wouldn't be surprised if she had changed her will in his favour. She was always dropping hints – proof enough that she must be going barmy.

He had several times tried to get into Zak's room but Zak had had a very efficient lock fitted and never omitted to use it. This was fishy enough in itself but when Fergus had commented on it to his mother she had made a typical reply.

133

'You don't know how lucky you are, Fergus,' she'd said, 'to have been brought up in a place like Burr Ash where we all trust one another. Zak hasn't had that advantage. Grandmère told me he came from a poor area of Wolverhampton and went to a rough school. You can't expect him to change overnight.'

'He's been here ages. You'd think by now he'd know no one was going to pinch his stuff,' Fergus had said sulkily.

'Let Zak alone. He works very hard for Grandmère and she doesn't like him upset.'

So that was that. Afterwards he'd said no more about it and though he had watched his adversary like a hawk he failed to discover him in any activity that looked remotely shady, apart from sucking up to Grandmère; but waiting until Grandmère snuffed it in the hope of being left something in her will had to be a waste of time when he really thought about it. Grandmère was careful with money but everyone knew she wasn't rich.

He was watching his grandmother now, pressing himself against the studio door and peering through the narrow gap he'd created. She was sitting in his grandfather's chair on the studio dais. On her lap was his grotty old corduroy jacket. Fergus had been unproductively through the pockets already and found it as useless and disgusting as it looked, stinking of tobacco, paint and the powerfully lingering smell of his grandfather's body odour. Grandmère was stroking it fondly as if it were a favourite cat, and her lips were moving. If he hadn't known her to be an atheist, he would have said she was praying. Jacko hadn't been a bad old guy, but during the months of his illness he had become nothing much more than an object, and a pretty disgusting one at that. Fergus could remember the time when he had dominated the conversation at mealtimes but it had never been obligatory to listen; Jacko liked the sound of his own voice and had been satisfied with a semblance of attention. In any case, Fergus hadn't known what he was on about most of the time. Grandmère was different. It was expedient to pay attention to Grandmère; there was never any doubt about her meaning, however much she wrapped it up in French phrases or long words.

The telephone purred through the echoing studio, making Fergus jump. In Jacko's time, calls were rarely put through to the studio, now Grandmère insisted on it as she and Zak spent much of their time here; a fact which Fergus was well aware irked his mother, though she said nothing.

Regine lifted herself from the chair and went over to the desk in the far corner, moving like a swimmer or a sleepwalker. They said she had once been a dancer, which Fergus thought might account for the weird gliding walk she effected. He listened attentively, trying unsuccessfully to fathom the gist of the conversation from his grandmother's replies.

'Regine Monk speaking. Oh hallo, Zak dear. Have you? That's splendid. *Oui, oui, bon.* From her brother? I see. Will you? Ring me from there then, dear. And Zak, please be very, very careful.'

She put down the receiver and stood in thought, her nails tapping a hollow tattoo on the desk top. Then she sat down and, unlocking a drawer, took out a black book which Fergus knew must be her current diary. His mother had said that Grandmère had kept a diary ever since her life with Jacko had begun. Fergus thought it must be the most boring book in the world. And now she and Zak were actually going to make a biography out of it and what's more, publish it!

It was late evening and though not yet dark outside, the drawn blinds created their own twilight. Regine reached over to turn on a reading lamp. It cast a yellow pool of light, like a diver's torch in an underwater vastness. From her bag the old lady drew a pair of spectacles and, balancing them on her nose, she made an entry in the black book, which she afterwards closed and returned to the drawer, locking it. Then she folded the spectacles and put them back in her bag.

Fergus was surprised. He had never suspected she was short-sighted and neither did anyone else at Burr Ash. Except perhaps Zak. After all, Grandmère liked to give the impression she was perfect. He speculated about this new discovery, filing it away in his retentive memory. Then he thought of all the withering inspections that had come his way.

'Shit!' he whispered to himself. 'I bet I've been pissing myself for nothing!'

The family had gathered round the long dining table and Arlette was serving out stew into a pile of dishes. At one time, when she was much younger, she had been an adventurous cook but as the years passed and the amount of sheer hard work needed to keep Burr Ash ticking over increased, her enthusiasm waned. Now she stuck to a nourishing though monotonous menu that demanded no extra thought. The evening meal, though culinarily uninspired, had become a kind of ritual; no one was expected to miss it unless they were ill. For Jacko it had been an opportunity to expound his philosophies; Regine used it to extract an account of the day's activities, directly from the young, more subtly from the adults.

Fergus watched his grandmother keenly and was gratified when he heard her ask if there were any maps in the house. She would need glasses to read a map, though he supposed that when it came to it, she'd be crafty enough not to do so in full view of the family.

'I have a school atlas,' Andra offered. Fergus noticed she was eating one-handed so that she could fondle her cat and secretly pass it pieces of unwanted meat.

Regine smiled at her kindly. '*Non, ma petite.* That's not quite what I had in mind. What d'you call the kind that have marked all the roads, rivers and towns in the British Isles?'

'You mean Ordnance Survey, Maman?' Donald said.

'Do I? Have we one in the house?'

Everyone looked vague. Fergus knew there wasn't but he kept quiet. No one at Burr Ash had much interest in the outside world as a rule.

'You want one of this area. Maman?' Donald enquired. He received his dish of stew and began to scoop up chunks of meat and potato, helping them on to his fork with lumps of his wife's wholemeal bread. He had a good appetite.

'I would like one that shows the South-West.'

'If you tell me which part of the South-West you're interested in, I'll bring one back from the shop tomorrow,' Donald said importantly. It was rare, Fergus thought, that Grandmère needed his father for anything.

'Is there more than one?' Regine wanted to know.

Fergus smiled to himself. So his grandmother didn't know everything. He looked back to his father.

'There must be twelve or thirteen. Would you like me to bring them all?'

Fergus felt the faintest glow of pride in his father, an unfamiliar sensation. No one at Burr Ash ever appeared to read except his father and himself, though Donald would have disapproved of both Fergus's choice of books and his method of acquiring them if he had known. Fergus simply helped himself to all the Colin Dexters, Dick Francises and Alastair Macleans he wanted from the shop and put them back on the shelves, slightly dog-eared, when he had finished with them.

'Would you do that? How sweet of you, Donald,' Regine said.

'We don't sell very many.'

Fergus was surprised his father sold any at all. The maps were kept on a dark shelf at the back of the shop and were mostly out of date anyway. He wondered if he should risk asking Grandmère why she wanted the maps. He knew very well that no one else would, but having found a weakness in his grandmother that she was so obviously anxious to keep from the family gave him a dangerously exhilarating sense of power.

He risked it. 'What do you want to know, Grandmère?' he asked in the voice of innocence. His hooded eyes, so like hers, were wide.

'Fergus!' Arlette said sharply. 'Don't be impertinent.'

'The child has an enquiring mind, for which we should be grateful,' Regine said. 'An enquiring mind is a great asset.'

Fergus breathed again.

'But such a pity,' Regine continued, addressing the company in general, 'that he doesn't make more use of it at school. I've said this before but one still hopes that an expensive education is not being wasted.'

It always came down to this, Fergus thought, biting on his lip to hold back a scalding fury. One day he would get the better of Grandmère. One day. However, his new feelings of superiority had already dried up the rush of tears which were so often and so humiliatingly the result of tangling with his grandmother.

Auriel envied Fergus. She could see already that he would be one of the ones who escaped. Like Alain. There was hope for him since he had never knuckled under, even if it meant facing a daily barrage of criticism from Maman. Like last night, for instance, when she had once again threatened to take him away from his school.

She sat down on her bed and pushed a damp draggle of hair back from her face. How she hated the drudgery of washing. Why wasn't it possible for them to have a washing machine like everybody else?

'It's insidious,' her mother had said severely when she had once suggested it, and Arlette had taken Maman's side, naturally. 'If we give in over that, all the other trappings of modern life will follow. It would just be an excuse for the children to start demanding television and music centres. As it is, you know I don't approve of them going to the cinema.'

'But Maman!' she had cried recklessly. 'You have a car and a computer.'

'They are unfortunate necessities. Burr Ash is not in the middle of a conurbation and frankly, Auriel, I'm surprised that you question the word processor. It's Jacko's life we're recording and unfortunately time is not on my side. Besides, I depend so on Zak who is of the younger generation and wouldn't undertake the work at all without modern technology. You do understand that, dear, don't you?'

Auriel immediately felt awash with guilt and Arlette's reproachful expression hadn't helped.

She looked at the glass in her hand and realized that she had helped herself too liberally from the bottle in her bedside cabinet. She would have to be more careful.

Naturally, she had apologized to Maman. 'That was stupid of me. Of course you have to have those things.'

But the resentment wouldn't go away. Arlette didn't seem to mind how hard she worked or for how long. The domestic routine depended entirely on her and she obviously enjoyed the power it gave her, albeit dimly perceived. Having a husband helped too, even though he was ineffectual. Then there were the children. Auriel had none of these status-improving aids. Vincent had left so long ago it was as if he had never exited.

Above her bed was a small oil sketch Jacko had done of her when she was twelve. It had been one of the studies he'd made for a large and somewhat preposterous painting that purported to illustrate some kind of Golden Age. It had been exhibited at the Royal

Academy that year. Such paintings had been anachronisms even then, she thought, but the sketch, if not the finished painting, still contained much of his old flair, the exuberant brushwork of his early years. It was to go into the retrospective, of course. Gazing at it, her eyes filled with tears. Unbelievably, the same eyes that gazed back at her from the painting; huge, limpid eyes, full of the tenderness and trust of a protected childhood. She had indeed been a beautiful child.

Auriel dashed away the tears with the back of her hand and rummaged in the bedside cupboard for the bottle of Gordon's; she poured a measure into her tooth glass, carefully this time. Musn't overdo it again, however much she needed it. She drank.

The idyll had gone sour long since. Jacko had descended into irascible old age. Maman had become ever more obsessed with her husband so that everything and everyone was subordinate not only to his needs but to his whim as well.

Arlette appeared quite content to take complete charge of the domestic affairs of Burr Ash, however much it wore her out. She, Auriel, had become steadily more peripheral. Yet she would never leave. In spite of everything she loved Burr Ash with every part of her being. In fact, she really believed that she was actually part of Burr Ash and inseparable from it. Her boring round of drudgery was lightened only by the astonishing, heart-stopping beauty all round them and the magnificence of the changing seasons. The translucent greens of spring, the gold and viridians of summer, the tans and earthy hues of autumn and winter, all sustained her in their own particular way. The most astonishing thing of all was that no one but her appeared to notice them. Arlette was too busy and Maman was in any case blind to anything else besides Jacko.

'Auriel! Where are you?' Arlette's gruff shout reached her from somewhere below. 'We haven't finished yet, you know.'

'I'm just coming. Came up to get a hanky,' she called back. Without thinking she poured herself another quick snifter of gin and drank it, forgetting that she had already had two. The glass and bottle clattered together as she hastily hid them away at the back of the cupboard. She wrenched open the bedroom door clumsily and went unsteadily downstairs, back to the washing.

* * *

Joss Kingsnorth

Zak Stratton was dyeing his hair in the en suite bathroom of a Lyme Regis guesthouse where he was staying the night. He was using a temporary hair colouring he'd bought in the town. He had chosen a colour called Burgundy Brown, a shade or two darker than his real colour and a great deal darker than the ashy blond he'd maintained over the last two years. At the same chemist he had purchased a pair of faintly tinted sunglasses with tortoiseshell frames. He was already experiencing that buzz of adrenalin that he had been forced to forego almost entirely for two weary years. Now, unexpectedly, the chance had come to do what he liked doing best. Taking risks.

Extracting Emily Troy's address from her brother had caused some delay and a certain amount of effort but he had at last accomplished it. Some deft faking up had produced a convincing enough letterhead for Francis Troy to be persuaded that his sister had indeed won some money on a premium bond. All in all it had turned out to be by far the quickest way to his goal. He had discovered that Emily lived in Devon, in a place called the Saltings. Regine had assured him that Emily had attended the funeral, though he himself had only a vague recollection of her; he had put her down as some eccentric ex-mistress of Monk's. However, batty or not, the woman would most certainly recognize him unless he took steps to make sure she did not. Hence the spectacles and the hair dye.

Living on the edge of the law and sometimes a good way outside it, had started when Zak was still at school. About the time he was born his mother had heard that her hero, Ringo Starr, had named his child Zak, and promptly followed suit. His father had moved out of the family home soon after and Zak and his mother had finished up in a council flat. Leonard Stratton had bequeathed his child only a surname and a flair for duplicity and fraud. From his mother, Zak inherited a creative talent that had taken him to art school, at least for a time. As far as his mother was concerned, her only son could do no wrong. She believed in him implicitly; deceiving her was a breeze. Having managed to keep out of the hands of the police was something else, a real matter of pride. He intended to keep it that way.

Confident in his newly acquired camouflage, Zak set off on the

A3052 in his hire car, but as soon as he arrived amongst the chalets and wooden bungalows of the Saltings, he realised that he had been misinformed. Going by Regine's information he had been looking for a seaside residence, if not in the grand manner, at least of some consequence and style. Emily Monk was supposed to have been supported all these years by her rich ex-lover, hadn't she? Zak had certainly not been prepared for a slum.

He stopped the car alongside a shabby old man and his snuff-coloured mongrel.

'I'm looking for Sandplace,' he called through the window.

The man surveyed the new arrival with a disparaging air, apparently chewing over this piece of information.

'Be 'ee?' he said at last.

'Do you by any chance know where it is?' Zak made an effort to stay civil.

'I dare say I might.'

'A Miss Troy lives there.'

The man still hesitated.

'Well, do you know or don't you?' Zak said impatiently.

The man pointed with his stick. 'You might try downalong,' he suggested.

'Sandplace is down there, is it?'

'I dare say 'tiz,' the man said slyly, watching complacently while his mongrel, who had been sniffing round Zak's hire car, lifted a leg against the front wheel and let fly with a yellow stream.

'Bloody hell!' Zak spat out. 'Can't you control that tyke? Isn't it supposed to be on a lead or something?'

The man appeared to be mouthing obscenities as Zak drove off but he instantly forgot him as he resumed his search. He left the car in a sand-blown dinghy park while he continued on foot, scanning every crazy beach dwelling that had any indication of being occupied. He found what he sought at last and very unprepossessing it looked too. All he could do for the moment was to return to the car and work out a completely new strategy. Nevertheless, he was only half convinced that it was worth going on with his employer's mission.

He drove to East Ashpool, where he had previously noticed a reasonable-looking pub. He would have to stay the night since it was too late to plan and execute a fresh approach. That evening he telephoned Regine to tell her that he would be delayed. She was not dismayed. His absences from Burr Ash for research purposes were, in any case, fairly frequent. Regine never minded since the book was progressing well. Besides, she didn't know about the additional private business that he managed to conduct while he was away.

On the same evening Gideon was also on the telephone. His father, at Riversfoot, took the call.

'I'm ringing about Miss Troy,' Gideon said.

'About time too,' his father scolded him. 'I've been trying to reach you but you always seem to be away from the phone. I thought you had one of those frightful mobile contraptions.'

'So I do, but it's not always convenient to have it on me when I'm out on a job.' This was a slight fudging of the facts. At the risk of putting off potential clients he had deliberately left the phone at home on several occasions. Sarah hadn't forgiven him for missing the party, and his hints that all was not well between them had not gone unnoticed. Later that evening he was taking her out to dinner, when he planned to make the break. He was not looking forward to it.

'Well, now that you have condescended to get in touch you'd better tell me what you were able to discover. What did she say about my invitation to stay at Riversfoot?'

'I'm afraid it's no go.'

'What do you mean, "no go"?'

'I mean she respectfully declines your offer.'

A silence.

'Did you hear what I said?'

'Yes, yes,' irritably. 'Did she, by any chance, say why?'

'She doesn't want to leave Sandplace. She's not keen on travelling.'

'You told her about my offer to send a car?'

'Yes.'

'But you did see her in person, didn't you? I mean you didn't just telephone her?' Aiden was suddenly suspicious.

'She's not on the phone and yes, I did see her in person and used every inducement, but she still won't budge.'

'And what are her circumstances?'

'A bit dodgy but she seems happy enough.'

'Gideon, please don't be difficult!' Aiden burst out. 'For goodness' sake explain what you mean!'

'She lives in a converted railway carriage down by the sea.'

'A railway carriage? This isn't one of your jokes, is it, Gideon?'

'Absolutely not. It's a very nice railway carriage. She appears to be very happy in it.' Gideon hesitated. 'But it seems she might have to get out in the near future. Perhaps you should wait a bit and see what happens.'

'What are her plans? Has she somewhere to go?'

'I don't think she has any plans. She doesn't seem too bothered.'

'I expect she didn't choose to discuss them. But I must say I don't understand this railway carriage business. Emily was always a little eccentric but why should she choose to live in such a place?'

'Because it's cheap, I imagine. She evidently hasn't much money.'

'No money? I don't understand,' Aiden repeated.

'I know it's a tricky one, Dad, but yes, I think that would be a fair description of her circumstances.'

'Are you making fun of me?' Aiden was piqued, and not solely because of the suspected teasing. Gideon had called him 'Dad' again. 'But you must be mistaken. She told me Jacko was supporting her. And besides, she has the Modigliani drawings. She could sell those.'

'Drawings?'

'She stayed with me for a while once. When she left she took a couple of drawings with her.'

'When was this?' Gideon queried, puzzled.

'I can't remember. About 1945.'

'Christ, Dad! That's fifty years ago! She would have sold them long since.'

'Yes, I suppose you're right. However, according to her brother, she has some money coming to her.'

'Oh yes, her brother. Chap we were introduced to at the funeral.'

'Yes. He telephoned. I'm not quite sure why. He talked about money most of the time,' Aiden said with an air of distaste. 'And he made some suggestion that I should become a governor of his frightful little school. Can you imagine!'

Gideon chuckled. 'So, do you want me to see Emily again? To keep you posted?'

There was a surprised silence. 'I thought you were too busy.'

'I'm considering offering her granddaughter a lift there this coming weekend. Holly visits her fairly regularly.'

'That would be kind, yes. Do that, Gideon. By the way, William is here this weekend. He's advising me about additional security.' Gideon's cousin had taken over much of the stewardship of the Riversfoot collection.

'Good. That reminds me. Has there been any progress with the stolen paintings?'

'William still clings to the notion that their disappearance was not dissociated with the visit of that young student but I'm not sanguine. Time runs on. I'm afraid I shall not see them again.'

'Dad, I have to go.'

'Very well. But may I make one last request?'

'Another one?'

'Would it be at all possible for you not to address me as "Dad"? I think I've mentioned this before.'

'So you have. Sorry, I forgot.'

'Since I am well aware that we have never been close, I think "Father" would be perfectly acceptable. Or now that you are adult, my first name. As you know I'm not of a naturally paternal disposition.'

'I'll bear it in mind. Goodbye, Father.'

An hour later he was facing Sarah across a pristine white tablecloth, with only a slender glass of anemones between them. The deep carmines and purples blazed dramatically against her corn-gold hair; the tips of her lashes were bleached almost white and her love of tennis and outdoor sports generally had also dashed a healthy glow across her cheekbones. In a few years' time her delicate skin would begin to lose the battle and become weatherbeaten. Gideon couldn't imagine Sarah losing any sleep because of it, as long as she was happy. But he was not offering her happiness. At least, not the happiness she was currently counting on. He had planned to broach the subject over coffee but was well aware that she already knew something was amiss.

She dipped her spoon into a crème caramel. 'I'm sorry I jumped down your throat over the party the other night, Gideon,' she said. 'I know you've been mega busy lately.'

This made his task even more difficult. Did she guess this?

'I needed time to think,' he prevaricated. 'About us, I mean.' He paused. 'You see, I don't believe this relationship is going anywhere.'

She smiled. 'Should it go somewhere?'

'I think so. Shouldn't it get deeper or more meaningful or something? We still seem to be two quite separate people, doing our own things, getting together when we have time.'

'Isn't that what most affairs are like?'

'I haven't the remotest idea. But for me it's not enough.'

'Most people have a solution to this.' She grinned. 'Though far be it from me to suggest it.'

'A solution?'

'Don't act thick, Gideon!'

'You mean marriage?'

'Well, you did say you wanted things to *go* somewhere. It's the next step for most people. We could live together, which would be fine by me but I think Douglas and Elizabeth wouldn't be too keen on the idea. As far as they're concerned it would have to be marriage or nothing.' She held him in a blue stare.

Gideon put down his spoon. 'Then I'm afraid it has to be nothing, Sarah. I think we should split up.'

Skilfully she disguised her sense of shock. 'You're prepared to chuck up what we've had together because of a few temporary problems?'

'Sarah, these problems aren't going to go away.'

Sarah reached over and removed a deep pink anemone from the vase. Systematically she removed the petals, one by one. 'So you don't think there's any love left?'

'No.'

'Or affection?'

'Yes, there's affection.'

145

'Some people would say that was enough at the stage we've reached.'

'Not for me. There has to be passion.'

'Fuck passion. It doesn't last.' The dismembered flower lay on the cloth. Her elegant fingers were stained black and pink.

'I'm sorry, Sarah. I've changed in the last two years. I believe we want quite different things out of life.'

'Such as?'

He was silent. He hadn't the heart or the words to tell her how enormous he thought the gulf between them had become. All he wanted to do was to pay the bill and leave the restaurant, like a coward.

'Such as?' Sarah persisted grimly.

He shook his head. 'Everything.'

The waiter approached the table. 'Coffee?'

'No, thank you,' Sarah said. 'I think we should go.'

In the car Sarah sat in icy silence. Gideon put the key in the ignition and hesitated. 'I'm sorry, Sarah,' he said.

'Sorry!' she cried, her hurt souring the words. 'Tell me, when did all this come on? One minute everything's fine and then you say you want to end it all.' She turned on him. 'I take it there's someone else?'

He was silent, not knowing for sure that there was.

'Right. Now we know where we stand,' she said bitterly. 'Gideon, you're an absolute bastard. An absolute fucking bastard. And I'll tell you something else! I'm glad it's over because I think, basically, that you're a loser.'

'Perhaps I am. Basically.'

'Don't mock me, you shit! And there's no perhaps about it. In fact, I believe my parents might be rather glad about this. Look, start the bloody car, will you? I want to go home.'

When Zak set off from The Green Man at East Ashpool the following day, his appearance had altered yet again in line with a new plan of action. His hair remained a dark auburn but he had added some fresh touches. The local shop doubled as a chandlers and from it he had acquired a pair of distressed jeans, a navy knitted hat, a navy guernsey and a pair of yellow sea boots. As soon as he was out of sight of the pub he had taken the precaution of dirtying up his new outfit with dust and mud from the side of the road.

He left the car by the dinghy park. As soon as he stepped out of the lee of the meagre tamarisk bushes the stiff breeze snatched at his hat and fluttered the papers on the clipboard he carried. Another half-hour and it would be raining. He strode pusposefully up to the door of Sandplace and banged the greenish, pitted knocker once or twice. There was no answer. He lifted the knocker again. It was in the shape of a bearded head that looked not unlike Monk himself. He wondered if the old bat got a kick out of the thought that her visitors did violence to the image of her ex every time they called.

'Who are you?' The voice came loudly from behind him, but Zak was not easily disconcerted.

He remembered her now. It was the woman he had seen at the funeral, her hair escaping from a milk-white knot and her rugged figure draped in what appeared to be a horse blanket. He adjusted his tortoiseshell rimmed spectacles, watching her closely from behind them for signs of recognition. She looked at him blankly and he reckoned he'd passed the first test.

'The name's Shuttleworth,' he said, holding out his hand.

'Are you from the housing department?' she said suspiciously, ignoring the hand.

'No – you're not expecting someone, are you?'

'That depends,' she said frowning. 'You're not, by any change, from that crowd of crooks?'

Zak grinned engagingly. 'I think I can guess who you mean. And in a way, that's what I've come about.' He brandished his clipboard. 'I wonder if you'd sign our petition? It's against the sale of the Saltings and on behalf of all the chaps who use the dinghy-sailing facilities.'

'Bit late for that, aren't you?' Emily pushed back a skein of hair that blew across her weatherbeaten face.

'Late, but not too late. It'll be easier to get signatures now that the season's starting. I already have a few.' He held out the fluttering pages, raising his voice against the brisk breeze. In the pub last night he had not only discovered a convenient local issue but had taken the precaution of committing a few names to memory.

'Do you live here? I haven't seen you before.'

'I live in Dorchester. And you might have seen me before; I keep a Mirror in the park up the road.' He pointed to where the small coppice of masts showed above the bushes.

'I should have thought you sailors would be all for a scheme like this,' Emily said. She was looking at him rather too intensely for his peace of mind.

'Not at all,' he said, making an effort to smile. The woman had not seen him smile at the funeral. It would throw her off the scent. 'We're only small-time sailors. None of us could afford to keep our boats in a marina. Have you heard what these places charge? We should have to try to find somewhere else, though God knows where. I think it's a scandal. We want to stop it if we can. Will you sign the petition? It would be on behalf of the residents too.' He tried not to let his impatience show but he was desperate to get inside her place, not least in case a bona fide sailor should turn up. He had already noticed one or two pottering about round their craft.

'I think you're too late,' Emily said, making up her mind. 'But I'll sign your petition if you like.'

He handed her the clipboard and fumbled in his pocket for a nonexistent pen. 'Sorry, I seem to have dropped the blasted Biro,' he said, grinning. 'Not much good as a canvasser, am I? First time I've done anything like this.'

'Oh, well, you better come in,' Emily said. 'I've got one somewhere.'

So he was inside at last. And while the old girl went off in search of a pen Zak imprinted the look of the kitchen and its contents on his memory. There were no paintings by Monk here, just one or two assured and colourful gouaches by another hand. He moved to the door through which she had vanished and glimpsed bedrooms beyond. The only other exit from the kitchen appeared to be into a sitting room; through its window he just had time to catch the restless glitter of the sea before she came back.

'The house of an artist,' Zak said ingenuously.

'There are no artists here,' she said crisply, 'and I can't find a pen.'

'Never mind,' Zak said. 'I'll call again.' He looked round him. 'It would be such a shame if the Saltings were knocked down. I think it's charming. And there's something about the way you have this place arranged – perhaps that's why I thought you were an artist.'

Emily moved over to open the door for him. 'Good heavens! I don't have time to *arrange* things.'

'That means it's instinctive. I do envy people who have that flair. I have none whatsoever though I'm a keen gallery-goer. What I know about art is self-taught and full of errors, I'm quite sure. I like the moderns. In fact I'm a collector in a small way. I was most fortunate in picking up a Matthew Smith and a Graham Sutherland recently.'

'They are hardly considered moderns now,' Emily said shortly and Zak experienced the sudden rush of adrenalin when he knew a scam was beginning to take.

He leaned against the dresser. 'I thought you must know something about it. You were being too modest.'

'Modesty is not one of my failings,' she said.

'In that case,' Zak said carefully. 'I wonder if you could give me some advice. I have been offered a Monk but I have to say I'm not sure about it. Someone told me that only his early paintings are any good. Do you know the painter I mean?'

Emily narrowed her eyes thoughtfully. 'I might do.'

'I must confess I like all his stuff, even though it's not generally appreciated these days. I'd give a lot to lay my hands on more.'

'Why don't you ask his widow?'

'I have also been told that she is unlikely to have any of his early work.'

Instinct told him that his quarry was getting restless. In any case he had laid the trail, all he had to do was wait. The old girl was patently short of cash.

He shook hands politely, left one of the cards printed with a variety of names that he always carried, and departed, saying that he would be at The Green Man for another night and would call again, expressing a hope that she might by then have had some more thoughts about the possible whereabouts of Monk's early paintings.

His almost infallible instinct for when he was on to something made the risk of remaining one more night at the pub worth taking. It was quite apparent that the crazy old bird had nothing in the run-down shack but he had received some unmistakable vibes from the new-looking shed that lay alongside. Besides, it had a suspiciously efficient padlock.

Emily had her swim earlier than usual. The wind had persisted so it had just been a matter of being tossed about in the surf for a while, unafraid and perfectly in accord with the formidable element, before she allowed a great apple-green breaker, its crest a seething white maelstrom, to hurl her ashore. Then she padded back inside and dried herself briskly.

She had things to do that she had obviously postponed too long already. A little business that she didn't want even Holly to know about. It was fortunate that this was the day it was to be implemented.

The moment the young man had left the previous afternoon, she had been overcome with feelings of deep unease. She had had few visitors over the years and now suddenly they were arriving thick and fast; this last one, though apparently sincere and personable, had left her with a sense of foreboding, as if he was a harbinger of some unknown disaster. And she couldn't get over the impression that they had met somewhere before. Within an hour of his leaving she was on her bicycle pedalling to the telephone box, where she rang an Exeter number.

The arrangements had been made previously, so it was just a matter of checking that all was to go forward as planned. Now, as soon as she had dressed, she made her way across the patch of salt-scorched grass, took a key from her pocket and undid the padlock of the wooden building that lay a few yards from her back door. Inside, she folded back the shutters that masked the windows and the daylight streamed in. A moment or two later she heard the erratic whine of a van approaching down the uneven road. Two men got out and she led them into the building. 'They're all ready,' she said. 'Take everything that's wrapped and labelled. Mr Tallboys has the inventory.'

'Right,' said the larger of the two men, the one in charge. 'Any special order.'

'No. But do take care. They are all extremely fragile.'

There were a great many flat, bubble-wrapped packages stowed round the walls and the men started work on them at once, carting them out to the van three or four at a time. As the room became emptier, Emily swept the remaining rubbish into a pile at one end: fragments of dusty old canvases, oily rags, picture wire, flattened tubes of paint, their labels long gone. There was no sign of emotion on her face as she strode about with the broom.

'That's the lot is it, then?' the large man asked at length.

'That's it.' Emily signed his piece of paper and the man clumped out to join his mate in the van. The door slammed and the van reversed erratically back up the road, leaving Emily standing in the echoing room with the dust of the morning's activities hanging in the air in a million shining motes.

That was the end then; the sum total of what the struggle, pain and anguish amounted to. All that was left of Jacko was a small cache of decaying flesh around a few insignificant bones and several hundred canvases whose true worth only a future generation could decide, if indeed one could count on there being future generations. As for her and Regine, they were nothing much more than a couple of old bags of bones themselves; she didn't know what Regine would have to show for her existence on the planet and as for her own legacy, that had yet to be tested. But at least the morning's exertions had given her a sense of being disencumbered, her duty discharged. All that was left to do was to give Mr Tallboys his instructions.

No sooner had the van disappeared than she saw a car draw up at the dinghy park. The young man who had called on her yesterday got out and made his way purposefully towards her. She at once clapped the shutters to, relocked the shed and went back into the kitchen. Closing the door behind her, she reached for the whisky bottle and poured herself a generous slug. She sat at the kitchen table where the windows were too high for her to be seen by the casual observer, resolutely ignoring the young man's knocking. When he went round to the verandah door and knocked again, calling insistently, she felt her misgivings about him were somehow justified. She ignored his entreaties and eventually he went away.

* * *

Half a lifetime ago Emily had arrived at Sandplace intoxicated with the wine of her new freedom while at the same time desperately vulnerable to the realization of what it cost her. On the occasions when this struck home she was ready to do away with herself, swimming out to sea and never turning back. She had lost a good, kind lover but most of all she had lost her children. After making one final attempt to persuade Muriel to let them take their chances with her, she had at last become reconciled to the fact that she would now never get them back. The children had been too much indoctrinated with the belief that their mother not only harboured a disgusting and infectious disease but that she was also loose-living and unreliable, and they could not now be persuaded to think otherwise. They were actually unwilling for her to take them away, having appeared to accept Muriel's strictness and religious fanaticism as the norm; and if they seemed lacking in *joie de vivre* yet they were apparently not unhappy. So she had given up at last and left, determined to put as great a distance between them as her resources allowed.

At first she had been so lonely and miserable that she almost hoped Aiden would track her down and carry her triumphantly home to Riversfoot. After all he had been in Army Intelligence, hadn't he? Didn't that make him good at things like that? Perhaps remorse at losing her would put a match to such a conflagration of passion in him that he would overlook her need to be done with stuffy social norms and manfully bear having the children underfoot as well as the sight of her painting in scruffy old clothes; just so long as he could be near her.

But of course he had not tracked her down. Now that he had tested the reality against the painted image he was no doubt beginning to see the advantages of the latter. It had evidently proved impossible to reconcile the two Emilys after all. For all she knew, his squeamish sexuality had its roots in the same obsessions that governed his mania to collect and possess beauty, particularly of the undemanding variety. It was the image he valued; for he hadn't the least idea how to cope with the flesh and blood reality. As for herself, she had known all along that she didn't love Aiden. She valued his friendship, she was grateful to him for providing a roof over her head when she most needed it, but she was never in love with him. She had no alternative but to leave.

What first struck her about the Saltings was the quality of the light. Light, and the alchemy that turned it into colour and back from colour into light. How it bounced from sky to sea and from the pale sand, dissolving and reshaping the angles and patterns made by the shacks among the dunes. The colours had none of the hot intensity that she remembered of the Provençal landscape; these were cool and northern, pearly greys, indigos and azures warmed by earthy ochres and siennas and the occasional hot blue. Sometimes there would be drama; soot-black clouds, the tossed foam reaching back almost to the horizon, luminous by contrast; or a sun dipping below the horizon, bathing the beach and the whole of the Saltings in rose red. There would be days when rain and low cloud obscured even the line of the surf, days when the gale blew sand under the door and into every nook, so that it found its way into Emily's bed and into her food; but she learned to live with this for the seclusion the place afforded.

Now the seclusion was at an end. The tentacles of the modern world had reached her at last as they were bound to. It was not unexpected. She had known all along that it had to happen.

CHAPTER FOURTEEN

Holly was kneeling on the floor of her room surrounded by large pieces of grey card. In front of her was a drawing board. With a Stanley knife and a metal ruler she made a cut and lifted away the surplus card from the centre. Window mounting was tricky but presenting her most successful drawings to the best advantage could make a difference. On the other hand she could be marked down for it. Too craft orientated! Rolled up beside her were several huge charcoal cartoons, far too big to mount, which would have to be pinned to the wall of her final display. The three-dimensional work would stand on the floor or on plywood pedestals. She crawled round on the floor, fixing the drawings to the finished mounts.

Outside, the rain continued to beat down as it had all afternoon and evening. To save money, the heating in the flat had been turned off for the summer two weeks ago so Holly was wearing a vast jersey over leggings and a pair of fisherman's socks she'd bought in the chandler's at East Ashpool.

She packed the mounted drawings back into their folder and dumped it on her bed. Then she padded along the passage and into the kitchen.

'Tea?' She called through to where her mother was watching late-night television.

'Yes, please, darling.'

Holly helped herself to a bowl of cornflakes. She always used the same bowl. Once, when they were arguing, Fern had pointed out that this habit was only different in scale from the compulsions that drove her, which had given Holly some indigestible food for thought. She put the bowl and the two mugs of tea on a tray with some ginger biscuits and took them through to the sitting room. A

155

film of extreme banality was playing itself out on the screen in the corner of the room.

Holly put the tray down between them. 'This is gross,' she said. 'Can I switch it off?'

'Yes, do. I wasn't really watching.' At one time Fern had been a choosy viewer and then only when she could spare the time from marking. Now the television seemed to be on most of the time that Fern was alone, like a verbose companion wittering away in the background. Also, Holly guessed, it was an excuse to put off going to bed. Fern did not sleep well lately.

'Have you finished what you were doing?' Fern asked.

Holly nodded, pouring milk on to her cornflakes.

'What about the dissertation?'

'That went in weeks ago. I told you.'

Fern looked abashed. 'Yes, of course.' She forced herself to pick up her tea without the usual silent ritual. Another victory? It certainly didn't feel like much of a victory. Hardly worth putting in her diary.

'How was today?' Holly asked. She glanced across at her mother who was curled up in her armchair wrapped in a man's dressing gown, her pepper-and-salt hair drawn back from her face with an elastic band. Holly remembered her mother as a very attractive woman. There were early photographs of them holidaying in Cornwall and the Isle of Wight in which Fern, though already in her late thirties, looked slim and pretty with a cloud of dark hair. Although some of the good looks remained, she was gaunt, her olive skin was sallow and her dark eyes had bruised shadows under them.

'All right, I suppose. But sometimes I think I'm not making any progress at all.'

'Isn't that what your diary is supposed to be for? So you can check back?'

'I know. I know.'

'What does Celia say?'

'She thinks I've come on. But it's so slow.'

Fern sipped her tea, enfolding the mug in both hands. The rain could still be heard beating down into the small area outside the windows. A group of youths, too drunk to notice the wet, passed noisily along the pavement.

'Mum, listen,' Holly said, spooning up cornflakes. 'What will you do when you're better?'

'Go back to school, of course. They're keeping the job open for me.' Fern looked away to hide her fear from her daughter, for the thought of going back to school was like an approaching cloud of impenetrable blackness. She wondered if that alone accounted for what she thought of as her slow recovery.

'Why go back if you don't want to?' Holly said.

Fern stared at her daughter. 'Darling, I have to,' she said. 'There are only a few years left before I retire.'

'You could do something else.'

'But it would affect my pension, don't you see? I just can't afford to.'

'Sod that! I don't see the point of knocking yourself out for it. Why don't you make some enquiries?'

Fern shook her head. 'No, it's quite impossible.'

Holly shrugged. 'I think you're crazy.'

'I think perhaps I am,' Fern said succinctly.

Holly banged her spoon down in the bowl. 'You know what I meant. Sometimes I think you just give in too easily. You simply accept everything as if it were beyond your power to do anything about it.'

'That's life, Holly,' Fern said.

'No it bloody isn't!' Holly cried. Abruptly she went down on her knees in front of the gas fire. 'And it's frigging cold in here. I'm lighting the fire.'

Fern drank her tea in hurt silence making no protest. Frowning, Holly held her hands to the glow.

'Will you be going to see Emily this weekend?' Fern asked at last.

'I might, if you don't want me here. It'll be my last chance until after the degree show.'

'It would also be an opportunity to see where she's planning to live. I really wish she'd take Aiden up on his offer. Will Gideon be there?'

'He said something about picking me up here and travelling down together, but that's a crackbrained idea. He'd be driving miles out of his way.'

'If he wants to, let him.'

'You know I'm not into all that male macho stuff. No, I'll borrow the car if you don't want it.'

'Of course. Take it. I don't feel up to driving yet. In any case Audrey's asked me if I'd like to go to Cheltenham with her.'

In fact Holly was desperately anxious to get back to Devon. She had come to love her grandmother to a degree that surprised her, and the Saltings itself had a hypnotic and slightly loopy attraction for her. The bracing nature of her encounters with both always left her feeling invigorated; it pained her to admit that they were the perfect antidote to the depressing atmosphere in the flat and her mother's maddening lassitude.

Holly picked up her mug of tea. 'Perhaps I will. And I wish you'd at least think about leaving that sodding school.' Her deep attachment to her mother made her sharper than she intended.

'For Christ's sakes, shut it!' Fergus croaked. 'They'll bloody hear us!' He grabbed the three-quarter-full bottle of gin from the bedside table and stuffed it inside his jacket. Then he and Russell belted along the corridor for the sanctuary of Fergus's room.

Russell Galpin was not a particular friend but, like Fergus, he existed outside any of the recognized groups of boys at school; which was why the two occasionally spent time together. They hadn't much in common; both were intelligent – Russell highly so – but Fergus was secretive and sedentary while Russell was restlessly curious and bookish, destined no doubt for later academic success. Both were underdeveloped physically, at least compared to their classmates; Russell wore spectacles but Fergus noticed that this didn't appear to be an obstacle to his being unnervingly observant. He lived with his grandmother, who paid his school fees. This was something else that set him apart from the other boys.

His object in asking Russell round was because Russell had boasted that he could crack locks, and with Zak away it had been a golden opportunity to have another go at Zak's room. However, Russell had admitted defeat almost at once.

'Bloody hell, Pollock,' Russell muttered. 'You didn't say it was a five-lever Legge. And it's no good looking for the number on the key, even if you could get hold of it.'

'Why not?'

'Because there isn't one, dumbo.'

Fergus was bitterly disappointed. On an impulse, by way of an alternative entertainment, he had suggested pinching the bottle from Auriel's room instead.

'She'd never say anything,' he assured Russell. 'No one's supposed to know she drinks.'

'Pass it over then.' In the comparative safety of Fergus's room Russell motioned to Fergus to part with the bottle.

'You dickhead! Have you gone bananas? We can't drink it here! My mother'll be up nosing around any minute.' In fact Arlette could already be heard calling for Fergus to fetch more logs for the Aga.

With muffled guffaws they skedaddled down the back stairs and into the yard out of sight of the kitchen.

'Shall we go in there?' Russell suggested breathlessly, pointing to the studio.

'You joking? Grandmère'll be in there. Sure to be. We'll go to the old stables. But you better take a stick, there's rats in there.' Fergus's fear of rats generally kept him out of the stables but, with Galpin beside him he suddenly felt much braver.

'I'm not scared of rats,' Russell said scornfully.

'Nor am I.'

'Let's go and kick some rat-arse then,' Russell spluttered in a fit of giggles. 'Hear that? Rat-arsed. You know what getting rat-arsed means, don't you?' He pointed to where the bottle of gin resided under Fergus's jacket.

'Oh, very whimsical, Galpin. Come on.'

'Don't drop the frigging bottle then.'

They vanished into the dusty dark of the disused stables which smelled of old cobwebs, slowly decaying timber and bird droppings. Arming themselves with an old broom handle and a broken rake, they climbed the unsteady ladder to the hayloft and collapsed giggling on to a heap of antique straw that lay rotting into powder on the boarded floor.

'Pass us the bottle then.' Russell reached out his hand.

'Piss off. My turn first.' Fergus held the bottle to his mouth.

'What's in here?' Russell was on his feet again, trying a plank door at one end of the loft.

'I dunno. Come on, let's get stuck in,' Fergus said impatiently, unwilling to penetrate further into rat territory.

'No. Let's go in here. It's more private.'

'You can't, dickhead. It's locked.'

'Why?'

'Don't ask me. It's been locked for ages. There's nothing in there anyway.'

'Perhaps there's a mouldering body. In any case, it's only a padlock. I can do padlocks.' Russell saw an opportunity to redeem his reputation.

Fergus, intrigued at last, got up and came over. 'It should be easy,' he scoffed. 'It's an ancient old thing.'

'No, it isn't. It's quite modern.' Russell poked about with a piece of metal that he'd originally tried on Zak's door.

Fergus took a second swig from the bottle. 'Come on, get a move on, if you're so sodding clever.'

Suddenly the padlock eased open. Both boys crowed with delight and crashed into the small room beyond. As Fergus had promised, there was nothing of interest. Certainly no mouldering bodies and fortunately, no rats. Just some broken old furniture and a heap of moth-eaten carpets.

Fergus cuffed Russell round the head. 'Satisfied Einstein? For that you can have first swig.'

'Who you kidding? I saw you just now, slurping away.'

They sat side by side on the carpet, taking alternate gulps from the bottle.

'Pity it wasn't full,' Fergus said, wiping his mouth with his sleeve.

Russell was quite glad that it wasn't. He was not at all sure that he liked the stuff. He took smaller swigs than Fergus and to put off taking another turn he picked up the broom handle and began rootling around behind an armchair from which the stuffing protruded like a grey wound.

'Don't do that!' Fergus said nervously.

'I bet there's rats in here,' Russell said. No rats emerged so he shoved the armchair to one side. 'There's more of your grandfather's old pictures back here,' he said, 'or what's left of them. I think the rats have had a go at them.'

'Best thing for them, if you ask me.' Fergus said. The gin had made him feel braver. He again held the bottle to his lips and drank deeply. 'They're rubbish.' He held out the bottle. 'Want some more?'

'In a mo.' Russell started poking about among the tattered canvases with his stick. 'What's in here?' He pulled out a flat packing case.

'Leave it, for Christ's sake. You're churning up a duststorm, Galpin.'

Russell had dragged out the packing case. 'I bet it's guns,' he said. But he was disappointed. After fiddling with yet another lock, he flung back the lid only to discover more paintings.

'I told you. It's just more of Jacko's crap.' Fergus drank again.

'Doesn't look like his usual.'

Russell cast himself down on the carpet next to Fergus. He drank gingerly from the bottle, feeling slightly sick. Luckily there wasn't much of the gin left.

Fergus was now leaning against the armchair.

'If these are just rubbish, can I take them back to my grandma?' Russell asked. 'She likes stuff like this.'

'Sure, go ahead,' Fergus said. His words came out slurred, which sounded hilarious to Russell. He began to giggle and to beat his stick against the carpet, raising clouds of dust.

'Rat-arsed, rat-arsed,' he burbled. He picked up the paintings from the packing case and lumbered unsteadily to his feet. 'Come on, Pollock. What shall we do now?'

The only reply he received was a retching moan. He looked down as the bottle tumbled from his companion's hand, spilling the last remaining drops on to the crumbling floorboards. Little by little Fergus lowered his head on to the carpet, then he passed out.

As the Metro lurched about among the pot-holes, Holly, peering through the windscreen, thought that the Saltings could hardly have looked bleaker. The rain, which had lashed the car ever since she had left Bath, had now eased, and moist low cloud drifted forlornly around the shacks and chalets. The wind bowed the tamarisk and sculpted the sand into sodden undulations amongst the marram. The new green of the hinterland that she had just passed through was heavy with great drops of moisture, some of the tenderest buds scorched by the salt wind.

The wet sand scrunched under her tyres as she pulled into the relative shelter of the ragged hedge. Beyond it a torn plume of smoke from the metal pipe that served as a chimney was the only indication that Sandplace was occupied. She dragged her bag out of the boot and hurried through the gate and up the steps. She grabbed the head of Neptune and banged it against the door. It was some time before there was an answer.

'Oh, it's you.' Emily sounded surprised.

Holly stepped inside and closed the door on the wind and rain. 'Who did you think it was?'

'There's all sorts turning up lately. You'd be surprised.'

'You mean the property developers? Those guys you call the Midianites?' Holly started to remove her old black coat.

Emily didn't answer at once. She turned her back and filled the kettle at the sink. 'I suppose you want tea?'

'I should say! Are you all right for milk?' Holly opened the door of the minute fridge and fished out a carton. 'I can go into Ashpool in the car for more if you like.' She leaned over and kissed Emily on the cheek. 'Hallo, Em.'

'I thought I'd seen the last of you,' Emily said gruffly.

'Not unless you want to boot me out. I was rude to you, wasn't I? I'm truly sorry. I was out of order when I said those things about wasting your life and so on. What do I know about anything?' She gave a small ironic smile and Emily knew that she would find it very hard indeed to forgo the visits of this persistent young woman.

'We'll have some tea and say no more about it,' Emily said. 'Only I'm afraid it's a waste of time coming to the Saltings in weather like this; it could go on for days.'

'The forecast said it was going to clear up,' Holly said, fetching mugs.

'Hm. They don't know everything on the wireless.'

'Television actually.' Holly grinned.

'I wouldn't know anything about that,' Emily said dismissively. She put a loaf of bread on the table with jam and a tub of margarine. 'I expect you're hungry.'

Holly cut herself a slice of bread and spread it liberally. 'What do you do here when it's like this?' she asked, looking through the window at the tumbled surf.

'I go on as usual, of course,' Emily said, pouring tea. 'In fact I cycled into Ashpool this morning to make some telephone calls.' She passed a mug of tea to Holly. 'I received an extraordinary letter from my brother.' She reached over to the dresser and shoved an envelope across the table. 'Read that!' she commanded.

Holly opened the single folded sheet without much interest and read.

'He says you've won a packet on the premium bonds!' she exclaimed. Fleetingly she thought how wonderfully this might solve her grandmother's problems.

'I thought at the funeral that Francis might be losing his marbles, now I'm sure of it.'

'Why? Isn't it true?'

'Of course it's not true.'

'In any case, how come he knew and you didn't?'

'Precisely. Even though I never in my life purchased a premium bond I contacted the Stocks and Bond office in Lytham St Anne's just to make sure, and of course they say the number doesn't exist. There! You see it was a hoax as I suspected. Sometimes I despair of Francis. I wonder if he's fit to look after children, he's like a child himself.'

Holly sipped the hot tea. She was glad of it after her long wet drive. 'I'm sorry, though,' she said. 'What a pity. A win might have solved your problems.'

Emily shook her head. 'Money doesn't solve everything,' she said scathingly. 'It wouldn't save Sandplace.'

'It would if you had enough. You could buy out those rotten property developers.'

'Now you're fantasizing!' Emily snapped. 'Let's take our tea into the sitting room.' She led the way, selecting her favourite cane chair while Holly took up her usual station on the windowseat with the view of the beach. Clouds like dirty cotton waste continued to drag themselves low across a grey-green sea.

'Have you decided what you're going to do when you leave here?' Holly said, putting her empty plate on the floor beside her.

'If they want me out of here, they'll have to carry me out bodily,' Emily said, her eyes blazing. 'I refuse to even contemplate making plans.'

Holly gazed at her grandmother anxiously. She looked indestructible, sitting there with her feet, in their rugged sandals, planted foursquare on the wooden floor. She was wearing a faded red fisherman's tunic over trousers cobbled together from a number of disparate pieces of fabric. She radiated energy, a zest for life that struck an echoing chord in Holly, a vitality that was so much missing in her mother. All the same, she was flesh and blood like anyone else.

'But surely—' Holly began.

'I don't want to talk about it, is that clear?'

'Well, at least tell me when it happens. I'll come and sit in with you. If I put a notice up about it at college, I expect I could get a whole crowd down here.' She thought for a moment. 'Or maybe not,' she added sadly. Her friends had recently become amazingly serious and conformist.

'I forbid you to put up a notice and I don't want a crowd of your friends down here, thank you very much.'

For the remainder of the weekend, Holly failed to extract any more information from her grandmother, however obliquely she framed the question. Emily started to talk about Gideon.

'He may be coming down tomorrow,' Holly said. 'Will you mind?' At the last minute Gideon had phoned to say he had been delayed and would drive down later. Not that she cared one way or another, naturally.

'He must please himself,' Emily said. 'I'm sure the two of you will find something to do together. He's in love with you, of course.'

Holly had been about to drink her tea. She stared at Emily. 'You're joking!'

'Don't be naïve, Holly. It's not like you.'

Holly put down her mug. 'I don't believe in love. As a matter of fact, I think it's a load of crap.'

'It's up to you what you believe, but it's a fact all the same.'

'You don't believe in romantic love, do you? After what you went through? And look at Mum. As soon as I arrived on the scene, the love of her life, my dad, did a runner, didn't he? Nothing personal, Mum says. So much for love!'

'That's as may be. Old fogies like your mother and I have an excuse to be cynical but when young women in their teens and twenties are already taking the attitude I fear there is little hope for the human race.'

'Don't worry. Plenty of us still fall for the old routine. Besides, I thought you believed that there isn't much hope for the human race anyway?'

Emily drank the last of her tea. 'For our present civilization perhaps not. But it seems that we're so extraordinarily good at adapting to the most unpromising of conditions that, as a race, we can survive almost anything.'

'I don't consider myself cynical, you know,' Holly said, turning from the contemplation of a narrow crack of lemon light that had opened up on the horizon. 'I just think one has a better chance of happiness if one looks at life as it is. Realistically.'

'The trouble with that is that reality has a habit of presenting a variety of aspects of itself not only to us as individuals but to each individual according to mood. So it would seem to have infinite permutations, don't you see?'

'But facts are facts, aren't they, however you look at them?'

'And so many of them! Have we taken them all into consideration? Are we actually in possession of them all?'

Holly grinned and shook her head. 'To hear you talk anyone would think you were a reasonable, balanced person. A sitter on fences. As level-headed and conventional as they come. But I know you're not like that at all, are you? You go to extremes. I believe you always have.'

Emily put down her mug. 'You are at liberty to believe what you like,' was all she said. A smile played about her lips as she regarded Holly through the blurred vision that was now ever-present. Not for the first time, Holly wondered what her grandmother was thinking.

But when Emily spoke it was to enquire about Fern. 'And how is it that you can be spared this weekend,' she said, 'when you were in such a hurry to leave last time?'

'Mum's going to Cheltenham with a friend. And I wanted to

come because this will be my last chance before the term starts and there's all the hassle over the degree show.'

Emily rose from her chair rather stiffly and Holly was reminded that, when all was said and done, her grandmother was an old woman.

'We must think about what we're going to have for supper,' Emily said. 'I think I may have some tuna in the cupboard, if that suits.' She spoke as if it was a totally unexpected item to find in the Sandplace kitchen.

'I've brought a few things with me,' Holly said diplomatically. 'I thought we might have an omelette. Just for a change.' She got up from the window seat and collected her plate and mug. The crack of light on the horizon had widened to a band of kingcup yellow that turned the distant sea beneath it a vivid turquoise. 'The forecast was right after all,' she said with a grin.

That night Emily lay awake for some time before sleep came. Beyond the window the remains of the cloud was evaporating to reveal a great yellow dinner plate of a moon. The weather had been very similar to this when she had first arrived at the Saltings except that then it had been much colder. So soon after the war the place had an air of neglect even worse than at present. Its heyday, if it could be said to have had one, had been later, in the fifties. In the late forties it still manifested traces of rusty barbed wire that had previously cordoned off the beach; she had found, lying half covered in sand, a notice stencilled with a faded skull and crossbones that had once warned of mines.

She had spent the first winter tramping the coastal dunes and cliffs and the inland footpaths and lanes, finding her way in a landscape still largely free of traffic. She bought a bike and managed longer trips. When bouts of exhaustion overtook her she spent the time lying on the narrow bunk in her railway carriage home reading, or sitting on the verandah making gouache sketches of the ever-changing prospect.

When her energy came back for longer and more reliable periods she began working for David Hannaford who owned a farm within easy cycling distance. Her job was to help the only remaining labourer, an old man called Jobie Dunsford, in all the routine work.

She picked fruit, dug ditches, helped with the hay-making and the harvest, patched up the roof of the pigsty and learned to plough, riding the ancient Fordson. David paid her three pounds a week, of which she sent one pound ten shillings to Muriel towards the children's upkeep. She managed on what was left and on generous handouts of eggs, milk and vegetables. She was content with a life in which she shuttled to and fro between the farm and Sandplace.

David Hannaford's wife had left him at the beginning of the war. As a Waaf she found she had a much better time than on the farm, where the work was hard and unremitting. She had never come back. David himself was a quiet self-sufficient man in his early forties and with no great to-do he and Emily had become lovers and remained lovers until he died twelve years later. He never insisted she gave up Sandplace to live with him and he never demanded to know what she did with the hours they spent apart. Neither of them desired or expected marriage (he had never had the time, the money or the inclination to trace and divorce his wife), but his love for Emily and hers for him was enduring and exclusive. With grave ceremony he had presented her with a ring that had belonged originally to his grandmother, a huge art nouveau affair with a garnet in a swirly gold setting.

'I'm not one for speeches,' he'd said. 'You know how I feel about you and I want you to have it. Fortunately for both of us Viv hated it and thought it old-fashioned.'

'David, you are the "verray, parfit gentil knyght",' she said, admiring it.

'I don't know what you mean by that,' he said in his soft Devon accent. 'But it sounds all right to me.'

After Jacko and Aiden she had thought that she would never love another man but she had loved David more than either. He was neither tempestuous and temperamental like Jacko, nor clever and analytical like Aiden; he was accepting in a way that generations of Hannafords had learned to be in those gentle South Devon hills. When he died the loss was incalculable and she knew she would never meet anyone like him again. She never had.

In his will he had left the farm to relatives (he had known she didn't want it anyway), but to Emily he had bequeathed a sum of money that was enough for her to live on in the frugal style of

Sandplace, which in any case she couldn't imagine changing for any other. But she missed him desperately even now, nearly forty years later.

Each time she visited Sandplace Holly quickly became accustomed to the noises of the Saltings: the wind, the roar of the surf or, with the weather in a more moderate mood, the steady splash and rustle of waves breaking on the beach. And the other sounds: the pattering feet of gulls roosting on the roof, the creaks of the old wooden structure, the slap of the loose canvas against the leaning hull. Compared to the flat in Bath it was actually quite noisy.

She thought about Gideon and wondered if Emily was right about his being in love with her. She didn't believe it for a moment. Men talked about sex and, coarsely, about shagging but in her experience, not much about love. His interest in Sandplace was sure to be caused by his father's pressure to persuade Emily to stay at Riversfoot; the old guy probably had a guilty conscience about something that happened in the past, about which Holly wished she knew more. Emily might hint, but she never really came across. Holly slept.

It was not one of the usual noises that woke her. She listened, sticking her head out from under her sleeping bag, trying hard to catch the tail end of some sound that seemed to betray an unfamiliar presence. Just as she was convincing herself she had been mistaken, it came again: a muted and stealthy creak and a faint metallic click.

She pushed the sleeping bag down round her waist and thrust her feet on to the floor. Wearing only what she slept it, knickers and a tee shirt, she crept barefoot to the window and looked out. The moon had passed behind a dense cloud but there was enough light to make out the whiteness of the beach and the pale line of the surf. In front of it were the jagged silhouettes of bushes and the block shape of the shed which stood by itself in the corner of the weedy patch enclosed by the paling fence. For a moment everything appeared normal, until a darker shadow detached itself from the blackness of the shed and melted away into the night. Nothing else moved until a faint breeze caught the door of the shed, which she now saw had been open, and blew it shut with a gentle bang.

She humped on her coat and went into the kitchen, rummaging in the dresser drawer for the very efficient torch which Emily kept there together with a powerful magnifying glass which Holly suspected her grandmother used for reading. She opened the outside door and shone the torch towards the shed.

'Is that you, Em?' she called. There was no answer. Nothing and no one stirred. Cautiously she made her way across what Emily pleased to call a garden, swinging the torch to left and right. She glanced into the shed, which to her surprise was empty; up to now she always imagined that it had accommodated her grandmother's surplus possessions. The torch picked out nothing of the shadowy figure she thought she had seen and she began to think she had imagined it; the shed door had simply come loose and had been swinging on its hinges. She closed it. The padlock was hanging open on its hasp, which was odd; she had never known Emily leave it unlocked. She pondered whether she should wake her grandmother, who certainly wouldn't thank her for doing so if it was a false alarm. On the other hand, because she had always been convinced that the shed had things in it, she woke Emily.

Emily appeared, with her cloak pulled round her naked body. Her hair flowed round her shoulders, wild and white as the surf, like some mythical creature summoned from the deep.

'There better be a good reason for this,' she grumbled.

'I heard a sound. I think someone's been tampering with the shed.'

Emily took the torch from Holly's hand and examined the padlock by its light. 'It's been forced,' she said. 'Look at these marks.'

'Is anything missing?' Holly asked anxiously.

Emily scarcely bothered to look into the interior. 'There wasn't anything there to steal. I'm afraid they were wasting their time.'

'I expect it was a someone hoping to doss down for the night and I scared him away.'

'You're quite wrong there. I know very well who it was.'

'You know?'

'It was a spy with red hair and a woolly hat,' Emily said, for she now remembered that the first time she had seen the man with the clipboard had been at Jacko's funeral when the grieving widow had been leaning on his arm.

Holly glanced at her grandmother, hoping that she was mistaken in thinking that Emily was going off her trolley.

CHAPTER FIFTEEN

'Sudden intakes of large amounts of alcohol can lead to alcoholic shock,' Dr Griffith said. 'Especially if one isn't used to it. Fortunately in this young man's case all he needs is time to sleep it off.'

'I can't imagine where he can have got it from,' Arlette said with an attempt at ingenuousness. The fact that Auriel had declared herself unwell and had taken herself off to bed soon after the commotion was evidence enough, but Arlette could not yet bring herself to acknowledge that her sister drank, let alone associate her drinking with this latest escapade. 'I wonder if Russell could have brought it with him?'

Russell was not there to defend himself since he had cleared off quite smartly in the confusion after he had reported Fergus 'unwell'.

Dr Griffith refrained from comment though he had ideas of his own as to the origins of the bottle of gin.

'I shan't mention this to my mother,' Arlette said as the doctor was leaving. 'I'm sure Fergus had learned his lesson.'

'Yes, I think so.' The doctor grinned and, more seriously, enquired about Mrs Monk, who had not appeared.

'She's well. She likes to work on her diaries or write letters in the afternoon. You knew she's been preparing the material for a biography of my father?'

'Yes, she told me. She's a remarkable lady; but do insist that she doesn't overdo things, won't you?'

Arlette could not imagine insisting on anything where her mother was concerned. 'She has Zak to help her. He does most of the running about.'

'Good. I'm glad about that.' Behind the wheel of his car again,

Dr Griffith glanced at Arlette, her feet planted stolidly on the doorstep, her red work-roughened hands still holding a drying-up cloth. Her skirt was made out of some shaggy material and over her peasant-style blouse she wore a waistcoat made out of small crocheted squares of brown and grey; her coarse black hair was, as usual, escaping from its pins and combs. Not for the first time he marvelled that such an earthy-looking creature could have sprung from the loins of a woman like Regine Monk. Although Arlette had the stocky build of her father she had none of his charm or audacity. Stoical endurance without an atom of imagination was how the doctor saw Arlette Pollock. And how she needed those qualities! he thought. And how the Burr Ash household needed them, for it would be difficult to see how the place would survive without them. She had taken the news that her son had collapsed in a drunken stupor with her usual impassive calm, doing whatever was necessary. All the same, Evan Griffith thought he wouldn't like to be in young Fergus's shoes if his grandmother did eventually find out.

And Regine did find out, naturally. Arlette never entertained much hope that she would not. Supper was a subdued meal. The girls sensed the atmosphere and had little to say except when Regine spoke sharply to Andra for having her cat on her lap at mealtimes. Andra hastily tipped the cat off. It crept under her chair and waited until the unease was over.

'Sorry, Grandmère,' Andra said. They all knew that Regine disliked animals about the place, particularly cats, and had only put up with them because Jacko relished the idea of their endless fecundity.

Fergus and Auriel were, of course, both missing, Auriel ostensibly with a migraine. It wasn't until the end of the meal that Regine at last dismissed the girls, who had not been told the reason for Fergus's indisposition, and opened the subject.

'Donald, you do realize that this can't go on?'

'What is that, Maman?' Donald said, pouring milk into his coffee from a large white jug.

'Fergus's wilfulness. I'm not a complete fool. I know what happened today.'

Donald helped himself to two spoons of sugar before he

answered. 'I'm sure this is quite exceptional,' he said. 'Children like to experiment. He wasn't to know what the outcome would be. He's not as worldly-wise as most boys of his age. I think he's learned his lesson.'

'I realize that it's quite natural for you to defend your son,' Regine said. Her small cup of black coffee remained untouched before her. 'But for him to understand the seriousness of his actions, it will be necessary to punish him. Strict measures now will save both you and the boy a great deal of suffering later on.' They were all aware that her long-term, and mostly successful, campaign with Jacko's alcoholism gave her words particular weight. 'He and this young friend – and I hope you will see to it that the child is not invited to Burr Ash in future – must somehow have managed to purchase the intoxicant, since we have always kept so little on the premises.' She only rarely alluded directly to Jacko's weakness and then only as an unfortunate allergic reaction. The fact that Auriel may have inherited the allergic reaction was likewise glossed over. Regine had her own plans to deal with Auriel, but as her daughter had greater access to the outside world than Jacko had in his later years the problem was proving to be a troublesome undertaking, one for which she could hardly spare the energy. At least this latest episode would give her the power she needed to bring Auriel to heel.

'Obviously we'll deal severely with Fergus as soon as he recovers,' Donald said mildly.

'I am well acquainted with what you consider to be "dealing severely",' Regine said, 'and I have to say that, in my opinion, it is woefully inadequate. The boy has to learn his lesson now if his future life is not to be scarred by this regrettable weakness.' She fixed her eyes on Donald in a mesmeric stare which immediately made Donald feel as if the regrettable weakness had been passed down through his own genes.

'Don't worry, Maman. I will see to it,' he agreed.

'No. *I* will see to it,' Regine said brusquely and with finality. Donald shrugged and abandoned the argument.

A dull misery troubled Arlette. It lay like lead somewhere so deep inside her that she couldn't work out the reason for it.

Later, after Arlette had washed up, helped by two silent girls, she heard Regine go upstairs and enter Auriel's room.

'So I've been trying to suss out what she meant ever since,' Holly said. With a putty rubber she let light into a densely black area of her drawing. 'She swears nothing was taken yet insists she knows who the intruder was.'

Gideon was sitting beside Holly on the beach, absent-mindedly tracing the outlines of a current garden scheme in the sand with a stick. He glanced at Holly. Because the day had turned out warm he was glad to see that she had shed her hideous old coat and was wearing a black tee shirt. Her neck rose out of it smooth, strong and caramel-coloured.

'So who does she say it was?'

'A spy.'

'A spy!'

'She says so. From the property developers, I take it. But what would they be wanting in her hut unless they were planning a little sneaky arson?'

'A bit far-fetched, wouldn't you say?'

'You never know these days.'

'Do you remember smelling paraffin or petrol?'

Holly sat back to appraise her drawing. 'No. I can't say I did. Though, now I come to think of it there was a slight whiff of turps. Perhaps I disturbed the would-be arsonist before he got that far.'

'You say you saw someone?'

'I can't be sure now.'

Gideon continued to scratch at the sand. 'I don't see the point of firing an empty shed.'

'They probably didn't know it was empty. Ever since I've been coming here the shutters have been closed.'

Gideon threw his stick into a pool where it made a gentle splash; he lay back against a rock, his hands behind his head. 'She hasn't mentioned any more about her future plans?'

'Not a word. She's like a clam. But, who knows, you might have more success than I have. You seem to be flavour of the month.'

Gideon laughed. He let his eyes rest on Holly. There was something wonderfully down to earth about her; he could imagine her coping with anything. The more he saw of her, the more he knew how disastrously unsuited he and Sarah had been. He'd heard no more from Sarah herself but Elizabeth had rung and given him a very uncomfortable quarter of an hour.

'I suppose you know you've broken her heart?' she'd blazed. 'Sarah's far too proud to give way to her feelings but I know when she's hurt. I am her mother, after all.'

'I'm sorry it had to happen, Elizabeth,' he'd said placatingly. 'I'm very fond of Sarah and I wouldn't have hurt her if I hadn't thought it was for the best for both of us. I think she will come to the same conclusion eventually.'

'Well, I think you might have thought of this before you took two years out of her life.'

'It's not always possible to know these things straight away. I wish it were.' A quiet voice in his head was contradicting. With Holly, he'd known.

'I suppose someone else has taken your fancy, is that it? Perhaps I should warn this young woman that you are not to be relied on, Gideon. But I should have taken more notice of my instincts right from the start. If you must know, I've always thought that pigtail was pure affectation.'

'Elizabeth, I don't think there's anything to be gained by this conversation.'

'And don't call me Elizabeth! You've forfeited that privilege by your appalling behaviour. I'm Mrs Henderson to you now and don't you forget it.' She banged down the receiver and the line went dead. Gideon sat at his desk staring moodily at the planting scheme he'd been working on. He'd always known that Elizabeth Henderson could be vindictive but he'd never been on the receiving end until now. Besides, he didn't really blame her. He'd acted like a shit, hadn't he?

'You've gone quiet. What are you thinking about?' Holly asked, turning to look at him at last.

'I'm thinking that I missed you last week,' he said, picking up a stone and flinging it across the sand.

'Oh, yes?' Her eyebrows shot up.

'Why don't you believe me? Don't you think you're missable?'

'You hardly know me.'

'What difference does that make? I want to see you again.'

175

'With finals coming up I won't be able to see anyone,' she said roughly. 'Not even Em.'

'Even for an hour or two?'

'I live in Bath. You live in Dorset, or did you forget?' Holly put in some broad sweeps of dark with the side of her charcoal.

'So what? An hour in the car, nothing to it.'

Holly grinned. 'You're mad.'

'Why do I get the feeling you're not too keen on men?'

'It's just that they don't have a very good track record in my family.'

'Your famous grandpapa and your dad, eh?'

'You could say,' Holly observed and then applied herself industriously to finishing her drawing.

Gideon watched some gulls floating overhead, their yellow eyes on the lookout for intimations of picnics. This time he would have to go carefully, not rush things as he dearly would like to have done.

'I've been thinking about how to display my degree work,' Holly said suddenly. 'I want to make a glade. Or at least I want to suggest a glade.'

'A glade. I like that idea.'

'There's a problem.'

'Tell Uncle Gideon.'

'Obtaining the wherewithal. Legally, if possible.'

'If you mean branches and so on? I can get you as much as you want.'

'That'd be great!' Her voice and her eyes were bright with enthusiasm when she talked about her work. He lay on his side, leaning on his elbow, and watched her, fascinated. She appeared to be entirely without consciousness of self, a quality he found endearing. Sarah, though neither vain nor shallow, was never forgetful of what impression she was making; it could be said that it was part of her professional conditioning.

Two hundred yards away Emily sat on the verandah writing a letter to her solicitor, in answer to one that had arrived from his Exeter office in which he'd assured her that the items sent by carrier had arrived safely and that he'd checked them against the inventory and found everything perfectly in order. He had confirmed that the consignment would remain in store until such time as she gave him further instructions.

Letters were a problem, necessitating a measure of resourcefulness with the magnifying glass.

She wrote in reply:

Dear Mr Tallboys,
  Thank you for your letter. Take no further action until such time as I kick the bucket. As you know, the rest is in my will.
  Yours sincerely,
  Emily Troy

She put the letter in an envelope, sealed it down with a gnarled thumb and tossed it beside one to Francis she'd written earlier.

Some way down the beach she could see that Gideon, who'd turned up an hour earlier, had found Holly and that they were now deep in conversation. It would be nice to think that Gideon would be another David Hannaford rather than a replica of his father. Perhaps, because of his contact with the soil and his sound practicality, even his defiant pigtail, he had more to offer than a cool intellectual like Aiden. Holly apparently had little in the way of favourable experiences of the male sex, so the blighter had better not let her down.

Emily rested her hands in her lap and gazed out to sea. It was odd, this lack of activity. All this time spent in contemplation.

As the sun rose in the sky, the light changed and the sea acquired its summer colours. Even with the general blurring of her vision Emily could still detect the broad sweeps of delft blue that were being chased by chartreuse and purple, which in turn gave way to pale turquoise. Where the waves broke, patterns of silver, sepia and aquamarine jostled each other, only to be inundated with a tumbling mountain of white spume. The tide was out and the beach was a receding buff-coloured plane streaked with sienna and interrupted by great slabs of blue-black or rust-red outcrops. It was too late now to record anywhere but in her head what she saw, but the sensual pleasure it gave her was for the moment as sharp and lucid as it had been long ago in what now seemed like another life, in Provence.

* * *

Fergus had a splitting headache. The new term had already started but today no one insisted that he get up or be driven off to school in his father's second-hand Fiesta. His breakfast had been brought up on a tray but he hadn't felt like anything except orange juice; he certainly couldn't face his mother's stodgy porridge. Breakfast at Burr Ash normally consisted of porridge and toast and marmalade with an occasional fried egg.

There was an ominous silence about the house. His mother said very little as she collected his empty glass but she looked at him with a curious expression on her face. He hadn't seen his father since last night, or anyone else for that matter. But he had recovered just sufficiently to be worried and his anxiety soon turned out to be well founded. He had just closed his eyes, laying his aching head tenderly on the pillow, when the familiar click of the door opening and the smell of his grandmother's scent alerted him to her presence. He kept his eyes firmly shut, feigning sleep.

'Fergus, I know that you are awake. I would appreciate it if you would open your eyes and sit up.'

Fergus lay doggo but he felt his lids tremble with the effort of remaining so tightly closed.

'Fergus, I'm speaking to you.'

He made a small pantomime of waking and discovering her by his side. 'Oh, Grandmère! It's you.' He put his hand weakly to his head.

'Sit up, Fergus!'

Groggily, he obeyed.

'I understand you have a headache?'

'Yes, Grandmère. An awful headache. Terrible.'

'I don't suppose that surprised you?'

Silence.

'Does it? I'm told you drank a great deal of gin.'

'No. And, yes, I did.'

'Brought into the house by your friend, I assume?'

'No!' Fergus fixed his eyes on the large dangling tassel of the onyx necklace that rested on a level with his grandmother's waist.

'Then, where on earth did it come from, this bottle?'

Fergus was silent. He knew she was hoping for the satisfaction of making him say that Galpin had brought the stuff, or better still, grass on his Aunt Auriel. It would give her power over all of them. But his secrets were all he had and he had no intention of relinquishing them without a fight.

'Fergus. I'm waiting for an answer.'

'We found it,' he said sulkily.

She smiled disbelievingly. 'And where could you possibly have found it, I wonder?'

'In the barn.'

'In the barn! I see. That is not the truth, is it Fergus?'

'Yes, it is. We found it in the barn.'

'Come now. You can't expect me to believe that you found a full bottle of gin in the barn?'

'Well, we did. I expect someone hid it there. Anyway, it wasn't full.'

Regine moved closer. 'So someone hid it in the barn, did they? Who would have done that, d'you suppose?'

Silence again.

'Who, Fergus?' Her voice was sharp.

'I don't know. One of those travellers, I expect.'

'We've had no travellers here.'

'Then it was probably Jacko,' Fergus said. It was his trump card but an astounding risk. But she'd pushed him to it, hadn't she?

'What did you say?'

'I said it might have been Jacko. He used to hide bottles.'

The silence was probably the worst minute of Fergus's entire life. For a moment he thought his grandmother was going to strike him. His fear was so terrible that he felt himself losing control of his bladder, something he had assumed he'd grown out of, and the ultimate humiliation.

But to his utter relief and astonishment she turned abruptly and left the room as silently as she had come, her face a white mask. A moment later he shot out of bed and along the corridor to the lavatory at the far end. He relieved himself into the ancient, crazed porcelain with a trance-like sigh. Then he set about washing his wet pyjamas, a task he once associated with abject feelings of shame. But this time, for some reason, he had a distinct sense of exhilaration.

* * *

Francis emerged from an exceedingly trying staff meeting and returned to his office where he began, distractedly, to open the post he hadn't yet had time to attend to. The staff were being more than usually recalcitrant and uncooperative, no doubt because he'd had to postpone the pay rise they'd expected last month until the following academic year. Well, he couldn't help it. The school wasn't made of money and he dared not raise the fees again. He'd already had one or two warnings from influential parents that if he did, they'd remove their sons altogether and send them to rival establishments.

He turned over an envelope addressed in his sister's wild, rambling script. Her thanks for his part in the premium bond win, no doubt. At least *someone* was appreciating him for *something*. A sudden audacious hope gripped him that a very great deal of money could be involved; he knew money meant almost nothing to Emily so she would be sure to put some of it his way. Frantically he slit the envelope with his paperknife, a somewhat miserly gift from a leaver some years previously.

But the letter brought him no comfort.

My dear Francis,

For goodness' sake, have you gone completely gaga? Whatever else am I to suppose when you don't know a hoax when it's staring you in the face? A win on the premium bonds indeed! Or were *you* hoaxing *me*?

Otherwise I am glad to say I am well and enjoying my granddaughter's presence once more. As you see, I am for the moment still at the usual address. Write and let me know how you are for I fear the worst.

Yours affectionately,

Em

Francis dropped the single sheet of paper and put his head in his hands. A sound almost like a sob escaped him. Would it be altogether beyond the wit of Providence to allow *one* thing to go right for him? Quite apart from the difficulties with staff and parents, Mrs Bessemer was being impossible and now the doctor had suggested that Francis probably had asthma as a result of urban pollution, and had given him an inhaler. No wonder his fits of depression were worse and more frequent. And now Emily was calling him a senile old fool. Perhaps after all she was cross with him for raising her hopes unnecessarily, for the money would undoubtedly have got her out of a hole. But what could *he* do about it? He thought guiltily of the money he'd salted away from the sale of the engravings; some would say that by rights it belonged to Em, disregarding the fact that he had been their conservator all these years while under her care they would most certainly have come to grief.

Impulsively, he reached for his cheque book and made out a cheque for the full amount he'd received for the engravings. As he was about to put it in an envelope with a hastily scribbled note to his sister, an element of caution came over him. He tore up the first cheque and wrote another for half the sum. Neither amount would have solved her problems; all she needed was the reassurance that he had her interests at heart and was most definitely not potty.

As he sealed the envelope a bell shrilled. Prayers. And he'd had neither the time nor the inclination to prepare a reading or the usual little talk and prayer that went with it. Fumblingly, he opened the dog-eared Bible on his desk at random. He shut his eyes and stabbed the page with his finger. Lamentations: chapter three, verse four: 'My flesh and my skin hath he made old; he hath broken my bones He hath builded against me, and compassed me with gall and travail. He hath set me in dark places . . .' Francis closed the book.

'God help me!' he muttered. It was by far the most sincere prayer he was to offer that day.

Audrey expertly negotiated a roundabout on the way back from Cheltenham.

'My dear, you do realize that next week will be the latest to book up for this holiday?' she said, glancing at her passenger. 'They're frightfully popular. It's only because I know the people that they agreed to hold the extra place.'

'Oh, yes. You told me,' Fern said after a lengthy silence. 'I hadn't forgotten.'

'What does that clever daughter of yours say about you going? Surely she's all for it?'

Fern twisted her fingers together in her lap. 'Yes, yes, of course.'

'And you seem much better. It'll give you something to look forward to. Cheer you up.' To Audrey, the cure for being what she would call down in the dumps was something to cheer one up. At the moment her mission in life was clearly to make sure Fern got taken out of herself.

'I will let you know in the next few days, I promise,' Fern said as they whirled past a huge juggernaut. 'But there is the expense to consider.'

'You didn't go anywhere last year or the year before,' Audrey reminded her. 'I should think it's patently obvious that you can't afford *not* to take a break. Look, you'll be fine by July even if you couldn't manage school this term.'

'I hope so.' Fern looked at her friend thoughtfully. 'Audrey, may I ask you a serious question?'

'Fern, of *course* you can!' Audrey tail-gated an old man in a Maestro and then slipped by. Fern closed her eyes momentarily.

'Do you like teaching?' she asked when the road was clear.

'That's a strange question. Naturally I do. I wouldn't do it if I didn't enjoy it. Obviously, like all jobs it has its down side, like the wretched National Curriculum pickle and the school inspections. But these things come and go.'

'What if you stopped enjoying it?'

'I must say I never seriously considered that possibility. I suppose I'd do something else. Social work or something, I expect.'

'At our advanced age, I don't suppose that would be an option,' Fern smiled wryly.

'Don't worry, I'd find some way of occupying my declining years,' Audrey laughed. Then she said, 'What's all this about?' But they had reached the crowded environs of Bath and Audrey had to concentrate on her driving.

She turned into the street where Fern lived and pulled up outside the flat.

'Will you come in for a cup of tea?' Fern asked tentatively, wondering if she would be able to cope with the business of actually making it and getting it on the table without making a complete fool of herself.

'Yes, I think perhaps I will.' Audrey looked faintly startled, as well she might; it was the first time for nearly a year that Fern had invited her in.

The tea was lukewarm by the time the cups were in front of them but Audrey kindly appeared not to notice. Fern's cheeks were pink from the effort but also from surprise that she had managed it at all.

'I gather from what you were saying that you want to give up teaching,' Audrey said when they were both settled. 'Take early retirement? Is that it? Lots do.'

'Yes, I suppose they do.' Fern was amazed that Audrey wasn't shocked at the idea.

'I can't say I blame you. It wouldn't be for me. I love teaching, even with all the occupational hazards.' She took a sip of her nearly cold tea. 'Why don't you look into the pension provisions? You'd lose a bit but I dare say you might get some dispensation on health grounds.'

'Yes, perhaps I would.' Suddenly the edge of the darkness lifted the smallest degree. When Fern put her cup down it rattled slightly in the saucer. 'About that holiday—' she said.

CHAPTER SIXTEEN

Arlette finished hanging out a monumental wash in the walled vegetable garden and humped the empty basket on to her hip; not for the first time lately, she had been dreaming of washing machines and spin-dryers, of vacuum cleaners and freezers. When she came into the yard she saw there was a visitor; a small grey-haired woman was peering through the kitchen window.

Visitors were not welcome at Burr Ash, especially casual ones. As far as Arlette was concerned they were a time-wasting nuisance. Since the incident with the gin, Auriel's help was even more erratic than usual so time was shorter than ever. The housework at Burr Ash had to be done to an inflexible routine or things got quite out of hand. Regine would not allow Arlette to employ paid help because she was of the opinion that the household chores were surely not beyond the powers of two grown women. Beside, Regine objected to the idea of some village person carrying tales to the local community.

Because the visitor had surprised her in the middle of the guilty reverie, Arlette's greeting was even more abrupt than it would normally have been.

'Mrs Pollock?' The woman held out her hand, apparently undeterred by the cool reception. She put her head on one side, which heightened the birdlike impression created by her small stature and bright little eyes. The resemblance to her grandson Russell was so marked that even Arlette, emerging from her wistful wool-gathering, noted it at once.

'Mrs Galpin.' Arlette's expression changed to one of stubborn self-justification. If the woman had come to complain about the recent incident she'd get nothing out of Arlette Pollock.

'I hope you don't mind me calling round like this but I have something I'd like you to look at.'

'Yes?' Arlette said discouragingly.

'If I might come in it would be easier.'

The woman seemed determined so Arlette reluctantly stepped aside and allowed Mrs Galpin inside the kitchen, noting immediately the way she scanned the room like an inquisitive robin.

'How's Fergus?' she asked with the hint of a smile.

'He's much better, thank you.' Arlette did not return the compliment and ask after Russell but stood with her pink arms folded across her chest, waiting.

In fact, Fergus was in the hall listening. He had heard someone knocking and had peered out of his bedroom window to see who the insistent visitor could be. That it was Russell's grandmother gave him little comfort; he had hoped she would go away before his mother returned from the garden, or even that Grandmère might emerge from the studio where she worked on her stupid diaries and letters as if her life depended on it. Now that Mrs Galpin was in, it was vital that he heard what she was on about.

'Russell recovered fairly quickly, I'm glad to say,' Mrs Galpin was telling Arlette. 'I don't think he drank quite as much.' She shook her head. 'The rascals! What will they get up to next? Still, I think they've learned their lesson and will not be making a habit of it.'

Arlette grunted but she was beginning to relax.

'But that's not what I called round about, as it happens,' Mrs Galpin went on.

Arlette was wary again.

'No, it's this.' Mrs Galpin had been carrying a plastic bag which Arlette had supposed contained shopping but which her visitor now laid carefully on the table. She took from it two objects wrapped in old pillowcases. 'Russell brought these home with him,' she said, busily unwrapping.' He claims to have found them in the barn – along with the gin, no doubt.' Her bright eyes gleamed mischievously. 'But of course he couldn't have. If these aren't valuable paintings, I'm Michelle Pfeiffer.' Two unframed canvases lay revealed on the kitchen table.

Arlette's brow wrinkled. 'Michelle Pfeiffer?'

'Just a silly joke, Mrs Pollock. I take it these do belong to Burr Ash?'

Arlette stared at the two paintings that lay exposed on the table. She had never seen them before in her life. They were certainly not the work of her father.

'Your grandson says he found them in the barn?' she said noncommittally.

'That's right.'

Arlette felt completely out of her depth but was unwilling to admit her ignorance.

'They *do* belong to Burr Ash?' Mrs Galpin enquired.

Arlette breathed heavily. 'Would you mind if I just go across the yard and see if my mother is free? I expect she'll know more about this than I do.'

She left the puzzled woman standing in the kitchen while she hurried to the studio and knocked anxiously at the door, reluctant as ever to disturb her mother.

Regine had been speaking to Zak on the telephone and was not in a good humour. Zak had been unable to trace any of Jacko's work at the home of his first wife and was convinced that if she ever had possessed any it was more than likely she'd long since sold it.

'She's not as well off as we thought,' he'd added.

'But what about Chase? I assumed she had money from him.'

'If she does it can't be much. Besides, there are plans to bulldoze the whole area. It's an eyesore. Not a place one would choose to live if one had money.'

'But how can you be absolutely certain she has none of Jacko's work?' Regine was unwilling to relinquish a notion she'd cherished for so long.

'I made it my business to be certain, Maman, believe me.'

'Thank you, Zak dear. You're very resourceful. But now we have to start all over again, don't we?'

'Not quite. There's a sculptor. The one you wrote to.'

'A very poor prospect, I'm afraid. He's very old now and probably has a failing memory.' Regine had first met the sculptor in the Burr Ash kitchen when he had stepped in to stop Emily attacking Jacko with a knife. He was one of the few friends who had remained faithful to Jacko and who had once been a regular visitor to Burr Ash. Not now, though. Now he was incapacitated with arthritis like so many of his profession. She hoped his memory for the whereabouts of Jacko's early work wasn't equally enfeebled.

'But I remember you said that he may actually have a few paintings in his possession. I could go straight to Highgate from here,' Zak suggested obligingly.

'Yes, dear. I wish you would. And be sure to explain why it's not possible for me to come in person, won't you? He has my letter.'

Arlette's timid knock interrupted the conversation. Frowning with disappointment over Zak's lack of success and the grinding physical pain she had suddenly been made aware of, Regine went to answer it.

Arlette explained her unusual dilemma and Regine reluctantly accompanied her to where the paintings were displayed. She saw at once that it would be as well to take them seriously. Arlette and Mrs Galpin between them rehearsed the details of their discovery and Regine made an instantaneous decision and insisted that Arlette carried them to the studio where she suggested the light was better. Left alone, she examined them with the aid of her spectacles. She was no expert, except when it came to anything painted by her husband, but it seemed to her that the smaller of the two, an unfinished landscape consisting of meticulously placed squares of blues, greens and ochres, representing rocks, trees and sky, was so like one of Cézanne's paintings of the quarry at Bibémus that it made the hairs on her head rise. The other was a dreamlike composition depicting a little town in the snow with strange floating animals in the sky. She fixed her eyes on it in an effort to recognize the style. Then she summoned Arlette to convey the two canvases back to the kitchen, where she treated them with dismissive amusement.

'How kind of you to bring them back, Mrs Galpin,' she said, with all the graciousness she could muster. 'They do in fact belong here. They were done by a visiting student years ago to prove he could paint like any of the great masters. As a joke, you know. I had completely forgotten about them.'

'Oh.' It was clear that Mrs Galpin was disappointed.

'They were put in the barn because one couldn't allow them to be sold, naturally.'

'Yes, I see.' Mrs Galpin was doubtful as well as disappointed but she could hardly argue.

'I trust your grandson has recovered from his indisposition?' Regine walked to the door with the visitor.

'Yes, thank you. What naughty boys!'

'Indeed. I'm sorry you've been troubled, Mrs Galpin.'

Regine saw Mrs Galpin off and returned to the kitchen and her favourite high-backed chair, her pallor quite pronounced. Arlette gave her tea without comment but her gaze lingered on her mother. For the first time it crossed her mind that there might be something wrong with Regine other than the usual failing powers of old age.

Fergus sidled into the room and went immediately to the table.

'Are you sure you found these in the barn?' Arlette asked him in a low voice. She was now thoroughly bewildered.

'Yeah.' Fergus had his eyes fixed on the two canvases, seeing them for the first time in a sober state. 'And I know how they got there.'

'And how do you think they got there, Fergus?' Regine asked suddenly from behind them.

'Zak must've put them there. The padlock on the door was new.'

There was a prolonged silence.

'I bet I'm right,' Fergus insisted defensively.

When Arlette turned to look at her mother she was shocked to see that her eyes were not only closed but seemed to have sunk into purple hollows in her head and that she was swaying slightly. She rushed to Regine's side.

'Fergus, how could you?' she said, not even sure what she was reproaching him for.

Supported by her daughter but with her eyes still tightly closed, Regine whispered, 'No, don't. It's perfectly understandable that the boy should think that they are somehow connected with Zak, even if he happens to be wrong. As I said, the paintings were done by a friend of Jacko's many years ago and are worthless.' Her eyes suddenly opened and she gave them both a chilling stare. 'All the same, they are absolutely not to be discussed, or mentioned, to anyone, is that clear? Not to anyone.'

Startled by her tone, Fergus and Arlette looked first at each other and then back to Regine. There was a prolonged silence while Regine finished her tea.

'Now, Fergus,' she said at last, seeming to recover, 'I believe you said that they taught you about computers at school?'

'Yeah,' Fergus said suspiciously.

'And about how to transfer information to disks and printers?'

'Yeah.' Fergus stared at his grandmother.

'Well, then, I'd like you to come with me to the studio and show me how to do it.'

'The ones at school are different.'

'Never mind. I'm sure the principle's the same.'

Fergus, reluctant yet intrigued, since this was the first time his grandmother had asked him to do *anything*, followed her to the studio.

'Thanks, you're a hero,' Holly said, puffing with the effort of helping Gideon heave the huge blocks of carved wood into place.

Gideon brushed bits of bark and greenery off his shirt and stepped back to survey the general effect of Holly's hours of work.

'It looks OK,' he said. 'Like the endeavours of a rather butch bower bird.'

'Thanks,' Holly said again but with a different inflection.

She had turned the space she'd been allotted for the display of her degree work into a suggestion of a woodland glade so that her great earthy sculptures were seen through a light screen of willow branches. Gideon had shown her how to bend them so that they formed arches overhead. The sterility of the white walls and harsh light from the studio windows had been alleviated by the slender tracery. Last of all she had arranged her drawings outside the glade, leading the eye inwards. The tutor who talked about 'rationale' had stood before the display expressionless for a moment before shaking his head and walking away.

'They remind me of Celtic standing stones,' Gideon said, smacking a huge thigh-like plane disrespectfully. After showing her how to fashion the willow he had, at her command, left her to it until it was time to heave the sculptures into place.

'Geroff!' she said. 'In any case, I thought you didn't know anything about art.'

'I don't, much. Look, I could murder a beer.'

'Me too.' But she continued to tweak and fuss. 'Don't you think that large cartoon would have been better on the other side?'

'No. I don't,' he said firmly. 'We already went through all that. Now leave it!'

He prised her away at last and they made their way through the chaos where degree students were struggling with last-minute emergencies. A young man with a shaved head was being screamed at for pinching the staple gun of a female student with multi-studded ears; a girl with long tangled hair was weeping in a corner, comforted by another; a young man was up a ladder, hammering, putting the finishing touches to what appeared to be a padded cell. What with Björk playing at top volume the racket was deafening. In the space next to Holly's a young woman with shining hair and expensively tailored shorts was sitting, apparently oblivious to the din, in contemplation of her finished display which consisted of two white envelopes on opposite walls, one open, one shut, attached by two pieces of thread to the centre of a huge enlargement of a piece of printed text that took up most of the floor space. Gideon took all this in, looking baffled.

'It's a madhouse,' he shouted in Holly's ear. 'In more ways than one.'

'What d'you expect?' Holly answered. 'Screw up on this one and it's four years' work up the Swanee.'

'I don't think you entirely understood what I meant.'

All the same, compared to some of the temperament on exhibition Gideon now saw that Holly's fussing was as nothing.

'All things considered, I've come to the conclusion that you're actually quite laid back about all this,' he said as they reached the main entrance and a pleasant draught of fresh air reached them, untainted by the smell of turps or resin.

'Mum says I'm a stoic,' she said.

'Perhaps you've needed to be,' he said, more perspicacious than he knew.

She shrugged and led the way to one of the pubs not usually patronized by students. In its dark depths, where at least two of the walls dated from the time of the Caesars, they ordered beers and packets of crisps, which Holly insisted on paying for.

'I owe you one, don't I? After all your efforts bringing the branches for me. I would never have been able to do it on my own; our garden is OK for terracotta pots but not well supplied with willow branches.'

'Glad to be of service, ma'am. I'll send in the account later. Let's see. My hourly rate is—'

'You'd be lucky, buster!' she said gruffly. 'Though seriously, you must be missing out on jobs?'

'Don't worry about it. I rearranged my schedule a bit, that's all.' He drank half his lager straight off. 'I think it worked out well, very well, don't you?'

She nodded and sipped her lager, wolfing down some crisps. 'I'm happy with it but that doesn't mean a thing. I'll be lucky to get away with it at all.'

Gideon shook his head. 'I must be way out of touch. To me your display was by far the best I saw. It was brilliant.'

She shrugged philosophically. 'Nevertheless, I was flying in the face of repeated advice. I expect I'll be punished. I'm pinning my hopes on the visiting tutor whom I suspect of liking my stuff.'

Gideon gave up trying to make sense of it all. 'So what about the future?' he asked. 'Any plans?'

'Nothing yet,' she said. 'I've sent out a few applications for artist-in-residence places, stuff like that. But it mostly depends on my results.'

'You should bloody well get a First after all this.'

'Not a chance,' she said dispassionately.

He leaned across the table. 'Listen. I have some news. Have you ever heard of King's Melcombe Hall?'

'Vaguely. In Dorset, isn't it?'

'It's a big house with great grounds and an arboretum. It had gone to pot but was rescued three years ago by a private trust and is now run by a mate of mine. One of their rich sponsors left a bequest to fund an artist-in-residence to make sculptures for the gardens and arboretum – on the lines of that place in the Forest of Dean, I believe. What do you think?'

'Of course it sounds great. But it'll obviously be advertised.'

'I imagine so. But you're sure to get it if you apply. You're just the woman for the job.' Gideon sat back against the wall with an air of triumph. 'In fact, I'm almost certain that a couple of the board are coming to see your exhibition. So you had better apply!'

Holly looked aghast. 'Why didn't you tell me this before, you sonofabitch?'

'Because I wanted you to put up your show with some degree of cool, that's why.'

'Holy cow!' Holly's face flooded with colour. She hardly dared to hope.

'And you being at King's Melcombe would have another great advantage.'

'Yes?'

'It's only ten miles from Winterbourne Valence.'

'Winterbourne what?'

'I live there. Remember?'

'So you do.' She frowned. She was not at all sure she was keen to be in the debt of someone about whom, after all, she knew so little.

He scribbled down the address where the application forms could be obtained.

'Thanks,' she said laconically. 'It's worth a try.'

'Out in the big, bad world,' he said.

'I have a feeling it might be a doddle after life as a student.' Holly finished her crisps. The last four years had been more like an obstacle race than anything, but she would miss the friends with whom she'd shared the failures and successes; she imagined she might even miss the students who invariably got on her tits. In a sense, it would be like leaving the womb.

If she got a job away she would also miss Fern. It would be the first time they'd ever lived apart. Since she was about fifteen and even before, always in some respects old for her years, Holly had been depended on by her mother for moral support. Sensing her mother's vulnerability she realized early that she had to acquire the sense of responsibility of an adult. She admired her mother's courage in securing a teaching qualification and a job, even though the process terrified her, and then bring up a child unaided, but the struggle had cost the painfully shy Fern dear. A fact of which Holly was now well aware.

She had not inherited her mother's insecurity. Although she had never met her father, she imagined him as a phlegmatic type, not given to emotional displays. In some ways she guessed she was like him, the difference being that while he had been content to dump a wife who hadn't lived up to his expectations, Holly adored her mother and would have fought like a lion to defend her. She was hardly aware of the fact that at some point her mother had sensed this, and had gratefully surrendered the role that had cost her so much anxiety during her daughter's early years.

'How's your mother?' Gideon asked, uncannily tuning in to her thoughts.

'Better, I think. But it's slow. Two steps forward and one step back sort of thing. I'm trying to persuade her to take early retirement but she's worried about the money. Sod the money, I say!' Holly tipped the remaining drops of her lager down her throat. 'She was losing her bottle about going back in September. I reckoned that was why she wasn't getting better as quick as we hoped.'

'Money is a consideration,' Gideon opined solemnly.

'We're both used to being poor.'

Holly talked of her own work with the kind of enthusiasm he knew was rare in their generation but which he understood since he shared it. But in spite of her personal difficulties one could not get away from the fact that they were two of the lucky ones. They had both at least had a chance.

He would have to make this sight of her last for at least two weeks since he was just about to embark on a huge landscaping job in Devon while she would still be involved with the show and its aftermath.

Today Holly was wearing a loose-fitting, sleeveless black tee shirt which was somehow irrelevant to the body it covered; her arms were rounded and strong and browner than ever; her ragged denim shorts revealed sturdy legs, her feet crammed into bright red socks and black boots. Beads of sweat still glistened on her top lip and she was lightly dusted all over with the evidence of their morning's work. Suddenly two weeks seemed an eternity to him.

'I shall miss you,' he said, which was a gross understatement. What he wanted to do was to whisk her back home with him right away, take her brown body into his arms and make passionate love to her in the small white bedroom of his cottage, or even in one of the fields or hedgerows on the way if he couldn't wait that long.

But he had promised himself that he wouldn't rush into things as he had with Sarah. He had slept with Sarah within a week of meeting her, thinking himself madly in love; for a time they had been totally obsessed with one another, a feeling that had worn off, on both sides, in a disconcertingly short space of time. He had no intention of making that mistake again if he could help it. The problem was – how long did one have to wait to be sure? It bore the same uncertainties as the length of a piece of string.

He reached across the table and removed a small leaf that had become lodged in the dark mass of her hair. With great ceremony he reached for his wallet and placed the leaf tenderly inside.

'What was all that about?' Her teeth gleamed in the dim light.

'A keepsake.'

'Bullshit,' she said, laughing. She looked at her watch. 'I have to go.'

'Must you?'

'I promised Fern. I don't like to leave her longer than I absolutely have to. Thanks for your help.'

Outside the pub, but just inside the railings that separated them from the hurrying pedestrians, Gideon took Holly's elbow and pulled her to him. For a moment he placed his mouth on hers, savouring its fullness and a faint taste of crisps, lager and sweat. 'Good luck with the degree show,' he said. 'I'm really going to hate this separation.'

For a moment she looked at him consideringly and with a slightly enigmatic smile.

On the way home she popped into the covered market and bought her mother some sweet peas and, after rooting through the coins in her purse, a quarter of a special tea that Fern had long since given up for reasons of economy or a hopeless kind of apathy or both. She thought about Gideon's kiss, disturbed by the effect it had had on her.

At the far end of the Saltings the JCBs clattered and grumbled away as they had all day. Dust rose like a sea fog and drifted into the

tamarisk bushes, turning them into ghosts of their former selves.
Emily kept an eye on the distant dust cloud from the open door of
her kitchen. The diggers were as yet nowhere near Sandplace since
the work was scheduled to proceed in two stages. This first stage
evidently required the shifting of large amounts of the beach from
one place to another as well as the flattening of all the properties
that had once peacefully coexisted there. The faceless characters
behind the mayhem doubtless believed that the continual uproar
would eventually see off old man Watts, herself and a few other
recalcitrants, leaving the Saltings to them.

Emily waved to Mr Watts as he shuffled by, accompanied as
usual by his tan mongrel. In all the years they had lived in the place
they had never done more than exchange a neighbourly salute or a
greeting, it was almost an unwritten rule that no one asked
questions or embarked on a round of socializing in the Saltings,
which was what had attracted Emily to it right from the start.

'Bloody racket,' Mr Watts shouted. Extenuating circumstances
evidently called for more than the usual 'Morning'.

Emily nodded and went to hang her swimming things on the
verandah. The brisk breeze across the beach tempered the heat of
the sun, discouraging all but the hardiest of the summer visitors
but not the usual flight of windsurfers, skimming like bright
butterflies across the navy-blue sea. A few of the dinghies were out
but not as many as the weekend would bring. Besides, she rather
fancied that many of them had already taken themselves off to
pastures, or beaches, new.

Since Holly's last visit, her peace had been shattered not only by
the JCBs but by several individuals who claimed to be from the
social services or the housing department and who bothered her
with specious arguments and glossy brochures laying out the
advantages of something called 'sheltered housing'. Sheltered
housing indeed! What a diabolically cosy, sterile image that
conjured up! She had sent them all packing, or hadn't opened the
door to them in the first place. All the same, she would have to
think about things soon.

The oddest visitor of all had been the young man with the
clipboard who had most certainly been the night-time intruder. She
cursed her failing sight that she had not recognized him sooner but

his disguise, minimal though it was, had been clever. He had even appeared to change his stance and his walk. Undoubtedly he had been sent by the Queen of the Night. Emily hadn't been aware that the woman knew where she lived, but she had evidently found out and the Queen of the Night never did anything without a reason. Emily was glad she had taken the precaution of emptying her shed. Let the silly old bat rake over dead embers as much as she liked as long as it didn't impinge on Emily Troy; at the funeral it had been all too apparent that the woman's whole existence had revolved round Jacko and that she had dedicated her considerable will to the greater glory of his monstrous ego.

That was the trouble with artists, Emily thought. Ever since they began to scribble their names on their work, had become creative geniuses instead of artisans, the cult of the ego had taken hold. There was no escaping it.

She had complained grumpily to Holly during the course of a conversation they'd had. 'Now it allows any Tom, Dick or Harry with a smattering of talent equal status with the greats just as long as he's prepared to entertain his public with his eccentricities. When it comes right down to it, the artist nowadays has to be something of a performing dog. I consider that too high a price—'

'How apt that you said "his" just now. *His* public,' Holly had interrupted, grinning.

Emily had waved away the observation as if it were too obvious to require comment. Then suddenly: 'Do you believe in the isolated creative genius?'

'Yes. Surely you have to slog away in isolation just to get the work done.'

'I didn't mean that. I was talking about cultural isolation.'

Holly shrugged. 'I don't think that's possible these days, is it?'

Emily wagged her finger at her granddaughter. 'You've heard of Sickert, I presume?'

'Of course I have.'

'Sickert said, "These things are done in gangs", meaning movements in painting. In his day it went without saying that he meant gangs of *male* artists. You're in the thick of it. Have things changed?'

'Women do get more of a look-in. The problem as I see it is that the whole scene was already set up years ago to suit male attitudes and male expectations. It makes it bloody hard if you're coming from somewhere else altogether, if you see what I mean, right from the start. Needless to say, most of our tutors are male and it makes a difference, whatever they say. No female role models.'

'Yes, that I understand. All the same, surely we now have a *few* women who have hewn out a niche for themselves, even against these odds?'

Emily thought about that conversation as she gazed towards the lavender-coloured horizon, shading her eyes, and wondering whether the odds would have been different if she had never met Jacko.

She had last seen him in Trafalgar Square. Against Muriel's better judgement she had allowed Emily to take the children to the Festival of Britain. She was on her way back to Paddington station when she heard her name roared out above the din of traffic.

'Em! My God. Em!'

He had his arms round two women. Now he raised his hands high as if in benediction.

Emily had stood rock-still. She was shaken by a sensation that was very like panic, followed by an unreasonable impulse to run, which she might have obeyed if the crowds round her hadn't pressed so close. He approached and it was like seeing a character from a vividly remembered film or play. But it was a character changed. His mane of dark and rumpled curls had become iron grey and his handsome features were like a familiar sculpture on which a subsequent hand had chased a network of new grooves, folds and puckers. It was also apparent he had been drinking. She knew the signs: the puffiness, the wonderful amber eyes bloodshot, though they still blazed at her as before, filling her with unease. Just a few years spent with David, a man of such a different calibre, had made her oversensitive, she thought.

The two women, whores he'd picked up God knew where, ogled her; one with studied boredom, the other with the unfocused animation of the slightly squiffy.

'Bugger me if it isn't the divine Troy!' he shouted, still holding out his arms as if he expected her to run into them. 'Girls, this is the original Emily of Troy. Did I ever tell you the tale of how I laid siege to her and scaled her walls and all without the aid of a wooden horse?'

The young woman who had been smiling vacuously, groaned, 'He's off again!' To Emily she said, 'You the one in the flipping painting he's been on about? The one who tried to murder him?'

Jacko attempted to throw his outstretched arms round Emily. She stepped back. Passers-by were looking at him curiously.

'Still fantasizing, I see?' Emily said.

'Bugger all that. How are you? And what have you been doing, best beloved? And why don't you ever come to Burr Ash these days?'

'You must be well sauced up to ask that! How did you manage it? I didn't think the Queen of the Night let you out of her sight, or did you escape?'

He shouted with laughter. 'The Queen of the Night! That's a good one.' He leaned forward and whispered hoarsely, 'Ah, Queenie! She spins her web and runs my life and worships the ground I walk on. Did you get that? You never bloody worshipped me, did you? You looked into my soul and gave it the evil eye; now see what I've come to.' He rolled his eyes towards the two tarts, shaking them by the shoulders. One opened her eyes wide and giggled, the other made a fretful *moue* of disgust.

'Come on now, Em,' he continued. 'Throw off the simpering Chase and come back to Burr Ash with me. We can live like three sparrows in a nest.'

'Sparrows, you think? A vulture, an eagle and a cuckoo would be nearer the mark.'

Jacko roared again. His strong teeth were hardly less white than before. 'Ah, but which is which, that's the question?' He squinted at her through an imaginary eyeglass in parody of an expert examining a painting. 'You look countrified and alarmingly healthy. Has Chase tucked you away in some bucolic love-nest?'

'My good health alarms you? That's interesting.'

'Come on then, where's he hiding you?' He suddenly seemed less drunk, more threatening.

'What's it to you?'

'Wouldn't you be delighted if I searched, though? I've a bloody good mind to.'

'I have a train to catch,' she said abruptly. 'I'll leave you in the company in which you are obviously so much at home. All whores together.'

His face darkened. 'Then kiss me for old times' sake.' Roughly he reached for her and she evaded his grasp, marvelling at how disgust could have so entirely replaced desire.

'There are no old times I could conceivably want to celebrate.' She grabbed the arms of the two tarts and shoved them against him. 'If you want to kiss someone, kiss these two,' she said fiercely.

The smiling girl relapsed into a more characteristic form of expression. "'Ere!' she exclaimed. 'Piss off, can't you!'

Emily left Jacko standing on the pavement between his tawdry companions and strode off. His shouts were lost in the general racket of the London square.

So what she had once imagined had been an overwhelming passion, an abiding love, a bonding of two souls had ended in a mundane and sordid encounter. On the train heading west again, she thought of David with delight and gratitude.

Zak faced the man across the scruffy table that served as a desk, thinking how startled the dealer's usual clientele would have been to know that he operated in these dingy surroundings as well as the hushed and elegant establishment beyond the firmly closed door.

'I told you right from the start that Chagall might be difficult,' the dealer said, fingering his immaculate lapel. 'There are already too many knocking around purporting to be the ones that went missing from his La Ruche studio.'

'But this is the genuine article. I know that and you know that. Chase would hardly have fallen for a fake.'

The dealer looked pained at such outspokenness. 'Anyone can make a mistake, Standish. Anyone. Besides, that's not the point since we will be unable to declare our sources. Provenance, my dear young friend, is all.'

'All right. But you said a receipt from a country auction would be perfectly OK. I touched the paintings up a bit with watercolour like you said, and they went through like a dream. I have the bill of sale to prove it.' In fact Zak had spent several days in his room at

Burr Ash, carefully covering the original paintings with slightly altered landscapes of his own devising. He had since carefully sponged away his work to reveal the originals.

The dealer was evidently not pleased at being reminded either of his promises or his suggestions. 'I may have a client who could be interested in the Cézanne but that's the best I can do.' In fact he had a buyer who had been waiting impatiently for nearly a year.

'So what the bloody hell am I supposed to do with the Chagall?' The dealer shrugged.

'You promised,' Zak said, his mouth a hard line. 'And I said all along that it was a mistake not to get shot of them out of the country straight away.' He glanced round the dim room, thinking on his feet. Round the walls were stacked canvases, their faces turned to the wall and never seen by the dealer's legitimate buyers. Some of them had been there years.

'It's the way I like to work, waiting until the publicity has died down. You knew that. And you are mistaken about what I said, I never make a binding commitment. How could I? Certainly not for the Chagall. But there are other methods of disposal.'

'You mean an arrangement with the insurance company, I suppose? Not on your life! Too sodding dangerous.'

'It's not a safe profession you're in. If you wanted "safe" you should have been a bank clerk,' the dealer said dismissively.

'Even a bloody bank clerk's job isn't safe these days. Too many frigging villains about.' Zak spoke entirely without irony.

'All the insurance people are worried about is getting the stuff back. They're most unlikely to inform the police, believe me. Of course you could always contact Chase. A private arrangement, no questions asked.'

Zak was silent. He had already thought of this if the worst came to the worst. He wasn't as green as not to know that the dealer might go back on his word.

'What about the Cézanne then?' he said. 'Chase paid a million for it in 1985. And nearly as much for the Chagall. They're worth a bloody sight more now.'

'Don't be naïve, Standish. As for the Cézanne, obviously I shall have to see it first.'

'That's not a problem. You know the painting anyway. But I

have to have an undertaking from you if I take the risk of moving it.'

For a few tense minutes they wrangled, the dealer suave and implacable, Zak tense with a steely determination not to allow his cunning and his risk-taking to go cheap. If all else failed and the dealer got cold feet there was always the possibility of threatening to expose him. Not that he ever would, since it had taken a long time to find and cultivate a reliable means of disposal. Besides, he didn't know if the dealer had friends whose methods were less fastidious.

No firm conclusion was reached about a price for the Cézanne but at the last moment the dealer said, 'Bring the Chagall as well, Standish. I may be able to dispose of it for you.' He'd had plans for the Chagall all along but he was not going to reveal these to Standish, any more than 'Standish' would reveal his true identity to him.

He let Zak out by a rear door into the small, seedy yard where Zak had parked his hire car. The appearance of the yard was as different from the ostentatiously tasteful frontage of the gallery as it was possible to be; the dealer's glittering Mercedes, parked tightly in beside a row of dustbins looked as if it might have fallen, by accident, from some celestial showroom.

Impatient and grim-faced Zak edged the hire car through the narrow, affluent streets, heading for the M3. He wasn't altogether disappointed with his day. He had a feeling that if he played his cards right he would be able to call the dealer's bluff – for he was sure the man was engaging in a cat-and-mouse game with him – and besides he'd had some luck with the antique sculptor in Highgate.

The old codger had welcomed him very civilly and, even though he was bent and twisted by arthritis, his memory appeared to be functioning perfectly. He talked knowledgeably (though at greater length than Zak could be bothered with) about the early days during and just after the Second World War. He shared the general view that Jacko's early work was the best and most interesting, after which he agreed, the painter had come unstuck.

'Seemed to miss the boat somehow,' he'd said, 'in spite of having a good woman to look after him and keep him on the wagon. Pity.

But maybe the artist in him thrived on the drink. Or perhaps it was the original model he needed.'

The sculptor still had two of Jacko's paintings in his possession. Both were of Emily in a landscape, one done in Provence, the other in Dorset at Burr Ash.

'A beautiful woman,' the sculptor said. 'Temperamental though. I expect she's snuffed it by now.'

Zak did not volunteer a comment.

'So how are you doing?' the sculptor said. 'Got enough for a decent retrospective? Because I know the whereabouts of two more early ones if you're interested.'

Zak implied that he was and asked the sculptor if he would be willing to loan the two in his possession and to allow them to be photographed.

'Of course, laddie.' He put a smeary glass of whisky down in front of Zak. 'Anything for that sweet lady. How is Regine? I'm afraid it's been more time than I like to think of since I saw her.'

'She gets very tired, which is why we have to get this show on the road as soon as possible.'

The sculptor drank from his generously filled glass. 'I know how she feels. Well, she's welcome to my two. Just say the word.'

'Thanks.' Zak took a cautious mouthful of whisky. Belying the appearance of the glass, its provenance and the general shabbiness of their surroundings, it was very good whisky indeed. Zak finished it.

At least he had some good news for Regine, for as far as she was concerned this part of his mission had been successful, he thought as he eventually drove into the Burr Ash yard.

Regine was not in the studio but in her room. She seemed to take her time coming downstairs.

'Ah, there you are, Zak,' she said, meeting him in the hall. 'I wondered where you'd got to.'

'It all took longer than I expected,' he said, wondering that she didn't at once ask him about the results of his various activities. 'I'm sorry about drawing a blank down in Devon but I had better luck with the sculptor, you'll be glad to know.'

While he was explaining about the possibility of running to ground two further paintings, Regine studied his face keenly.

'Thank you. That's very good news. I must thank him.'

Zak was puzzled. She'd hardly acknowledged his efforts at all. He gazed after her savagely as she went before him into the kitchen with her upright, gliding walk.

Then she surprised everybody by pressing a letter and a five-pound note into Fergus's hand and sending him off to the village to catch the last post.

CHAPTER SEVENTEEN

The degree results were pinned to the board one morning when Holly had come into college to finish clearing up. All her possessions except her sculpture, which was still on display, had to be removed from her locker as well as from the share of the studio she had called her own for three years.

The crowd in the entrance lobby attracted her attention at once; laughter, tears, shouts of relief, silences. Della Gillespie, a girl she knew well but who was not quite a friend, broke away, her face streaked with tears. She came up to Holly and laid her head on Holly's shoulder without a word. Holly put her arms round her. Della had been a particularly industrious student but she had rebelled, like Holly, so there was a bond of sorts between them. She specialized in studies of elephants, drawn and painted, but she had never been able to find anyone willing or able to teach her to draw.

In spite of all her work and the lengths she had been to to research her subject, Della had only managed a Third. Holly, listening sympathetically to Della's distress, feared the worst for herself.

She took Della out for a comforting cup of coffee.

'It's all very well for you,' Della said, blowing her nose. 'You've done quite well.'

Holly held her breath. 'How do you know?'

'I looked at your marks. You've got a Two-one.'

'Are you sure?'

Della nodded. 'It's not fair,' she said bitterly. 'Sorry. You deserved it, of course. You deserved a First, actually. But I bloody well didn't deserve a pathetic Third!'

Holly felt inadequate. No words would really help. But when she could, she went herself to the noticeboard to make sure that what

Della had told her was true. She sighed with relief, gratified that *someone* somewhere along the line had been on her side. A First would have been nice but in the circumstances it would have been unrealistic to expect it.

She took a load of stuff back to the flat, feeling a sense of anticlimax. She'd been to the pub with Joel and Lottie, both of whom *had* achieved Firsts; Joel for his 'padded cell' and Lottie for her 'envelopes'. Now there seemed to be no one else to tell except Em, who wasn't on the phone, and Fern who was on her way to Italy. Her mother, to Holly's relief, had at last decided that she would go with Audrey on the painting holiday but had to be strongly dissuaded from changing her mind when she discovered she would not be there when Holly's results came through. So that left Gideon.

He was in the middle of a discussion with some clients, an affluent young couple who ran a design business and who had just brought a converted barn. It was not the most convenient moment Holly could have chosen.

'Gideon? It's Holly.'

He sounded pleased but busy.

'I have something to tell you. Guess what?'

'You've had the results. Quick, tell me.'

'It's not the right moment is it? Ring me back.'

'Don't be aggravating. At least tell me if it's good or bad.'

'Good-ish.'

'Mm. Listen, I'll get back to you. About half an hour.'

He turned back to his humourless clients, and realized with amusement that they probably believed he had been discussing a pregnancy test.

Later, that evening he drove up to Bath and took Holly out for a celebratory meal.

'Here's to Holly Wyatt, BA Fine Art,' he said raising his glass. 'And to her future, especially if I fit into it somewhere.'

'Holly Wyatt might have made the grade up to a point but her future as a sculptor is a bit iffy to say the least.'

'Any news from King's Melcombe, or anywhere else?'

She shook her head. 'I haven't even heard if I'm short-listed or not.'

'You will be. I'm sure of it. And I know the King's Melcombe chap saw your degree show.'

'Along with half a dozen other degree shows, I'll bet. But in the short term I shall be working at Palladian.'

He raised his eyebrows.

'Gift shop just round the corner.'

'Ah.'

The vegetarian cannelloni arrived; her choice. It was stuffed with cheese, spinach and sun-dried tomatoes. They began to eat. It was the first time they'd been together for ten days. The fifty or so cross-country miles that separated them made casual meetings impossible.

'You've never had to worry about money, have you?' Holly said matter-of-factly, tucking in hungrily; lunch had been an egg sandwich.

'No,' Gideon said. 'I confess I haven't.'

'Won't you be madly rich when your pa dies?'

'Not madly, no. Riversfoot will go to my cousin, Will, since he's the one interested in my Dad's collection and actually knows about art. I told Dad years ago, when I was eighteen, that I didn't want the collection or the house. It would mean I'd have to give up my work.'

'Don't you get anything?'

'He's settled some capital on me, which suits me perfectly.'

'Some people would say you were off your trolley.'

'Then they wouldn't understand that I love my work. I expect it's arrogant, but I've always fancied the idea of being able to improve the landscape while working with it. Giving it a little tweak here and there, rather like you and your carving, wouldn't you say?'

'Mm. You may be right.'

'Anyway, the collection and the house were my father's obsession, not mine. Fortunately for me it's an obsession that Will shares and I must say, he's welcome to it. Eventually, I expect Will will give up his work and spend all his time at Riversfoot.'

'I thought you said he was a policeman. How does that fit in with being an art historian?'

'Quite conveniently as it happens. He's in the Art and Antiques

207

squad. Dealing with theft and fraud. He's after my Dad's stolen paintings just at present.'

Holly smiled slyly. 'Well, I hope he doesn't arrest Em. She told me the other day that she pinched some drawings from your dad once, when she was skint. Donkey's years ago.'

'Did she? He's never mentioned it. But then he wouldn't. He's been so uptight for a couple of years over losing the Cézanne and the Chagall. Apparently you can claim tax benefits if you allow scholars and students access to your collection; he suspects they were nicked by this young guy posing as an art student who probably collaborated or bribed a couple my father employed as housekeeper and handyman at the time.'

'I expect the paintings are in America or somewhere, in someone else's collection.'

'Will thinks they're still in the country. He says thieves sometimes sit on nicked stuff until the heat's off, though, according to him, exporting it is a doddle. He's in contact with Interpol and an outfit called the International Foundation for Art Research. He says the trail's hotting up lately. All very cloak-and-dagger.' Gideon shook his head at the unaccountable absurdity of it all.

'Would you believe, some of the degree work was heisted. Not mine, but then they'd have had their work cut out lifting that,' Holly said.

'That was pretty mean.' He grinned. 'Someone run out of envelopes, did they?'

Holly laughed. 'You're a very cynical person.'

He filled her glass. 'What time do you get off this weekend?'

'Saturday lunchtime. Why?'

'Are you going to see your grandmother?'

'No. I went last weekend. I don't want to outstay my welcome. Em's getting pretty wired about what's happening down there but still doesn't say what her plans are. It's infuriating.'

'What *is* happening?'

'Stalemate. But I'm afraid the wheels of bureaucracy are grinding on inexorably.'

'I thought you might come and stay with me.'

Holly considered the idea. She had been surprised that he hadn't suggested sleeping together before, since that was what it would mean. She had put it down to the fact that he was older than the other guys she'd known, who had all been students. Their main preoccupation had been to jump into bed *at once*, evidently regarding actually getting to know each other as an optional extra. Mostly they and their sexual competence had eventually been such a turn-off that, these days, she didn't bother. Now she had to decide if she wanted to change her mind.

'I could, I suppose,' she said doubtfully.

'Don't go completely overboard, will you?'

'I'll have to think about it.'

'Haven't you already? It must have occurred to you that sex would come into it?'

'Of course. But – I have to ask you this – are you any good at it?'

'At sex? What a question!' He grinned suddenly. 'Always the pragmatist. Well, let's see. All I can say is that although I'm no Don Juan, I think I'm patient and considerate and—' he chose his words carefully — 'I'm also very fond of you.' His thoughts briefly encompassed Sarah. There had been no complaints about his sexual competence from her anyway, only the one about them breaking up. He wondered if she'd found someone else.

'So how about it?' he said aloud. 'You don't have to be at home for your mother do you?'

'No. She'll still be in Italy.' Holly carefully aligned her knife and fork on her empty plate. She would never have thought, six months ago, that her mother would actually go for it. Go with Audrey to Umbria. 'Thank goodness. Not that I wanted to get rid of her. I just think it will give her a break.'

'You think deciding to take early retirement helped?'

'I'm absolutely certain of it. And a *painting* holiday!'

'Why not?'

'She was supposed to have been very good at art when she was at school but she never went on with it. I think she believed that she shouldn't set herself up in competition with Jacko.'

'That's absurd.'

'Yes, isn't it?'

Their desserts were brought. Holly had decided on a vast, exotic ice cream decorated with chocolate leaves.

'Bet you fifty pence you don't finish it,' Gideon said.

'Bet I do.'

'So what's the verdict,' Gideon said, dipping his fork into his blackcurrant cheesecake. 'You've had at least ten minutes to think about it.'

'Me coming to Winterbourne Thingy?'

'Mm.'

'I've decided I'll come,' she said, and went on to finish her ice cream. She held out her hand 'Fifty pence, please.'

Gideon reached for his pocket.

Surrounded by the scents of honeysuckle, thyme and old roses and the sound of distant sheep bells and nearby bees, Fern endeavoured to concentrate on the warm pinks and ochres of the eight-hundred-year-old walls of the Villa Verdi. She faced a doorway that was draped in jasmine and a pale apricot-coloured rose; on the steps that led up to it were pots of lilies and geraniums.

'Look for the structure first,' Kit had said, 'then tone, finally colour. And that's not to say colour isn't important.'

Being only a beginner she was bound to take him at his word. She obediently looked, then transferred her interpretation of what she saw on to the piece of paper that Marie, her tutor's wife, had helped her to stretch on that first evening. The mixture of cadmium and sienna she'd used for the walls established, she searched for the exact colour and tone for the cool shadows under the eaves, then for the indigo darkness of the open doorway.

Time passed and she was not aware of it passing, only of the movement of her new sable brush and the drift of colour that followed it across the pristine textured white of the paper.

She had brought a cushion from her room to soften the impact of the stone seat beneath the olive tree under which she had set up her borrowed easel. The other members of the party had disposed themselves in various patches of shade round the garden but Fern was not aware of them except when occasional bursts of conversation floated towards her on the hot scented air.

Audrey was somewhere at the far end, attempting a landscape with mountains, a distant hilltop town and the dark smudge of *macchia* that surrounded the hidden lush oasis where there had been a building or settlement since Etruscan times.

Audrey had urged Fern to 'do the view' too, but Fern didn't feel ready for mountains. In fact it had been several days before she had dared to do more than a few timid pencil drawings and only because she feared to look foolish in the face of the enthusiasm of the rest of the party did she finally break open her brand-new box of watercolours. She had only admiration for those who attempted oils, braving the difficulties of transporting the wet paintings afterwards.

Her first efforts had looked unbelievably childish but Kit had made a few useful suggestions and today's painting at least looked no worse than those of some of the others. Better than some even.

She sat back and, taking off her straw hat, brushed the sweat away from her hairline with the side of her arm. Then she lifted her bunched hair off the nape of her neck. The sun had gone round and when she put her hat back on she saw that the shadow it made on her paper was a violet arc pierced by a thousand tiny points of light, like an old painting of the universe. It was astonishing how many ordinary, everyday things she'd begun to notice; how could she have spent so many years of her life *not* noticing them? Now she considered it a criminal waste of sight, and drank in the visual prodigality like someone who had been dying of thirst.

She had never expected to be here at all; at one time Audrey's suggestion had seemed as preposterous as going to the moon. Quite apart from anything else, there was the expense. The holiday wasn't cheap. Although Kit and Marie were friends of friends of Audrey's, they couldn't be expected to make allowances; they had already kept their places open longer than they need have while Fern made up her mind. But she decided to worry about the money later, when she returned home.

The Head hadn't seemed surprised when she had given in her notice.

'I shall be, personally, very sorry to lose you. I always regret losing a good teacher – no, an excellent teacher.' Patricia Stover, an elegant woman in her thirties corrected herself. She was perfectly sincere. Losing teachers and finding replacements was a continual headache.

Fern detected relief too. She knew she'd been a worry for the past two years. Confused by the changes to the curriculum, slow and forgetful, her confidence and competence washed away in a flood of detail, her failure merely bore witness to the enduring expectations of her aunt.

The relief was hers too. There were moments of utter panic, when she thought about the future, that sometimes had the power to kindle old compulsions, but these were getting fewer. Encouraged by Holly and Audrey she had made enquiries about jobs, ordinary jobs, because quite apart from financial considerations, she would have to fill her days. She could not yet bring herself to imagine what life would be like when Holly left, as she must some day quite soon.

A swallowtail butterfly landed on her paper and flexed its wings. She studied its astonishing and exotic livery of black and cream, the wings splashed with flecks of blue and orange on their lower edge. It was as if it were presenting itself to her on purpose, so that she could admire it. Then it flew away, zig-zagging lazily above a clump of pinks.

The tranquillity of the place was beginning to seep into her. For the first few days Fern had been haunted by the idea that there was something else she should be doing – in fact that she shouldn't be here at all. She had done nothing to deserve being here. There had been a day of restless tension when she had been unable to settle, even to do the slightest of sketches. She had wept once, at night in her simple cell-like room; the room with windows that overlooked the garden which had been as full of glow-worms and nightingales as she had been of tears. She had thought weeping must mean she was caving in altogether. It was something she hadn't done for years for she had long since discovered that all it achieved was red eyes and a headache. But this time she had actually felt better the following morning.

'How's it going?' Kit stood behind her, his brown arms folded across his chest. According to Audrey he had got fed up with short-term lecturing contracts and, eight years before, had blued a legacy, bought the Villa Verdi, and launched the highly successful Villa Verdi Painting Holidays. Now he had become so integrated with life in Italy that he even looked Italian.

Fern leaned back. 'What you said yesterday helped a lot. What do you think?'

212

He crouched beside her. He wore a denim shirt faded almost to white, the sleeves rolled to his elbows. 'Tons better. You've got the tones this time and your colour is spot-on. Your strong point, I think, Fern.' They were all on first-name terms at the Villa Verdi.

Fern knew that it was his job to encourage timid amateurs but she was pleased all the same.

He sat on the wall beside her, relaxed. This nervy middle-aged woman slightly intrigued him. She was not quite their usual type of client, eager to pack every hour with meaningful activity, to enjoy the Italian food laid out in the shade of a vine and, of course, to pick his brains, since that was part of what they paid for.

'Will you carry on with it when you go back to Bath?' he asked her.

'I think so *now* but you know how it is. Good intentions and so on.' She gave a tremulous, unaccustomed laugh.

'There wouldn't be much point if you didn't really want to. The thing is only worth doing if you couldn't *not* paint.'

'We'll have to see. At the moment I don't even want to think of going home.'

He smiled. 'Good. I must remember to put that comment in our brochure.'

Holly's lunch consisted of the usual sandwich, which she devoured while she slung an assortment of summer clothes into her bag: shorts, tee shirts, a tunic-length jersey and one or two tops that skimmed her midriff. Until the following week when Fern came back, she still had the use of the car. Her mother had talked about selling it.

Working at Palladian had proved hectic, and on returning to the flat Holly had immediately thrown off the tie-dyed frock which was required wear for the shop and dived into the shower. Palladian sold cushions and quilts, novelty mirrors, amusing ceramics and candle holders of beaten tin, mostly the efforts of precarious economies worldwide. It had been hot, and the shop had been crowded with browsing teenagers from countries whose economies were relatively robust.

A reply had come through from the King's Melcombe estate. Holly had been short-listed and the interview was the following

Wednesday. The one thing that gave her a glimmer of hope was that two of her degree pieces had been bought by King's Melcombe's rich sponsor, a man by the name of Digby. She had been short-listed for an award too but she wasn't optimistic. The competition was fierce. She almost hoped that some of her more distant applications would come to nothing since she'd arrived at the awful conclusion that she didn't want to be too far from Gideon. This was a shock and she wondered if it meant that she was in love. She certainly spent a great deal of time thinking about him and trying to remember *exactly* what he looked like.

And now she was about to be reminded as she was driving down to Winterbourne Valence for the weekend. He had offered to fetch her but she had poured scorn on the suggestion.

'I'm not some infant you have to ferry about, you know!'

'OK, OK. I thought it would be nice to drive down together.'

'But you'd still have to drive up alone.'

The logic of that was unarguable and he shrugged, grinning to himself. 'Please yourself.' He lingered on the phone, needing to hear her voice. 'I'll have a meal waiting. Do you like pasta?'

'You know I do. I'm not keen on meat.'

'Right. No meat.'

She locked up the flat and tossed her bag into the Metro; she eased the car out into the traffic, the windows wide open because the weather was airless and thundery. The roads out of Bath were congested but gradually she left the worst of the traffic behind. To pass the time she tried to visualize Gideon's cottage from his description. He said he'd painted it all white inside, except the kitchen, which was blue, and taken out all the fifties Formica and the polystyrene tiles from the seventies. It sounded nice. Simple. He'd shown her photographs of the garden which was, as was to be expected, beautifully designed and planted. There was honeysuckle, clematis and roses, and plants with definite shapes, and places to sit and York stone paths.

The prospect of sleeping with Gideon, of spending a long period of time with him rather than an hour or two now and again, had become steadily more appealing. She wasn't on the pill; there hadn't seemed much point in taking it since the time she'd decided to give up sex. But to be safe, one had to use a condom anyway these days. The example of fellow students who had been either careless or unlucky was a continual reminder.

The village of Winterbourne Valence was prettier than Holly had imagined from Gideon's description; that is, after one had passed the garish filling station on the outskirts. It was entered between high banks thick with ferns and canopied with trees. From there various roads branched off, narrow and twisting as if to defy strangers to find the village at all. One of the lanes ran straight enough for long enough to accommodate a row of cottages, each approached by a plank bridge over a stream. At the end of the row Holly glimpsed the church behind some chestnut trees, dark green in their summer foliage, their trunks like great twisted ropes. Beyond, navy-blue clouds built up, their lower edges a murky sepia.

One of the cottages contained a shop and post office. A poster in the window entreated her to 'Save our Post Office'. She parked the Metro as near the stream as she dared and asked directions from the woman behind the counter.

'Left at the church and then right at the telephone box,' she was told. ''Tis about a hundred yards. You looking for Mr Chase?' she asked superfluously.

Holly grinned. 'That's right.'

It was more like a quarter of a mile but in the end she came upon Gideon's cottage abruptly. It was separated from the road by a small front garden, in which an archway of laburnum led towards the front door, its blossom now over. A small notice beside the gate announced 'Gideon Chase – Landscaping and garden design'. As instructed she pulled the Metro into a grassy lane beside the cottage and parked it behind Gideon's blue Volvo.

Gideon came out of the front door with a great welcoming smile. He was brown, his pigtail neatly plaited and his blue shirt freshly ironed. He grabbed her bag and steered her into the narrow hall where, tentatively, he took her into his arms.

'I've been looking forward to this all day – all week,' he said.

'Me too.'

He kissed her, feeling her response and then, leaving her bag in the hall, he led her into the sitting room and on into a small conservatory where he kissed her again. A few heavy drops of rain fell on to the glass roof.

'This is nice,' she said. Surprised by her physical need of him, wanting time to get used to it, she peered through the leaves of a plumbago to the exuberant garden beyond.

'Like some tea? Or I've some lemonade if you'd rather?'

'I'd prefer lemonade. Then could I have a shower, please? I'm disgustingly sweaty.'

'Have whatever your heart desires.' He went to fetch the drinks.

A bronzy light filtered in as the sun dipped beneath the lowering cloud. They drank the lemonade sitting on green-painted wooden chairs with striped cushions faded by the sun.

'I'm doing a vegetable lasagne and an enormous salad,' he said. 'That suit you?'

'Sounds great.'

'Holly, I—' he began. He kneeled on the floor in front of her, his arms each side of her thighs. I wanted to tell you that I meant it when I said I was looking forward to this.'

'So have I.' For almost half a minute it was impossible for either of them to look away.

'I'd planned to be sensible,' he said eventually, 'for us to have drinks, for me to show you the garden and then for us to have a leisurely meal here in the conservatory.' He leaned forward and kissed her. 'But I'm awfully afraid I'm not going to be sensible at all.'

But before she had a chance to answer, the front doorbell jangled through the house, making them both jump with the unexpectedness of it.

'Bugger,' Gideon said, without moving.

'Aren't you going to answer it?'

'No.'

The bell rang again.

'I think you'd better.'

Gideon got to his feet and strode impatiently through the hall to the front door.

Sarah stood there. She looked wonderful in a wisp of a cotton frock worn fashionably over a skimpy white top. Her skin was the brown of honey, her hair as gold as a new coin.

'Hallo, Gideon,' she said. 'I'm sorry but I had to come. There seemed to be too much unfinished business between us for things to be just left as they were.'

Gideon continued to stare at her dumbly.

'May I come in?' she asked.

'Well, it's not very—'

'I have come especially.' She stepped inside. 'You see, I tried another relationship briefly but it didn't work. I just had to see you one more time. In case you'd changed your mind but were too proud to get in touch.' She held out her hands with a slight, wry smile. 'As you see, I'm not too proud if it means saving something precious.'

He managed to speak at last. 'Sarah, I really meant it when I said it was over between us. I haven't changed my mind.'

'How can you be so sure?' She looked about her. 'Do we have to discuss this in the hall?'

'You should have rung. I have someone here.'

'Oh, a client.' She looked momentarily nonplussed but then her social poise took over. 'That's all right. I'll wait outside.'

'It's beginning to rain.'

'In the car then.'

'No,' he said more loudly and abruptly than he meant.

His manner had stirred her curiosity and she was at the door of the conservatory before he had time to stop her. Holly had risen from her chair and was standing, her glass still in her hand, looking faintly belligerent and not at all like a client. Her expression told him that she had heard everything that had gone before since small cottages do not allow for much in the way of privacy.

'Oh,' Sarah said slowly. She turned to look at Gideon. 'I see.'

'Sarah, this is Holly Wyatt,' Gideon said desperately. 'Holly, Sarah Henderson.'

Sarah just nodded.

'Have a drink?' Gideon said, trying to behave as if the situation was absolutely normal.

'No, thank you. I wouldn't want to break up your little tête-à-tête.' She looked critically at Holly, who was immediately aware how scruffy and sweaty she looked after her long, hot drive. All the same, she gazed defiantly back.

'I suppose the most obvious comment, Gideon,' Sarah said, 'is that you don't waste much time. Off with the old, on with the new, sort of thing.' She sat down on the chair Holly had vacated. 'I think, if you don't mind, that I will have that drink after all, Gideon. My usual please.'

Gideon went to fetch it, glad of a chance to think. While he was in the kitchen he slurped some brandy straight from the bottle. He felt in need of it. He poured Sarah's usual, a white wine spritzer.

'It looks as if he hasn't told you about me,' Sarah was saying meanwhile, in a conversational tone of voice. She wasn't absolutely sure how important this girl was to Gideon but it was imperative to get rid of her as soon as possible. She had psyched herself up for this encounter and might never have another chance to talk to Gideon face to face.

'No, he didn't,' Holly said stiffly.

'We're engaged, or at least we were engaged,' Sarah confided. A small lie in a good cause, she thought. 'I think he must have been leading you up the garden path,' she smiled and glanced briefly out of the window. 'No pun intended.'

'You've known him a long time?'

'Oh, we go back years, Gideon and I.'

'I see.'

Gideon came back and passed Sarah her drink without a word.

'I don't think Gideon bargained for this encounter,' Sarah said, sipping her drink appreciatively. 'Mm, you always mixed a mean spritzer.' She laughed. 'Look at him! He's wishing that one of us would fall through a hole in the ground.'

Holly went to the door. 'Gideon, I think it would be better if I left you two alone while you get this sorted.'

'No!' Gideon said loudly. 'Come back. Where are you going?'

Holly went and picked up her bag. She returned to the conservatory, standing in the doorway.

'I don't like muddles,' she said, and to Sarah, laconically, 'Great meeting you.'

Gideon was beside her in the hall whispering despairingly. 'Look, just give me five minutes. Sarah won't stay long.'

'It doesn't look like a five-minute job to me.' Holly opened the front door.

'But you can't go, you mustn't.'

'I think it would have been more honest to have told me about her in the first place.' She looked beyond him. Sarah was now standing in the hall, drink in hand, almost like a hostess seeing off a departing guest. 'I'm going home,' Holly added.

'You can't drive back to Bath tonight!' Gideon said, horrified and feeling that the situation was now quite out of hand.

'Bath!' Sarah said. 'They *do* come a long way to get fucked. That was your car outside, then?' She deliberately made it sound as if Holly had left something disgusting on Gideon's doorstep. She knew she was being bitchy but it couldn't be helped. The girl was an irrelevance; Gideon couldn't possibly mean anything to Holly while everything that was vital to herself hinged on this meeting. Desperate situations, desperate measures. For weeks she had brooded over the loss of Gideon Chase. She had set her heart on marrying him eventually. She didn't like to admit it, even to herself, but the fact that he was the son of a rich and eminent father was terribly important to her; marriage to him would bring kudos to her whole family. She knew nothing of her mother's telephone call to Gideon and would have been grieved and angry if she had.

'Goodbye, Gideon,' Holly said. 'Sorry, but I think this visit was a mistake.'

Even at the car, while Holly attempted to put her key in the lock Gideon tried to dissuade her. 'It's not as she says and it's not what it seems. For Christ's sake, don't be a bloody idiot. Stay. It didn't even occur to me to mention Sarah because it was all over between us.'

'She doesn't seem to think so.'

'She's trying it on, that's all. Holly, don't be an idiot. Stay, for Christ's sake.'

'Another time perhaps.' Holly slid into the driving seat, tossing her bag into the back. 'Or maybe not.'

It was raining properly now, which didn't even begin to cool the hot, sticky air. As Holly backed the Metro out into the lane she saw Sarah watching from the front door while Gideon stood at the gate, getting wet, and punching an anguished fist into an open palm, a look of utter frustration on his face.

Regine saw Donald and the girls off in the car, which was unusual and significant in itself, since they were only going into Dorchester for the morning, then she beckoned Zak to follow her into the studio.

She sat herself at the desk where the usual tidy stacks of diaries, letters and other papers lay beside the word processor. Piece by piece Jacko's life was being reconstructed; all his sayings (remembered and noted down at the time), quotes from well-disposed friends and art critics, the minutiae of daily life as well as momentous events, all meticulously edited and recorded. The account of his early life was, from necessity, as he himself had narrated it to Regine. Most of the rest she knew first-hand. She was too intelligent to omit Jacko's faults: his betrayals, his cruelties, his drinking and his womanizing, as well as his haphazard grasp of the knack of solvency, were all made light of, or subtly modified so as to make them appear positive virtues. It was vital that she completed the task before she was no longer capable and somebody less sympathetic presumed to take it upon themselves instead.

As Regine had seated herself at the desk, Zak hitched up his chinos and perched himself on the edge of the dais, his hands clasped loosely between his knees. He nodded towards the word processor. 'You don't want me to get stuck in this morning then, Maman?' he said. 'We lost a bit of time last week – though it couldn't be helped.'

'Never mind that now, Zak. I have something I need to discuss with you rather more urgently.'

'Oh? Right. Say on.'

Regine's hands strayed over the books and papers, realigning and straightening. Then she turned her attention back again to Zak.

'While you were away,' she said. 'I made an interesting discovery.'

'Yes?'

'If I said *La Carrière de Bibémus*,' she annunciated the French precisely, 'or *Vitebsk avec des Animaux*, would it mean anything to you?'

Zak's expression altered not at all but a tiny muscle at the corner of his eye flickered. 'Should it?' he said at last.

'I think so. You see, I can't imagine who else but you could have put these two very nice paintings in one of the old stables and secured them with a brand-new padlock.'

There was a long silence. Then Zak said, 'I see. And if I did know anything about them?'

'Well, then. That would make two of us, wouldn't it?'

Zak acted casual. 'So you haven't told anyone else – the police, for instance?'

'Indeed not. Why should I tell the police? I'm sure you have an excellent reason for storing two paintings in one of our outhouses. It seemed to me more pressing to talk to you.'

Zak frowned. He had been so sure that transferring the paintings from his room to the old stables had been a shrewd move. Fergus had shown a lot too much interest in the contents of his room and something had had to be done, just in case; since he'd learned of the kid's aversion to rats it had seemed the obvious solution. After all Fergus was otherwise the only one inquisitive enough to chance on them. Besides, in the remote eventuality of a police raid, his room would be found to be that of a citizen entirely above suspicion.

Zak grinned suddenly. 'All right, I'll level with you. They're copies, fakes. I made them when I was desperate for cash just after I left college but I hadn't the nerve, when it came to it, to try to pass them off.'

'In that case, Zak dear,' Regine said, intrigued at the way his mind and hers so often ran along identical lines, 'I'm sure you won't mind that I took the precaution of making sure that they're in a safe place. Just in case.'

'Right. But there's no need for that, Maman. Just as soon as you let me have them back, I'll put a match to them, I promise.'

'I'm afraid I can't do that at the moment. When the book's finished we'll talk about it again.'

Zak stood up and wandered over to Jacko's old chair. He gave the ancient corduroy jacket that hung over the back a savage tweak. 'It won't make any difference to the book, Maman,' he said. 'And I really need to have those paintings back.' His eyes raked the studio as if he expected to see them amongst Jacko's canvases.

Regine held up her hand. 'Don't waste time looking for them here, Zak dear. I sent Donald into Dorchester this morning on purpose to put them in a secure place. Although I have the utmost trust in you, it just wouldn't do for these copies to get onto the bona fide market. They're very good, Zak. You're a very clever young man.'

Zak went and stood over her threateningly. 'I want those paintings. I'm afraid if I don't have them life might become a bit less pleasant for you. I might even not help you finish the book.'

'I'm sure I could overcome that difficulty. There are others who would gladly step in.'

'I might even manage to accidentally lose what we already have in here,' he said, tapping the top of the monitor.

'That would be unfortunate but not catastrophic. I managed to master the secrets of that printer while you were away and, quite by chance, I happen to have a – what is it called? Hard copy, I believe – of everything we've done so far. And in case you had anything else in mind – which I'm sure you hadn't since I believe you are a nice person at heart, if misguided – I had Fergus post a letter to my solicitor which will put him fully in the picture should anything untoward occur.'

Zak was silent, thinking furiously.

'But look on the bright side, Zak dear. How much work would you say we have left to do? Another two months perhaps?'

'Ye-es.' Zak was cagey. 'And then what?'

'Then naturally you will have returned to you anything that's yours and I will give instructions for the letter I gave my solicitor to be destroyed.'

'How do I know I can trust you?'

'Young man, I am an old woman and you should know by now that my only interest in life – my absolute priority – is to finish this book. What you do after that is entirely up to you. Whereas, if you embark on reckless or injudicious action you will lose everything.' A hint of a smile played round her mouth. 'Even of having your name associated with Jacko's biography.'

'Having my property back won't interfere with my work here,' Zak said petulantly.

'I can't take the risk. Zak Stratton in prison is no earthly use to me.'

'Why do you mention prison? Anyway, there *is* no risk.'

'I wasn't born yesterday. I happen to think there is.'

'What d'you know?'

'Nothing I'm prepared to discuss with you – or anyone.'

'Even the police?'

'As far as I'm concerned the police do not even enter into it. Now or later.'

'How do I know I can trust you?' he repeated insistently.

'You don't. But if you're intelligent you'll understand that I'm just not interested in your private affairs. I can't impress on you strongly enough that they do not concern me in the very least.' She fixed him with a penetrating and purposeful stare. 'So, do we have a bargain?'

'Who found the paintings?'

'I'm not at liberty to say.'

'Because if it's that sodding boy, how are you going to guarantee he'll keep his trap shut?'

'Fergus has seen the paintings. He thinks they're copies. And in any case, you must know by now that the child has no interest in art.'

Zak took a turn or two about the studio, wondering if he could stall the dealer. It might even be to his advantage to keep the man waiting, or even dispense with him as an intermediary altogether. After all, the dealer hadn't thought twice about buggering *him* about.

He glared at his employer aggressively. 'You know what you are, don't you?' he said at last. 'You're a cold-blooded old boiler with a face like a horse's arse.'

'I'm glad we are being honest, at last,' she replied calmly. 'I take it then that we have an understanding?'

He came over to her and she held out her hand. He took it reluctantly. 'I suppose I shall have to trust you,' he said. And, crazy though it seemed, he did.

CHAPTER EIGHTEEN

Emily stood on the verandah and dabbed impatiently at the runnels of salt water that drained from her hair and chased down her cheeks. After her swim she had thrown a fisherman's smock of faded orange over her trousers. This patchwork garment was made up of the cornflower checks of what had once been a tablecloth, the peacock-coloured remnants of some curtains and various scraps of purple and yellow cotton.

It was a hot day and the breeze, which was scarcely less hot, was whipping twists of white sand along the road where they eventually lodged in the verges amongst the mallow and the steel-blue foliage and yellow flowers of the horned poppy.

Old man Watts lifted his stick in greeting as he shuffled by with his mongrel. He had worked as a rat-catcher for the local authority before he retired and gave the impression that he was still going about his business. His dog was evidently convinced of it.

'I zee they'm still at it,' he said indicating the clattering JCB now nearer than previously. 'They won't be zatisfied 'till they 'av us all riddled up.'

'So what will you do, Mr Watts?' Emily asked, her damp towel still in her hands.

'They'm gonner 'av to shove I out on the end o' that bliddy dractor,' he vowed.

'And then what?'

'I dare say I'll 'av to bide wi' my little maid over to 'Oniton.'

'Honiton's not too far.'

''Tis var enough. Var enough,' he said darkly.

'I'm sorry, Mr Watts. I'm afraid we're too old to make a fight of it.'

Mr Watts departed, shaking his head. It was the longest conversation they had ever had.

This summer there were noticeably fewer visitors, though it was now the height of the season. With most of the chalets and shanties standing empty and shuttered, the weekend sailors stayed in more salubrious accommodation in East Ashpool or further afield and appeared each morning for another day of painting, tinkering and winching dinghies up and down the beach. Most of them put to sea sooner or later and in evidence a sprinkling of white and coloured triangles moved silently across vivid patches of kingfisher blue and jade far out beyond the surf. Small groups of figures punctuated the wide stretch of beach left by the receding tide. As always, the shoreline in summer was a gentle playground for the human species, its sombre winter aspect forgotten.

Emily turned away and began to rummage in the dresser drawer for notepaper. She had been putting it off but now she really would have to write to Francis to thank him for the blasted cheque. What a nuisance he was with his spontaneous gestures! She had a good mind to send it back, she had no use for it now, though there had been times in the past when she could have done with it. Why hadn't he offered it then? As it was, he hadn't explained this sudden rush of generosity or by what reasoning he had arrived at this apparently arbitrary figure, which was a great deal of money to send on impulse. It wasn't like him to act on impulse, especially one that led him to part with large amounts of cash. He was probably regretting it already. But perhaps it was to compensate for the premium bond fiasco; however she was not one to deny her brother the sharp pleasures of self-sacrifice. She would write to him, thank him nicely and put the money aside. While she was about it she would attempt to buck him up a bit. Her brother's situation fretted her but nothing she could say would induce him to get shot of that ghastly little school; it was all too evident that it worried him to death as well as being far too much for a man of his age to handle, especially one as neurotic as he.

She was still searching for the notepad when there came a whisper of tyres in soft sand and a car with dark-tinted windows drew up outside. Its polished blackness gleamed like jet against the smudged pastels of the encompassing sandscape. To Emily its sudden appearance had all the sinister connotations of every black saloon in every gangster movie since film-making began. Harbingers of evil, always. The driver leaned across the empty passenger seat and squinted at the name on the gate. Then his face disappeared and the engine was switched off. There was no doubt that the car, a hired BMW, had arrived at its destination.

So they had sent in the heavy mob! Not unexpected, but she had no intention of giving in without a fight. With no attempt at concealment she slammed the outside door and drew the curtains across the windows on that side of the house. Then she retreated to the sitting room and closed the glass doors that led on to the verandah; they wouldn't trouble the hired muscle for long but it was the principle of the thing. Without question the noise involved in getting her out would alert everyone on the beach and in the dinghy park.

Emily ignored the knock on the door when it came and continued to ignore it when it was repeated. The third time it was louder and quite evidently impatient. There followed a longish silence but because there was no sound of a car re-starting she wasn't fooled.

'Sod it all,' she muttered to herself. 'How can I be expected to concentrate!' She had, in any case left the magnifying glass in the kitchen.

A shadow fell across the room from the glass door of the verandah. Someone was outside, peering in.

'Piss off!' Emily roared. 'Is it too much to ask to be left alone in one's own house?' The someone tapped on the glass and at the same moment Emily recognized the silhouette.

'Hell's teeth! It's the Queen of the Night!' She went to the door and flung it open as if to make certain that her vision wasn't as far gone as she feared. Without being invited Regine stepped into the room and with a cursory glance at her surroundings, sat herself down in the nearest chair. Emily looked on in horror as Regine crossed her ankles in their fine black stockings and rested her blue-veined hands on an envelope-shaped purse on her lap. She was all in grey, the grey of pigeon feathers with a hint of violet: silk suit, her silver necklace with its large onyx beads and shoes of Italian leather. She was hatless but with no hair out of place in spite of the fitful breeze outside. But Emily noticed, or thought she noticed, that Regine had allowed the tide of ink-black to recede; round her hairline had appeared the merest suggestion of white.

Emily peered, cursing her failing eyesight. The woman was not quite as she remembered, even with so recent a reminder as Jacko's funeral. Her face was a mere spectral echo of Jacko's much-painted model. The flesh had been pared away leaving a bone structure that was more apparent than before, and her eyes, which had always been large, now seemed to both occupy the greater part of her face and at the same time to have sunk into their sockets.

'This is an abomination!' Emily spluttered, finding her voice at last. 'Absolutely the last bloody straw!'

Regine appeared unmoved. 'Emily!' she commanded.

'Isn't it enough that you sent your dreadful little toady to spy on me? Didn't he tell you all you wanted to know or did you have to come and check up on me in person? I dare say you would have been here before, wouldn't you? Only Jacko wouldn't have let you. Was that the way it was?'

Regine held up her hand. 'Emily,' she said, 'will you just listen? I have come a long way to see you and I don't propose to waste time and energy wrangling over the rights and wrongs of the past. I have something to say to you and I'd like to say it in as civilized a manner as possible; so perhaps you'd consider all your objections to me being here, all your cries of outrage, et cetera, to have been expressed so that we might have a cup of tea and talk about what matters to us *now*. It's been a hot and tedious journey and I'm extremely tired.' She stopped talking suddenly and sighed.

Bluntness and straightforwardness were so unlike the woman Emily remembered that she was taken aback. Then, with belligerency returning, she said, 'I can't think of a single thing you and I could have to talk about after all this time so I'm afraid you've had a wasted journey.'

'Please, Emily. Let's be sensible. I need to talk to you,' Regine insisted calmly.

'Well, I don't need to listen. You can get in your great black hearse and bugger off.'

'You wouldn't deny even your worst enemy a little refreshment on a day like this, would you?'

'You *are* my worst enemy.' Emily moved to the door leading to the kitchen. 'But as you look as if you're about to peg out I'll get you some tea.'

She left the room abruptly. In the kitchen she filled the kettle and reached for the teapot and mugs. Outside the black car still lurked; the driver was reading a tabloid newspaper and smoking. He had the door wide open to catch the breeze. Emily set out an extra mug for him. When the kettle boiled she put everything on to a tray with a bottle of whisky and carried it into the room where Regine was sitting. No further words passed between them as Emily poured the tea. It wasn't for her to break the ice, Emily thought fiercely.

'No milk for me,' Regine said at last.

'That's all right. There isn't any. It went off.' Emily relented. 'You can have some whisky in it if you like.'

Regine declined.

'I'll pour a mug for that poor sod of a driver.'

'That's thoughtful,' Regine said. 'His name is Mr Simmons.'

Emily poured the extra mug and carried it out to Mr Simmons, who was duly grateful for it, even without milk. When she returned she sloshed a generous measure of whisky into her own mug and then sat back, waiting.

We're old, both of us, she thought. Two old women drinking tea together. What could be more harmless and ordinary?

Regine sipped from the mug, reluctantly supporting its unaccustomed weight with one finger of her left hand. Then she put it down on the table beside her. She had come to a decision.

'I'm afraid I've been a fool,' she said.

'Surely not?' Emily said sarcastically.

'There is no one else in whom I can confide and it's necessary for me to talk about one or two matters.' For the first time in many years she had dropped her French accent.

'It seemed to me at the funeral that you had more than enough relatives and hangers-on,' Emily said, 'who would be only too delighted to be confidants. And what about doctors and lawyers – aren't they the traditional guides, philosophers and friends of old women? What d'you want with me?'

'I want the truth. Not flattery or cosy reassurance. As I said, I've been a fool and allowed myself to be duped and betrayed. Pride, you see. I heard what I wanted to hear. And besides, a great deal of what I want to say concerns you and me alone.'

Emily put down her mug impatiently. 'For goodness' sake stop speaking in code and spit it out. I haven't time for beating about the bush.' She gave Regine what would have been a penetrating stare if only she could have focused properly. 'And I shouldn't think you have either by the look of you.'

'So you've guessed?'

'Guessed?'

'I'm dying, Emily.'

Emily was unmoved. 'Aren't we all? I'm over eighty, for God's sake, and you're not that much younger. I suppose you could say that the grim reaper has his beady eye on both of us.'

'The difference is that few of us know precisely the time and manner of our end. For all we know you could still have another ten years. I don't. What I have is more like ten weeks, a little longer if I'm careful.' She seemed without emotion. 'But that is not what I came to see you about. As you rightly said, we are all mortal.' She took up her mug again with all the steadfast courage of one who is used to Earl Grey in a cup of the finest bone china. 'If it's all the same to you I'd like to change my mind about the whisky.'

'Good idea,' Emily said gruffly, reaching across with the bottle. 'Bad luck about your illness. Bloody rotten.'

With her tea fortified, Regine continued, 'A few weeks ago I sent a young man, who was in my employment, down here hoping he could discover if you had any of Jacko's work. I believe he may have used subterfuge.'

'The spy, you mean? Yes, I remember him well. I sent him about his business.'

'Tell me what happened exactly.'

Emily related the sequence of events, including the break-in. 'He damned nearly took me in so I suppose I have to congratulate you on choosing such a clever young toad to do your dirty work for you. Didn't he report back?'

'In a manner of speaking. But I had good reason not to believe what I was told. I sent him down to talk to you and to ascertain if you still had any of Jacko's paintings, not to deceive you and steal from you. I have since discovered that duplicity is his stock-in-trade and that had I been as astute as you have obviously been, I could have seen him for what he is, a thief and a con man.'

'Cheated you, did he? Swindled you out of your life savings and so on?'

'Not quite. But I think that perhaps the intention was there.' Once again she set her mug down as if holding it was an effort. 'Emily, what did he steal from you?'

Emily looked surprised. 'From me? Why, nothing!'

'Nothing?'

'Not a sausage.'

Regine looked nonplussed. 'Oh. Well, that's something at least.' She frowned.

'You look as if you hoped he had. Anyway, where is this enterprising young rascal? Got away, no doubt.

'I do apologize for sending him here in the first place, I'm relieved to hear that you got rid of him before any real damage was done.'

'He was good, I'll give him that. But fortunately, just in time, I noticed his ears.'

'Ears?'

'I remembered them from the day of the funeral. My eyesight was better then. Have some more tea?'

Regine shook her head. 'Not just now, thank you.'

Emily felt the hair at the nape of her neck. It was still slightly damp. She removed a hairpin and stuck it in more firmly. Regine noticed the large garnet ring on Emily's finger and in spite of her determination to put such things behind her, she experienced a fleeting pang of jealousy. Jacko's ring! She immediate'y thought. And Emily still wearing it!

'Is that all you wanted to say?' Emily enquired. 'It seems a very long drive just for that.'

'No, it's not all. It's only the beginning. Emily, I have to ask you this straight out. You may have heard that I'm planning a retrospective of Jacko's life's work which I may well not live to see but which I must at least finish organizing before it's too late. We are experiencing difficulty in tracking down some of his early paintings and, as I said, one of the reasons I sent our dubious young friend down here was to find out if you had any in your possession. I was so sure you had.'

'Me! Any of Jacko's paintings? Don't talk hogwash.' She glanced round the room, chuckling. 'See for yourself!'

'I do see.' Regine followed her gaze. 'I'm sorry. I so hoped you had. You had the best of Jacko. I thought you might have some of what is considered his finest work too.'

'I had the best of Jacko? What *can* you mean?'

'Home truths, Emily. What I came down here for.'

'Home truths! I don't like the sound of that. The airing of home truths is a very overrated pastime, in my opinion.'

'Necessary in this case.'

'All right. You'd better get it off your chest.' The whisky was causing Emily to feel better disposed towards her visitor. It was also loosening Regine's tongue.

Regine paused for a moment, looking through the window at the view which she seemed to be seeing for the first time. 'I wanted to confess to you,' she said at last, 'how much I've always envied you. How jealous of you I still am.'

Emily stared in disbelief. She had picked up her mug; now she replaced it on the table.

'That amazes you, doesn't it?' Regine said. 'You thought I had everything – Jacko's love, his children, money, Burr Ash.'

'So you have – had.'

'Emily, listen to me. Yes, I had Burr Ash but latterly it's been a desperate struggle to keep it going. I've always had to be responsible, to keep an eye on what we spent, which with Jacko, wasn't at all easy. He loathed it when I rationed his spending money so that he couldn't go drinking. If he drank, in the end he didn't work. Sometimes I think he hated me for it. It made me harsh with the children, preoccupied as I was, so that they were either frightened of me or couldn't wait to get away. But even losing the children seemed worth the sacrifice, just so I could keep Jacko. All I ever wanted, you see, was that Jacko should be great and that my name should be linked with his for ever. A sort of immortality by proxy, you understand? For that I was willing to do anything, bear anything. I ploughed in all the considerable alimony I got from my first husband, Inky Petheridge, to make sure Jacko would be happy and comfortable; so that he could work undisturbed by domestic worries.' She gave a small dry laugh. 'I used to blame you for not protecting him from them as I intended to do.'

Emily grunted. 'Is that what he told you? Well, you got your wish. You got Jacko, and hung on to him through thick and thin as I understand. That must have taken some doing.'

Regine shook her head slowly. 'Do you remember when I first came to Burr Ash? The day you went for him with a knife?'

'Correction, Queenie. The day Jacko went for *me* with a knife. And that was a result of home truths, so watch out.'

'Why do you insist on calling me that?'

'Queenie was your name, wasn't it?'

'That was a long time ago. It was all a long time ago, so I don't suppose any of it matters in the least now. But whichever way round it was I know you won't believe me when I tell you how much I envied you then – and went on envying you. Not only for having Jacko but for yourself. I could see all too clearly why Jacko worshipped you.'

'Worshipped me! Now you *are* talking balls!'

'He worshipped you. There you were, as statuesque and fiery as an Amazon, your hair as wild as a Medusa's. Your sort of beauty didn't depend on being soignée. Mine did, and with such as remains, still does. And it wasn't only that. It was your fearlessness, your audacity, your contempt for conventional behaviour. I tell you, I took one look at you that day and cursed you for implanting in me an inferiority complex that I would never grow out of if I lived with Jacko for a thousand years.'

'I don't believe you.'

'Nevertheless, it's true. You don't imagine I'd be swallowing my pride to tell you something that wasn't true, do you? What do you think it was like for me, having worked so hard to prise him away from you and set everything else in my life aside, to know that after all, he still loved you? To have him regard me as some kind of prison wardress who denied him his drink and rationed his mistresses, even if I did put up with his mania and his black depressions. Do you think I enjoyed that? And then to know that I could never inspire him as you had done?'

'That's a load of tripe. Jacko and I fought like gamecocks. It was all you-step-on-the-tail-of-my-coat-tra-la! All the time. In any case, that business about being his inspiration is just a lot of sentimental poppycock. You've been reading too many romances, my girl. Jacko was already played out, we both knew that. And would have been played out even if I'd stayed. The truth is, Queenie dear, that he had one or two ideas and as soon as he'd rung all the possible changes on them he exhausted his talent. The rest was just hot air. We have to face it but I'm sorry to say that his was not a great gift. The poor old bugger was a small fish in a very large pond. Did you know, by the way, that he was colour-blind?'

Emily stopped speaking abruptly. 'What's the matter?'

'No, Emily, no!' Tears were welling up in Regine's tired eyes. They trickled down her waxen cheeks, leaving snail-like tracks in her skilful *maquillage*.

'But he was, you know,' Emily said gently, as if to a child.

Regine opened her purse and drew out a folded white handkerchief which she pressed to her eyes. The tears continued to flow. 'I knew about his colour-blindness,' she sobbed. 'It wasn't that.'

'You mean about his not being a great gift?'

Regine nodded as she struggled to stem the river of tears.

Bewildered, Emily endeavoured to offer some crumbs of comfort. 'Don't be upset, Queenie. You know his work fetches quite decent sums with a certain kind of dealer. And I'm told there's been an increase of interest since – well—'

Regine moaned as if Emily's words were piercing her like a knife.

'You surely didn't believe,' Emily said, light dawning, 'that he was the great underrated genius of the age, did you?' Emily spoke softly, bending forward out of concern that the woman was making herself iller by the minute. 'Damn it all, you did!' She leaned back, letting out a noisy breath.

'I had to believe it,' Regine said, mopping her tears. 'Don't you see, I loved him. Why should I have sacrificed everything otherwise? Everything!'

'You poor old cow. Never mind, it's not so bad. Women are giving up their own identities every day of the week for much less worthwhile characters than Jacko. For violent chaps. Criminals, some of them. Since you were set on self-immolation I'll say this, you could have done a lot worse.'

This didn't appear to have the cheering effect Emily had hoped for. 'I loved him,' Regine moaned. 'I had to do what I did. I was good for him in so many ways but when it came right down to it I wasn't what he needed. He needed the woman he loved, which was you. He probably needed to fight and to struggle, he needed someone who would tell him the truth however much it hurt, even if he'd died of alcohol poisoning forty years ago.'

'Look here, that's all very well but aren't you forgetting something?'

Regine lifted her head, eyes pink-rimmed. 'What's that?'

'I would have thought it blindingly obvious. Jacko might have needed friction and struggle but *I* didn't. At least I'd had enough of it by the time the children were born. The struggle I've had here just to survive has been quite enough for me. You seem to have forgotten that marriage to Jacko bloody nearly polished me off. I nearly ruddy well *died* in that sanatorium.'

Regine shook her head. 'I didn't know that.' She continued to stare at Emily as she wrestled inwardly with terrible and novel ideas. She leaned back in her chair with a fearful sigh.

'Look here,' Emily said, getting to her feet, 'I'm going to tell your driver chappie to go away and come back later, tomorrow if you like. You're going to lie down now and have a damned good rest. You're not up to another car journey just now.'

'I can't. The expense,' Regine said faintly.

'Bugger the expense,' Emily said. She lifted Regine quite gently to her feet and with an arm under her shoulders, guided her to her own bedroom where she laid her visitor on her own bed and removed her shoes. Regine, too tired to protest, let her.

'It's not the Ritz but any port in a storm, eh?' Emily said to jolly Regine along.

'You're so kind,' Regine whispered.

'Kind! Balls! I'd do the same for old Watt's tyke!'

Emily went outside to send Mr Simmons away. 'Mrs Monk is unwell. I think it would be best if you came back tomorrow.'

Mr Simmons hesitated.

'Don't worry. Mrs Monk will pay you then.'

The black saloon lurched back up the sand-dusted road, the sun glinting on its tinted windows. Halfway along it met a Metro coming down and the two cars edged past each other gingerly.

Holly pulled into the scanty shade of the hedge. 'Hallo, Em,' she said.

'It's like Piccadilly Circus here today! I thought you were staying with Gideon this weekend?'

Holly got out and dragged her bag out of the back. 'Yes, well it didn't work out,' she said gruffly. 'Do you mind awfully if I dump on you instead? To tell you the truth, I'm knackered.'

'You better come in,' Emily said sensing that her granddaughter was not quite her usual stoical self. 'But I have to warn you, I'm not alone.'

After Sarah left, Gideon allowed enough time for Holly to have arrived back in Bath before he rung the flat. He tried again several times but always with the same result. No answer. By ten o'clock he was beginning to get seriously anxious, a feeling exacerbated by guilt. Either she had gone out, or she was refusing to answer, or, and this was when he began to understand what the phrase 'cold sweat' really meant, she'd had an accident and was now lying in hospital, or worse. He considered ringing the police and all the possible hospitals to which she may have been taken.

To say that Sarah couldn't have chosen a worse moment to turn up, was a gross understatement. It seemed to him like the act of a malevolent Providence, for Sarah could hardly have known that Holly would be there, unless she hoped to catch him unawares with someone else anyway. She had even apologized.

'I didn't do this on purpose,' she said. 'How was I to know that you'd have another woman here? Who is she? Is it serious or did you just pick her up?' There was the merest hint of disdain. Sarah could be quite good at disdain when she chose.

'That's my business now, Sarah. But, no, I did not just pick her up.'

'Darling, I'm sorry. I didn't mean to be a cow but I had to know. Look, I have two tickets for a summer concert in the grounds of King's Melcombe. Why don't we go? No strings, just a pleasant evening—'

'No, Sarah.'

'You said that as if you meant it.'

'I do. Look, however one rakes over old embers, there's no bringing them back to life.'

'So that's really it, then?'

'Yes.'

Without warning she lifted her arm and struck him across the face with what felt like all the force of her tennis forearm. His head spun and his cheek smarted. He put a hand up to his face, his eyes watering, but he didn't retaliate. Somehow her action made him feel less of a heel all of a sudden.

'I just thought you'd better know how I feel,' Sarah said, picking up her shoulder bag. Then she burst into tears and flung herself into his arms.

He held her cautiously, as if they had been strangers thrown together accidently. She pressed herself closer to him as if seeking comfort. The situation was more emotionally loaded because he had never seen Sarah cry before; she wasn't the crying type.

'Please, Sarah,' he said. 'Don't.'

'You're a bastard, Gideon,' she wept. 'But I'm sorry I hit you.' She wiped her eyes with the back of her hand.

'Here, I'll get you a tissue,' he said, if only to distance himself from her.

'No, no, stay. I need you.' She lifted a tear-stained face and pressed her mouth against his neck. He was conscious of her thighs adhering to his as if glued there. The state of arousal brought on by his exciting nearness to Holly was suddenly and fatally rekindled. He kissed her, murmuring comforting words. What happened in the next hour or two was one of the bigger mistakes of his life to date.

It was much later, after Sarah had driven away in her smart Golf convertible, that sanity and anxiety over Holly surfaced and Gideon began to ring the flat. By half-past ten, when there was still no answer, he rang the police. He had to know if there had been any accidents on any of the roads he would have expected her to take. There hadn't; at least none that had involved ambulances, Metros or a young woman driving alone.

Gideon felt desperate to speak to Holly again, yet tainted and unworthy of her. He had won her trust over the weeks by a slow and careful process, then cruelly discarded her. He vowed, if she could ever bring herself to speak to him, never to let her down again. Besides, although he had tried to explain, he wasn't sure if Sarah understood that what had just occurred was merely a postscript, a final coda. All his fault if she didn't. How could he have been such a fool?

CHAPTER NINETEEN

From the window of his study Francis stared gloomily out at the bobbing heads of the returning boys, their caps like so many cherries in a bowl. Another academic year beginning. Endlessly the procession of pupils came and went: some were the sons of former scholars and some, God help him, were grandsons. They changed so little that he frequently found himself confusing the generations, ascribing the successes and failures of a father to the son and vice versa.

Outside the gates, half obscured by the now purplish red foliage of the copper beech, the procession of expensive cars arrived, parked, and double- or even triple-parked. Every year in his address to new parents he had gone on, humorously of course so as not to offend, about how this practice could put the lives of the boys at risk and every year he was completely ignored.

In the last decade of the school's existence he had been obliged to admit an increasingly mixed bag of new boys; indeed the incoming tide of children reminded him vaguely of the nursery pictures of which his sister Muriel had so much approved, that depicted Christ blessing a sort of United Nations of infants thronging around him and into the distance as far as the eye could see. Muriel had no objection to the throng as long as it wasn't thronging round her, Francis thought cynically; she had actively campaigned amongst her neighbours to make life uncomfortable for a polite and unobjectionable Indian family who moved into the locality in the 1960s. She had been successful and they had moved on.

He had become used to this new departure for the school, not least because the standard of achievement and behaviour had risen because of it. All the parents, of whatever ethnic origin, who sent

239

their children to Rudyards were ambitious for them to 'get on'.

Francis was brooding. Usually he looked forward to the beginning of a new term, the end of loneliness and too many opportunities for introspection and of being at the mercy of Mrs Bessemer for weeks on end. He would have liked to go away for a protracted holiday but funds just didn't run to it. To add to his discomfort there had been yet more murmurings, even from erstwhile loyal supporters, hints that he was past it and should give way to a younger man. Some merely suggested that he step down as principal, others had the nerve to propose that he sell out and retire completely from the scene.

The knock on the door was, as always, more like an assault with a deadly weapon – actually the tray Mrs Bessemer used for fetching and carrying his coffee and biscuits – and as always, the door flew open before he had time to answer. Mrs Bessemer surged in.

'I thought I'd let you know straight away,' she said without preamble, 'that I shall be leaving tomorrow week.'

Francis stared at her bemusedly. He sat down at his desk.

'That's right. Leaving,' she said as if he'd queried it. 'I'm giving in my notice as of this minute.'

'But – Mrs Bessemer. Why?'

'I think you know why, Mr Troy. He that soweth sparingly shall reap also sparingly.'

'I don't—'

'And he that soweth bountifully shall reap also bountifully. D'you get my drift, Mr Troy?'

'Yes, I certainly do, Mrs Eh—' Francis took a deep breath. 'So you will be leaving us after all?'

Mrs Bessemer hesitated for a moment, clearly taken aback. 'That depends on you, doesn't it, Headmaster?'

But the future without Mrs Bessemer had all at once taken hold of Francis's imagination and his heart leaped for joy. After all, it was so easy. He could never had taken the initiative and given her notice himself, so helpless did he feel in the hands of Fate, but now that the decision had been taken from him completely, it was a different matter. In spite of the irksome process of readvertising and interviewing a succession of possible candidates, he felt like a man reprieved. Surely in all the teeming population of Greater

London, there must be someone more amenable than Mrs Bessemer.

He stood up and was conscious of an involuntarily straightening of his spine. He handed her his empty coffee cup and said, 'Well, now, Mrs Bessemer, we shall be sorry to lose you, naturally, but I suppose that on the subject of your remuneration we shall have to agree to differ, won't we? Of course, I shall be only too happy to supply a reference should you decide to try for another position.'

Mrs Bessemer sucked in her breath and gazed at Francis with eyes like marbles. For once she was utterly speechless.

'Tomorrow week, did you say?' Francis continued. 'It doesn't give me much time to find your replacement but since you've made up your mind, so be it.'

'I could perhaps—'

Francis held up his hand. 'No, no, Mrs Bessemer. I wouldn't hear of you altering your plans. Tomorrow week it is.'

For a moment she stood holding the tray as if she'd been turned to stone, then without a word she turned and left the room. She even forgot to slam the door.

Francis paced about the room, feeling like one of his boys on the last day of term. The enormity of change affected him like a draught of a forbidden elixir. For so long he had been in thrall to the status quo but now that the possibility of things ceasing to be permanent and unmovable, perhaps even improving, had entered the equation who knew where it would lead? It had been a summer of discontent. There had been the perennial worries over finances, in particular the funding of the new science block; then the proceeds from the sale of Jacko's two engravings had been so much less than he anticipated and besides he had sent half of it to Emily (who hadn't been as grateful as he hoped either). Added to that was the disturbing business of being hoaxed over Emily's supposed premium bond win; he was still unable to understand the point of that little episode. Perhaps a disgruntled old boy?

However, now he would put these things behind him. Mrs Bessemer was leaving and that was a giant step in the right direction. For a few minutes he allowed his pessimistic soul to feed on a few crumbs of hope.

The boys he passed on the way down to Prayers were surprised to see 'Old Horsy' smiling benignly at them. The story circulated that he had won the lottery.

Holly lay in a slight depression in the ground surrounded by ferns and the tapering trunks of young ash trees. With her hands behind her head she gazed through the canopy above her towards the powerful cobalt of the September sky. Every now and again a winged seed would spiral down from one of the dense clumps attached to the branches like pendulous nests.

The park ranger had left her to wander about on her own to 'get the feel of the place'. He was a pleasant young man; shy and obviously very keen on his job.

It was Holly's second day at King's Melcombe and there were enormous adjustments to make. The appointment had come as a surprise at the end of a day in which she was competing with five others. In spite of the fact that Richard Digby had bought her work, she had been certain they would offer it to a mature student with what appeared to be every advantage. For all she knew, Digby had bought some of his work too.

The appointment was for two years initially, longer if more funds became available. The salary was laughable but she was to be provided with a flat and one or two other perks from the estate; and fortunately there was the eight hundred pounds from the sale of her degree work. The flat overlooked the old stables and was dark and in dire need of a coat of paint; however, any amount of white paint was available so long as she did the work herself, which naturally she didn't mind.

Lying in her little dell she felt a great sense of energy pouring into her from living things. She determined to give back some of what she received; glimmerings of creative ideas absorbed her. Later she began to think about what had happened since the end of her degree course. An awful lot had changed.

On the day that she had arrived unexpectedly at Sandplace she and Emily had walked along the shore so that their conversation shouldn't disturb the strange woman who lay asleep on Emily's bed. Holly had been astonished to learn that it was Regine Monk.

'I thought you detested her,' she said.

'Yes, well. She's a poor old thing, you know. Couldn't sling her out.'

'Why did she come?'

'I'm not absolutely sure but I'm afraid I inadvertently disillusioned her about Jacko.'

'Inadvertently?' Holly glanced slyly at her grandmother.

Emily was offended. 'Yes. Inadvertently. Poor old cow.'

'It seems to be a day for being disillusioned about men.' Holly bent and picked up a flat pebble with odd mottled markings. She gazed out across a sea so calm that it perfectly mirrored the piled thunderclouds on the horizon.

'So that's why you're here. You've fallen out with young Chase.'

'Right.' Briefly Holly told Emily what had happened. The telling made her realize for the first time that she felt stupidly tearful. But crying in front of Emily just wasn't on. She bit her lip.

Emily strode on in silence for a while. Then: 'Most men look at things in an entirely different way. You have to get used to this if you're going to take one on.'

At any other time Holly might have laughed. 'A man's for life, not just for Christmas, you mean,' she said. She skimmed her pebble violently into the sea. It bounced five times and then sank. 'Anyway, I didn't say I was going to take him on,' she said fiercely. 'But I think the least he could have done was to tell me that this woman existed.'

'Have you told him about your old flames?'

'No, but that's different. They're history.'

'Gideon evidently thinks this one is too.'

'Not if she's still around, which she clearly is. It makes me wonder about him. She seemed pretty mad at him. What if he's the type who gets fed up with women very quickly and then treats them badly?'

'I can't imagine you ever giving a man permission to treat you badly,' Emily said drily.

Holly chuckled suddenly and bent to pick up another object from the cluttered high-water line. This time a distorted piece of driftwood. 'All the same, I hate muddles,' she said.

'I can believe that.'

'I was disappointed. That's why I was so mad.'

'Yes.' Emily tripped slightly over a rock, righting herself quickly without fuss. Not for the first time Holly wondered about her grandmother's sight. She glanced at her, trying not to register concern, which would only annoy Emily.

'I find it easy to talk to you,' she said. 'Mum gets too involved and upset if I tell her stuff like this.'

'I won't always be here,' Emily said. 'You realize that?'

Holly didn't want to face this possibility. No, certainty.

'I'm old, Holly,' Emily continued. 'I haven't got long. Old people have a habit of snuffing it.'

'I know. I just don't like to think about it.'

Emily laid a hand briefly on Holly's shoulder. She so rarely made a spontaneous gesture of affection that when she did, it was doubly significant. 'Don't worry. I dare say my shade won't be so easy to get rid of. I'll footle around for a bit on purpose to give you the pip.'

Holly smiled. 'Is that a promise?'

'You can be sure of it. I'm not one for religion but I have a nasty suspicion that this life is just a passing phase. A fitful fever.'

'You believe in reincarnation?'

'I don't know about that,' Emily chuckled. 'Who was it who said that if life had a second edition, how he would correct the proofs?'

'I bet he wouldn't have got it right even then.'

Hesitantly, reminded by the great scarred beach at the far end and the temporarily abandoned JCB, Holly brought up the question of where Emily was to live.

'It's all fixed,' Emily said dismissively. 'I went to see these little boxes they're offering us in East Ashpool.'

'And you don't mind?' Holly looked at her grandmother suspiciously.

'I don't suppose a year or two in what they please to call "sheltered housing" is going to hurt me.'

'That's not what you said before. Have they been getting at you?'

'Not at all. I make up my own mind.'

'I'd like to go and see where they're proposing to house you.'

Emily shrugged. 'Please yourself. You can give the show flat the once-over if you insist, though I'd rather you didn't.'

Holly fully intended to look at the place but not necessarily to tell Emily. They plodded back up the beach. It was deserted and silent except for the sluggish plop of swells unrolling on to the shore and the very distant murmurings of thunder. A hot wind had begun to blow, agitating the flat calm.

'I suppose, I better go to the phone box and ring Gideon,' Holly said. 'If there's no reply from the flat he'll call out the marines.' But she didn't seem in a hurry. 'What are you going to do about the Queen of the Night?'

'I suppose I'll have to feed her when she wakes up. Do you think she likes tuna?'

Holly rose from her quiet couch in the 'green shade' and made her way back to King's Melcombe House (available for conferences, concerts and functions). In what had once accommodated the family carriages, underneath her flat, an area had been cleared to make a studio in which she would be able to work; it was sheer luxury to have this amount of space, even though it would probably be freezing in winter. She would have to ask about heating. At the moment it was still warm enough to have the great double doors wide open. Along the back wall a bench had been installed to house her tools and equipment but nothing had been done to the floor, which consisted of granite sets which would be sheer agony. Wooden planks set across them would do for the moment; something else she'd have to negotiate for.

After being in a group for four years she would have to get used to working alone. There would be no one with whom she could discuss her ideas. On the other hand there would be no one offering destructive criticism either, or trying to persuade her into another approach altogether.

Of course there was Gideon, ten miles down the road. She had let him know of her appointment as soon as she heard but in spite of her jubilation their conversation had been stilted.

'Thank you for telling me about it in the first place,' she'd said dutifully.

'Don't mention it. Look, this deserves a celebration. How about it if I came up and took you out?' They hadn't seen each other since the Sarah débâcle.

'Mum's treating me tonight.'

'Oh.' There was a pause. 'What's wrong with another celebration tomorrow?'

'Well, I'm busy right now. I have so much sorting out and packing up to do.'

'Holly. This is ridiculous. We have to talk.'

'What about your engagement?'

'For Christ's sake!' Gideon exploded with rage. 'I'm not engaged. I never was engaged and I never intended to be engaged. At least not to Sarah. I'd just appreciate a chance to explain. For a start it's all over and it was all over just after I met you.' He went cold inside at the lie. He'd resolved not to let Holly down again. Already he was being selective with the truth.

'Sarah didn't seem to think so.'

'Well, she knows it now. I have the bruises to prove it.'

'What d'you mean. Bruises?'

'Never mind. As I said it's all over. Past history. I never mentioned her because she was no longer part of my life. It's just that she found it harder to let go than I anticipated. And it's not even that she was in love with me.' They had talked before Sarah had left and she seemed to agree that going to bed together had meant nothing; that he had only been trying to comfort her. He hoped she believed it; not that it meant he felt less of a shit if she did.

'Look, it's OK. You don't have to go on about it. I understand. These things happen.'

'So. Will you let me take you out?'

'I'd rather leave it for the moment. There's so much to think about. Arrangements to make—'

'What about the arrangements for Emily?'

'She's still refusing to move though she told me that, when it comes to it, she'll accept one of the flats at East Ashpool.'

'Have you seen them? What are they like?'

'Yes, I looked at the show flat before I left. They're all right, I suppose. Poky. I just can't imagine Em in one of them, that's all.

'Do you think I should make one more attempt to persuade her to accept my dad's hospitality?'

'Do you honestly think that would work any better?'

'No. I suppose not.' Gideon sensed she was about to ring off. 'Look, let me come over when you're installed at King's Melcombe, won't you?'

246

At least she agreed to that arrangement. Gideon resigned himself to another wait.

So now that she *was* installed at King's Melcombe she was, as promised, seeing Gideon again – not at his place but somewhere altogether more neutral, a pub precisely halfway between King's Melcombe and Winterbourne Valence.

The pub was old and timbered. Logs blazed in a huge hearth, somewhat unnecessarily as it was a mild evening, filling the air with a faint haze of wood smoke.

Holly and Gideon took their drinks to a corner table. Gideon was attentive, scrupulously avoiding physical contact.

'I want to explain about Sarah,' he said.

Holly shrugged. 'It's OK. I don't need to know.'

'I think you should give me the chance, at least.'

'All right. I'm listening.' Coolly.

Briefly, Gideon sketched in the history of his affair with Sarah.

'Even before I met you I knew things between Sarah and me had run their course. We'd been thrown together, it was fun while it lasted, but we were fundamentally different and expected quite dissimilar things from life. I thought she had accepted that a parting of the ways was inevitable. Obviously I was wrong.'

'Do you still love her?'

'No. It really is all over.' He thought about the last time he and Sarah had been together, but he could hardly tell Holly about the way in which he had tried to convince Sarah that he no longer loved her. He felt, wretchedly, that all he had done on that occasion had been to re-light a fuse that left to itself, would have eventually gone out of its own accord. He could still not altogether banish the notion that he was sitting on a bomb.

All the same, before he and Holly separated that evening, he risked a kiss and was relieved and delighted that this time she responded. He departed for Winterbourne Valence conscious of the feeling of warmth the imprint of her lips had left on his.

'That one is cheaper but this one is better value for money if you could possibly run to it,' Fern said.

The girl thought hard, looking from one candle holder to the other. One was ceramic, one was painted tin.

'It's for my mum, you see,' she said.

'Does she like trendy things?'

'No. She's more into the Laura Ashley look.' The girl, who was obviously not into the Laura Ashley look, was wearing a skimpy sweater and a long waistcoat over black leggings and her hands were encrusted with silver rings. Her hair was cut sharply and expensively short.

'I think she would prefer the ceramic one,' Fern said decisively. 'But she could always change it if you keep the receipt.'

'Oh, yes. So she could.'

As Fern took her money and put the candle holder in a one of the smart Palladian bags the girl said shyly. 'Do you like working here, Mrs Wyatt?'

Fern smiled. One of the hazards of the job at Palladian was that it was so well patronized by pupils from the independent girls' school where she had so recently taught. But she had got used to it now and had her answers ready.

'I'm breaking myself into retirement gently,' she said. 'Just part time, you know.'

'I bet you're glad you've left,' the girl said. What was her name? Michelle? Melanie? Melanie. And now Fern remembered the mother. Laura Ashley, definitely.

'I hope your mother likes the candle holder,' Fern said, passing over the leading comment as she handed Melanie the bag. 'Remember to tell her that she can change it if she brings in the receipt.' The habit of reiterating information dies hard, she thought wryly. Once a teacher, always a teacher!

'Thank you, Mrs Wyatt. I will.'

Fern at last felt quite used to dealing with credit cards, change, indecisive or obstreperous customers and being on her feet several hours a day. She had actually been astonished that she could cope at all. Not that she intended to stay at Palladian indefinitely, but it would do for the time being. Since Italy it was slowly sinking in that teaching was very probably not her only skill.

Deciding to take a leap into the unknown and retire early had been only one of the string of decisions Fern had been forced to make in the last few months; not without a great deal of pushing and shoving from Holly and Audrey, she had to admit. Celia had remained infuriatingly noncommittal.

'Are you asking my permission?' she had said.

'No. Of course not.'

'It's a decision you have to make for yourself.'

'Yes. I realize that.'

There had been a long silence. Celia was good at silence. They trained you to be, probably. To demonstrate the contrast between the futile busyness of her own mind and the composure of normality? But she couldn't put her hand on her heart and claim that the choices were hers alone.

Once in Italy she had gradually set aside her habitual anxieties as she removed her jerseys and cardigans and donned summer clothes and the straw hat she'd bought in a little hilltop town. It wasn't so difficult. The shape of her days had been decided for her: meals around the long table in the courtyard under the vines, painting, rests, lectures, demonstrations, outings. Back at the flat it would be different. She would have to arrange her days to fit her new circumstances. On this point Celia was much more forthcoming.

'You have to create your own structure,' she'd said. 'You've lived for years with the routine of teaching and caring for Holly but that's all changed now.'

'You think I didn't do the right thing, giving up teaching?'

'That's all behind you. You've dealt with that. It's past.'

For the first time Fern felt a stirring of resentment towards Celia. She wasn't much more than a kid. What did she know about the problems one faced as one got older?

Celia was smiling. 'You look cross.'

'Do you have to be a mind-reader as well?'

'It's supposed to be part of the job.'

'Well, I wish you wouldn't.'

Celia felt a rush of optimism about her client. At last she was showing signs of rebellion, or at least something other than the initial all-pervasive apathy. 'Your holiday's done you good,' she said. 'What now?'

With a continuing sense of stubborn independence Fern decided not to tell Celia about the possibility of a job at Palladian. Holly had told her that as soon as the new term began the students who had been working there for the summer would leave and that there would be vacancies as a result.

'I never worked in a shop,' she said immediately Holly had suggested it.

'I never worked in a shop either until two years ago.'

'Don't you have to be young and trendy?'

'The boss is getting a bit fed up with young and trendy,' Holly said. 'She says they aren't reliable. Besides, you're not untrendy. You've looked really good since you came back from Italy. Sort of continental.'

'Well, thank you.' She reached across and laid a hand on Holly's strong brown one. 'I shall miss you, won't I?'

'You'll be all right?' The thick, dark eyebrows registered anxiety on her behalf. Fern had seen that expression too often.

'Of course I will. I've been such a pain lately. And, darling—'

'Yes?'

'Thank you for all you've done. I know it hasn't been easy for you.'

Holly cleared her throat, shrugged. 'It wasn't anything.'

'And then there's Emily. You think she'll be all right in the sheltered housing? Now I'm better I can at least take that responsibility off you. Do you think I should go down to see?'

'Not for that reason, no. She hates fuss. And I got the impression that she doesn't want too many people to see what the great Emily Troy's been reduced to. Though it would be nice if you went to see her before she moves.'

'The new place can't be worse than an old railway carriage, surely?'

'In her eyes it is. But she would have had to accept it sooner or later anyway.'

'Why?'

'She tries to hide it but I think she's losing her sight.'

There was a silence. 'I see,' Fern said at last. 'Oh dear. Poor Emily.' For the first time for many years she felt a stirring of a feeling for her mother. She wasn't absolutely sure what the feeling was.

So she hadn't been down to see Emily. She knew that the visits to her grandmother had become important to Holly; she decided not to interfere. Instead she went to see Holly's boss at Palladian and, much to her surprise, had been taken on.

On the way back home at lunchtime she stopped at Waitrose. At the newsagents round the corner from the flat she bought a *Guardian* and some stamps; as she left the shop she scanned the noticeboard, filled as always with items and services for sale or wanted: large pine kitchen table and set of chairs, £250: student wanted to share flat, non-smoker: your ironing dealt with, will collect and deliver. At the bottom was a fuzzy snapshot of kittens: 'Good homes required for kittens. Two left.'

Fern passed on, hurrying home with her purchases. Kittens indeed. Whatever next!

'These are all the remaining letters,' Regine said. 'I've marked the relevant passages and where I want them included. It shouldn't take long.'

Zak, crouched over the word processor, grunted.

'I shall lie down for an hour or two but I shall be available at half-past four if there are any queries.'

Zak glanced at her. There was no doubt in his mind that the old girl was headed for the last round-up, was about to hand in her dinner pail. Not a word had been said to him (though it wouldn't be, would it?) but as far as he knew his employer's condition wasn't discussed by the family either. Could it be that the disintegration had been so gradual they hadn't noticed or had noticed but couldn't accept the fact that even Regine Monk had to pop her clogs sometime? The thought cheered him up no end.

'You're doing well, Zak. We've practically finished,' she went on. 'Perhaps you'd be so kind as to post that letter to the publisher.'

As she passed his chair on her way out, she brushed a hand affectionately over his hair, which was blond again, just as she used to do before the business over the paintings. It was weird. While virtually holding him to ransom she still occasionally touched him in the same way as she always had; as if nothing had changed. He used to wonder if she fully realized their sexual nature but had come to the conclusion that of course she did. Nothing Regine Monk did was accidental. And he couldn't claim that she had failed absolutely to turn him on, ancient though she was. He wondered if that made him some kind of pervert. But now it was as if she were playing a game. He didn't completely trust her, it was possible her game was too devious to comprehend, even for him. He had been forced to rely on her word that, once the book was finished, the paintings would be restored to him unconditionally, and without a word to the police. Or anyone with an interest in them. He was inclined to believe her if only because he knew that she was not the sort of conscientious citizen who would see it as her duty to call in the authorities no matter what. All her actions were calculated to benefit Regine Monk first and foremost and secondly to preserve the memory of A. J. Monk himself. At one time he would have reversed those priorities but lately it had become very apparent that she was a great deal keener to emphasize her own part in the great man's fortunes than previously; and very much more likely to include some of his less endearing traits than before. The new image of the painter that was emerging as a result was almost human. Zak wondered what had precipitated the change.

Of course he could have played the whole thing differently. He could have employed the threatened strong-arm tactics but, besides being not quite his thing, it would certainly have endangered the whole setup. Enquiries would have been set in motion and he would most probably have lost the paintings anyway, might even have finished up doing time. As it was, things were panning out almost better than he could have hoped. The delay in actually producing the Chase paintings had worked to his advantage in the end. The dealer had been mad as hell over their non-delivery and had accused Zak of stalling to raise the price. In the interim he had been approached directly by the buyer, or by his representative, who suggested that they cut out the dealer altogether.

Zak had agreed that he would consider this offer seriously, which had the advantage of giving him more time. The buyer, who was a rich American collector, anonymous not surprisingly, was very keen and didn't mind waiting. These leisurely dealings suited Zak far better than negotiating with the tetchy dealer who behaved like a nervous rat.

A penultimate meeting with the collector's man had been fixed, when final details would be ironed out: how payment would be arranged, how the paintings would be handed over. It pleased

Zak's sense of theatre that the meeting would take place on the Cobb at Lyme Regis; and the collector's representative hadn't even raised an eyebrow, as if he were in the habit of doing business on windswept breakwaters.

Zak pressed the keys that would store another batch of material on disk, leaned back and rubbed his hands over his short thatch of hair. He caught sight of Fergus standing at the door.

'What you want?' he growled. He had never been a hundred per cent sure that the boy hadn't in fact had something to do with the discovery of the Chase paintings. Could he have got over his fear of rats and gone poking about in the old stables?

'D'you want some help?'

'No. Sod off.'

'I could put all those papers back in the box files.'

It was a job Zak detested. 'OK,' he said laconically. 'Only make sure they go back in chronological order. You do know what chronological means, I take it?'

'Sure I do. Then can I have a go on the VDU?' These days he was sometimes allowed to play Solitaire or Battleships.

'Maybe,' was all Zak said.

Fergus's status at Burr Ash had been subtly upgraded. Ever since he had shown Grandmère how disks and the printer worked, her attitude to him had changed and it occurred to him that her attitude to Zak had changed too. Like in a game of snakes and ladders. Almost as if while Zak had slid down a snake, Fergus had ascended a ladder. He wished he knew why. He had made every effort to find out in what way Zak had fallen from grace but was still as much in the dark as ever. All he knew was that it had started soon after he'd got pissed. Perhaps it was because he'd stood up to Grandmère.

'You leaving soon?' he asked Zak boldly.

'Why d'you ask?'

'The book's nearly finished and the exhibition's fixed up.'

'Yea, well. Probably.'

'Where'll you go? Have you got another job?'

Zak shrugged hugely, as a man who could afford to take another job or not, as he pleased. 'I might go into the City. Or I might travel around for a bit.'

'What would you do for money?'

Zak looked at Fergus contemptuously. 'You're a nosy little bugger, aren't you? Anyway, as it happens, I shan't be short of the folding stuff.'

'Won't you? I didn't think Grandmère was paying you that much.'

Zak crowed with laughter. 'That old skinflint! You're joking!'

Fergus was shocked. He'd never previously heard Zak utter a breath of criticism of his grandmother. 'Have you won the lottery or something?' he asked.

'A sort of lottery. Only there's a bloody sight more skill attached to this one.'

'What is it?'

Zak realized abruptly that his desire to impress the kid was getting the better of his judgement. He turned his attention to the screen.

'Never mind,' he said, signalling that the conversation was at an end by a flourish of tapping on the keyboard.

'Forget it.' He shoved the letter to the publishers to the end of the desk without taking his eyes off the monitor. 'Here, take this down to the postbox, will you? And don't for Christ's sake lose it. It's important.' It was doubly important to Zak. It informed the editor that the biography of A. J. Monk would be on her desk in a little under ten days. And it signified his freedom.

Inside the house there was an unusual flurry of activity. Arlette had taken up her mother's customary tray of tea and had found her sprawled, shockingly inelegant, across the bed, retching drily. Auriel had been roused from a torpor of potato peeling and ordered to telephone Dr Griffith without delay.

Half an hour later Dr Griffith's dark blue BMW slid into the yard.

The chain saw ripped into the massive piece of oak, practically half a tree, slicing off a branch, leaving only a small stump. The air was full of the resiny smell of sawdust. Holly, wearing protective visor, gloves and boots, was reducing the giant log to a rough shape to be worked on later. Probably two years later, but oak was kinder to tools when it was green. It became harder as it seasoned. Her tutor – ex-tutor – would have had a seizure. Not only was she not getting rid of the craft aspect and what he described as 'the object', she was positively exulting in the despised activities of the *artisan*. In between times, when she hadn't been feeling vitriolic towards him, she had a certain sympathy with her tutor's point of view. At least part of the intention in theory had been to get rid of the art product, to defeat the acquisitive art market, but in practice it simply hadn't worked out like that. When Marcel Duchamp had jokingly exhibited a urinal as long ago as 1917, it was immediately claimed by the art establishment as a desirable thing of beauty. His cultural descendants were still the darlings of that same establishment.

Meanwhile, not being one for games of irony and wordplay, Holly went her own way, hoping to get to grips with the substance, make her own discoveries at a level other than the intellect which 'knew' yet didn't understand. At least so she believed.

She was indulging in a little forward planning, as one had to. The immediate projects would begin to take shape in the next few weeks, the most important being a living summerhouse in an existing clearing at the end of a long irregular avenue of trees called The Glade that was one of the sights of King's Melcombe. The summerhouse was to be made of planted saplings which would eventually be canted over at an angle and the branches pruned and woven to create the roof. As well as her own creative activities, and in spite of her declared aversion to teaching, the part of her programme she was becoming very enthusiastic about was a series of visits by local school children when she would be talking to them about her work and putting on demonstrations in which they could take part.

Loneliness hadn't been much of a problem after all. The estate was a community in itself, most of the employees were friendly, interested in her work and ready enough to talk about theirs. It wasn't so different from college after all.

This morning she was busy in what had once been the stable yard. The weather was overcast and misty but not cold, and although it was early October King's Melcombe was very far from closing down. In fact the Visitor Centre on the other side of the house was at its busiest at this time of year. The autumn colours in the arboretum were a big attraction and the car park was packed with cars and coaches every day from ten until five. The limes already wore a livery of sulphur yellow and the maples would soon be at their best; a blaze of crimson, orange and gold.

The Visitor Centre was a new building, circular in design and constructed with timber from the estate. Inside was a huge plan of the grounds with a number of suggested walks. It indicated trees of special interest, amongst them a massive tulip tree, a dawn redwood, a handkerchief tree and, in a sheltered dell, some tree ferns, all rescued from threatened annihilation by the years of neglect. On a separate noticeboard was a photocopy of the press release concerning Holly's appointment. There was also a slightly out-of-focus photograph of her, together with very much clearer ones of her degree work. She had been invited to supply a short comment in which she outlined some of her plans.

'It's a nice change not to be asked for a bloody "rationale",' she'd told Emily. 'Here they at least trust me to act as a professional.'

She pushed up her visor and glanced at her watch; then she laid down her chain saw, took off her gloves and dusted the fragrant sawdust from her arms. There would be just time to clear up, shower and change before Gideon turned up. Now that Fern had reclaimed the Metro, Holly was left with her bicycle as chief mode of transport so had been obliged to accept lifts from Gideon. They had met only twice since the evening in the pub, and the atmosphere between them had become steadily easier. They had talked mostly about their work, the Sarah affair was receding. At about eleven he would drive her back to King's Melcombe, kiss her, ever more passionately, promise to phone and would then disappear down the long drive that led to the lodge gates.

Today it was to be different; today he was coming to help her paint the sitting room of her flat which she had left until last; she had already spent a large part of her weekends sloshing white paint on the kitchen, bathroom and bedroom. She admitted that white was not very enterprising but her creative talents were engaged elsewhere at the moment and besides, anything was better than the dismal ochre colour (that might once have been cream) with which the whole flat had been smothered, as if it had been dipped in a vat of mouldy custard.

After her shower she put on another set of working clothes, thrust a handful of spaghetti into boiling water and put on the sauce

to warm through. As she grated some cheese she saw Gideon's blue
Volvo turn into the yard. He came bounding up the stairs and kissed
her.

'How's it going?'

She handed him a glass of plonk. 'Fine.' She carried on grating.

He wandered round, glass in hand. 'It looks like a different place
already. Furniture's a bit basic but you can't have everything.'

'It's how I like it. Clutter does my head in. It's ready. Come and
eat.'

The spaghetti didn't detain them for long. Afterwards they took
their coffee into the sitting room where she had already covered
what furniture there was with dustsheets. They contemplated the
task in hand as they drank their coffee.

'There's still some sanding to do. Then I thought we'd get a first
coat on and finish off tomorrow. Can you spare tomorrow?' she
asked him. Gideon had had to work through the last two weekends
to get an urgent job finished.

'The downside of being self-employed,' he'd said then. Now, he
said, 'For you, anything.'

'Oh, yes?'

For two hours they sanded and painted. Holly had tied a scarf
over her hair and was wearing a man's checked shirt which just
skimmed the bottom of her shorts. Her brown legs, increasingly
speckled with white, disappeared into the thick black cuffs of her
socks and a pair of disreputable trainers. Gideon found the sight
distracting but he struggled manfully on, recharging his roller and
spreading white over the corpse-coloured walls.

Holly laid down her paint tray.

'I've finished my wall,' she said. 'I'll make some tea.'

'Good thinking, Batman.' Meticulously, Gideon began to fill in
round the edges with a small brush.

Holly went into the kitchen, made the tea and put the mugs out
on the kitchen table together with some buns she'd bought in the
Visitor Centre café.

They drank the tea and ate the buns perched on the only two
chairs the kitchen possessed. From a side window they had a
glimpse of the park beyond. In the mist the crimsons and the
yellows and greens were like a dissolving tapestry.

'So you won't be going back to Bath this weekend?' Gideon said, studying her over the rim of his mug. 'Or down to see Em?'

'Not with all this painting to do. It'll take all tomorrow, even with you helping. Besides, it's not so easy without the car, though I'm sure Mum would let me borrow it if I asked.'

'You should get some wheels of your own.'

'Oh, yeah? I suppose my year's salary would just about cover it.'

'I'll look out for something cheaper for you, if you like. There's a chap in the village who has a repair shop. I could ask him. Anyway, I reckon we could knock this painting on the head by lunchtime tomorrow if we started early, say eight thirty. Then we could do as we pleased, even go down to see Em, if you like.'

'Eight thirty?'

'If I stayed the night we could manage that, couldn't we?' He glanced at her. She had pulled off her scarf and was thrusting her fingers into her black mop of hair, massaging her scalp.

She re-filled their mugs without answering.

'What d'you say?' he persisted.

'I suppose you could use my sleeping bag.'

'Bugger your sleeping bag! I wasn't thinking of using your sleeping bag.'

She paced round the room, her mug clasped in paint-smeared fingers.

'OK,' she said at last.

'Don't go hog wild!'

She grinned. 'I said OK, didn't I?'

'Well, thank God for that.'

Standing behind his chair she gave his pigtail a tweak. He reached round and captured her by the waist, sliding her onto his lap. He kissed her ear. 'Let's go to bed.'

'What about clearing up the painting things?'

'Sod the clearing up.'

They went into her spartan bedroom where the only furniture was the bed Holly had brought from her bedroom in the Bath flat, her old desk and some cheap kelims. On the windowsill stood a pot of geraniums; that and the patchwork counterpane on the bed had come from the spare room in Sandplace; on the walls hung Emily's two paintings. Because she would have only one bedroom and a small sitting room in her sheltered accommodation, Emily had been through her possessions, either ruthlessly discarding or insisting that Holly take anything she fancied.

Gideon removed the counterpane and folded it, placing it on the chair Holly had cobbled together from driftwood picked up on the beach at the Saltings and which was remarkably sturdy.

Holly held up the scarf she had recently taken off. 'Now it's your turn,' she said.

'What's this? Strip poker? OK then.' Grinning, he removed a shoe.

She took off her watch.

'That doesn't count,' he said.

'Take yours off then.'

'I already did. I didn't want it covered in paint.'

'Tough.'

He removed his other shoe.

They continued until Holly was reduced to her knickers and Gideon, for some reason, to one sock. By this time the game had become of secondary importance.

'You're like your carvings,' he said, running his palms down her rounded thighs. 'All chunky and brown.'

'Oh, great,' she murmured.

'In a sort of sensational way.'

She pulled him gently towards her, her hands behind his shoulders. His physique reflected his profession; it had made his shoulders well-muscled while his hands remained those of a draughtsman. She felt them on her breasts.

They took their time, time to get accustomed to one another's bodies and rhythms.

Gideon had not been entirely successful in banishing the memory of the evening he'd spent with Sarah. He'd been a complete bloody idiot. And a shit, treating Sarah as a sort of substitute for Holly. His actions did not in any way coincide with his previous image of himself as a decent bloke who respected women. He had sweated blood at the thought of the hold Sarah might now feel she had over him. She might even see it as her duty to tell Holly.

His guilty feelings began to subside as he held Holly close. Other,

259

more powerful, urges took their place. All the same, he must be careful not to rush things; he had looked forward to the moment for too long. Last time he had made the mistake of planning it too carefully; he had been in a hurry. Today, nothing had been planned, it was all happening spontaneously; he could allow his fingers the leisure to explore the strong contours of her body. Having to learn to rely on him not to behave in the rough-and-ready manner of her former lovers, she was slow to arousal but once excited she was fiery; he realized that under the sensible, pragmatic exterior was a highly passionate woman. A woman who could be hurt. He wasn't surprised that she was wary of men. He hoped he wouldn't let her down.

Exhausted by their final fierce ardour, they lay side by side, holding each other on the narrow bed. Before he slept Gideon turned to look at her. Her eyes were closed and a few beads of sweat lay along her upper lip. Something about being allowed to witness her off guard made his heart, an organ to which he'd so far paid little heed, contract in sympathy. It was a new and slightly disturbing experience.

Emily swept an accumulation of sand off the verandah. Sandplace had been well-named, for sand was the one drawback of living there, especially after a stiff westerly. Even set on its brick piers it still seemed to be subject to the beach's determination to transfer itself to Emily's verandah, her kitchen, even to her bed.

She had spent the morning clearing up. During Holly's last visit Emily had casually hinted that she could help herself to what she wanted for her new flat, never believing that any of her possessions would have any appeal whatever to the young. She'd been surprised when Holly had taken the ancient and now quite fragile patchwork counterpane and the two paintings.

'I want to have something you made yourself,' she'd said. *Not* adding, Emily noted with a smile, 'to remember you by.'

There was still a phenomenal amount of rubbish to be thrown out for the dustmen; how could she have accumulated so much? But Sandplace was now pared down, stripped of everything except the few possessions that would fit into the miserly space she'd been allocated. The usual clutter had disappeared from the dresser: the pieces of driftwood and the interesting pebbles had been returned to the beach whence they'd come; the pots of geraniums had been emptied or handed on to Holly.

The broom was still. Emily shaded her eyes, gazing towards the horizon, but the beach, the sea and the sky melted into undifferentiated bands of sepia, chartreuse and smoke grey, a soft-edged abstract. Monet must have had a similar view of the world in the last years but it hadn't improved his work. He destroyed the panels painted at the time a cataract had dimmed his sight.

Sometimes she sat on the verandah, oblivious to the cool autumnal weather, her hands in her lap, forcing herself to face the kind of truth Monet himself had once had to come to terms with, fighting down the storms of panic. She was not one to lose her head. She had come eyeball to eyeball with goodness knows how many hopeless situations in the past, and survived; but each time at a cost. Each time something had been lost, been stripped away: her children; David, the only man she'd ever truly loved; now her sight.

She had put off going to the optician's for glasses because she couldn't believe she really needed them – her sight had always been exceptional. And also because such a visit would mean cycling to East Ashpool followed by a tedious bus journey to Exeter; but when reading a letter from Francis became almost as troublesome as the journey and took almost as long, she gave in. Last March she had finally made the appointment.

The ophthalmologist had broken the bad news gently.

'Senile macular degeneration is not uncommon,' she said, 'but unlike most cases of cataract there is no cure or corrective measures available at the moment.'

Emily had not quite taken it in at first. 'So I'll need glasses?'

'Certainly spectacles will help in the short term.'

'Do you mean to say I'm going to lose my sight entirely?'

'You may well retain some sight until the end of your life. It appears to be developing quite slowly.'

'But it *will* get worse?'

'Gradual loss of vision is the usual pattern but I'm afraid I couldn't possibly say how long the process will take. I'm sorry I can't be more specific – or more reassuring.' The ophthalmologist glanced at her client; she was used to all kinds of responses to news of this kind, tears, shock, disbelief, resignation.

Emily stood up. 'When do I call back for the spectacles?'

'We'll do them while you wait. Have you any shopping?'

'No.' She had gone to see an exhibition at the museum instead. English landscapes. Green blurs. It had been a mistake.

Senile degeneration indeed. Although she didn't go in for looking-glasses much at Sandplace, one was bound to notice the ageing of one's body if by chance one should be unfortunate enough to catch sight of it. On the whole she reckoned hers wasn't too hideous for an octogenarian, though naturally she wasn't comparing her appearance with other eighty-year-olds but with herself at forty, at thirty, at twenty. Senile degeneration of any sort was what happened to other people; to the old.

She had long ago decided that although she expected no special dispensation that made it possible to deny the years, she would never be the sort of 'old' that gave other people the right to visit all manner of indignities upon one. Not losing control was the thing. The last independent choice one had was that of determining, as far as one could, the manner of one's going. She loved life. Given the choice she was game for as many healthy years as fate decreed but now it looked as if she'd rather outstayed her welcome on the planet. 'They' were already dictating where she should live and what possessions she should take with her. But she had outwitted those faceless fates because she had a secret weapon. And because she had Holly, who was part of it. As for her, Emily Troy, it would soon be time to get on to the next thing. Whatever that was.

She heard the clatter of the JCB. It was nearer now, an amorphous yellow blob.

'I'm tellin' 'ee,' Mr Watts had said. ''Tis a proper scoud-up, downalong. They don't know what they'm up to.'

But today, except for the unknown JCB operator, the beach was devoid of all human presence. The surge of the waves breaking endlessly and the plaintive call of seabirds remained.

CHAPTER TWENTY

Auriel folded her hands together in her lap, tightening them until her knuckles showed white. Her hands had once been a matter of pride, graceful and long-fingered, but now they were reddened, the joints knotty, the nails worn down and chalky.

She had slipped upstairs to her room, away from the atmosphere of suppressed consternation that prevailed in the rest of the house, meaning to fortify herself from her bedside cupboard; but she had changed her mind, needing to savour to the full, just this once, the import of what was taking place. Alcohol provided not an absence of pain but a veil between the pain and her full realization of it. A life without edges. Suddenly she had needed to know, if only briefly, what her feelings actually were, for there was something about them she didn't understand.

Maman was dying. This was a fact.

Maman was dying and she, Auriel, was grieving. They were all grieving, especially Arlette, whom everybody acknowledged was closest to Maman. Yet Arlette carried on tirelessly, working even harder than usual because of all the extra washing, the running up and down stairs, remembering Maman's tablets, taking up trays of tempting morsels, which were inevitably returned with their contents untouched. Poor Maman. Poor Arlette.

It went without saying that Auriel did her share. She also was kept busy from morning till night, and took turns with Arlette through the night too. But unlike Arlette's selfless activity, Auriel knew hers to be guilt-driven.

She clenched her hands even more tightly together as if she held within them the terrible explosive joy; an exultation that would keep surfacing through the grief. The brightness in her eyes she hoped would be put down to unshed tears as Regine slowly withdrew to a place where no one, not even Arlette, could reach her.

Auriel had no idea where this ignoble and wholly unexpected exhilaration came from; she would never have suspected herself of harbouring such a heartless and unfilial reaction to the prospect of Maman's imminent death. It couldn't possibly have originated merely from that last intimate scene with her mother when Regine had accused her of being an alcoholic and told her to pull herself together or get treatment.

'If Jacko could rise above it, so can you,' she'd said, her contempt apparent. 'And don't think I haven't known all along. For it will certainly please you that Fergus refused to tell me where he obtained that bottle. I must say, I was quite impressed by the boy's loyalty. There's more to him than I thought.'

Since then Auriel had tried to be especially kind to Fergus even though previously she had rather disliked him.

Now Regine had only days to live, according to Evan Griffith. Each day and sometimes twice a day he came to administer the injections of morphine. He nevertheless remarked on the clarity of Regine's mind and her tenacious hold on what life remained to her.

When Dr Griffith had broken the news it had shocked the household. Nobody believed that Maman would live for ever – of course not, she was an old lady – but in the last few months she had seemed so full of energy, applying herself tirelessly to finishing Jacko's biography, driving Zak to extra effort quite remorselessly. With hindsight it had to be acknowledged that it was almost as if she knew death was on her heels. Auriel suspected that not only had Dr Griffith known beforehand, but Maman too. The doctor certainly hadn't appeared surprised. The change in Maman since the book had been finished and packed off to the publisher had been dramatic. She shrank before their eyes. Now it was very nearly the end.

Auriel forced down the invasive visions of life without Maman but they would keep breaking through like hot springs through mud, bursting unbidden through the layer of shock and grief. No wonder she was consumed with guilt. She felt like a betrayer.

Another member of the Burr Ash household was contemplating

Regine's last illness almost completely without dismay. For him it was a deliverance.

Zak was packing. It would not take long, he was a man who liked to travel light. The last two weeks had tested even his steady nerve but it had all turned out right in the end. The old girl had come across after all. As soon as the manuscript was submitted she had written a letter to her bank who duly released the attaché case that contained the two paintings. He had examined them minutely, still suspecting that she'd pulled a fast one at the last moment. But it was all in order; he'd be able to deliver as agreed and the money would be handed over. Months, years, of effort and planning would pay off far more handsomely than if he'd negotiated through the dealer. In a very short time now he would be a very rich man. Certainly richer than the dreams of a boy from a Wolverhampton estate would normally aspire to.

Tenderly, he padded the bottom of his bag with his underclothes and laid the case containing the paintings on the top, which he then covered with his folded shirts and chinos. This time next month he'd be able to bin this pathetic clobber; by that time he'd have some pretty expensive gear on his back. He pushed his sponge bag down the side and zipped up the bag. He was ready for the off.

The man he'd met on the Cobb in Lyme Regis hadn't been what Zak had expected. He was much younger than he'd anticipated, about his own age in fact, and informally dressed in faded jeans and an old ski jacket with 'Gstaad' embroidered on the sleeve.

At the last moment Zak had worried about the weather and cursed himself for a theatrical idiot for not thinking of it before. It could be raining or blowing a gale for all he knew and there was too much at stake to be distracted by extraneous detail. Elemental considerations did not usually come into his scheme of things.

But the weather had come good. Dull and overcast but no rain. There weren't many people about either, the summer visitors had departed, and though there were a few Saga coaches in the car park, few of the passengers braved the walk along the Cobb. Zak and the representative of the American collector, who said his name was Guy, were in almost sole possession.

'Ever see *The French Lieutenant's Woman*?' the man asked. He was fresh-faced, like an overgrown schoolboy.

'No.'

'It was filmed here.'

'Oh, right.'

'Meryl Streep. Good actress.'

'Yeah.'

'Did you see her in *Postcards From the Edge*? That was a cracker of a film.'

'Look, let's cut the Barry frigging Norman spiel and get the show on the road, shall we?'

Guy got the message at last and broke off his movie reminiscences. 'Right,' he said briskly. 'My employer has studied the photographs you sent. He says they look good.'

'They are good, dammit.'

'Of course you realize my employer won't expect to pay the inflated prices the paintings would fetch at auction? There's a risk attached, you know.'

'Very little for him. A lot for me, as I'm quite sure he realizes.'

'He understands. He's a fair man.' Guy grinned boyishly. 'Besides, he might want to do business with you again.'

Zak lowered his lashes on the brightening of his eyes. 'Suits me. So what sort of figure are we talking about?'

'My employer suggested a million and a quarter for the Cézanne.'

Zak looked disdainful. 'I'm surprised. They were fetching more than that ten years ago.'

'At auction. Remember that for you it'll be clear profit.'

'Not entirely. I've had to sit on them too long for my liking.' All the same, one and a quarter was a better offer than he'd expected. It would be to his advantage to clinch it rather than to haggle and risk losing the deal. They paced up to the end of the Cobb while Zak thought. Below them the sea creamed over rocks and besieged the massive blocks of Portland stone of which the Cobb was built. A crabber negotiated the narrow entrance to the harbour. The two men stood watching.

'I'll go for it,' Zak said.

Guy nodded. 'Great! I think it's a fair offer,' he said, adding coyly, 'in view of the circumstances.'

'What about the Chagall?' Zak asked, watching the crabber tie up.

'Well, less, I'm afraid, but you expected that, of course?'

In low voices they came to terms over the Chagall.

'Now about the handover,' Guy said. He reached into his jacket and fished out a notebook, leafing through the pages. 'I take it you are now in possession of the paintings?'

'Yes.' Zak squinted at his companion, thinking how the man's appearance and manner concealed the cool business-like brain ticking away underneath.

'How about today week? That suit you?' It was all so matter-of-fact; as if he were arranging an appointment with the doctor for a minor ailment.

'Suits me. Same place?'

'I think not. Just a bit too public, don't you think? And if it's raining—'

'Yes. Right. Of course. What about the car park at the top of the town?'

'Brilliant. Ideal.' Again the public schoolboy.

At Burr Ash Zak looked round the room without regret. In less than a week now he would be a millionaire. After two years of enough boredom to last a lifetime, incarcerated with a family of basket cases in the backside of nowhere, he frigging well deserved to be rich. At least the chap Guy hadn't turned out to be acting for some bloody insurance outfit when he would have been paid off with a pittance for delivering the goods, under the threat of being reported to the cops. Caution remained absolutely vital but he would hardly be human if there weren't moments when he almost lost his cool at the prospect of the final pay-off. He'd come a long way but this was only the start.

He picked up his bags and turned his back on the room that had been his for longer than he had at first reckoned on. In the passage outside he met Fergus.

'You leaving?' Fergus said.

'Yes. Glad to see the back of me?'

Fergus looked suspiciously at Zak's bags. 'There's a car in the yard.'

'It's my taxi.'

'Where're you going?'

'What's it to you? Don't worry, your mother has a forwarding address.'

Zak tilted his head towards Regine's room. 'Tell her I said goodbye,' he said. 'I had quite a soft spot for the old girl.'

'Tell her yourself.'

At that moment Arlette came out of the sick room carrying a cloth-covered bowl. She looked distractedly at them both for a second before she spoke.

'Are you off, Zak?' she said in a whisper, glancing over her shoulder.

'Just going. Goodbye, Arlette.'

'Oh, yes. Goodbye,' her attention already elsewhere. 'Thank you for helping Maman. Fergus hurry. Grandmère wants you.'

In the kitchen Auriel was pouring hot water into a large brown teapot. Donald came in with his arms full of logs. He had left his assistant to mind the shop for a couple of days.

'You leaving now,' he said to Zak, dumping his logs into the sagging basket.

'Yep. That's my taxi.'

Donald actually came across and shook hands. 'Well, all the best. We appreciate the way you helped Maman with the book. Most grateful. And you've left a forwarding address?'

'Arlette has it. It's a friend's place in London but it'll find me for the time being. Right, I'm off. Ciao.'

Without looking back, he strode out of the kitchen, chucked his bags into the back of the waiting car and slid in after them. The taxi swept out of the yard and disappeared.

Inside the kitchen Donald stood at the window staring out. 'That's funny,' he said. 'I was convinced he'd stay until after Maman's will was read.'

'Maman's will!' Auriel stared at her brother-in-law, her eyes wide. Just in time she realized the teapot was about to overflow. 'Maman's *will*?'

'Auriel, you know Maman can't last above a day or two. You have to face it.'

Auriel's eyes filled with tears. 'Sometimes you can be absolutely heartless, Donald,' she said.

Donald lifted his shoulders fractionally, studying his worn suede boots.

'Did Alain say when he would be arriving?' Auriel said. She

arranged four cups while she waited for the tea to brew.

'He didn't commit himself. Just said he wanted us to ring tonight after Dr Griffith had been.'

'But you told him how ill poor Maman is?'

'Oh, yes. But you know Alain. He wouldn't want to waste time and money coming down before it's absolutely necessary.'

Unsteadily Auriel began to fill the cups. 'If he leaves it much longer it'll be too late.'

'Now who's being heartless?' Donald said.

Regine reached out a hand to touch Fergus. Realizing what was expected, Fergus took it cautiously as if afraid at its fragility. He found it hard to believe that anything so insubstantial could actually be alive, for the hand was just a collection of mouselike bones and some threads of blue veins encased in a skin so fine that it was no more than a mist over what lay beneath. His grandmother's face had altered dramatically as well; her round forehead and high cheekbones jutted like miniature mountain ranges about the great blue hollows into which her eyes seemed to have sunk. Almost worse was her hair. It had been arranged in two plaits on either side of her head. There was a lot less of it too, confirming Fergus's belief that she had previously worn some kind of hairpiece. Round her temples half an inch of white now showed. Her head was resting on a great heap of pillows and she looked like an incredibly ancient schoolgirl. Fergus could smell not only her lavender oil scent (his grandfather would tolerate only flower perfumes on his women) but something else underlying it, something he found both sinister and repellent.

Yet he continued to sit beside her bed, holding her hand.

'Fergus?' Regine spoke in a whisper. The enormous marble-veined lids lifted and a cat's-paw of pain disturbed her features.

'I'm here, Grandmère.'

'I'm afraid I asked your mother to keep you home from school. I wanted to talk to you, you see.'

'That's OK.' In fact this was one occasion when Fergus would have been glad to go to school. His father had driven the girls off to theirs an hour ago.

'How old were you last birthday?' Again the whispering voice.

'Thirteen. I'm nearly fourteen.' Extraordinary, her not remembering.

'Thirteen. You're growing up.'

'I take GCSEs the year after next.'

'So you do.' Her eyes burned into his in the old way for just a moment but he wasn't afraid. On the contrary, he felt strong and full of life.

'Listen,' she said. 'Burr Ash will be yours some day. You'll be master of all this.' She moved her head ever so slightly.

'Will it? What about Uncle Alain?'

The veined lids drooped. 'Alain is not interested.' There was just a hint of the usual asperity when she spoke of her only son.

A long pause followed while Regine gathered her strength. Then: 'But you will have to work hard at school. If you don't prepare yourself all this will be taken away.'

'Who will take it away?'

'It's the way of the world. Do you understand?'

Fergus nodded, then doubtful about how much she could see he added a 'yes.' It dawned on him that his grandmother had lost her French accent while they'd been talking.

'Of course you do. You're a bright boy. I've always known it.' There was another long pause. She seemed to have gone to sleep but just as he was about to disentangle his hand, her eyes were open again.

'I wanted to see you in order to thank you for helping me out with the computer. I couldn't have done that alone.'

'There was Zak,' Fergus said, hoping to lead his grandmother into an explanation as to why precisely it had been important that Zak's help had *not* been sought on that occasion. But he was disappointed. She merely called him a 'good boy' and reiterated her thanks.

'That's OK,' he said. 'Anytime.' Then realizing the fatuousness of that remark he flushed crimson.

She smiled. Another spasm twisted her features and she turned her face away as if to hide it. When she'd recovered she said, 'I expect you know I'm dying, Fergus?'

Fergus didn't know what to say. He looked at the floor.

'It's all right, you know,' she went on. 'We all have to die sometime. It's not something of which we should be afraid. A very wise old lady reminded me of that quite recently.' She paused, waiting for another spasm to pass. Fergus guessed that her injection was wearing off. She seemed to sleep. The smell that he'd noticed before, beneath the masking scent of lavender, potpourri and clean linen came to him again like an acrid reminder. He knew it was the odour of dying. He laid her hand aside as a preliminary to making his escape.

'I'm proud of you, Fergus,' her voice came suddenly. 'I think you will do well in whatever walk of life you choose.'

'Thanks, Grandmère.' He hesitated feeling that something more was required of him. 'I'm going downstairs now. Is there anything I can get?'

Regine moved her head from side to side. 'No, dear. Thank you.'

For a moment he stared at her, then awkwardly he bent down and kissed her forehead. It was the first time he had done any such thing except under duress. The autonomous action and the compassion he had genuinely, and for the first time, felt for his grandmother suddenly made him feel very adult, no longer a child.

Half an hour after Dr Griffith had left Arlette knew that her mother had taken the first step across the threshold between life and death and was waiting to take the next almost eagerly. The suffering that she had endured for the last few days, in spite of the drugs, seemed suddenly to be behind her. She called Auriel.

'Hasn't Alain arrived yet?'

Auriel shook her head. 'I rang again but there was no reply.'

They took their stations on either side of the bed but their mother did not regain consciousness.

Fifteen minutes before Alain's BMW drove into the yard, Regine died.

CHAPTER TWENTY-ONE

Fern was driving with more than customary concentration, leaving it to Holly to take in the way autumn was changing the hues of the countryside, where green was giving way to gold, russets and crimsons. Not spectacularly as at King's Melcombe where the fiery maples were putting out their banners of yellow and scarlet but subtly as if not absolutely certain that summer was over or that winter was imminent.

Holly had declined to drive, thinking that if her mother had something to do she'd have less time to think; think and possibly change her mind.

'You turn left about half a mile up here where the signpost says East Ashpool,' she said.

Fern made the left turn but a few minutes later without warning she stopped the car in a layby and switched off the engine.

'God, I wish I had a cigarette,' she said.

'You haven't smoked for three years. Why now?'

'You know why.'

'Mum, you've been through worse than this.'

'How would you know?' Fern answered testily.

There was silence except for the sound of a fitful wind gusting through the hedge. The country lane lay ahead, empty except for a cock pheasant who strolled casually from one side to the other, ignoring the car.

'Do you want to go back?' Holly asked. She didn't think she could bear it if her mother decided on retreat; it had taken her months to set up this meeting.

'I suppose Emily's expecting us?'

'Sort of.' Holly had asked Emily if she minded if she brought Fern with her one day. She hadn't actually specified the day.

273

'In any case, she wouldn't come,' Emily had said brusquely.

'She might.'

Emily glowered in the general direction of the horizon. 'I'm not at all convinced it's a good idea. It's been far too long. Much better leave things as they are.'

'Of course it's a risk,' Holly said blandly. 'Don't think I don't appreciate that. I'm not sure I'd have the courage either if I was in your place.'

Emily turned from her contemplation of the blue distance. 'And don't think I don't know what you're up to, you scheming little toad!'

Holly made a grimace of resignation. 'OK, OK. I just thought it was a good idea.'

'In whose interest. Yours?'

'Is that so awful? And anyway, no. Not entirely.'

'And whose idea *was* it? That therapist woman's, I've no doubt.'

'Celia? Goodness no. Just me kite-flying again.'

'Then you'll be disappointed. Fern would never agree to it,' Emily said with finality.

When Holly broached the subject to Fern her reaction had been precisely the same.

'Emily would never agree to it,' she'd said.

Work kept Holly busy for the next few weeks and she saw Emily only once, when she and Gideon drove down for a fleeting visit, but she and Fern were in touch by telephone and Holly never lost an opportunity of reintroducing the subject. If she suggested to each in turn that the other was marginally more enthusiastic about the scheme than she knew was the case, she justified it stoutly to herself, and to Gideon, to whom she explained it. 'I believe it's better to goof up than spend the rest of one's life saying "what if",' she said when he expressed doubt.

'I know *you* believe that,' he said, grinning. Then, looking solemn, had added, 'It's a responsibility all the same.'

Now that resolve was about to become reality Holly began to see Gideon's point. What if Emily behaved as gruffly as only Emily could? Her mother would never understand. And what if her mother retreated into her shell again, went back to her old compulsions? What if she'd mistimed things and it was all too soon. But too soon or not, time was not a commodity in unlimited supply. As Emily kept reminding her, her grandmother was an old woman. And although she was as tough-minded as ever (not to say bloody-minded), it was impossible not to notice that Emily was less strong physically. Her sight was quite poor, though when Holly had suggested stronger glasses she'd been roundly ticked off for interfering.

Fern dug into her bag for a hair brush which she used to tidy her hair, retying the thick bunch at the nape of her neck.

'If you can't face Emily yet we could always go and take a look at the sheltered housing they've offered her,' Holly suggested. 'I'd like to know what you think about it.'

'Yes, perhaps we should,' Fern agreed, tossing her bag over on to the back seat.

'Then you need not make up your mind straight away.'

Fern started the engine. 'Let's go then. You'll have to direct me.'

In another few minutes they arrived at the raw brick housing development, dignified by the name of Beaufort Court, whose architect appeared to have quite meticulously avoided any similarity to any other building in the locality, either in materials or style.

'Oh, Holly. It's ghastly!' Fern said as she stopped the car. They were in a kind of courtyard punctuated with raised brick beds full of dismal-looking dwarf conifers. They were surrounded on three sides by two-storey blocks and expressionless rows of windows.

'I did warn you,' Holly said, getting out of the car and stretching her limbs.

An unpredictable wind funnelled into the courtyard after them, corralling another consignment of leaves into one corner. A curtain or two was tweaked aside in the flats already occupied.

'We have to get the key from the warden,' Holly said as they hurried along a paved path and under an archway to the warden's office.

The warden was youngish middle-aged with a firm but pleasant manner, rather like Audrey, Fern thought.

'Hallo, Miss Wyatt,' she said. 'How nice to see you again.'

'This is my mother, Mrs Meyrick,' Holly said and the two older women shook hands. If Mrs Meyrick thought it somewhat strange that Emily Troy's daughter should have taken so little part in her rehousing, she gave no indication of it.

'I expect you'd like to see the flat,' she said, taking a key from a locked cupboard behind her. She led them along a corridor, flanked by a line of identical flush doors and up a staircase to the next floor. Here the corridor looked exactly like the one on the floor below.

'There are lifts, of course,' Mrs Meyrick explained. 'All the same, we tend to put our more able-bodied on the first floor.' She unlocked the third door along and stood back to let them through into the flat.

Fern's first thought was that 'flat' was a misnomer. The accommodation consisted of a bedsitting room, with a bathroom and kitchen leading off a hall so tiny that there wasn't enough room in it for the three of them at once. The kitchen was minute. Everything was decorated in various tones of beige.

'You see they have everything to hand. All the rooms are fitted with alarms and all have radiators; the radiators are the first thing some of our residents notice.' She smiled. 'Some of them were used to cold, draughty cottages so it's quite a luxury for them. The bathrooms have been specially designed with the elderly in mind, as you see, and the kitchens are very easy to keep clean; handy for making the odd cup of tea.'

'What about meals?' Fern asked, studying the rudimentary cooking facilities.

'Meals are generally taken in the dining room downstairs, which we'll see in just a moment. That way we try to encourage our residents to socialize.' She went to the window and looked out. 'There's quite a nice view. You can just see the tops of the trees in the village.' She turned round and looked at Fern with an expectant smile. 'I'm sure Mrs Troy will be very happy here.'

'It's Miss Troy,' Holly said.

Mrs Meyrick shot a puzzled glance in Holly's direction but awaited Fern's verdict without further comment.

'It's – it's very small,' Fern volunteered tentatively.

Mrs Meyrick looked momentarily shocked. 'Oh, but Mrs Wyatt, these rooms are considered beautifully spacious compared to some. Beaufort Court is thought to be quite a model of its kind, you know. Of course there are more luxurious facilities available but I understood that Mrs Troy's compensation was not as generous as she'd hoped. Or perhaps you were thinking of having her to live with you instead?' She gazed at Fern with an unmistakable air of triumph, knowing that her closing words usually put an end to criticism.

As was the case here. Fern and Holly followed the warden downstairs again in silence. The dining room was pleasant; carpeted, with seating arranged around small tables.

'And the lounge is through here.' Mrs Meyrick led them into a large room where a few residents dozed in armchairs. A few others read or indulged in desultory games of scrabble. There seemed to be very little conversation.

Fern nodded in apparent approval but depression had settled on her like a fog.

As soon as she and Holly were back in the car and doing up their seat belts, she said, 'I'm sure the woman is right and that the place is a model of its kind; so why does it frighten the life out of me?' She turned on the ignition. 'All the same, it's not me who'll have to live there. Emily's presumably made up her mind.' She drove out of the courtyard with a sense of relief.

'So where to now?' Holly asked.

'Now I have to see Emily, don't I? You better tell me where we go from here.'

They pressed on to the Saltings. It seemed to Holly that Beaufort Court had managed to inject into her mother an uncharacteristic purposefulness; she tackled the ruts and potholes between the remaining shanties with dogged determination.

Holly had to admit that the Saltings could hardly have looked bleaker. The sun was making pale, infrequent appearances through a hustling procession of ragged cloud. Khaki-coloured breakers hammered the shore, the white spume snatched from their tops driven forward on to the beach where it formed shivering mounds amongst the plastic bottles and blackened seaweed.

Fern looked about her in dismay. 'Where *are* we getting to? You can't mean that Emily lives *here*?'

'It's not looking its best,' Holly said, springing to its defence. 'Most of the residents have left. Besides, the bulldozers have stirred it all up. It used to be so nice. Park here under the tamarisk hedge.'

As they emerged from the car, the wind buffeted them more fiercely than in the comparative shelter of Beaufort Court. Blown sand gritted their eyes.

'Honestly, Holly, this is frightful. I must say I'm beginning to see the merits of Beaufort Court.'

They staggered up the wooden steps but before Holly could raise her hand to the knocker the door flew open and Emily stood there, impressive in her man's trousers and the multicoloured jersey with the fraying sleeves.

'You had better come in quickly, the sand is everywhere.' She raised her voice above the noise of the wind and the racket of the tarpaulin slapping the sides of the cruiser.

'I see it's come loose again,' Holly yelled.

'Bloody thing,' Emily said, closing the door firmly behind them. They stood in the kitchen facing each other.

Holly kissed Emily on the cheek. 'Hallo, Em.'

Fern and Emily stared at one another without speaking. Then: 'You had better both go and sit in the other room. I'll put the kettle on,' Emily said gruffly, turning down Holly's offers of help.

If Holly had ever entertained hopes of an impassioned reunion she would have been disappointed; there were no emotional fireworks whatever. Emily and her mother behaved like polite strangers. They drank tea and ate the digestive biscuits Emily had laid on in expectation, as a treat. Emily enquired about their journey; neither Fern nor Holly mentioned their visit to Beaufort Court.

'I'm going for a walk along the beach,' Holly announced, after gulping down her tea. 'I want to see what a pig's ear they're making of the Saltings.' And she bundled out of the door before anyone could volunteer to accompany her.

After she left there was silence. Fern sipped her tea, flicking continual small glances at her mother.

'I gather she was trying to be tactful,' Emily said. 'Have another cup of tea.'

Fern held out her mug. 'Thank you.' She did not actually want more tea, it had a peculiar brackish taste, but the activity masked the significance of their extraordinary circumstances.

'Holly says you're better. That the holiday in Italy did you good.'

'Yes, I think so. It was an exceptionally beautiful place.'

'You've chucked in the job, I hear?'

'Taken early retirement, yes.'

'I don't see as well as I used to but it seems to me that you look younger than I imagined.'

'So do you.'

'It must run in the family.'

There was another long pause. Fern gazed round her at the white-painted plank walls. Then turned to look at her mother.

'Did you mind my coming?'

'Mind? Of course I didn't mind. I imagine that if either of us had violently objected to the scheme we wouldn't have allowed that headstrong girl to persuade us into it. Where did she get her bloody-mindedness? Not from you, I take it. From that husband of yours, perhaps?'

'Jonah? No, I don't think so,' Fern smiled.

'I expect you'll say from me.'

'I don't know you well enough to say, do I?' Fern gave up on the tea and put her mug on the floor beside her chair.

'Are you sniping?' Emily said impassively, refilling her own mug to the brim.

'Of course not.'

'Wouldn't blame you,' Emily mumbled.

There was another silence.

'Do you hear from the twins?' Fern asked.

'Only at Christmas. They send me extremely effete cards of the sort they obviously foist on to their clients.'

'They've been quite successful, I believe. They were always so self-sufficient.'

'Still in Toronto, I take it?' Emily gulped her tea.

'I presume so. They must be coming up to retirement themselves by now. I have the impression they would really prefer to discontinue the family thing altogether. Even Muriel found it hard to penetrate their mutual exclusivity, though she tried hard enough.'

'And you?'

'As time went on they kept me at a distance too.'

'But Muriel treated you well?'

'She was very religious in a narrow sort of way but that soon came to seem normal. According to her own lights she was fair, never knowingly unkind. She couldn't bear children, you know.'

Emily's eyes opened wide. 'That's funny. She certainly tried hard enough to hang on to you lot!'

Fern giggled suddenly. 'No, I didn't mean that! I meant that she couldn't have any of her own.'

'Oh, I see,' Emily chuckled.

'She used to imply that your illness was somehow caused by loose living. We believed it at the time.'

'Loose living!'

'She assumed it was because you belonged to what she called "the arty set".'

'I'm afraid my sister never did forgive me for allowing Jacko to paint my fanny – and put it on display, what's more.'

Fern smiled, trying not to betray that her mother had momentarily shocked her. She said, 'Later, I realized that your TB was more likely to have been brought on as a result of living in that damp farmhouse, even though I had wonderful memories of the place. To me it was like the paradise from which we had been expelled, but by the time I was old enough to guess the truth it was too late. Up until then I was so indoctrinated by Muriel's opinions that I know I must have been absolutely vile and priggish. I'm not surprised you gave up coming to see us.'

'You think I abdicated too easily?'

'You had a living to earn. You had to keep body and soul together somehow.'

'The least that could be said was that I contributed to *your* keep as well. But that meant that there was no money left over for the train journey to London to see you.'

'You sent money for us?' Fern said abruptly.

'Didn't you know?'

'No.' Fern looked aghast. 'Muriel didn't say.'

'She probably thought of it as immoral earnings or the wages of sin or something.'

'But you worked on the land. She knew that.'

'Of course I worked on the bloody land,' Emily said irritably. 'I was joking.' Poor Fern never did have much sense of humour.

Fern left her chair to stare out across the beach towards the churning sea. 'I'm glad I came,' she said. 'Injustices have been done. False assumptions made.' She turned to face Emily. 'I'm sorry for my part in perpetuating them.'

Emily began to collect the mugs and the biscuits and put them back on the tray. 'One can play the game of "what if" till the cows come home. It never did anyone any good. Of course I'm sorry that I had to leave you with my bigoted sister. But what's done's done.' She carried the tray out to the kitchen.

Fern followed. 'Let me wash up.'

'No, leave them, for God's sake. We shall be having lunch directly.'

'I'd like to take you out somewhere.' Fern had heard about the tinned tuna and knew she couldn't face it.

'There's nowhere decent for miles unless you count The Green Man.'

'What's wrong with The Green Man?'

'It's all right if you like pub food.'

Holly arrived back, letting in a gust of wind. She looked anxiously at the two older women.

Emily let out a gutsy laugh. 'It's all right. We haven't gone for each other with the bread knife.'

She glanced sharply at her daughter. But then Fern wouldn't remember the incident involving a bread knife that remained so crystal clear in her own memory, for the children had been in bed at the time.

Fern paid for drinks and three ploughman's at The Green Man. Towards the end of the meal she felt confident enough to broach the subject of Emily's removal to Beaufort Court. She mentioned that she and Holly had been to see it.

'Then you had no business to,' Emily snapped. 'Just because we're in touch again doesn't give you the right to interfere in my affairs.'

'Do you think you'll like it there?' Fern asked cautiously.

'I've made my decision. There's no more to be said.'

'All the same, if after a trial period you discovered that you absolutely couldn't bear it, you could always come to live with me in Bath. We have a spare room beside Holly's.' As soon as she'd spoken Fern wondered what on earth had possessed her to make such a patently unworkable suggestion.

Holly stared at her mother open-mouthed.

Emily laughed loudly, attracting even more attention to their table by the window. Her eccentric style of dressing had already caused something of a stir amongst the lunchtime drinkers who were not already acquainted with her. 'There's no need for that,' she said, hugely amused. 'Poor Fern. Can you really imagine us sharing quarters? Personally I can't conceive of anything more likely to produce disaster.'

Fern bristled. 'There's no need to laugh! I just wouldn't like to think of you stuck somewhere you absolutely loathed. Now we've made the connection we just can't go on as we did before. It has to make some difference otherwise what's the point?'

'Good for you. I thought you had some spirit in you somewhere. And you're good-hearted in spite of Muriel's attempts to turn you into a holy roller, but if you think I'm about to make any claims on your filial sensitivities after all this time, you've got another think coming.'

'I'd like to keep in touch all the same.'

'Let's not make any promises we'd afterwards regret. In any case I dare say I won't have any more success in the future than I've had in the past at keeping this obstreperous granddaughter out of my hair.'

Afterwards Holly drove the three of them back to Sandplace. By the time they eventually left the Saltings the wind had dropped and was replaced by sudden calm; the sun was dipping through strips of plum-coloured cloud, staining the sky and the sea blood red. The barren beach had been transformed into a rose-pink border round the dark land. All at once Fern began to understand what had kept Emily here for so long.

'You must let us know when the moving date is,' she said regretfully. 'We'll come and help.'

'It's all arranged,' Emily said. 'But you can come all the same if you like.'

Holly looked about her. 'I'm not sure I could bear it,' she said with a thunderous frown in the direction of the mess at the far end of the beach.

Emily put a hand on her shoulder. 'Perhaps I might come up and see you for a change.'

Holly brightened. 'Would you? Would you really? That would be great. I could put you up in my flat, you know. I don't mind a bit sleeping on the sofa.'

'Don't rush on so. I said I might.'

Holly had to be content with that. 'No more visits from the Queen of the Night?'

'Unlikely now, poor old coot.'

'Why's that?'

'Snuffed it. Read about it in the paper.'

'Really. She didn't look so hot when she was here.'

'Who is the Queen of the Night?' Fern asked, feeling out of it.

'I'll tell you later,' Holly promised.

Before they left Holly flung her arms round her grandmother, holding her tight and rocking a surprised Emily on her feet. It was the first time Holly had dared to embrace her so affectionately. She kissed her on the cheek and was gratified to be kissed in return. It was like the thawing of ancient permafrost.

On the return journey Holly drove; as the car floundered up the road she waved from the window. In the side mirror a tiny vignette of Emily's gaunt cloaked figure appeared beside the blue-painted GWR carriage, while behind her the sunset blazed in strips of vermilion and gold.

They turned the corner by the dinghy park, now practically empty, and Holly pulled into the side.

'What's the matter?' Fern asked.

Holly scrabbled in her pocket for a tissue and blew her nose. 'Mum, do you realize that's the last time we shall see Emily in Sandplace.'

'Yes, darling. I'm afraid so.' In spite of everything Fern was quite unable to see the Saltings as anything but a desolate scatter of makeshift shanties. She put a comforting hand on Holly's arm. It wasn't like Holly to cry. She'd always been a stoic, even as a little girl. Fern reached into her bag for a packet of her own tissues. She handed them to Holly.

'Emily's been there for ever,' Holly said, fishing into the packet for another tissue and wiping her eyes. 'It's like she and Sandplace belong to each other.'

'Darling, we have to face the fact that it couldn't have gone on for much longer anyway. Emily's not getting any younger. It struck me that she was having more trouble with her eyesight than I expected from what you told me.'

'That's just it. I suppose I didn't want to face it.'

Fern put an arm round Holly's shoulders. She rested her chin on Holly's springy dark hair. It was a long time since she had held her daughter as close as this; been able to offer comfort rather than receive it. She stared out of the window at a clump of stunted pines and felt warmth seeping back into her life.

Holly blew her nose, shoved the tissues back in her pocket and restarted the car. 'We'd better get going,' she said. 'Though I'm afraid it'll be almost dark before we get to King's Melcombe.' Fern was to drop her off and continue alone to Bath.

'I don't mind driving in the dark. I rather like it,' Fern said. 'And don't worry too much about Emily, darling. Now I've met her again, I see her as a woman in charge of her destiny.'

Holly glanced at Fern as she drove. 'I didn't think you believed in that.'

'I think I may be changing my mind,' Fern said.

Although it was not actually raining there was enough airborne moisture spewing over the Cobb to make the notion of having any serious meeting there out of the question. Zak was glad that, given the critical nature of his mission, he had decided against theatrical props of any kind.

He had arrived early and had left his hire car in an inconspicuous corner of the large car park at the top of the hill. Carrying the attaché case, with its precious contents, he had walked down the steep road to the pub near the Cobb and ordered a lager; he was tempted to indulge in something stronger to steady his nerves, but there would be time for that later. And it would have to be a good deal later for as soon as the money was finally in his possession he would have to see most of it safely stashed in a string of building society accounts he'd opened in the last two years and the rest used in one or two money-laundering schemes he had up his sleeve. He intended to reach the safe anonymity of London before he allowed himself anything in the way of a celebration.

Normally he found no difficulty keeping cool under pressure; throughout the entire process of relieving Mr Aiden Chase of two of his most valuable paintings, his pulse rate had hardly risen a fraction, so sure was he of himself and his meticulous planning. But now that, finally, all his efforts were about to be rewarded and in addition, far more of the proceedings were out of his hands than he would have liked, he found himself taut as an overwound spring. His breathing had quickened and his hands had become clammy with sweat. Surreptitiously he wiped them on his handkerchief before he lifted his glass and downed his lager. He glanced round, wondering if any of the drinkers would turn out to be his contact. For this important transaction he was to meet someone further up the hierarchy than the one who called himself Guy, some tame expert who would know enough to vet the paintings before he handed over the money. But Zak had no fears on that score. If the expert knew his stuff he'd see immediately that these were the real McCoy.

He glanced at his watch. It was too early to make a move. He ordered another lager and drank it while the hands on his watch stood still.

At last he knew it was time to trudge back up the hill to meet the man. Waiting for him to make contact and half hidden by the bole of a huge Scots pine, he checked out the car park. He pulled the knitted hat he had bought in East Ashpool more firmly over his ears and partly unzipped his jacket. From an inside pocket he extracted a recently purchased device and switched it on. With it he scanned the local radio frequencies, including police transmissions.

All was very quiet indeed. Everything else appeared normal. He imagined that summer would see every parking space taken but on this grey autumnal day there were just a few shoppers loading their purchases into the boots of cars.

A gust of wind brought with it the beginnings of rain and just at that moment his mobile phone bleeped.

'I'm in the black BMW on the far side of the public conveniences,' a voice said in his ear, giving the registration number. 'Perhaps you'd like to join me here.'

'I'll pull up alongside,' Zak said, his heart jumping.

He went to his hired Ford Escort and reversed it over to where the man waited in his BMW, parking it so that it faced the exit.

The man was young but not as boyish as the fresh-faced youth Zak had dealt with up to now. As Zak slid in beside him, clutching the attaché case to his chest, he could well believe that he was negotiating with a shrewd operator. The man had a long, intelligent face with dark blond hair trendily cut, though with a slight air of the military about it.

'We'll keep this as brief as possible,' the man said. 'First perhaps we'll take a look at what you've brought.'

Before he opened the case Zak leaned out of the door and once again checked out the car park in the manner he had before and once again everything was almost boringly normal. He took out the first painting, the Cézanne, and handed it to his companion, who examined it meticulously in total silence, even taking out a magnifying glass to study it in great detail. The wind soughed round the car while Zak twisted in his seat to keep the whole car park under surveillance, but the man appeared completely oblivious. An attaché case very similar to Zak's own lay temptingly on the back seat. His pulse rate quickened. It was as much as he could do to prevent himself snatching it up and making a run for it. Except that the man had taken the precaution of activating the central locking.

The examination of both the paintings seemed to take an age but at last the expert turned to him with a confident smile. 'Good,' he said. 'Everything appears to be in order. He closed the case and reached into the back for the one he had brought with him which he laid on Zak's lap. It was heavy.

With trembling fingers Zak snapped up the catches and revealed the bundles of notes. His first reaction was that it seemed a lot; he had never seen that much money in one go before. Swiftly he counted the bundles of high denomination notes, extracting one here and there and perusing it for signs of counterfeit or of being marked.

'That seems to be OK,' he said, barely controlling his voice. 'I reckon we have a deal then.' He held out his hand as if to seal the bargain, but the man had turned to place the attaché case containing the paintings on the back seat. Zak dropped his hand.

'Do we have a contact number in case we're interested in further business?' the man said.

'No. I don't quite know where I shall be, but that shouldn't be a problem. I'll phone you as soon as I have one.'

'Excellent,' the man said, releasing the door locks. 'Hope to see you again.'

Zak scrambled out. Bending down he raised his hand in salute. 'Ciao.'

He unlocked his own car and slid into the driving seat in a state of shocked elation. As he placed the case containing the money beside him on the floor, the black BMW slid away. He watched it leave the car park. After wiping his sweating palms on his handkerchief for the second time he started the engine and revved the car, making for the exit at speed. A second or two before he reached it, a police car appeared from nowhere and blocked his path while at the same time a maroon Ford Sierra pulled up alongside and two men in plain clothes bundled out. With a jolt Zak recognized them as two of the drinkers at the pub.

'Holy shit!'

For a fraction of a second Zak froze in disbelief. He had been so sure the man in the BMW had been on the level. He found himself acting involuntarily. He had grabbed the case and was out of the car before he was conscious of his decision to make a run for it. And he was almost halfway across the car park before his pursuers began to give chase.

Thankful for his trainers and casual clothes, he found himself hurtling down a private drive between well-kept gardens and cliff-top houses. He expected any moment to arrive at someone's front door but quite suddenly the drive gave way to a rough path that in turn led to a field. As he negotiated a kissing gate, the case held aloft, he was bewildered for just a second by a signpost with a choice of destinations, but opted almost by instinct for the arm that directed him to the coast path. Light rain was already making the grass slippery underfoot and at one point he had to make a wild leap across an overflowing stream. Cursing their determination to hinder, he forced his way through yet another kissing gate. The next field rose steeply to a viewpoint; behind him Black Venn and Golden Cap glimmered in the misty rain while distant Portland was out of sight altogether. Behind him came the police, though he saw, with a stab of hope, that he was leaving them behind. He stampeded on along a track bordered with bracken and nettles, over a plank bridge and through another fiendishly delaying gate. He experienced a twinge of dismay when he unexpectedly came across a house but from here the track widened and became more like a unmadeup road where both mud and puddles laid traps for the unwary. He saw no more houses.

Sycamore and ash closed in on each side. Zak glanced behind. The police were just emerging from the gate. His hand was slippery and sore from clutching the case, which now felt as if it were stuffed with lead.

He arrived at a point where the road gave out and was replaced by three paths. Two looked as if they led to a farm or back to Ware. He took the third, which was the coast path leading straight on. Zak was too relieved to gain the cover of the trees, and in too much of a hurry, to bother with the notices that warned of the length and severity of the walk, especially in adverse conditions.

A few yards further along the narrow, ankle-twisting path a stile, with a steep slope on one side, barred his way. He hurled himself at it, guessing it was the last man-made obstacle. Halfway over he swopped the case to his other hand, lost his footing and then his hold on the case. As if in slow motion he watched it arc over and down the precipitous slope to disappear into dense thickets of ivy, fern and bramble. Given time he might eventually have retrieved it, but time he did not have. He could already hear the voices of his pursuers. For a moment longer he hesitated, torn by terrible indecision.

Then with a choking sob he ran on through the trees, tears of frustration and fury mingling with the rain on his face. He was soaked through, dirty, scratched and exhausted. A quarter of an hour later he stopped and listened. The only sound was the sighing of the wind in the trees which closed round him protectively. Or was it menacingly? He couldn't be sure.

The plain-clothes men saw that they had been outpaced and concentrated their efforts, with the help of a sergeant and a PC, on retrieving the attaché case.

The patrol cars were contacted and one of them shot off in the direction of Axmouth, seven miles along the coast where the tangled Undercliff ended. A helicopter was summoned.

'He was across the car park like a ruddy Exocet,' the sergeant told the DI apologetically.

'No point going after him without dogs,' the local DI said. 'We could look for him for a year in that lot and never find him. There are only a couple of possible exits, and we've covered them and set up roadblocks in case he cuts across the fields. But there's no hurry; he'll be in there a while yet, poor bugger. Besides, I reckon he left some handy fingerprints on that mobile phone.'

Will phoned his uncle from the police station.

'It's all over,' he said. 'We have the paintings.'

'Thank God.'

'And the money's safe too.' He didn't mention the close shave that the painfully garnered cash had been exposed to; he was certainly in no hurry to pull another stunt like that, especially not one involving family money. He noticed that his uncle didn't ask if he, Will, was safe. His cousin, Gideon, would have made some pointed remark but Will was more detached, and without Gideon's sense of humour.

'The paintings are the main thing. I suppose it was that person posing as a student?'

'I'm afraid that's where we slipped up. He's got away, at least for the moment. I never met the student in the first place so I couldn't tell you for sure if it was the same chap.'

'They're sure to catch him, aren't they?'

Will cleared his throat. 'Ah. Well, you see they had to call off the search.'

'Call off the search! How could they be so asinine?'

'I'm afraid it's the same old problem. Money. Overtime and helicopters don't come cheap.'

'Is it really as bad as that?' There was a silence.

'Anyway, we're holding a chap for questioning. A crooked dealer. But I'm afraid the name of his accomplice was just another alias.'

Aiden wasn't interested in the nuts and bolts. 'The paintings are undamaged, I sincerely hope?'

'As far as I can see.'

'When will you bring them?'

'I'll be on my way as soon as I've finished here.'

Just before he put the phone down Aiden remembered to thank Will for his sustained efforts to retrieve the paintings. He had resisted his nephew's initial suggestion that details of the paintings should be publicized on the Internet as too much like advertising the vulnerability of one's collection. Now he was glad; it wouldn't have helped anyway.

He let out a long sigh of relief. There had only been one saving grace in the whole situation, although it would have sounded like sacrilege to express it to any normal collector. It was that neither of the stolen canvases had been *Emily Asleep*.

CHAPTER TWENTY-TWO

Holly gave up working in the arboretum just after lunch. She had been warned by the head ranger that it was too dangerous; one or two of the more vulnerable trees were down already. The last leaves of the autumn whirled round her head in a colourful swarm, like maddened birds. The wind roared in the branches with the sound of an approaching train.

She returned to the stable workshop and spent the rest of the afternoon completing the drawings for the design of the living summerhouse. It would include planting and would take years while the trees grew but even if the job here came to an end she intended to come back or at least to leave her drawings so that the work could be continued. The idea of being able to design a long-term project appealed to her; like the early gardeners who planned but never saw the mature grandeur of their planting schemes. She had been glad of Gideon's help in devising the project.

At five o'clock she made herself a cup of tea and sat at the kitchen table writing a postcard to Stan, whose instruction had been so invaluable in the last three years. Even now she sometimes phoned him if she had a problem with her carving. Making herself more tea, she gazed out of the window that had a view over the park. The wind howled round the building, whistling through cracks and creating draughts where none had been before. The wind made her restless as she watched it ripping the leaves from the trees and hurling them before it. Tomorrow they would form an ankle-deep carpet on the woodland floor.

It was spectacular but it was bad news for the arboretum; there would have been a week or two left for visitors to admire the last of the autumn colour. Now what was left of it was underfoot.

She had an early supper, worked on a maquette for a carving for

291

an hour or two and then went to bed, lying awake listening to the wind. Once or twice before she dropped off she thought she heard the distant crash of a falling tree.

Sometime later Holly awoke with a jolt. An anxiety which had been latent was now bringing her out in a prickling sweat. The gale continued to buffet the old stables but it was not fears for her own safety that disturbed her sleep but for Emily in her precarious berth. There had been storms before, including the storm of 1987, but Emily had dismissed even that as not affecting the Saltings as much as it had places further east. In any case, Emily had been younger then and her eyesight had been more reliable. And there had been neighbours to call on; even three weeks ago, when Holly had visited Emily with Fern, the only other resident that she knew of was old Mr Watts. The most aggravating aspect of her concern was that Emily was due to move to Beaufort Court during the following weekend; Holly and Fern had planned to go down to help.

Sleep was impossible now. Holly turned on the light and sat up in bed, hugging her duvet to her chest and staring out into the tumultuous night. If she'd had the car she could have driven at once to the Saltings. As it was, all she possessed was a clapped-out old bike. A fat lot of good *she* was in an emergency! Her heart thudded uncomfortably as she thought about the south-westerly pounding the beach within yards of where Emily lay.

An even fiercer squall had her reaching for the phone and dialling Gideon's number.

'Thank God,' she said when Gideon's sleepy voice at last answered.

'Do you know what time it is?' he growled.

'Of course I do. Gideon, what shall I do? I'm frantic.'

'What d'you mean? Where are you? Are you all right?' He sounded more awake now, and anxious.

'I'm fine. It's Emily.'

'Emily?'

'I'm so worried about her in this storm. You know what the Saltings is like now.'

Gideon thought for a moment. 'Right. I understand. I'll pick you up as soon as it's light and we'll get down there and check it out. I probably won't be able to carry on with the job in hand anyway.'

'No, no. That's no good. We have to go now.'

'Now? You're mad!'

'What would be the point of turning up tomorrow morning if she needs help now?'

'Holly – darling – be realistic. Even if we made it down there without having a tree flatten us, what d'you think we could do? I mean, it's not as bad as the '87 blow. You know Emily. She wouldn't thank us for making a fuss.'

'Things are completely different now.'

'All right. We'll set off earlier if you insist but there would be no point going now. Absolutely none. If you're worried I could get on to the local police.'

'I think we should do that anyway. But we couldn't rely on them having time to check on her. They're sure to be busy.'

'It's a crazy idea.'

Half an hour later Gideon was driving through the gale to King's Melcombe. Holly had spent the time waiting in trying to get a message through to Ashpool police; a polite voice had promised her concern would be given priority. An hour after Gideon picked her up they were still on the road, having been diverted several times by fallen trees. As he backed up to turn round for the third time Gideon glanced at Holly's set face as she sat beside him, the road map on her knee and a pocket torch in her hand. He decided against reminding her that he thought this whole scheme a wild-goose chase – and dangerous into the bargain.

She was hurrying anxiously down unfamiliar corridors searching for Room 27 where she was supposed to have been long since. After endless minutes, or it could have been hours, she arrived, flustered and disorganized. The class she was scheduled to teach were mercifully still there though in total chaos; but since her voice would not seem to carry above the din she was reduced to wittering ineffectually, ignored by everyone. Since in any case she had mislaid her notes for the lesson she'd hoped to give, she was reduced to ceaselessly counting and recounting the shifting individuals, knowing that the inspectors would be arriving any minute. She prayed for the bell. When it did at last ring, insistently, it woke her up. For a moment she was simply dazed with relief that the nightmare was over. Then she realized that the phone was ringing. She picked it up.

'Mum. It's Holly.'

'Holly! What's the matter? What's wrong?'

'I'm fine. Listen, the storm's pretty bad down this way. I'm on Gideon's mobile phone. Gideon and I are on our way to Emily's to see if she's all right.'

'Why? Darling, has something happened?' The gale that was blowing so strongly on the south coast and even as far inland as King's Melcombe was merely a high wind in Bath, and in Fern's basement flat it hardly registered at all.

'I'm hoping not. I just want to make sure.'

'Holly, it's the middle of the night. If it's as bad as all that I don't think you should be on the road. It could be dangerous with all the falling trees.'

'Don't worry about it. But I think someone ought to check out the situation.'

Fern hesitated. 'Do you want me to meet you there.' Driving to the coast on such a night would be a nightmare worse than the one from which she had so recently woken. But she would go if she had to.

'No point. I at least have Gideon with me. I'm just ringing to tell you what's happening. I'll phone again tomorrow morning. Sorry to have woken you but I thought you ought to know. I've left a message with the police but they don't know anything. Do you think you could get on to them again? Tell them it's urgent.' Fern heard Gideon's voice in the background. 'Look, I have to go now.'

'Darling, please take care.'

'Sure.'

'I'll try the police again.'

'Thanks, Mum. Be in touch.' Holly rang off.

After half an hour on the telephone Fern managed to get through to someone in police headquarters, who assured her that the message had already been passed on. Feeling vaguely dissatisfied with this response but now thoroughly awake, she went to the kitchen to make tea, taking it to the sitting room to drink. She switched on the television with the sound down, hoping she wasn't beginning to revert to her old habit of having it on most of the time she was alone. But tonight was different; she needed distraction and at least a semblance of company.

She was sure that Holly was overreacting. Storms must be a frequent occurrence at the Saltings. But Holly and Emily had formed a bond over the last two years for which she must surely be happy, mustn't she? Holly was not well endowed with relations, after all. It was just that occasionally, just occasionally, Fern felt a little excluded. It was her own fault, of course. Holly had nagged her to go with her to Sandplace almost from the day she'd found out where her grandmother was living.

In the end, meeting Emily had not been as disturbing as Fern had expected. Anticipating the resurgence of all kinds of feelings long since buried, she found her reactions had been remarkably subdued. She had liked Emily, though she was a little afraid of her, but only as one would like or be afraid of an acquaintance. The memory of the mother that had haunted her dreams for years when she was a child had finally been eliminated by Muriel's insidious propaganda. It had been a severe disappointment to their aunt that neither Fern nor her brothers had ever come to regard Muriel as a mother or even to like her very much. The whole process had succeeded in depriving the growing children of anyone they could truly think of as a parent.

While knowing that damage had been done, Fern had never dwelled on the loss, for she believed there were traumas in most people's lives. Some people had far worse things to adjust to. Or not adjust to. One simply had to get on with the business of living as best one could, accommodating oneself as one would to a physical injury. Given time, she thought, she might grow to feel affection for Emily, as Holly had done, though it was easier for Holly. She hadn't to come to terms with the past first. For her it had just been a matter of deciding to make a friend of her grandmother and then acting upon that decision. It was not in Holly's nature to look for complications; her sculptures were a highly accurate reflection of their creator, Fern thought, smiling over her teacup. She'd claim that all she had to do was, with the minimum of interference, extract a shape from a piece of timber that had been laying dormant within it all along. She saw no obstacles in befriending Emily so there were none.

Fern looked at her watch. She had about three hours in which to attempt sleep, though she doubted if sleep would be possible now. Perhaps in the morning Holly would ring to say that it had all been a false alarm. After all, Emily was due to move from Sandplace that weekend. Which was just as well; Fern didn't think she could bear the prospect of an increasingly infirm old lady to worry about every time the wind blew.

Emily put two teabags into a mug and lifted the kettle from the camping gas stove. The electricity had been off for half an hour which was not an unheard of occurrence, the supply to the Saltings was somewhat vulnerable. Residents always had their stoves and hurricane lamps ready for these emergencies. Actually she liked the soft light of the lamp swinging gently over her head and the Robinson Crusoe feeling of making do and being independent of the outside world. There was no milk in the fridge; she had forgotten to get any. Instead she sloshed in a measure of Johnnie Walker; it was going to be one of those nights when sleep would be elusive. Usually she snoozed peacefully through all kinds of weather but tonight it was exceptionally rough. The ropes fixing the tarpaulin cover on to the cruiser had come loose yet again. They were probably rotten anyway; best let the damned thing blow away altogether. As it was, it was flailing monotonously against the side of the boat. Even before she'd finished her tea she was aware of small stones, as well as the usual sand and spray, being flung against the windows by the force of the wind. But the windows on her railway carriage home were tough and she was not concerned. It was a nuisance though that water as well as sand was being driven under the verandah door; she heaved a long sausage of fabric filled with sand across the bottom and pushed it into place with her foot. She shrugged herself into her cloak for added warmth and poured herself a finger or two more whisky, neat this time.

Outside there was a continuous hollow booming and the piercing scream of air being drawn at high speed through the rigging of the cruiser. A series of bangs and crashes made a harsh accompaniment as loose objects were hurled at fences and cabins.

The railway carriage itself shuddered from time to time. Sitting in her chair wrapped in her cloak, Emily dozed.

Sometime later she was awoken by a more insistent banging and hammering. Astonished, she came to the conclusion that there was someone outside. She got complainingly to her feet and went to open the door. At once the wind all but snatched it from her hands; she hung on, squinting into the roaring darkness.

Old man Watts stood on the top of the steps, enveloped in glistening oilskins and clutching the tan mongrel in his arms.

"Tis a praper heller, this ol' wind. I be gwain ter git out of yur. My darter's got the car up yonder so I reckon you'm best come wi' us,' he yelled.

'No thank you,' Emily shouted back. 'I shall be perfectly all right.'

"Tis gwain ter git worse. Doan ee bide yur, missus. 'Tisn't safe.'

'The Saltings has weathered worse than this,' she shrieked to make herself heard.

'I'm telling ee. Git a few things together and come directly. Th' car's waiting. 'Tis a powerful gurt wind we got.'

'I said I'm staying.'

'Then you'm a praper vule and a peg-headed ol' 'ooman.'

'I know, Mr Watts. It can't be helped. You go along with your daughter. I'm going to shut this door now. The wind's blowing everything about.'

His glittering oilskins disappeared into the night accompanied by his shouts of disapproval, as she heaved the door shut again.

Mr Watts was proved right. The storm did get worse. Sometime after he left she heard the tarpaulin go completely; it made a noise like a giant bird taking off. Then one of the windows in the verandah door exploded with a rattle of broken glass as a result of something heavy being blown violently against it; the room filled with salt spray, sand and the demon baying of the gale. For a moment Emily fancied that she felt Sandplace shift slightly on its brick piers but she was too busy struggling to nail a piece of hardboard across the window to give it a second thought.

As she returned to the kitchen there was a deafening grating noise as the cabin cruiser stirred, as if answering the call of the sea. Its side began to scrape along the outside of Sandplace and this time there was no mistaking that the floor beneath her feet moved. It was taking her home with it. She went to the window and stared out. She couldn't be sure but it seemed to her fading sight that the beach had gone and that the sea itself was outside her door. In fact she could hear it; and some of it was already pouring across the floor.

Then she knew it was time. Feeling very calm she went and helped herself to another generous measure of whisky.

'Pity to waste it,' she said, half to herself and half to David Hannaford. For she had been aware for a while that he was there, standing beside her, offering her his hand. Quiet, reliable David, whom she loved. He spoke.

'Ready, old thing?' he said.

'You bet,' she answered. 'Just as soon as I can get this bloody door open.'

For a moment she struggled, then the door flew open of its own accord. The sea was below her and all round her. She felt no fear, for it was her friend. As the wall of water approached she felt an exhilarating recklessness, knowing that it had come especially to fetch her. She wrapped her cloak more securely round her, seized David's hand and stepped serenely out into the welcoming dark.

CHAPTER TWENTY-THREE

The huge copper beech lay on its side. The lateral branches that had once cast an arboreal gloom over the drive now thrust themselves skyward or had become wedged, split and shattered between the massive trunk and the ground. The crown of the tree had been driven by the force of the fall deep into the north wing which contained the science laboratories and the boys' changing rooms. The roof had exploded in a mess of slates and rafters and a large chunk of wall had been gouged out, leaving the interior with its rows of benches open to the sky.

Francis surveyed the damage from the vantage point of his study. His hands were thrust into his trouser pockets and he jingled the loose coins inside them as if he found satisfaction in the sound. In fact, it would have been true to say that, apart from a few minor grumbles, he was perfectly content; smug even.

The events of the past thirty-six hours had been momentous ones. The gale that had brought down the tree so neatly on the science labs had also stripped off a few tiles and toppled a chimney or two, but otherwise the school and the boys had escaped unscathed. For the first time in his life Francis was almost ready to believe in a benign Providence. For the one thing he had never cut corners on had been insurance – mostly it was true, on the insistence of the governors, but never mind. He had already been on the telephone to the insurance people and they were to send a man round that afternoon. Their promptness seemed to him a good sign.

The fallen tree had not been the only augury of a more well-disposed Providence. It had all started when Mrs Bessemer had finally taken herself off and he had appointed Mrs May in her place. Mrs May had turned out to be a paragon of virtue, not

299

particularly efficient in her housekeeping as she tended to become flustered under pressure, but all the same painfully eager to please. Recently widowed, she was not used, as Mrs Bessemer was, to the hurly-burly of the workplace, the hirings and firings, the bickerings over the hourly rate, the precise terms of employment. What was more, she had a very flattering respect for places of learning and those involved in the academic process, particularly headmasters. She fussed over Francis like a cat with one kitten. His coffee came hot, on time and unspilled. Since her arrival he hadn't had a single recurrence of hay fever.

Mrs Bessemer had a habit of steaming into his study like a juggernaut; Mrs May stepped in as timidly as a deer. Which was what she did now, after a polite knock.

'Your coffee, Mr Troy.'

Francis turned from the window, rubbing his hands together.

'Not a beaker full of the warm south, but just as welcome, I'm sure.'

Mrs May took this to mean that he was pleased and ventured a comment.

'What a shame about the damage,' she said. 'But what a wonderful example of cheerfulness you've been to the boys, if I might say so. Calmness in an emergency is *such* an asset, I always think.'

Francis beamed. He was well aware that in emergencies he went completely to pieces, but fortunately this was not an emergency. This could be a God-given exit visa from his academic career. Indeed, in his mind he had already begun to draft the regretful end-of-term speech in which he would announce his departure. It would be a speech so moving that Mr Chips could have come to him for lessons. He would put in an acting head and sell as soon as possible. It was all decided. Then he would buy a small place, not in the sticks like Emily, but somewhere in Central London, a flat overlooking one of the parks perhaps, handy for the West End and the British Museum. He found he was still beaming at Mrs May.

'It's very kind of you to say so,' he said.

Mrs May was at the door, prepared to leave. He held up a hand to delay her.

'Oh dear. Have I forgotten something?' she said, her hand flying to her cheek.

'No. Not at all,' he said, dropping two lumps of sugar into his cup. Sugar lumps! Mrs Bessemer's speciality was a crusty bowl of granulated, stained with past coffees and stiff with insoluble concretions.

'I was wondering,' he began. 'I was wondering – and I hope you won't take this amiss – how you get on living alone?'

Mrs May blushed to the roots of her grey perm.

'Well, now, Mr Troy,' she said. 'I can't say I enjoy it exactly. Not after being married for thirty years, you know. That's why I took the job. To get me out of the house.'

'So you don't think you'll get used to it? In time, I mean?'

The tide of peony red was receding. 'I suppose one does,' she said shyly.

'You might marry again,' Francis suggested.

Mrs May giggled and the blush returned. 'Mr Troy! I'm not in the first flush of youth, you know. No one takes on an old bird if they can have spring chicken!'

Francis, surprised by her uncharacteristically racy comment, observed, 'That is not necessarily the case, if I might contradict. I would have thought you had every chance, a lady with your charm and capability. Unless you choose not to remarry, of course . . .' His voice petered out as he wondered where his gallantry might be leading him.

It was too late. Mrs May was visibly flattered by his clumsy chivalry and by reading into it more than was meant she obtained the strong impression that her employer was preparing the ground for a proposal of marriage. Francis, though he was not aware of it was, in fact, in the early stages of preparing his own mind for just that possibility.

As she left the room the telephone rang, for fortunately the line had escaped damage.

'Rudyards School. Headmaster speaking,' he intoned automatically.

'Francis, this is Holly speaking.'

'Holly?' Francis searched his memory.

'Emily's granddaughter. Fern's daughter. You remember, we spoke before, when I asked you for Emily's address.'

'Oh, yes, my dear. She said you'd been to—'

She cut him short. 'Listen. Em's missing.' Her voice cracked on the last word so that it was almost inaudible.

'Did you say missing?'

'Yesterday's storm,' she said. Then angrily: 'Didn't it occur to you that she might have been in danger? I take it she's not with you?'

'With me? I'm afraid not. We've had our own problems here. A tree fell on—'

She interrupted him again. 'I'm ringing from the Saltings. Everything here's in a state of chaos. I've been in touch with the police and all they'll say is that they're checking hotels to see if she went to one for the night. I was so hoping she might be with you—' Her equilibrium failed her again.

'Look, my dear,' Francis said soothingly. 'I'm perfectly sure that Emily's safe. If there's one thing I know about my sister, it's that she's a survivor. She'll turn up, you'll see. I'd come down myself only I'm waiting for the insurance people to arrive. There's a lot of damage here too, you know. Trees down, buildings destroyed and so on. But naturally I'd like to be kept informed. Let me know as soon as you have any news.' The silence on the end of the line was total. 'Holly?' he queried. But she had hung up.

Francis frowned. He would not for a moment allow himself to believe that Emily's disappearance was anything but temporary. From the window he noticed a small knot of boys inspecting the fallen beech tree when they had been given specific orders not to go near it. Irritation shattered his former tranquil mood. He opened the window, gesticulating and shouting peevishly. The boys obediently scattered, waiting until they were out of sight round the corner of the building before they began imitating him, clutching their stomachs to hold in the excruciating sniggers.

Gulls screamed over the scene of devastation that had once been the Saltings. By the time Holly and Gideon had first arrived, before it was even light, the police had erected barriers to keep out the expected sightseers. With the tide out, torches hovered over what was left of the beach as the police made an initial and necessarily cursory search.

As the grey day dawned Holly and Gideon surveyed the scene

speechlessly. In any case Holly had no words to express how she felt and Gideon knew better than to try to inspire her with false hope. The tears that sprang to her eyes were dried on her cheeks by the wind, as if to prove that it could be harmlessly playful, that last night had been an aberration.

Gideon put an arm round her shoulders and gazed at the place where a small community had once thrived. This was annihilation. Nothing recognizable remained. Even the beach itself had been scoured as if to make sure that the job had been thoroughly done. All that was left was a stretch of wind-seared ground dotted with salt-water pools and sudden craters. Spiked mounds of wet sand and driftwood indicated the spot where a shanty may have once stood, or an escallonia or tamarisk hedge. The JCBs of the developers could hardly have done a better job, for it was quite impossible to guess even the approximate spot where Sandplace had once existed. Gideon was viciously pleased to see that a JCB had itself fallen victim to the storm and lay helplessly on its side, a twisted heap of yellow metal. Beyond the wilderness, the sea creamed restlessly on the littered beach; it was the colour of chocolate sauce, caused by the sediment brought down by the nearby river.

They were at last allowed through the barrier to wander hopelessly among the flotsam. Holly stirred a patch of feathers with her boot, only to disinter the remains of a very dead kittiwake. She broke from Gideon's arm and paced on ahead, searching for any recognizable relic of Sandplace. She dropped to her knees and dug in the sand. She had to find something, anything, to convince herself that Emily had ever existed, did exist even now. The police had drawn a blank at all the hotels and guesthouses she could possibly have reached on foot. They were apologetic for arriving too late to check that all the residents were safe, but their manpower had been stretched to the limit that night. Holly guessed that her message was also too late by the time it had percolated through the system.

'It was about here,' she said wildly. 'I'm sure it was. Look, here are the bricks it rested on.' She uncovered a broken pile that might or might not have once been a brick pier and which might or might not have been one of those that supported Emily's house.

'Don't,' Gideon said, kneeling beside her. 'She isn't here.'

'I have to know! A person can't just disappear. The police should have come here last night and rescued her. They should have!'

'They did their best. I don't think there was anything anyone could have done.' The policeman on duty had told him that by the time Mr Watts managed to get to a working phone the damage was done. When the emergency services arrived the Saltings was completely engulfed.

Holly remained on her knees, raking the beach with her eyes.

'Don't give up, darling. Emily could be safe. She might have taken shelter in someone's house.'

'You know you don't believe that. Local people would have said.'

'It's early yet.' Privately Gideon thought that since Emily had refused help from Mr Watts when assistance was available, they might have to face the fact that she could have wanted it this way – unless she'd made a huge error of judgement, which he couldn't believe.

Holly stared at the place where she had been clawing at the sand, the surmisings that occupied Gideon already beginning to tumble wildly in her head. A tan dog pushed past her and began to assist in the digging. Holly rubbed the coarse fur on its neck. It wagged its stumpy tail, pleased at renewing their acquaintance.

'Hallo, Percy,' she said dully.

Mr Watts stopped when he was a few feet away.

'A rum ol' business, so 'tis,' he observed, shaking his head.

Gideon got to his feet. 'You've no idea why she opted to stay?' he asked.

Watts shook his head. 'Daft ol' besom! Pardon me, missus,' he said as Holly stood up. ''Er was warned. But by the time the coppers got yur 'er was gone, d'you see.' He thought for a moment. 'I reckon 'er thought 'er might as well git swept away by a bloody gurt wave as end 'er days in a council 'ome. An' I doan say I blames 'er. I'm staying wi' my daughter but the dog's getting on 'er bloody nerves already. Us ought to 'ave gone too, if you ask me,' he ended bitterly.

'I'm sorry you lost your place,' Holly said.

'So now it's all been most conveniently cleared for the

developers.' Gideon nodded towards the moonscape before them.

Mr Watts chuckled gnomishly. 'They interfered wi' nature, that's what they did, wi' they bulldozers. I reckons they'll 'ave second thoughts wi' this ol' marina job. Tis all to do wi' global warming, they do say. Like when they bloody icebergs d' melt.'

'Yes, I see what you mean,' Gideon said absent-mindedly, watching Holly, who had wandered off and was continuing her search.

Mr Watts leaned towards Gideon and assured him in a gruff whisper that the old lady would turn up at Black Tout in a day or two. 'All the drownded fetch up t'Black Tout,' he said, before making his way back to the barrier, whistling for his dog, who ignored him as usual.

Fern arrived at the barrier at the same time; breathlessly she scanned the remains of the Saltings.

Holly was brushing the sand away from a half-buried object. When she eventually tugged it free she recognized it at once. It was part of a gate and it bore the faded letters SANDPL.

The morning after the storm Fergus pedalled energetically down the lane on his new bicycle, skilfully dodging the litter of fallen branches that lay in his path. He was going to see Russell since they'd planned to reconnoitre the district to check out anything interesting in the way of damage. Since the beginning of term he had spent more time with Russell. Russell wasn't too bad, though his jokes were the pits. Even school wasn't quite so crappy this term, in fact.

Just before he reached the village his way was barred by an enormous fallen tree which was being cut up by a man with a chain saw. Fergus lifted up his bike and struggled through the maze of branches by the hedge.

'All right, squire?' the man said, and Fergus grinned. It was funny, the man calling him 'squire' like that. Since Burr Ash was the biggest house in the district he supposed that one day he might be the nearest thing the village had to a squire. The idea amused him.

Nothing had been said but Fergus couldn't help noticing that, in spite of his mother's depression over Grandmère dying and her going round red-eyed, things at home had improved. His mother had more time to spend with him and the girls. He suspected that this might have something to do with the spanking new washing machine and dryer which had mysteriously appeared in the scullery, or perhaps the new chest freezer which stood resplendent (and full) in the dairy. Perhaps the labour-saving bungalow he'd visualized wouldn't be necessary. And another thing: his Aunt Auriel had been as nice as pie lately and had given him a safety helmet to go with the new bike.

Uncle Alain hadn't appeared very upset by Grandmère's dying but he was absolutely gutted when he discovered that all she'd left him was a few of Jacko's less good paintings, including some of himself when he was little, and no money. Not that there was much left over after one took into account what was needed to keep Burr Ash going, and such necessities as the washing machine and his own new bike. He wouldn't even get to share in the royalties from Jacko's biography, not that that would piss him off particularly, for, as Fergus had thought all along, it was sure to be the most boring book in the history of the universe and would probably finish up on the remainders table in his father's bookshop.

Zak had disappointed him since Fergus had never been able to discover what he'd been up to. And he was convinced he'd been up to something; what's more he wouldn't have been surprised if Grandmère knew what it was, but Grandmère had never said and now she was dead. But maybe it wasn't anything much, hardly worth the police paying them a visit since whatever it was was too pathetically small-time for them to bother with, which was pretty sick-making. He'd had high hopes of Zak. One thing that intrigued him was that, contrary to everyone's expectations, Grandmère had left nothing to Zak in her will; just a part of the royalties from the book.

Fergus grinned to himself. 'Tough titty, Zak.'

By the time Donald drove to Dorchester that evening most of the major roads had been cleared. He dropped Auriel off near the centre of the town.

'You will pick me up again just after nine?' Auriel asked anxiously as she got out. 'You won't forget?'

'Don't worry, I'll be here,' he assured her. It would just allow him time to complete his business besides giving him a good excuse to leave promptly. Gwen was getting far too possessive lately and kept dropping hints about divorce. His divorce.

He was coming to the end of his excuses. In any case Gwen was beginning to lose her charm for him, especially now that she had become querulous and demanding. At one time she hadn't seemed to bother about regularizing their relationship but she had a close chum at the library whom he guessed had been having a go at her. Besides all that, Arlette was so much more relaxed these days and had much more time for him; he had even begun to glimpse some of the earthy appeal that had drawn him to her in the first place. He realized how comfortable he felt with the earth-mother type, a description that could hardly be applied to the spiky Gwen.

Tonight he planned to put an end to his relationship with Gwen. There was nothing now to be gained from an 'outside interest' and everything to lose. He admitted to himself that getting shot of Gwen would be quite a relief.

He grinned slyly to himself as he watched Auriel hurry away towards her mysterious rendezvous. It was the third time he had dropped her off in Dorchester, though lately she had started to talk of having driving lessons so that she could drive herself. 'Auriel' and 'driving lessons' were not two concepts that he could even begin to put together but far be it for him to interfere, as long as she didn't expect him to teach her. Leave that to the new boyfriend! Auriel with a boyfriend was as odd a notion as her having driving lessons. No wonder she was so secretive about it.

Auriel waved to him as he passed her. Then waiting until he had turned the corner she slipped into the place in which she believed lay her salvation. It was only the third time she had attended and she still felt almost paralysed by shyness. However, they had made her so welcome that this time she was determined she would pluck up the courage to speak. And later on she did.

Rising to her feet she said in a trembling voice. 'Hallo, my name's Auriel and I'm an alcoholic.'

Holly sat on a bentwood chair in Gideon's kitchen, resting her arms on the back, watching Gideon make scrambled eggs and a winter salad from his garden.

307

'Are you all right?' he asked, glancing at her. She still looked pale and had hardly spoken on the journey back to Winterbourne Valence. They had spent the day at East Ashpool with Fern, hanging about waiting for news which never came. Lunch at The Green Man had been a sombre affair. Nobody had eaten much or felt much like talking. At half-past four they arranged to call it a day and for Gideon to drive Holly back to Winterbourne Valence for the night while Fern made arrangements to stay at The Green Man. They would meet again in the morning, or sooner if there was anything new.

Holly nodded, in answer to Gideon's question. 'Thank you for coming with me,' she said. 'I'm afraid it's messed up your schedule.'

'You don't have to thank me, idiot. I wanted to come with you,' he said, breaking eggs into a pan. 'My schedule, as you call it, is shot to hell anyway after this storm.' As if to prove his words the telephone rang for the umpteenth time since they'd arrived back, then switched to the answerphone. 'I'll deal with them after we've eaten,' he said. 'No point in panicking.'

'Is that you wearing your philosophical gardener's hat?'

'Something like that.' He put two plates heaped with golden piles of scrambled egg on to the table. 'Come and eat,' he said.

She decided she liked watching Gideon in his own surroundings, his mudcaked boots beside the door, the shelves of well-thumbed books on every aspect of his work, the order in his apparently disordered kitchen. And she liked the way he wore his hair in a pigtail, reminding her of a nineteenth-century sailor, though the ragged twist of checked scarf faintly but unintentionally suggested a bandit. An improbable notion, she thought as she drew her chair to the table. He had laid bread and salad on a checked tablecloth and opened a bottle of red wine. He poured her some.

'I think we could do with this,' he said.

A minute before she would have said that she wasn't hungry and at first she only toyed with the food, but after a slurp or two of the wine and tempted by the delicious aroma of the scrambled eggs, she finally polished them off and cleaned her plate with a piece of bread.

Afterwards she sat twisting the stem of her wine glass, that

Gideon had refilled. 'Did you hear Mr Watts say that he thought Emily might have chosen to stay knowing she might be – might be drowned?' she said.

'Yes, I heard him.'

'Do you think he could have been right?'

'I shouldn't take too much notice of Mr Watts.'

'I've been thinking. There might be something in what he said.'

'I think your grandmother has always been a risk taker. It's true she might have decided to leave it to fate.'

'So that if she survived the storm she would go obediently to Beaufort Court without a fuss. Though she must have known no one could have lived in that bedlam.'

'I think I do believe something along those lines.'

'Because you know she's dead?'

'I don't *know*. But I'm afraid there can't be much doubt.'

Holly thought for a long time.

'I suppose I never did see her settling down like a lamb at Beaufort Court,' she said.

'Neither did I.'

Holly gave a wan smile. 'She would have driven the staff mad.'

'Without doubt.'

'If it's true that she's dead, then it was a terrible way to die but it sort of suited her. I always said she went to extremes.' She got up and started mechanically to clear the plates. Gideon grabbed her arm. 'Leave it,' he commanded.

'Look, I'll stack them on the draining board and make some coffee while you go and sort out your messages.' There was a frozen quality about her that made Gideon anxious.

Later, when they had finished their coffee, Gideon said, 'Your eyes are drooping. Time for bed.'

As soon as they lay down they were both asleep. Only later did Holly wake up to find herself weeping. She cried noisily and copiously, banging the pillow as if in rage. Gideon came out of sleep and took her in his arms, rocking her gently, feeling her wet face against his chest.

Her body was as sturdy as a young oak but now she cringed like a wounded animal. He enfolded her, feeling that he owed her comfort at least. One of the phone messages had been from Sarah, casually inviting him to a party at the house of a friend of the Henderson family by the name of Max Sadler. Sadler was forty, owned a haulage firm and had been infatuated with Sarah for years, much to her amusement. Gideon had not returned the call. He still couldn't think of Sarah without a gut-wrenching stab of conscience over what had happened last time they'd met.

After the tears were finally over he and Holly made love, almost soberly. It was a gentle, soothing process, urgent only at the last moment when Gideon found himself saying over and over, 'I love you.' For now he knew that it was true. One day he hoped she would repeat the words to him and mean them.

Holly felt at peace for the first time that day. Perhaps it had been the scene of devastation and the probability of tragedy that had increased her need of Gideon. He had been there. He had not only driven her down to the Saltings but during that terrible journey he had not complained once, nor blamed her for dragging him out of his bed on a wild-goose chase. The long shadow of her rejecting father began to recede.

CHAPTER TWENTY-FOUR

They had to wait nearly a week for news of Emily. Twice they drove down to the Saltings, hoping that there might be a fresh report. Fern remained at The Green Man. The police assured them that there was no need for this, that they would be told as soon as they heard anything themselves. Fern had telephoned Francis, who had received the news first in shocked silence, then in extreme agitation.

'Why don't you come down here?' Fern suggested. 'I'm putting up at the local pub. There would be room.'

'Oh, no,' Francis said in horror. 'I couldn't possibly. Besides there is so much to do here. The gale has done substantial damage to the science wing.'

Fern was relieved. Francis might be Emily's brother but there was evidently no resemblance between the two. She couldn't imagine what it would be like to have to deal with a neurotic old man; she was having enough trouble keeping a cool head as it was.

The woman PC turned up one morning as the three of them were having coffee in The Green Man. They listened to what she had to tell them almost with relief.

'Where was she found?' Gideon asked.

'At the foot of Black Tout,' the young woman said. 'But I'm afraid you will have to identify the body. We have to be sure.'

Fern went pale. 'Where is she?'

'She was taken the mortuary in Exeter, Mrs Wyatt.'

'Do you want us to come at once?' Holly asked.

'We have a car outside. We're going there now.'

'There's the problem of getting back,' Gideon intervened. 'I'll take you.'

'Then let's get it over with,' Fern said, getting up, her face set.

They drove to Exeter and were shown to the room of the coroner's officer who asked for proof of their identities and relationship to the dead woman.

'And who will be identifying the body?' he asked, looking at the two women doubtfully. To him the elder appeared to be at the end of her tether already; the younger was – well – very young to be subjected to seeing her grandmother in this sad state.

'I will,' Gideon said firmly.

'We prefer a blood relative, if possible,' the coroner's officer said.

'Then I'll do it,' Fern said, suddenly and resolutely.

They all looked at her in surprise. It wasn't like Fern to insist.

'I'll come with you.' Gideon took her arm.

After an initial protest Holly gave in. After all, what she really wanted was for her last recollection of Emily to be of her standing in the sunset, wrapped in her cloak, not as a cadaver on a slab. The real Emily was already somewhere else.

Fern and Gideon were away scarcely more than a minute. When they returned Fern was pale, Gideon grim. He nodded. Fern signed a paper.

Holly looked hard at the wall.

'What happens now?' Gideon asked the officer.

'I'm afraid that in cases of sudden death there has to be a post mortem and an inquest, sir.'

It would take at least a week before these arrangements could be made. Gideon drove them all back to East Ashpool.

He had to return to Winterbourne Valence urgently to sort out all the problems the storms had visited on 'his' gardens. Before he left, he held Holly close.

'It wasn't so bad,' he lied. 'And I'm certain now that Emily wanted it this way.'

'Yes, I expect you're right,' Holly said in a small voice.

As he drove away it dawned on Gideon that now he would have to break the news to his father. Which was going to need almost as much courage as identifying Emily.

Gideon's mind was so full of what he had seen that day, the memory of the poor bloated and battered remains of Emily Troy was grievously persistent, that when he stepped into the cottage he could not at first take in the scene in front of him.

312

Papers and most of his precious books were scattered about the floor, the gardening boots that stood by the door had been filled to the brim with, it turned out, the contents of all the bottles of wine, whisky and brandy from his modest collection. In the conservatory several of his prize plants had been snapped off: his Chilean Bell flower and the *streptosolen jamesonii* had both succumbed and lay wilting on the floor.

Nothing appeared to have been stolen and this was a puzzle until he went upstairs to his bedroom where similar chaos reigned; then he realized that the metaphorical fuse that he had so carelessly lit had, at last, reached the bomb.

Across the mirror, written in red nail varnish, were the words: Shits like you had it coming. S.

Gideon sat down on the bed, sighed and rubbed his hands over his face. He felt very, very tired.

Gaining access to the house would have been a doddle. Sarah was well aware that he kept a spare key to the conservatory under a slab in the garden. He would have to stop that all-too-convenient practice.

He roused himself and began to clear up, in slow motion, like a sleepwalker. Perhaps *now* Sarah would be content to call it a day; perhaps now his bad conscience would settle for calling it quits. Tenderly, he rescued his books from the floor, straightened their ruffled pages and replaced them on the shelf.

Holly and Fern stayed on for a day or two, waiting for the news of the results of the post mortem and the date of the inquest. Not until those were completed could they make arrangements for the funeral. Fern telephoned Francis again, then Piers and Perry in Toronto.

Holly rang King's Melcombe where clearing up was underway. It wouldn't have been possible for her to work in the arboretum in any case, they said.

Then she went to see the warden at Beaufort Court. As she walked into the sterile courtyard with its institutional planting and its drifts of dead leaves, she wondered how they could ever have thought Emily could live here. It came to her forcibly that Emily had never intended to; but what *had* her intentions been since she could not possibly have foreseen the storm? Standing in that bleak, man-made place, Holly believed she understood. Emily had lived for a long time close to the natural rhythms of the seasons; of sea, wind and weather. It wasn't in her character to plan, she had lived from day to day. Holly now had no doubt that Emily believed her fate would be taken care of in its own time without fuss.

She called to mind the evening when Emily had said goodbye for the last time. There had been something special about that leave-taking, as if she knew. Everything about the events during those last months must have suggested to Emily that she was nearing the end: the destruction of the Saltings, her failing eyesight, even Holly herself and then Fern arriving on the scene and so putting an end to a chapter. She mourned Emily but knew that what had happened had been right for Emily.

She blew her nose hard and then rang Mrs Meyrick's bell in order to cancel Emily's place at Beaufort Court. Her news was, of course, superfluous. It had all been in the local paper.

Gideon looked at his watch. 'We have plenty of time,' he said. 'Let's all have a drink.'

Fern was indecisive. 'Well, perhaps a tonic.'

'Half of lager for me, please,' Holly said.

The pub where it was arranged that everyone should meet was within easy driving distance of the crematorium in Exeter. Gideon, Fern and Holly had arrived first. The post mortem had produced no surprises and the inquest had been routine; accidental death caused by drowning during the extreme weather and the old lady's misjudgement of the situation, probably as a result of her failing eyesight. The funeral was the last ordeal.

As he awaited his order Gideon glanced back to where the two women were sitting. At this moment he could at last detect more than a trace of resemblance between mother and daughter. Up until now he had found it hard to see how the harassed, dowdy-looking Fern could have borne anyone as vivid as Holly; but today she looked almost elegant in a tobacco-brown suit and a paisley shawl. Her eyes were large, like Holly's, but the bluish shadows underneath them were less noticeable today. She had evidently had something done to her hair, cut perhaps, because instead of being drawn back and fixed with an elastic band, it lay like feathers on her forehead. He recollected a painting of Monk's that he'd seen reproduced somewhere; a portrait of Fern as a solemn-eyed child holding a tortoiseshell cat in her arms. One of Monk's better efforts. What a pity that the painter, having observed and recorded that expression of edgy sensitivity in his child hadn't treated her with more compassion. But then, if all Gideon had heard about the man was true, he had simply recorded without actually understanding what he saw. Which failing later became his downfall.

Holly's vigour was more attributable to her grandmother than to her mother. Her close-cut hair was hidden under a big squashy hat and she was wearing a short black skirt over black woollen tights, an oversized multicoloured cardigan and a very long bronze-red scarf wound several times round her neck. With her tawny skin she reminded him of a sturdy sort of elf. To him she was beautiful and her beauty stirred him. All at once and quite inappropriately, he desired her. He would have liked to have made love to her that minute. Instead, he carried the drinks back to the table where they were sitting.

'My father was grieved that he couldn't come,' he said, spinning a chair round and sitting down. 'But I'm afraid attending the funeral might have upset him even more.'

'I'm sorry,' Fern said, pained on the old man's behalf – an old man she didn't even know. 'Is he very distressed?'

'He used to be very fond of her, you know.'

'Yes, Holly told me.'

'And I've noticed he's much frailer. He says it's only the onset of winter but I've noticed a difference since he heard about Emily. Even having his precious paintings returned to him undamaged didn't cheer him as much as we'd hoped.'

'What paintings were those?' Fern enquired, sipping her tonic.

'A couple that were stolen two years ago, a Cézanne and a Chagall.'

Fern's eyes widened. 'Goodness! I didn't realize his collection was as valuable as that. How awful for him. And I didn't know anything about their being students together until Holly told me. In fact, I knew none of the details of my mother's life until Holly went to see her. I never had the courage to look her up myself.'

315

'I'm glad your dad won't be here,' Holly said gruffly. 'He would hate it. It's going to be neither moving nor impressive, I can assure you.'

'It will be the best we can do,' Fern said almost sharply. 'In the circumstances.'

The circumstances, as Gideon was well aware, were that neither Fern nor Holly could afford anything but the cheapest funeral and neither would allow him to help with the cost.

'I don't think anything grand would have suited her in any case,' he said soothingly.

'She used to say,' Holly said, remembering, 'she wanted to be recycled as bone meal or something.'

'Holly!' Fern exclaimed. 'How could you!'

'I can't help it. That's what she said.'

At that moment a man and a woman entered the bar and hesitated just inside the door. The man wore a suit that had begun to take on the shape of his stooped shoulders and the slackness round his narrow haunches. The woman hovered just behind the man's gaunt figure as if she wished to remain invisible.

'Francis,' Gideon said. He left his chair and went to meet them.

'So that's Francis,' Holly said. 'Who's that with him, I wonder.'

'I've no idea,' Fern said.

Gideon made the introductions. Francis ushered the small woman forward.

'And this is Mrs May. Doreen. A good friend of mine.'

Doreen blushed. She was neatly dressed in a grey suit and wore a small black hat on her tight perm. 'How d'you do?' She shook hands and Holly had the fleeting impression that she was about to curtsy.

Everyone moved round to accommodate the new arrivals. Doreen was full of apologies for disturbing them.

'What will you drink?' Gideon asked, still standing.

'Sherry please, old chap,' Francis said. 'Dry. And a sweet one for Doreen. Dear me, what a journey!'

'Were there hold-ups?' Fern asked.

'What's that?' Francis leaned towards her.

'Were you delayed?' Fern said more loudly.

'No. No delays, I'm glad to say, but three hours! I ask you!'

'We're here now,' Doreen reassured him. 'Safe and sound.'

Gideon brought the drinks. Francis sipped his as if his life depended on it, then took out his large handkerchief and blew his nose. The news about Emily had brought on an attack of hay fever even though the pollen season was over. He looked at Fern and Holly with rheumy eyes.

'My word!' he exclaimed, his gaze coming to rest on Holly for the first time. 'You're the spitting image of old Jacko. Female, of course, but all the same—'

Holly stiffened. Gideon grinned as he saw the familiar fire blaze up in her eyes.

'Be careful, Mr Troy,' he said. 'I wouldn't advise you to pursue that topic.'

'What d'you mean?' Francis said, misunderstanding. 'I'm not a racist, you know.'

'It's not that. I believe it's the personality of the man she objects to.'

'Oh, quite. Goes without saying. Couldn't stand the chap myself. Sorry, Fern, my dear. Mustn't speak ill of the dead, and he *was* your father. One forgets.'

'Yes,' Fern said drily. 'One does.'

'I take it your brothers will not be present?' Francis said, finishing his sherry and looking round hopefully in case someone should offer to buy him another.

'It is rather a long way to come, Fern said, 'especially as they never really knew her.' They hadn't attended either their aunt's nor their uncle's funerals either though they had known them very much better; leaving the arrangements to her.

Holly noticed an urbane-looking man hovering near the door, glancing about him in a business-like manner. He was well-dressed, even to the point of foppishness, in a pale grey suit and a maroon tie. He smoothed down his hair which was cut long and was a distinctive silvery grey.

'Do we know him?' Holly asked as he made for their table.

'It's Davidson,' Francis said, looking anxious. 'Bruno Davidson.'

For a moment Davidson looked surprised. He hadn't expected to meet anyone he knew, having just popped in for a quick drink before the funeral.

317

He was introduced to Fern, Holly and Mrs May. Francis shot him numerous agitated glances which puzzled Bruno for several minutes before he understood the cause. He smiled, remembering a certain transaction.

'We seem to be making a habit of meeting at funerals,' was all he said, to Francis's obvious relief.

Gideon fetched him a drink. Soon after that it was time to leave.

Outside, in the yard behind the pub, the transport was sorted out. Holly and Fern travelled in Gideon's Volvo, the others in Bruno's hire car.

'Why d'you suppose Mr Davidson came?' Holly said, when they were in the car. 'Don't you think it's odd, him turning up like that?'

'He used to exhibit Jacko's paintings,' Fern said.

'Perhaps he was another of Emily's lovers,' Holly speculated. 'I wonder how many more will emerge from the woodwork.'

'I met him at Jacko's funeral,' Gideon said. 'My father says he's organizing a retrospective for Jacko. So naturally he'll be interested in Emily. She was part of the myth, wasn't she?'

The chapel at the crematorium was small and discreet, the mourners were few. So were the flowers. Apart from a huge and hideous bunch of chrysanthemums from the twins, there were tasteful lilies from Gideon and his father and a spray of freesias from Fern. While she had been at the Saltings Holly had picked up what she could find, creating an arrangement made from the leaves of sea holly, horned poppy, some twisted driftwood and holed pebbles all tied together with some strands of orange rope; things that reminded her of Emily.

There was someone in the chapel when they arrived, a young middle-aged man who leaped to his feet as the coffin passed. Holly thought he must have come to the wrong funeral.

They were shown to their seats and the taped music came to an end. Holly felt nothing; she could not believe these proceedings had anything to do with her grandmother. Wild, untidy, colourful Emily could not be contained within these sanitized walls. They had asked for no clergy to attend, since Holly insisted that Emily would not have approved. Instead Gideon gave a short resumé of her life (what was known of it) and paid tribute to her courage and her freedom of spirit. When he sat down, Holly took his place.

'I'm not much good at words and I don't know as much as my mother does about poetry, but I remembered reading something ages ago that I believe Emily would have secretly liked, though she would have been bound to call it mega sentimental, and there are some bits she wouldn't agree with.' She looked at the others, smiling and there was an immediate lightening of the atmosphere. 'It's called "Crossing the Bar", but it's not the sort of bar most of us are used to.'

She began to read some words she had copied on to a piece of paper.

> Sunset and evening star,
> And one clear call for me!
> And may there be no moaning of the bar,
> When I put out to sea,
>
> But such a tide as moving seems asleep,
> Too full for sound and foam,
> When that which drew from out the boundless deep
> Turns again for home.
>
> Twilight and evening bell,
> And after that the dark!
> And may there be no sadness of farewell,
> When I embark;
>
> For though from out our bourne of Time and Place
> The flood may bear me far,
> I hope to see my Pilot face to face
> When I have crossed the bar.

There was a long silence. Mrs May wiped away a tear. Then Holly folded the piece of paper and stepped down. The taped music began incongruously to play and slowly they began to file out of the chapel and into the lobby where they stood feeling slightly dazed. Francis was surreptitiously wiping his cheeks with his handkerchief. Mrs May took his arm comfortingly, her own eyes red though she hadn't even been acquainted with the dead woman. The man who had sat at the back approached the small group hesitantly.

'Mrs Wyatt? Miss Wyatt?' he said. 'My name is Martin Tallboys, I'm Miss Troy's solicitor. May I take this opportunity to offer you my condolences?'

Still snuffling into his handkerchief, Francis peered at Mr Tallboys over Holly's shoulder. 'I never knew she had a solicitor.'

'I tried to get in touch with you at your Bath address,' he said to Fern. 'Without success, I'm afraid.'

'We've been at the Saltings,' Fern said, bemused.

'Yes, of course. Only you see, I was supposed to have arranged the funeral.'

'You?'

'Unfortunately I was on holiday and only heard about Miss Troy's terrible accident when I got back. All the same, I thought it might save you a journey if you could perhaps arrange to come to my office while you're still in Exeter. It's about the will.'

'The will?' Fern echoed.

'I didn't know she'd made a will,' Holly said.

Gideon looked round at a new batch of mourners who were just arriving.

'I suggest we go somewhere else to discuss this,' he said.

Mr Tallboys cleared his throat. 'As a matter of fact,' he said, 'although I was too late to make the funeral arrangements I have been able to see to it that tea is laid on at The Royal Clarence. In Exeter, you know. That was Emily's own idea and she specifically asked if Mr Davidson could be present too.'

Bruno looked puzzled. He had heard nothing of the events of the past week or two, or of Emily's death until, out of the blue, Mr Tallboys had telephoned him asking him if it would be convenient for him to attend the funeral. Naturally he was glad to pay his last respects to a woman he had once also respected in life. He was only sorry that her early promise had been so completely swamped by Jacko's monstrous ego.

As Mr Tallboys had said, tea was awaiting them in a private room in the hotel, overlooking the Cathedral precinct. Outside, the light from a low sun seemed about to dissolve the massively square shape of the Cathedral and the trees on the green in liquid gold. It reminded Holly of a Monet and her spirits rose by a degree.

'What's all this about, Mr Tallboys?' she said to him in a low voice as she accepted her cup of tea and cast herself down in a comfortable armchair next to him. 'I was under the impression that all Emily's wordly possessions went down the tubes during the storm.'

'That's essentially true, Miss Wyatt,' he said, helping himself to a cucumber sandwich. 'But she does mention a few outstanding items in her will. If you can spare the time, perhaps later this afternoon or tomorrow, I could go through the will with you.'

'What about the others?'

'Any member of the family would be welcome, naturally. It's just that she named you and me as executors.'

'Perhaps it had better be this afternoon before everybody goes home.'

'That's what I hoped.'

After tea they all trooped the few yards across the Cathedral Green to Southernhay where Martin Tallboys had his office. It was in a row of dignified regency houses, now almost all offices, with vermiculated freestone and neat black-painted railings.

Extra chairs were brought into Mr Tallboys' high-ceilinged office and they all sat down. Above the panelling Holly noticed some rather good modern etchings of local landmarks: Haytor and Becka Falls.

Martin Tallboys settled himself behind his desk and withdrew some documents from a box file. He was older than Holly had first supposed, nearer forty than thirty. He had fine, dark brown hair that was already receding from a high forehead; he was smooth-skinned and had intelligent hazel eyes. Holly hadn't had any experience of solicitors but this one didn't seem too bad.

'I am aware, of course,' Mr Tallboys began, 'that some of Miss Troy's effects have been lost as a result of the storm but we are here to allocate certain financial assets and see to the disposal of the remainder of her estate, after expenses have been taken care of. Perhaps you will bear with me while I read the disposition to you.'

It didn't take long. After the funeral expenses and the solicitor's fee had been paid, the remaining capital, boosted considerably by Francis's recent largesse, was to be equally divided between Francis, Fern, the twins in Canada and Holly. Two small engravings by A. J. Monk in her possession at the time of her death were to go to Francis, 'who had already appreciated at least some of Jacko's efforts'. The remaining paintings were left to Holly to dispose of as she thought fit, after consultation with Bruno Davidson.

'The remaining paintings?' Holly said. 'What paintings?'

'I knew that this may raise questions in your mind,' Tallboys said, diving into the file. 'Miss Troy left a message for you, Miss Wyatt.' He passed her a piece of paper.

Holly read it silently. 'I hope that, after all, you won't feel I've wasted my life, Holly. These are for you because you made time for your awful old grouch of a grandmother, who wants you to know she loved you.'

Holly folded the paper abruptly, forcing back tears.

'What did she mean?' she asked huskily.

'The paintings?' Tallboys got up from his seat. 'I have taken the liberty of removing at least some of them from store. They are in the next room if you'd care to take a look.'

With eyes still precariously full Holly went with Fern, Bruno and Gideon into the next room. Had Emily played some kind of posthumous joke on them? Francis followed behind, afraid that he might miss something; hesitantly Mrs May brought up the rear.

The room next door was a storeroom, lined with filing cabinets, but in front of the cabinets were a number of flat bubble-wrapped packages. Martin Tallboys bent down and began to remove the wrapping from one of them; After a moment Holly began on the next. Soon there was a pile of bubble-wrap in one corner and, facing them, about a dozen canvases. There was a second or two of silence.

'Oh,' Francis said, disappointed. 'More paintings.'

Bruno stepped forward and picked up the first one, turning it to the light. It was luminescent with colour: a limpid peacock blue trembled against a block of ochre, the ochre in turn was set beside a transparent jade; there were flashes of orange and a hint of red oxide. In this painting the underlying drawing was cobalt blue. It was a shimmering recollection of Sandplace in summer. Not quite defined, objects gave the impression of being just outside the field of vision, which when focused on might disappear, in particular a shape, no more than a stroke of the brush, that suggested a retreating female figure.

Holly, leaning over Bruno's shoulder, sucked in her breath. The signature, which was just decipherable in the left-hand corner was EBT. Emily's second name, Holly remembered, was Beatrice. The T was for Troy, of course. This was Emily's painting. She stared at the canvas, stunned.

Bruno picked up a second painting, a still life. Amethyst, dark green, a strident yellow, deep blue; flowers on the dresser at Sandplace with a glimpse of the sea reflected in a mirror, and also reflected in the mirror, the figure of a woman, walking away. This too was signed EBT. And it too had the hallmarks of the same style; colour and shape finely balanced but with a hint of risk, the suggestion of drama and passion, the touch of the brush unerring.

There were others. Paintings that alluded to the cliffs and the sea, some to woods and fields, others still to groupings of flowers, driftwood and other objects picked up on the beach. There were one or two in which the blocky shapes and colours suggested the shacks and shanties of the Saltings. Most of them had the same allusive retreating figure. Immediately, Holly recognized the style as the flowering of all the qualities already incipient in the two paintings Emily had given her earlier.

'This beats everything,' Bruno said.

'There are others,' Mr Tallboys said. 'These are just some of them.'

'And they're all of this quality?' Bruno said. He had put the canvas he'd been holding next to the others and had stepped back to view them together.

'You'd be more likely to be able to tell *me*, of course. But, yes, I would say so.'

'And how many are there?'

'About two hundred. I understand she destroyed anything she thought was not up to scratch.'

'Two hundred!' Holly exclaimed.

'It does represent about forty years' work. If you turn them over you'll see that they're all dated.'

'Why didn't she tell anybody what she did?' Holly wanted to know. 'And how did you come to have them?'

'She stopped painting altogether about two years ago,' Mr Tallboys said, 'when her eyesight began to fail, as I understand. Then earlier this year when she made her will she put them into store for safekeeping. And left them to you. You'd no idea she painted?'

'I knew she used to, when she was young. There were one or two of those at the Saltings. She gave them to me. But I didn't know she'd been painting all the time. The crafty old so-and-so.'

'Holly!' Fern said. But she was already beginning to understand her mother's need to work without the razzmatazz that accompanied Jacko's career. She knew at once that the paintings were exceptional. Presumably Emily was content to let posterity decide if it wanted her lifetime's product or not. Could it have been that while she lived, all she wanted was to be left alone to follow her own vision? Because *that* Fern could understand.

Holly turned to Bruno. 'They're good, aren't they? I mean *very* good. I'm not a painter myself but it seems to me they're pretty stunning.'

Bruno, who had taken up an attitude of deep study, nodded. 'Yes, Miss Wyatt. I think we'd agree on that. As you say, they're "pretty stunning".' With an effort he dragged his eyes away from the paintings and looked at Holly. 'What will you do with them?'

'I don't know. It's all such a shock. Maybe I could discuss it with you later, after probate's sorted out.'

'The two Monk engravings are here,' Martin Tallboys said, pulling the wrapping away from two smaller packages. 'The ones Miss Troy left to Mr Troy.' He was smiling and Holly could have sworn the smile betrayed a hint of real amusement, mischief even. When she saw the engravings she understood.

Mrs May gave a little gasp of horror. 'Oh, my goodness!'

Martin Tallboys replaced the wrappings.

Francis, aware of the subject matter of the engravings even without benefit of his bifocals, had gone brick red. 'Emily always did have a peculiar sense of humour,' he blustered. 'Of course I can't accept them. They're filthy.'

'Perhaps you'd like me to dispose of them for you when the time comes,' Bruno offered blandly. 'There are a number of collectors and dealers who specialize in this kind of thing, as you know—'

'I know no such thing,' Francis said huffily. 'But get rid of them, by all means.'

Holly caught Gideon's eye, her tears suddenly turning into a small explosion of laughter. Gideon was glad to hear the sound. He'd missed it in recent weeks.

'I tried to persuade Miss Troy to sell me one of her paintings,' Martin Tallboys said. 'But she refused. She said she wanted to leave you the collection intact, as it were. I asked her why she had allowed her painting to lapse while she was married to Jacko Monk. I thought, you see, that being married to a famous painter would have been an advantage.'

'Did you?' Holly said, staring at him. 'Did you really?'

'Anyway, she just laughed,' Mr Tallboys admitted, thinking that Miss Wyatt was a bit of an oddity and probably set fair to be as eccentric as the old lady.

The will having sprung no further surprises, the funeral party returned to the room at The Royal Clarence which Mr Tallboys told them had been hired until eleven p.m. and would include dinner. For at least three of the party no further surprises were necessary since the revelation of the paintings was quite enough to be going on with.

Bruno was very quiet as they sat over drinks.

'It was just like Emily to ask Mr Tallboys to organize all this,' Holly said, sitting herself in the armchair beside him.

He nodded thoughtfully, placing his drink on a side table.

'Are you sure you'd no idea she'd continued painting?' Holly said.

'Absolutely none. I reckon she must have had the last laugh after all.'

'Yes, that fits.'

'So what d'you think I should do with the paintings then?' she asked. 'I'm afraid they wouldn't all fit into my flat.'

Bruno roused himself at last. 'Fit in your flat! My dear young lady, those paintings are going to be exhibited. And, with your permission of course, I'm going to be the one who exhibits them!'

* * *

Joss Kingsnorth

When it came to surprises Francis was not to be outdone by his sister. After dinner, which included a delicious fillet of salmon with a carrot and cucumber sauce as well as chocolate fudge cake, all of which Francis tucked into with gusto, he rose to his feet and tapped on his glass for their attention.

'I fear this is not the most felicitous or appropriate occasion to announce our news,' he said, rather pompously. 'But as I'm sure Emily would have approved, I think I shall go ahead anyway.'

He looked at Mrs May, who smiled and blushed.

'Next Easter I shall be giving up Rudyards,' he went on. 'Selling out and retiring, you know. In fact negotiations are in hand at this moment. Through the good offices of one of my "parents" who is in the property business, I have been lucky enough to find a delightful apartment in Chiswick in which to spend my retirement. Which bring me to the most exciting part of what I have to say.' He paused to make sure he had everyone's attention. 'I am happy to be able to tell you that Doreen has consented to be my wife and, if all goes according to plan, the wedding will take place in six weeks' time.'

He looked round with an uncertain and slightly foolish grin but the news was not the sensation he'd anticipated. Since there appeared to be no other explanation for Mrs May's admiring presence everyone had evidently come to the conclusion, however improbable, that Francis and Mrs May had 'something going'.

'I expect you will think it very courageous of Doreen to take on a crusty old bachelor such as myself,' he said, after congratulations had been forthcoming. 'And I'm bound to say I agree with you – but there you are! This dear lady, bless her, seems prepared to take the risk.'

'Francis. Dear!' Mrs May protested fondly.

The news of Emily's death had had the effect of propelling Francis into a course of action that he had previously merely toyed with. While Emily had been alive she had unknowingly acted as a buffer, a bulwark between himself and the extinction he so much feared; now he had to face it undefended and alone. Mrs May, Doreen, was at hand; she was kind, docile and appreciative. Providence was now on his side, apparently.

'I think that's absolutely great! I'm sure you'll be very happy,'

Holly said, thinking that their initial reaction had been too polite and half-hearted.

'Come on!' Gideon said, rising to his feet and to the occasion. 'Let's order some champagne and drink a toast!'

'Oh, no. Gideon, please,' Mrs May gasped. 'Not with Miss Troy just—' She lapsed into an embarrassed silence.

'But that's a brilliant idea. Emily would have got a tremendous buzz,' Holly said. 'And she would certainly have taken first swig if she'd been here.'

Mrs May was shocked. Francis's family were certainly a little strange; but since Francis himself seemed to think it was all in order, perhaps she was just being too sensitive. Miss Troy, Emily, had after all, been very elderly. Her passing was to be expected.

Emily's wake turned out to be a celebration. Holly felt better; Emily would have given one of her gutsy shouts of laughter at such a turn of events. The occasion of her long-term bachelor brother getting hitched would have prompted some of her pithiest comments.

Francis, Mrs May – or Doreen, as they were now to think of her – and Bruno were staying overnight. Fern, Gideon and Holly were leaving for Bath.

As they joined the M5 Holly, in the passenger seat next to Gideon, said, 'I hope I'm doing the right thing.'

'The right thing?' Gideon accelerated past a slow-moving vehicle and the Volvo joined the glittering line of lights heading towards Bristol. In the back, Fern closed her eyes. She felt very tired.

'Letting Emily's paintings be exhibited.' Holly went on. 'After all, she wouldn't show them while she was alive.'

'That's because she didn't want the hassle. It's different now. Besides, don't you see, if she hadn't wanted them exhibited she would hardly have left them to you *and* got Tallboys to have Bruno hike all the way down here to see them. If she'd intended her work never to see the light of day she would have burned the lot of them ages ago.'

'Of course. I just wasn't thinking straight.'

Gideon reached over and put his hand over hers, which were clasped in her lap. 'It's been a tough day,' he said.

'Thanks for your help,' she said gruffly. 'I mean, you're no relation or anything. You didn't have to do all this.'

'I wanted to,' he said. 'And, one way and another, I almost feel I *am* a relation.' A small voice inside him reminded him that the activity had also conveniently removed him from the attentions of Sarah. He had at last begun to relax, feeling in his bones that Sarah had had her final say.

Claire Littlechild poured herself a drink while she prepared *moules marinières* and garlic bread for one and laid a small table with a white cloth; on the table she fastidiously arranged some designer cutlery and a single glass. These things mattered. Naturally they mattered, since she was in the business of design and display. She had worked hard and her monthly salary cheque and commission on top of that were substantial. Which was why she could afford a flat like this in Central London.

She had put her meal on the table and was about to pour herself a glass of Australian Chardonnay when the buzzer sounded indicating that there was someone at the front door.

'Shit! Who the sod's that!' She'd had a long, busy day and believed she'd earned at least three hours' peace before the party. Someone in the department was celebrating their twenty-fifth birthday.

She picked up the door phone and listened. 'Oh, it's you,' she said. 'I thought you'd died. OK, come on up.'

Zak looked very different from when she'd last seen him but then that was nothing unusual. He had allowed the bleached hair to grow out and wore it longer, though that wasn't all that was different. He looked drawn, grey and depressed; his normally trendy clothes looked shabby and there were small tears in his chinos. His hands and even his face had the scars of old scratches, small pink wheals that gave him a disreputable appearance.

Claire was so astonished that she forbore to make a joke about some woman catching up with him. She simply shrugged and said nothing.

He pushed past her. 'Don't say *anything*,' he snarled superfluously. 'Just pour me a drink.'

'I'm having wine.'

'Got anything stronger?'

'There's vodka. It's in the kitchen. You can help yourself. I'm going to eat.'

Having fetched his vodka, which he intended to drink neat, Zak flopped down on her monster white-upholstered sofa and put his filthy trainers on the arm. She glared but said nothing. Zak closed his eyes and lay like one dead for several minutes. When he opened them again to gulp from his glass, the pile of mussel shells on the side of Claire's plate was a little higher. For the first time he noticed the flat had undergone a radical transformation since he had last seen it. Gone were the primary colours and Mondrian-influenced décor; now everything seemed to be made of metal or wire. The sturdy scarlet-painted table had been replaced with something that appeared to be a hospital trolley with many years' service, and the battered metal chairs looked as if they'd be more at home in a East End sweatshop. From a galvanized rail fixed to the rough white wall hung a row of meat hooks from which depended various household objects, previously kept tucked away in drawers.

He put a hand over tired eyes. 'Oh Christ!' he said. 'Industrial chic.'

Claire's glossy red lips made a hard line. 'So?'

He made an irritable gesture.

Claire put the last shell on the side of her plate. 'I take it you screwed up?'

'Shut it, will you?'

'You never told me what you were up to but it doesn't take an Inspector Morse to see you've made a right Horlicks of it.'

'Look, for Christ's sake, shut up!'

'I suppose you want to stay?'

He grunted assent, then said in a falsetto voice. 'Don't tell me? You use this place like a doss house. I don't see you for months and then you turn up expecting me to drop everything! Blah blah blah blah blah.'

'What if I have a live-in boyfriend?'

'You haven't have you?' he said.

'As it happens, no.'

'That's all right then.' He finished his vodka and refilled his glass from the bottle which he had thoughtfully brought with him from the kitchen.

Claire finished her wine and refilled her own glass. She had no idea why she allowed Zak to treat her as he did. Their relationship hardly merited the description, it was more a series of one-night stands. He gave her nothing yet expected her to make herself, her food and her flat available to him at the drop of a hat. Friends who knew her situation said she was mad. In spite of her probings he never told what he did or where he lived between visits; she had given up even trying to find out but she presumed that his occupation was unquestionably illegal. All he would say was that it wasn't drugs.

'Drugs are out,' she'd said once, although she herself wasn't averse to the occasional joint. 'I'm not having my place turned over and my throat cut for you or anyone.'

'If you'd had your throat cut I don't suppose you'd mind about having your place turned over,' he'd said, grinning. 'In any case, it's not drugs. I can tell you that at least.'

She'd believed him then, though she knew, none better, that he could lie through his teeth. Now she was beginning to wonder.

It was later in the evening, much later, too late to go to the party even, that he got round to asking her for money.

'What took you so long?' she said, turning her wrist over to look at her watch. He leaned over her in bed, his parti-coloured hair flopping over his forehead.

'Because I don't just come for that. You should know that by now. And I always remember to pay you back.'

'Except when you don't,' she said, pushing her legs out from under the duvet and sitting up.

He stroked her bare back.

'I don't know why you don't stop arsing around and join our department,' she said, pulling on a kimono with a design of graffiti printed on it. 'You're good when you really try – and there's a vacancy as it happens.'

'And work under you, I suppose?'

'Not necessarily.'

'I'd rather work on top of you.'

'Don't be so unutterably vulgar,' she said snootily, making for the shower. 'By the way,' she called as she went, 'there's a heap of mail for you. It's in the wire trug in the other room.' She shut the door of the bathroom with a decisive bang.

Mail. For a moment Zak's mouth went dry. He had not yet recovered his equilibrium after his brick-shitting experience in Dorset. The discovery that he had been shopped to the Art squad had been bad, losing the money worse still, but the stuff of real nightmare had been trying to get out of the place they called 'The Undercliff', an innocuous enough name for hell if ever there was one. At the last possible moment, when he would have been overjoyed to see a living soul, even the fuzz, he had discovered an exit. In fact, he *had* seen a copper but by that time it was dark and Zak had given him the slip and legged it across a couple of fields to a narrow lane. He had trudged along a minor road for some time before hitching a lift from a chap towing a horsebox.

He slit open an envelope with a Dorset postmark and discovered it was from Regine Monk's solicitors. The letter informed him that, as instructed by their client, they were enclosing a cheque which represented his share of the delivery advance for the biography of Aurelius J. Monk. Zak turned the cheque over. It was for a thousand pounds.

'You're looking like someone's singing your song all of a sudden,' Claire said as she emerged from the shower, towelling her short hair. 'Is it me or the vodka?'

He caressed her bottom through her kimono. 'You. What else?'

She snatched the cheque from him and glanced at it. 'Oh, yes? A thousand smackeroos, eh? And legal tender by the look of it.'

He grabbed it back. 'Hands off, woman! That's going to be put to extraordinarily good use. I have an idea—'

She sighed. 'Here we go again! Well, bye bye, baby. It was nice knowing you.'

Arlette dropped her bombshell one evening when they were sitting round the table finishing their meal, which had been plain but good; steak and kidney pudding followed by apple and cinnamon tart, made with apples from the Burr Ash apple trees. Now that she had more time, Arlette's cooking had improved, helped along by the fact that she now spent a great deal of her day poring over English cookery books and trying out some of the recipes on the family. Now they all began to see why.

'I think we should open an hotel,' she said.

Everyone stopped eating at once and stared at her. Andra stopped fondling the ears of the tabby cat on her lap, the fork in her other hand suspended in midair.

'An hotel!' It was a kind of Greek Chorus with added astonishment.

'Well, not quite an hotel, perhaps. A sort of guesthouse specializing in good country cooking.'

'You don't know anything about running an hotel *or* a guesthouse,' Donald said, passing his plate for more apple tart.

'I can learn. Besides, I've already read some books on it.'

'Books! What books?'

'Books I got from the library. And pamphlets.'

'And then there's all the EU regulations.'

Calmly, Arlette cut another slice of tart and handed it back to her husband. 'I've been looking in the Yellow Pages, you'd be surprised at how few hotels and guesthouses there are just around here. Which is a pity because it's a very pretty part of Dorset.'

'That I grant you. But think of the work.' Donald's arguments were not particularly vigorous because he didn't believe his wife was serious.

Auriel chipped in without warning. 'I think it's a marvellous idea!'

Everyone turned to look at her. She so rarely volunteered an opinion that it took them all by surprise. She went red and turned her attention to her pudding.

'Yeah,' Fergus said. 'So do I. I think it'd be brilliant.'

'I've been thinking about it for ages,' Arlette said doggedly. 'Especially when I'm doing the accounts.' She looked meaningfully at her husband from under her thick brows. 'In fact, as far as I can see it would be the only way we can continue to live at Burr Ash.'

The two girls exchanged anxious glances.

Donald, too, looked worried. 'Are you serious?'

'About staying here, yes. *And* about opening a guesthouse,' Arlette said. She had finished her own meal and was sitting with her hands clasped over her stomach, an attitude that was both defensive and determined. 'Maman left us what she could and there'll be a little coming in from dear Jacko's biography but it won't be anything like enough to keep us all.'

'There's the shop,' Donald said. 'Don't forget that.'

'But you're always saying that it doesn't make much money, Donald.'

Donald frowned. It was perfectly true but he didn't like to broadcast the fact.

'So I thought,' Arlette went on stolidly, 'I thought that if you gave it up you could help me run Burr Ash as a nice, quiet country house hotel.'

'I think you've gone mad!'

'In beautiful surroundings,' Auriel said. 'People would love it, wouldn't they?'

'Of course we'd have to do it up,' Arlette went on as if there'd been no interruptions. 'Get it all renovated, put in more bathrooms and so on.'

The two girls looked at each other again. 'I think it's a lovely idea,' Adina said. She very much fancied the idea of living in a hotel.

'So do I,' Andra echoed. The cat on her lap dug in its claws in response to her tickling it behind the ears. Nobody said anything about her having the cat on her lap at mealtimes these days.

Donald continued to dismiss the notion out of hand, especially the bit about him giving up the bookshop. 'You simply haven't thought it through, Lettie. It's just a passing fad, a pipe dream.' He thought about the bookshop. That had been a pipe dream that had gone sour. 'And bloody hard work, if you ever did get it off the ground.'

'Don't swear, Donald.'

The girls giggled.

Arlette was unmoved and Donald began to fear that she was absolutely determined. Arlette determined was an awesome sight. 'As you know, Donald, I'm not afraid of hard work. It's the one thing I know. But working for ourselves would be quite different.

'Yeah,' Fergus put in. 'Right.'

'No need for you to put your spoke in,' Donald said to his son. He pushed his empty plate away and put his elbows on the table, frowning. Looking hard at Auriel, he said, 'You seem to agree with your sister. Are you saying you're keen on the idea too, given the hard work involved?' He had to admit that his sister-in-law was looking a good deal better lately, but he was beginning to have doubts about the existence of a lover.

Auriel saw the opportunity she had looked for but dreaded. She glanced round the table. 'I'm afraid that I've not always pulled my weight in the past but I would certainly support you to the hilt if you decided to go ahead with this idea.'

Even loyal Arlette could not deny that, up until Maman died, Auriel's help could not always be counted on, though lately there'd been a big improvement.

'But there was something else I wanted to say,' Auriel went on in a rush. 'I wanted to say that it was my fault Fergus got hold of that gin bottle. It could have been extremely serious, I see that now. It was a bottle I brought into the house and I might as well tell you now that it was just about the last.'

'It wasn't your fault I drank it,' Fergus said magnanimously. 'I did that on my own.'

'Anyway,' Auriel said, smiling at her nephew, 'it would be lovely having a proper responsibility after – after—' she faltered, but they all knew that what she meant to say was now that Regine and Jacko were both dead, they would be able to get on with their own lives in whatever way they pleased.

They all felt it. Even Arlette, who had adored her parents unreservedly, realized, if dimly, that while Regine and Jacko had been alive they had all gone about their own lives in a trance, as if mesmerized by the two overpowering personalities. It would take time but even now, they were emerging as if from a long tunnel, blinking, into the brilliance of the day.

'Just supposing I did give up the bookshop,' Donald said. 'What would my function be in all this?'

'You'd be the manager. The *maître d'hôtel*,' Arlette said craftily.

'More like a general factotum,' he blustered, nevertheless seeing himself in an entirely new light all of a sudden, with the possibility that other people would also see him in an entirely new, respectful, light as well.

'I'd go for it if I was you,' Fergus advised.

'You would, would you?' Donald said, standing up and pushing back his chair. 'Well, let's just say, I'll think about it.' He turned to

Arlette, who had begun to clear the plates. 'What we have to do, you see, is to get some advice about a scheme like this. Bone up on it. You just can't go into these things half-arsed, you know.'

'No,' Arlette said, earnestly. 'That's quite right, Donald.'

'Then perhaps we can talk about it again.'

'I think it'd be magic,' Fergus said, thinking ahead. He rather fancied himself as an owner of a hotel. Eventually, of course.

CHAPTER TWENTY-FIVE

The little waves folded over, broke and fanned out across the flat sand to spend themselves in an arc of bubbles. The tide was ebbing. Along the beach rocky outcrops stood like lumps of jet against the glittering morning sun; there was a stinging freshness in the air. Far out, a line of clouds marched along the horizon. The sea was the colour of pewter but with a million tiny suns reflected in it and cool jade glimmered intermittently in the curve of the waves.

Few people came to the beach these days and no one this early in the morning, when the sun was scarcely over the horizon. Holly had chosen the hour on purpose to avoid curious eyes.

Fern and Gideon watched her from their perch on what remained of the dunes, a solitary figure far out along the tideline.

'Best to leave it to her,' Fern said. 'After all, she knew Emily as well as anyone could be said to have known her.'

They watched in silence. Then: 'Are you glad you met Emily again?' Gideon asked.

'I believe that it helped both of us in some indefinable way, yes.'

'Mm. And how's retirement going? Are you glad about that too?'

Fern laughed. 'Let's just say that I wish I'd thought of it before. Before things got so impossible. It would have saved me a whole lot of grief; but it was a question of misplaced pride, you see.'

'Yes, I understand that.'

'Now my life is almost as busy. There's Palladian and I'm going to two art classes a week.'

'Yes, Holly told me. Do you enjoy it?'

'It's another thing I wish I'd thought of before. I've just switched to oils. Watercolours require one to be so much more decisive!' She laughed at herself. 'Anyway, talking of decisiveness, I've already booked up to go to the painting school in Italy. The one I went to last July.'

'That's fantastic. Good for you.'

She was silent, aware of seeming to be chattering. The one change she hadn't mentioned, because she believed, wrongly, that Gideon would laugh at her, was the arrival of Mabel. She had set out to acquire a kitten and had returned with an eighteen-month-old tortoiseshell cat. It had been nervous at first but was settling down well in the quietness of the flat. And it was affectionate, reminding her of one she'd had at Burr Ash when she was a child and that had given her comfort then. It sat among her paints in the evening, watching her every move, waiting for the time when she made herself a drink and retired to her chair, when it would immediately leap on to her lap. It gave her a warm feeling to think that the cat needed her as much as she had needed the cat.

Gideon watched Holly's distant figure. It was an astonishing relief to be able to do so without an undercurrent of guilt and unease. He had been released from these at last from a quite unexpected quarter which had been, in his eyes, totally undeserved and nothing whatever to do with his astute handling of the situation. He'd had another phone call from Elizabeth Henderson.

She'd come straight to the point. 'I'd just like you to know that Sarah is engaged,' she said in a voice so cold he wondered that his ear hadn't suffered from frostbite.

'Engaged?' His surprise obviously gratified her.

'We're thrilled about it, needless to say, since Max has always been such a good family friend.'

Gideon, recovering from the shock of both who was ringing him and the nature of her news, said. 'Max Sadler?'

'Of course Max Sadler. He's always adored her and she is very fond of him, naturally. To tell you the truth, Gideon, it's what my husband and I always hoped for.' He noticed 'Douglas' had become 'my husband'.

'I'm glad,' he said sincerely. 'Very glad. Congratulate them for me. I hope Sarah will be very happy.'

'*Do* you, Gideon?' she said across the frozen wastes. 'Do you really?'

'Of course, Mrs Henderson. In spite of what you think I always did care about her happiness.'

'Is that so? Well, I'm delighted to be able to tell you that your feelings no longer enter into it, since the family are all of the opinion that she's at last made the right choice. The wedding is to be quite soon and since Sarah is generous to a fault she may even invite you. However, Gideon, a word of advice. Speaking on behalf of my husband and myself, I have to warn you that you would not be made welcome. That's all I had to say.' The line went dead.

He really did hope Sarah had in fact made the right choice. Words like 'rebound' and 'marry in haste' immediately occurred to him. But, as Elizabeth had pointed out, it was no longer his business. Thank God.

'Us is all back yur, then?' Mr Watts appeared beside Gideon and Fern, gazing out at the place that had been his home.

Fern smiled. 'All the way from Honiton, Mr Watts?'

'A mate of mine wuz coming this way. Thought I'd give Percy a run 'stead of 'im getting under my darter's feet all the bloody time. Poor little bugger.'

By the last remark Fern and Gideon took him to mean Percy, not his daughter. Percy had already taken off and was tearing round after gulls, mad with joy at being in his old hunting grounds.

'We never thanked you properly for trying so hard to save my mother,' Fern said. 'We really appreciated your effort. It wasn't your fault that she was so terribly stubborn.'

''Twan't nothing,' Mr Watts said modestly. 'I reckon 'er stayed on purpose,' he added darkly.

'I suppose no one will ever know.'

'See the little maid's back. The ol' 'ooman was powerful fond of 'un, that's a fact.'

'Yes, I think she was,' Fern said.

Under her jacket Holly carried what the undertakers called an urn but which was, in fact, an ignominious plastic pot made to look like wood. It was unexpectedly heavy. She walked on, heading for the rocks. The beach was beginning to recover from the scarring inflicted upon it first by JCBs and then by the storm. The West Country news programme had recently been full of the reported bankruptcy of the consortium who had such plans for the marina. They had declared the site as, after all, unsuitable, but nobody knew whether or not this was true or a face-saving cover story. But the Saltings itself was safe from their predations, even if the shacks and shanties were no more.

A narrow spur of rock thrust itself out to sea, the remains of some ancient seam that had been turned, twisted, up-ended and finally eroded to the level of the waves. From this vantage point Holly could stand above the deeper water where a forest of oar weed swayed in time with the surge. Here the surf pounded more urgently, pouring over the rocks and seething in the pools and fissures.

She squatted above the turbulence and looked along the beach to where Sandplace once stood. The sand was already drifting back over the wounds, obliterating them, drawing a veil over the place where humans had, for a time, made their habitation. Now there was nothing left to show they had ever been here. And there would be nothing left to prove that Emily had ever existed if it had not been for the paintings, and a small piece of wood inscribed with the letters SANDPL. Emily would not have claimed either her children or her children's children as part of her contribution to posterity. She had regarded Holly as a friend first, rather than part of the family from which she had become alienated. Emily, it seemed had loved her in her strange, stoical fashion. There had been moments, gestures, hints which, knowing her grandmother's normal reserve, had seemed significant to Holly. It had been almost as if her grandmother were relearning the language of affection. And hadn't she, Emily, trusted Holly with the most intimate things she possessed? Martin Tallboys had told her that her grandmother's decision to leave her paintings to Holly had been a recent one. He thought, but he wasn't sure, that she had previously meant to destroy them.

Tears that she might have shed, that had been dammed up by a kind of numb shock, had now been evaporated by the drama of the discovery of the paintings. It was almost as if Emily had engineered it so that tears would not be shed, or at least not for long. Had Emily, after all, understood the nature of love better than Holly did? She twisted the garnet ring on her finger, now scratched and battered; it was too big for her. It hadn't been mentioned specifically in the will and it had even crossed her mind to let it stay on Emily's finger but in the end she had kept it. If all the paintings finally belonged to a wider public, the ring represented something tangible and intimate. She still had no idea where it had come from in the first place. Emily would never tell her. She assumed that the giver had been neither Jacko nor Aiden; perhaps Emily merely bought it for herself because she took a fancy to it. Holly would wear it, on special occasions, to remember Emily by.

The tide was abandoning the higher pools. She moved further down the rocks, with their accretions of limpets and barnacles, until her feet were within inches of the highest surges. Gulls wheeled round speculatively. She unscrewed the lid of the urn and, turning it upside down, energetically strewed the contents in a wide arc over the swirling, foaming water. Some of the ash was taken by the tide, the rest was whirled away by the breeze and then was gone.

Holly sat on the rocks for a long time looking out to sea, her arms resting on her knees. After today she would not return to the Saltings. It might not be turned into a marina after all but it would probably be changed. Concreted over to make a caravan site and a car park perhaps, with stalls for hot dogs and ice cream; public conveniences would be built and small shops that sold postcards and gifts made of stuck-together shells.

Never mind, she would never see it. The past was somewhere else, locked away inside her. Emily was not here, neither had she been in the chapel, nor even in the dust she had spread on the water. Bringing Emily's ashes here had been for her own benefit, not Emily's. Emily was someone she had only just begun to know; perhaps in the past there were others who had known her grandmother better but Holly could not believe that Jacko Monk had been among them. At least the fleeting friendship she and Emily had established had given Holly something of her inheritance to hang on to. She had so little, since her attempts to contact her father had met with such discouragement from him. Now it didn't seem to matter so much. She could even begin to forgive him at last, since his faults were part of his inheritance too.

Across the expanse of sand she saw Gideon talking to Fern and Mr Watts. Soon she would have to decide how she felt about

Gideon. All she knew at present was that life would seem very empty without him. Just as it felt emptier without Emily. Perhaps, after all, that was what love was.

She got to her feet and, in a burst of energy and exhilaration, began to leap across the rocks, vaulting the pools and putting the gulls to flight. They soared above her head, calling harshly. Percy, more animated than she'd ever seen him, came streaking across the beach towards her, barking as if to greet and old friend; she bent and fondled his ears roughly. He smiled idiotically and threw himself on the ground to allow her the dubious pleasure of tickling his stomach.

Gideon saw her coming and went to meet her. Fern stayed where she was, beside Mr Watts, leaving another generation to its own affairs.

EPILOGUE

The posters confronted Aiden everywhere, as bright and challenging as a flag of occupation. 'Paintings by Emily Troy at The Hayward Gallery'. By comparison, Jacko's retrospective had been a low-key affair.

Bruno Davidson had mounted what, of necessity, had been a small exhibition of Emily's work, but there was far too much of it for him to display in its entirety. The man was astute, he gave him that, running to earth what other people had overlooked for so many years. Both exhibitions had been reviewed in the quality Sundays with some excitement, heralding Emily Troy as that unusual animal, a British colourist. There had been fuzzy reproductions in the colour supplements and the manner of her discovery and death were, naturally, dwelled upon at some length, adding piquancy to an already newsworthy story.

It all irritated Aiden exceedingly. Emily had suddenly ceased to be his creature, his property, even if his monopoly was in his mind only. In addition, she was now to be considered in an altogether new light. Another dimension had accrued to her which was most unwelcome, so much so that he could not longer enjoy his pilgrimages to the Tate to worship at her shrine. This, then, would be his last visit.

'Don't leave me for more than half an hour this time, do you understand, Sears? Not more than half an hour,' he repeated irritably. 'Have I my pills?'

'They're in your pocket, Mr Chase.'

Aiden thrust two bony fingers inside his coat and extracted a pill box. Trembling, he opened it and took out a small pill which he placed on his tongue.

'Very well. You may leave me now.'

His chauffeur lowered him on to his usual bench. Aiden accepted the assistance, if not gratefully, then as a necessity. He had not been out for six weeks and to get this far had been almost too much for him. The events of the past year or two had taken their toll: the loss of the Cézanne and the Chagall had started it. Emily's death had been the culmination. Even the happy occasions in between, like hearing of Jacko's demise and having his paintings returned (thanks to the good offices of Will and his team), had been excitements that, at his age, he didn't need. However, a meeting with Gideon's new girlfriend, Holly Wyatt, Monk's granddaughter had intrigued him. Despite her uncanny resemblance to Jacko, she presumably had her share of Emily's genes, and appeared to be a young woman of character. Gideon was obviously smitten. Unfortunately, he himself would never live to see if his own and Emily's bloodlines ever commingled.

He deeply resented his own physical decline when, it seemed to him, his brain was as sharp as ever; the generally held opinion that he was 'astonishing for his age' brought no comfort. Thoughts of his own death were unwelcome and to be dismissed instantly. At least Jacko had predeceased him; to have outlived the man gave Aiden some satisfaction at least. He and Emily had been alive together on the planet for a period of time without the disagreeable presence of the man he loathed. He hated him for his talent, his irresponsible taking and discarding according to whim, and for having won Emily's love, even though that had turned sour eventually. For himself he would have accepted hate from her if that had been all that was offered. Instead he had had almost no impact on her life at all, even at the end, and with all his wealth he had not been able to give her anything that she could possibly desire. Now she had gone, leaving him only the image; and now that too had undergone a subtle metamorphosis in his mind.

He scrutinized the painting. It appeared to be as it had always been; seductive, tender, alluring. The real Emily, the flesh and blood Emily, was flesh and blood no longer, while the painted reflection lived on, powerful as a pagan fetish. Jacko had craved her as symbolizing the primeval female and earth-mother, receptive and fecund. Aiden himself had desired a spiritual icon of infinite beauty, untouched by man. The real woman had somehow eluded

344

them both, had evaporated like mist in the morning sun when they had put out a hand to possess her. For most of her life she had been inaccessible and unfathomable to both of them.

It was baffling and strange; today the painting offered him nothing, as if, when all was said and done, it represented only the surface and that the one seen by another man, and so ultimately unsatisfactory and sterile.

Besides, he felt old and ill and possessed by great weariness. He thought with longing of his comfortable chair, a hot-water bottle at his back, of his tea with a reviving dash of Armagnac. After all the striving, the acquisitiveness and the anguish, the assurance of these small comforts now mattered to him more than anything. For the first time in his life he was glad when his chauffeur reappeared.

'Are you ready, Mr Chase?'

'Yes, I'm ready, Sears. Take me home.'

A selection of quality fiction from Headline

THE POSSESSION OF DELIA SUTHERLAND	Barbara Neil	£5.99	☐
MANROOT	A N Steinberg	£5.99	☐
CARRY ME LIKE WATER	Benjamin Alire Sáenz	£6.99	☐
KEEPING UP WITH MAGDA	Isla Dewar	£5.99	☐
AN IMPERFECT MARRIAGE	Tim Waterstone	£5.99	☐
NEVER FAR FROM NOWHERE	Andrea Levy	£5.99	☐
SEASON OF INNOCENTS	Carolyn Haines	£5.99	☐
OTHER WOMEN	Margaret Bacon	£5.99	☐
THE JOURNEY IN	Joss Kingsnorth	£5.99	☐
FIFTY WAYS OF SAYING FABULOUS	Graeme Aitken	£5.99	☐

All Headline books are available at your local bookshop or newsagent, or can be ordered direct from the publisher. Just tick the titles you want and fill in the form below. Prices and availability subject to change without notice.

Headline Book Publishing, Cash Sales Department, Bookpoint, 39 Milton Park, Abingdon, OXON, OX14 4TD, UK. If you have a credit card you may order by telephone – 01235 400400.

Please enclose a cheque or postal order made payable to Bookpoint Ltd to the value of the cover price and allow the following for postage and packing:

UK & BFPO: £1.00 for the first book, 50p for the second book and 30p for each additional book ordered up to a maximum charge of £3.00.

OVERSEAS & EIRE: £2.00 for the first book, £1.00 for the second book and 50p for each additional book.

Name ....

Address ....

....

....

If you would prefer to pay by credit card, please complete:
Please debit my Visa/Access/Diner's Card/American Express (delete as applicable) card no:

Signature .... Expiry Date ....